LOVE IS A FERVENT FIRE

Robin Jenkins (1912–2005) studied at Glasgow University and worked for the Forestry Commission and in the teaching profession. He travelled widely and worked in Spain, Afghanistan and Borneo before finally settling in his beloved Argyll. His first novel, *So Gaily Sings the Lark*, was published in 1951 and its publication was followed by more than thirty works of fiction, including the acclaimed *The Cone-gatherers* (1955), *Fergus Lamont* (1979) and *Childish Things* (2001). In 2002 he received the Saltire Society's prestigious Andrew Fletcher of Saltoun Award for his outstanding contribution to Scottish life.

ROBIN JENKINS

LOVE IS A
FERVENT FIRE

Polygon

This edition published in Great Britain in 2005
by Polygon, an imprint of Birlinn Ltd
West Newington House
10 Newington Road
Edinburgh
EH9 1QS

www.birlinn.co.uk

First published in 1959 by
MacDonald & Co. (Publishers), London

The publishers acknowledge subsidy from

Scottish
Arts Council

towards the publication of this volume

British Library Cataloguing-in-Publication Data
A catalogue record for this book is
available on request from the British Library

Typeset by Hewer Text (UK) Ltd, Edinburgh
Printed in Denmark by Nørhaven Paperback A/S

'Lufe is ane fervent fire,
Kendillit without desire:
Short plesour, lang displesour,
Repentance is the hire;
Ane puir tressour without mesour:
Lufe is ane fervent fire.'

ALEXANDER SCOTT (1545–1568)

One

'He once remarked,' said Foulds diffidently, 'in fun, I suppose, rather bitter fun, perhaps, that so far as he could see there wasn't a single person' – 'bastard' was the word Hugh had used – 'prepared to make any atonement for what was done during the war.'

'Atonement?' Lured from his own safe, familiar beat of thought the Conservator raised his white brows and paused in his stirring of his tea. Where his own atonement should have been was a blank; but any man deserved warning. As a consequence his voice was peevish. 'Atonement? Does he consider his own conduct an example of atonement? Since he came home I understand there's not a public-house or hotel lounge in the whole of Edinburgh that hasn't seen him a dozen times, at least. What kind of atonement does he call that? No, John. Taking everything into consideration' – he repeated the phrase, slowly, with increasing solemnity – 'it still seems to me, basically, a revolt against authority. After every war it breaks out. Peace has its rigours and discipline, too. I mean,' he hurried on before his subordinate, the Divisional Officer, could speak, 'in our young friend's case, hasn't he gone out of his way deliberately to plague and perplex us who are his seniors and superiors? No man could have shown another more consideration than you have him. How has he repaid you? By letting you down all along the line.'

Two or three times during that display of well-laundered indignation, Foulds had glanced anxiously from clock to window.

'He's coming through by car,' he said. 'Likely the snow's held him back.'

The Conservator sipped his tea abstemiously. No doubt recalcitrance, aggravated by whisky, was assisting the snow.

'I hope nothing's happened to him,' said Foulds, unable to keep the fear secret.

The Conservator smiled. 'He's not a child, John. Even in snow the road from Edinburgh to Glasgow hardly bristles with dangers.'

In silence they looked out of the window. Over the city the sky was blue as slate, and snow was falling in large flakes. For the first time it occurred to Foulds as strange that in the water-colours on the walls, of forests under his jurisdiction, all were green or bronze, without snow. Yet at that moment the millions of young spruce and pine and larch would stand deep in it as in profuse blossom, with much more still unshed on their boughs. Simultaneously almost, in the fuggy office, he felt nostalgia for that chilly loveliness, and sympathy for young Carstares whose life, once so splendid, now lay in cold jeopardy.

'I understand,' murmured the Conservator, 'he never talks about his war experiences.'

'No.'

'I wonder why. I'd have thought disgruntlement of that sort would reveal itself in boasting, in shooting a line, as they say; especially where, as in his case, it could be so amply justified.'

'Disgruntlement?' Foulds set down his pencil on the desk with a deliberateness that revealed his disapproval, and indeed anger, more than if he had hurled it across the room. 'It's more than disgruntlement surely, much more. When Marion died he was thousands of miles away.'

The Conservator closed his eyes for an instant. He nodded carefully. That sorrow he had already conceded; it ought now to be let lie.

'And he couldn't be told for weeks,' went on Foulds, in an anguish of pity, 'because they thought he was going to die himself.'

Again the Conservator nodded, but this time he could not conceal his impatience at this naïve and reckless tampering with the balances of providence. Far safer to regard Carstares as a nuisance of a subordinate rather than as a victim of God.

Foulds gently played with the pencil on the desk. He heard again Hugh's one hoarse confidence: 'I can't forget her, Mr. Foulds. Christ, I know it's childish to keep regretting and blaming: might as well howl for a bubble that's burst. But everything I do's childish now; everything anybody does.'

'Let's keep in mind,' urged the Conservator, 'that he's young, with the future his for the taking.'

'His leg's not right yet. He might still lose it.'

'In that case is it wise to send him to Kinlochgarvie?' asked the Conservator. A stumble over a drain on the hillside could easily be arranged by those inimical forces, if provoked.

'I don't think disgruntlement's the word,' said Foulds.

His superior was nettled. 'All right, John, if it pleases you, I'll withdraw it.'

He jumped up and walked over to the window. There, with head courageously lifted, he watched the snow falling for almost a minute. Then, with his hair gleaming as whitely in the electric light, he turned and pointed.

'M.C.s aren't as common as snowflakes,' he said, urgently. 'God forgive me if ever I should withhold sympathy from any man who had won one, at such a personal cost; but I know that in our young friend's own interests, we must take care how we express that sympathy. At all costs he must be made to look forward, never back. He must be made to appreciate that, though he has disaster behind him, he has also in front of him magnificent advantages; yes, magnificent. Do you agree, John?'

Foulds made to disagree.

'Let me finish. What are those advantages? Let me mention some. He is young, only thirty-two. He is pretty comfortably off. He has recovered his health after being close to death. His leg was saved by miracles of devotion and surgery. And above all, while he lives he must be honoured by every decent man and woman in this country. Surely then he has far more to live for than drink, cynicism, and bitterness?'

Foulds was about to protest that it wasn't like a sum in

accountancy, with the assets comfortably outnumbering the liabilities; but he kept quiet, because he saw that where affection was missing it must indeed be such a sum. He could not resist saying: 'He hasn't touched a penny of Marion's money.'

The Conservator was sharply interested. 'Are you sure of that, John? I understand he's got a fine new car.'

'He hasn't touched it.'

Interest, keen as a ferret, searched for reasons. 'A kind of morbidity, do you think?' asked the Conservator. 'As you say, it was her money. Thirty thousand pounds or thereabouts, I understand; quite a fortune. Are you sure it's not barred from him legally? I know it's a practice in many business families to tie up the money on the female side to make sure it doesn't pass into strange hands. To the Branters, I suppose, young Carstares became a stranger the minute she died.'

'It was left to him. Marion saw to that.'

'You knew her, of course?'

'Yes.' Foulds could see her then, fair-haired and smiling, seated on the chair the Conservator had just risen from. How ill she had been, and how proudly had she spoken of Hugh whom she must have known she would never see again. He found the recollection unbearable, and realised, momentarily but profoundly, what Hugh must bear.

'Are you sure he's forsworn it?'

'I didn't say that. I said he hasn't touched it so far.'

'Odd. What I mean is, John, many people would think it was the possession of this money—'

He was interrupted by the outer door of the office banging open, and a stamping of feet. One of the clerkesses spoke. They could not make out what she said, but her relief, gladness, and admiration were manifest.

The Conservator's brows went up. Foulds nodded, smiling. Both listened.

Carstares laughed and spoke so quietly and amiably that the Conservator frowned in rather indignant surprise, as if he had been let down.

A clerkess knocked and put in her head. She looked anxious,

propitiatory, and at the same time curiously defiant. 'Mr. Carstares has arrived, sir.'

'Just send him in, Jean.'

'Yes, sir.'

'I must say,' whispered the Conservator, 'there's one kind of authority he seems to exercise.'

Carstares was in no hurry to come in. He chatted to the girls and had them laughing.

When he did enter it was with a peculiar cringe of apology that in another man, much smaller, say, with humbler physical presence, might have been regarded as the kind of joking subservience that placates superiors who are also friends. But Carstares, in the Conservator's view, was by no means good at playing the apologetic oaf. An intelligent, concentrated, and vigilant malevolence showed through. The Conservator was made to feel that only a fragment of it was directed against him; he wasn't important enough to merit its full force.

'Sorry I'm late,' said Carstares, without a smile. 'Snow.'

Without waiting to be asked he sat down, with almost truculent awkwardness. As he dragged his cigarettes out of his jacket pocket he let the packet fall. Picking it up wasn't for him the easy task it would have been for a child of three.

The Conservator was fascinated. Certainly there was now a strong aroma of whisky in the room, but Carstares, though he looked dissipated enough, was quite viciously sober. More than drink, and admittedly more than disgruntlement, caused that restrained desperation and clumsiness in the long pale fingers.

'Yes, Hugh,' said Foulds eagerly. 'I thought it would be the snow. You know Mr. McAndrew, of course?'

'Not well enough,' said the Conservator, officially hearty. Rising, he held out his hand.

Carstares without rising stretched, out and shook it briefly.

Then the Conservator, with a modesty he could not conceal, took up his position behind Foulds, where he sat smiling, prepared to be sympathetic in his scrutiny of his difficult young subordinate.

Carstares' past heroism and suffering, he thought, as well as his present contumacy and dissoluteness, could be plainly read in his face. Smooth and sallow, with the brow marked with curious boyish freckles, his face seemed charged with a weariness, mockery, and defiance, that combined to create, in the Conservator's mind, an unaccountably feminine effect. That must be a delusion, he knew, for Carstares' virility was not in doubt. His brown eyes were fallaciously mild, with long, dark lashes; indeed, his hair was as black, thick, and lustrous as any the Conservator had ever seen on a man; it glittered now with melted snow. But his long, lean, bony, yellowish hands were like hands remembered from a nightmare; their gestures, though small and restricted, all the time suggested passionate and utter abandonment.

The Conservator grew alarmed: surely he had been precipitate in agreeing to Foulds's proposal. The post of District Officer was not one of great responsibility, but a man possessed as Carstares evidently was could in it do great damage to the goodwill of the organisation.

'How do you feel, Hugh?' asked Foulds shyly.

'Not bad.' His voice had the same deceptive mildness as his eyes.

'And the leg?'

'As good as new, they tell me.'

'That's fine.' Foulds smiled and fiddled with his pencil. 'I'll come to the point right away, Hugh. I take it you're still dissatisfied with office work?'

The smoke from Carstares's cigarette seemed to the Conservator mockingly tranquil.

'That's right,' said Carstares.

'Well, Hugh, we've been considering your position.'

'Where's the trapdoor?'

'Trapdoor?'

'Where the body drops, after justice has been done.'

The Conservator laughed: such self-condemnation, fairly seasoned with wit, was, he thought, a sign of grace.

'No, Hugh, nothing like that,' said Foulds, laughing too. 'We're going to offer you a district.'

'On conditions,' chuckled the Conservator, holding up a firm, humane forefinger.

'Kinlochgarvie, Hugh,' cried Foulds, 'my own favourite in the whole division. If there's bonnier countryside I don't know where it is. The foresters, too, are all good men. You'll be able to take it easy until you feel settled in.'

'And it will soon be spring,' promised the Conservator.

'Kinlochgarvie?' repeated Carstares.

'Yes, Hugh. There are four forests: Garvie itself, Clashmore, Elrig, and Drummuir.'

'I thought,' remarked Carstares, 'Hector McIan was at Kinlochgarvie?'

'He's going further north,' said Foulds uneasily.

'Promotion?'

Foulds nodded.

'I happen to be senior to him, by three months,' said Carstares, 'if it's worth mentioning.'

Foulds was silent.

'I'll tell you what is worth mentioning, Mr. Carstares,' cried the Conservator, so earnestly he had to stand. 'You need have envy of no man. Your misfortunes have been hard to bear, but there have been compensations.'

'Name one.'

'Yes, I shall name one, with the greatest of sincerity. We must all honour you, Mr. Carstares, as we can never honour Hector McIan, or ourselves.'

In apparent acknowledgment of that tribute Carstares closed his eyes: he seemed indeed to be meditating almost religiously, so that the Conservator, in perturbation, was reminded of what Foulds had said about atonement.

'Christ,' said Carstares at last. He sighed the word rather than spoke it, in a revulsion so deep no tremor showed.

The Conservator, stripped spiritually naked, was disconcerted.

It was to Foulds Carstares apologised. 'I'm sorry,' he said. 'I used to be able to laugh at such guff, or salute, or bow the head, or shut my mouth.'

'I do not know what you mean, Mr. Carstares,' cried the Conservator, in a voice squeaky with petulance. 'What I said was the simple truth.'

'The simple truth,' said Carstares, patiently, 'is that Hector McIan's wife happens to be the daughter of one of our titled commissioners. Why be mealy-mouthed about it? It's done everywhere.'

'What is done everywhere?'

'I'm sorry if I haven't made myself clear. Arse-licking. We're adapted for it. Look how easily we can go down on our knees.'

Foulds was shaking his head miserably.

'That's one of the reasons I prefer trees,' said Carstares.

By this time the Conservator had rejected half a dozen rebuttals; somehow none had seemed effective. What Carstares had said was safely assailable, perhaps, only on account of its coarseness. To object to that might, in the circumstances, be unmanly. Also it was hardly permissible, though very pertinent, to point out that Hector McIan's wife hadn't brought him a dowry of thirty thousand pounds.

With a short wave of his cigarette Carstares absolved him.

'Will you go to Kinlochgarvie, Hugh?' pleaded Foulds.

'I'd like to, yes.'

'May I be frank?' cried the Conservator.

Another wave gave him permission, another smile stultified his frankness before it was uttered. Therefore he said what he had not intended. 'Drunkenness in Edinburgh might be regarded as a private shortcoming; in Garvie it would become a public nuisance.'

'The trees wouldn't mind.'

'No, but the local people would. And so would I. And so would Mr. Foulds. He'll tell you we have enough opposition there as it is without wilfully provoking more. You know how essential it is to an organisation like ours to build up and maintain goodwill.' He had to stop, otherwise he would have blurted out something demeaning to himself about Carstares' tie which hung so impudently outside his pullover. 'However, we all know you have fine qualities, Mr. Carstares. You have already displayed them, to your everlasting credit. It is Mr. Foulds's opinion that you will choose to display them again in Kinlochgarvie. I sincerely hope so. May I wish you the very best of good fortune?'

In the little cloakroom, as he was putting on coat and galoshes, he was upset. 'We're taking a bigger risk than we know, John.'

'He's entitled to it.'

'Perhaps he is. All the same, it might be as well to keep a close eye on him. For his own sake, as well as ours. Did you notice how he clowned as he entered your office? Was that to disguise his limp? Now if he has to limp crossing an office floor, how's he going to get on climbing a hill, walking among trees? Which is not to take into account the cynicism corroding him.'

'He'll be all right.'

'I hope so, John, I profoundly hope so.'

Carstares was standing in front of a large wall map when Foulds returned.

'I'm sorry, Mr. Foulds,' he said. 'I thought he was going to congratulate me on the money I've got in the bank.'

Foulds shook his head and tried to smile.

'But he was right enough,' added Carstares. 'You shouldn't trust me. It's possible I won't give a damn for his precious goodwill. And there's a hotel with a licence in Garvie.'

'There's a lot more than that, Hugh.'

Carstares stared at the map where his finger rested. Those green patches became in his imagination hillsides of young spruces, larch, and pine. He saw himself in one of the sunny aisles, watching roe-deer, those gentle marauders, flit past; that might be the kind of loneliness Marion could safely disturb. Among the trees surged the Garvie River, where salmon leapt. Far above them soared Ben Vorlich.

Foulds waited eagerly: it was his simple faith that winter, in men and trees, must be followed by spring.

'We've got magnificent larches at Garvie,' he said. 'Hundred-footers. We bought them with the estate.'

'Who's the forester?' asked Carstares.

'You'll find him very efficient and helpful, Hugh. Strone's his name.'

'Ezra Strone?'

'Yes, but he doesn't like to be called that. I think his wife calls him Ted.'

'Others call him swine, from what I've heard.'

Foulds frowned: he was aware of Strone's reputation and thought it unjust.

'I'd like you to wait and form your own opinion, Hugh,' he said.

'I will. It could be he's found swinishness the only successful policy.'

'Mrs. Strone doesn't enjoy very good health,' murmured Foulds.

'So he takes it out on the men?'

Foulds preferred not to answer. Instead he opened a drawer in his desk and took out a sheet of paper. 'Since you're going to be in charge at Garvie, Hugh,' he said, 'perhaps you should have a look at this. It was found in Strone's letter-box a couple of days ago.'

Carstares examined it. The paper was squared like that in a child's arithmetic jotter; indeed, it looked like a page torn from such a jotter. On it was scribbled in pencil, in block capitals: 'Last year 50 acres this year 5,000.'

'Looks as though one of Strone's kids has got his homework mislaid,' he said.

'Strone hasn't any children.'

'Some other kid then.'

'Strange place to mislay it, in a letter-box. It could be a joke of some kind; but it could also be a serious threat of arson. You see, fifty acres *were* burned last spring at Garvie, and we were never really satisfied as to how it happened. A spark from a passing train, we thought; but Strone had had all the embankment burnt beforehand, and his fire-track had been newly cleaned.'

'So it might be somebody who hates Ezra's guts?'

'Here's the note he sent with it.'

It was very short, written in tiny neat script: 'The enclosed was found in my office letter-box today. I shall myself make discreet inquiries, but I thought it better to inform you. Perhaps you may think the police should be informed.'

'The trees are well-established at Garvie,' said Foulds. 'It's one of our best forests. A big fire there would be a terrible loss.'

'Apart from the workers, is there anybody in the area with a grudge against Ezra's trees? Didn't I hear some mention of local opposition?'

'Yes. There's an old sheep-farmer called McKew; a cantankerous, hairy old rascal, like somebody out of the Old Testament. He's got a tribe of sons just like himself. Unfortunately, their land marches with ours. It's been a state of feud for years. He maintains we took over and planted a hill that used to rear champion sheep.'

'And did we?'

'It was years ago, before the war. Just last year we had to have him fined for burning his hill without giving us notice. That's the kind of thing he's always doing. His sheep are never out of our trees. Strone maintains gates are opened deliberately, and fences broken.'

Carstares grinned. 'I might enjoy a chat with old McKew.'

'Keep out of his way as much as you can, Hugh. I must say, though, anonymous notes aren't in his line. He'd be more likely to bellow his intention from the top of a hill.'

Carstares was studying the map. 'What's his farm called?'

'Creagan. It's across the hill.'

'Yes. Lonely spot, surely?'

'Yes, very. And you should see the farm; more like a border keep. It's a big place, carries thousands of sheep.'

Carstares was still gazing at the map. 'Is Garvie House occupied?' he asked.

'Yes, as a matter of fact it is.'

'By whom?'

'The Kilgours of Kinlochgarvie. They've been there for hundreds of years. You'll have heard of the impoverished gentry of today?'

'Can they afford just the one Daimler?'

'I doubt if they can afford a bicycle. They're the genuine article all right. The house was used during the war by a company of Commandos doing mountain training. They left it in a sorry mess, I understand, with bullet holes everywhere, and dry-rot. The Kilgours are living on the compensation. The house is falling to pieces.'

Carstares pictured it on its fine site overlooking the loch. 'We seem to have them hemmed in,' he said.

'Yes, it's planted right to their back door.'

'And to the front door, too.'

'No, not quite. We've left them a strip of natural wood between the house and the loch: for amenity reasons.'

Carstares, through the eyes of the Kilgours, saw the trees as besiegers that every year grew taller and more patient. 'I take it they're not very fond of us?' he asked.

'She's very bitter, according to Strone.'

'She?'

'Miss Kilgour, the laird's sister. He's something of a simpleton from all accounts. The rumour goes he was forced out of the army.'

'Not for being a simpleton surely?'

Foulds laughed. 'For incompetence, I imagine. From what I've seen of him I wouldn't say he's the military type, though he still calls himself Captain.'

'What's his sister like?'

Foulds shook his head, 'I couldn't say, Hugh. I saw her once, but it was from a distance.'

'So these two live alone in the big house, with their servants, of course?'

'They've got no servants.'

'So they're alone?'

Foulds was reluctant to answer. 'They've got a little girl living with them,' he said. 'About six. They call her their niece, but it seems she can't be, for there never was another Kilgour. I suppose she's really some far-out relation.'

'Is there any local theory?'

'Yes. They think she's really Miss Kilgour's daughter.'

'A bastard?'

'I suppose so.'

Grinning, Carstares gazed at the dot that represented the house. 'That's not so fashionable these days among the gentry,' he said. 'They'll think she's let the side down. Being poor's shameful enough, without that. Is there a local theory about the father?'

'There's talk she was engaged during the war to an airman; he was killed.'

'And he's given the credit?'

'By some.'

'And what do the others think?'

Foulds hesitated: the spokeswoman of 'the others' was, as far as he knew, Mrs. Strone, an insatiable gossip and romancer. 'Just that the father's still alive; that he jilted her; that he vanished abroad; that she's waiting in Garvie for him to return.'

Carstares was silent. 'So they feed on her?' he asked, savagely.

'I'm afraid we feed on each other everywhere, Hugh.'

Carstares, gazing at the map, had not heard. 'Poor bitch,' he said, and laughed. 'Well, when do you want me to go up?'

In relief Foulds began to discuss it.

Two

It was in the hospital in India, after one of the chaplain's futile but persevering visits, that the idea had first seeded in Carstares's mind that Marion's death, otherwise so unaccountable, had been his personal penance for the war. Since then, in spite of him, it had grown and ramified. Not even his recognition on his return home that no penance was considered necessary, and that none was being done at all, even by those who professed belief in God, caused his to wither.

As a consequence his grief, which might otherwise have been its own comfort and anodyne, had instead become an inquisitor, whose purpose seemed to be to demonstrate not merely the futility but the childishness also of every activity, aspiration, and belief. Often too, when he was tired or drunk, that inquisitor took the shape of a Japanese soldier whom he thought he had needlessly killed. This man, one of a patrol surprised in a village, had been found by Carstares inside a house, seated with his back against the wall, smiling. Carstares had fired, but afterwards he could never forget how the man's hands had been resting on the earth by his side. Those hands had become symbols of a peace and resolution forever beyond reach; often they were Carstares's own hands.

He had gone, as he had promised, to visit his friend John Ballantyne's parents in Hamilton. He had found them not only reconciled to their son's death, but even proud of it. They had begotten a hero, reared him lovingly, and yielded him as a sacrifice. Their memories were wholesome, and their expectations of meeting him again were patient but invincibly confident. As Carstares had drunk tea in their shaded and silent sitting-room, with their son's photograph on the piano in a silver frame inlaid with little Union Jacks, he had been as discreet as he could; he had kept his hands steady. He had not told them how the Japanese pilot had caught sight of them, as a child might grasshoppers in grass, and had swooped down, firing, as if making music to scare those amusing and impertinent insects. Then he had soared away again into the blue sky, delighted by his own recklessness as his wing-tip scraped a tall tree. In the distance the engines had sounded like chuckling. But John Ballantyne lay dying. And now, in the quiet room thousands of miles away from his jungle grave, his white-haired parents, with a faith as fantastically sure as a child's spoke of him as waiting for them to join him. They seemed to see him in the halls of heaven, wearing his officer's uniform, his shattered face whole again. Certainly they did not see him as the blasphemous, cheerful, fatalistic lecher Carstares had known. Perhaps if they had known about Marion they would not have asked him, with a sudden childish slyness and arrogance, if he, too, was sure of that reunion. He had not been able to restrain himself in the vehemence and absoluteness of his denial. They had quietly pitied him. Mrs. Ballantyne had wept and promised to pray for him.

On the wet, misty, April afternoon he drove to Kinlochgarvie, the rain-drops sliding down the windscreen reminded him of Mrs. Ballantyne's tears; they had the same sadness and insignificance. Belief in immortality was based upon stupendous conceit, the same kind that had mankind seeking new planets to conquer, although its own after thousands of years was still as chaotic as a spoiled child's playroom. Humility, that maturest of virtues, was nowhere to be found or achieved.

Under a great archway of dripping beeches he stopped the car and sat smoking. There were sheep with lambs in the field beyond the trees. Their bleating awoke a memory. In it the sun shone and the stubble glittered; Marion in her blue costume, with her fair hair shining, walked among the lambs.

Though he could not help smiling as he remembered, he had all over again to suffer the long, slow, penitential knowledge that Marion would not soon come back into the car, bringing into it, as visibly and innocently as a bunch of flowers, her love of the lambs and of the meekness they represented. For all her upbringing, her money, and her loveliness, she had been humble; and he had shared the joy that had been her reward.

As he sat, defeated by his loss, a lorry rattled by. It stopped a few yards along the road. Its door slammed. Footsteps were heard. Then there was the driver's face keeking in, long-nosed, coarse, inquisitive, smelling of beer.

'Onything wrang?' he asked.

Carstares shook his head.

'Sure?'

Carstares nodded.

The lorry driver touched the skip of his cap with apologetic forefinger.

'As the wife says,' he said, 'It's my long nose, cannae keep it oot o' folks' business. Thought ye'd fainted, or somethin'. Hellish day, in't it?'

Dabbing vigorously at his nose he swaggered back to his lorry, climbed in, slammed the door, and drove off.

He left Carstares in a strange agitation, remembering how, on a stretcher under a canopy of leaves, he had wakened from a nightmare of pain and fear and longing, to hear another Glasgow voice, rough, humane, and indomitable, and had seen a face like the lorry-driver's, though redder with the Burmese sun, winking in at him: 'We'll get you out of this f— hole, sir, or f— oorsels in the attempt.' And they had got him out.

The last thing they had looked for was gratitude. They had indeed forsworn it with heartiest profanity. Nevertheless, it still seemed necessary to be grateful. But to whom, and why?

About twenty minutes later he passed through Caldoon, which called itself the gateway to the Highlands. The rain was as heavy as ever. Mists, whiter and colder than smoke, hung over the houses and the crags above. Nobody moved in the gleaming street. A dog sneaked along the pavement, sniffing at nothing: all interest had been washed away. About to hate the town for its typical dreichness, he found himself remembering that the lorry must have passed through not so long ago.

Catching a glimpse of it through the lorry-driver's eyes, Carstares saw that this town, too, like the trees, would have its green buds of spring and its flowers of summer.

Beyond Caldoon the road twisted steeply into the hills. Near the top of the pass the rain turned to snow. Pine trees sprouted from rock. In its narrow gorge the river roared and frothed. It was the kind of scene that two years ago he had yearned for. Now this raw Scottish cold, this sleety snow, these austere hills, these bare rocks, and this long, dark, narrow loch represented only the necessity of endurance.

About a mile from the head of the loch he saw a woman walking steadfastly along the desolate road in front; with her head high and her shoulders back, she was enduring the heavy rain and desolation in a way that moved him. He thought she must be a farmer's wife or daughter or servant on an errand to some neighbour. Her legs were bare, with their backs reddened by the rain and cold, and her old fawn raincoat was black across the shoulders. She walked with a subtle lilt, especially of the left foot, as if she was singing to herself.

He slowed to walking pace and lowered the window, ready to offer her a lift.

The face she turned towards him astonished him. Instead of red-cheeked shyness there was a pale, aristocratic disregard, so intense that for a moment he thought she must be blind. The humour and simplicity that he had imagined in her walk and carriage were quite gone; in their place was a renunciation profounder and stauncher than his own. Not only the endurance, but the beauty and the nobility of the countryside were in her face. At the same time, remembering how her feet had lilted a minute ago, he felt sure there waited, locked deep within her, a warmth and brightness, as of sunshine.

'Good. afternoon,' he called. 'I'm going as far as Garvie Hotel, if you'd care for a lift.'

She intended to ignore him completely, but a sudden anxiety had her pushing back her soaked sleeve to glance at her watch. What she saw reassured her.

'No, thank you,' she said, in a voice quiet and refined.

'Quite sure?'

'Quite sure,' she replied, and walked on, dismissing him.

Yet as he drove past her he felt a relationship between them; so much so, indeed, that as he imagined the discomfort of her body his own shivered in sympathy.

The thought occurred to him she might be Strone's wife until he realised that though pale she could hardly be ill or delicate, walking so staunchly in such weather. Nor could Ezra's wife, no matter how cultivated a snob, have spoken with such refinement.

Half a mile along the road he met a forestry lorry drawn up on the grass verge. Men in black oilskins carried heavy logs down the hillside and heaved them up into it. They worked in sullen silence, like gigantic ants, except one, the brawniest, who stood on the lorry, stacking the logs. His shouts, though, were not of authority, as Carstares soon discovered when he stopped the car; they were of obscene banter at the gloom and misery of his sodden, staggering workmates.

They had all glanced back as the car approached; now that it was stopped across the road from the lorry they studied it with crafty peeps.

'Is Mr. Strone about?' cried Carstares.

'He's on the hill,' replied the red-haired man in the lorry, who then put his hands to his mouth and roared: 'Mr. Strone.'

Carstares noticed some of the men grinning, like schoolboys at the audacity of a classmate. Then they trudged away for another load.

The man on the lorry snatched off his cap and smacked it against the green logs; it was a curiously puerile gesture of defiance and contempt. Yet he was a powerful man, with barrel chest, heavy shoulders, and arms like a gorilla. He was vain, too, for he kept plucking at his moustache.

'Mr. Strone's coming,' he said, as if satisfied with the prompt success of his summons.

A small man was slowly coming down the hill among the scrub oaks and gnarled crotalled alders. He wore no cap, and his raincoat was slung over his shoulders, like a small boy playing at spaceman. Yet the rain hissed on loch, trees, and road. As he came he stooped and plucked a reed; this he carried as if it were a candle or a sceptre.

The man on the lorry bestrode a log as if it was a stallion.

'Gentleman to speak to you, Mr. Strone,' he cried, with gleeful mockery.

Strone glanced up at him. 'So I believe, Rab,' he said mildly.

He was not a mild man. It seemed to Carstares that in his every step he strove to make diminutiveness seem in him, and perhaps only in him, an advantage. His composure and self-assurance were so concentrated and aggressive that Carstares was reminded of other small men, with similar high cheek bones and narrow eyes, who had looked on themselves as demi-gods.

He held out his hand. 'Mr. Carstares?' he asked.

'Yes. Strone?'

Strone noticed the discourtesy, and grinned. He still held the reed in his left hand.

'Filthy day,' said Carstares.

Strone glanced about him. 'I never condemn the weather,' he said.

As they gazed at each other, both smiling, they heard the big man on the lorry shout to his mates: 'Bonnets at the ready, lads. Here she comes.'

Strone took his watch from his breeches' pocket. 'Late, surely,' he murmured. His smile was bitter.

The men had all stopped, some as they bore the logs, others as they were about to pick them up, others again as they were returning empty-handed. They watched the road. A tall, thin man, evidently ganger or foreman, ordered them to get on with their work. They paid him no heed. The man on the lorry had his hand at the skip of his cap; his other hand gestured obscenely.

'What the hell's up?' asked Carstares.

Strone did not answer, but waited, bleak with hatred.

Then Carstares saw the woman he had offered the lift to, passing. She still had her head high, and ignored them all.

A heron wailed on the loch.

'Miserable day, Miss Kilgour,' cried the man on the lorry. His cap was off in mock subservience; his gestures were filthier than ever.

Carstares was sure he had detected intense suffering on her face, beneath its mask of indifference. His fingers gripped the steering wheel so tightly they hurt.

'For Christ's sake,' he muttered.

Strone was again looking at his watch. 'When she gets round the corner,' he whispered, 'she'll hurry. Not in our sight, though. That would be admitting she's human, like us.'

The men were laughing. For the first time they were finding relish in their work. Their mate on the lorry was guffawing. He seemed for their delectation to be raping her in fancy.

Carstares thrust his head out of the car window.

'Shut your bloody mouth,' he shouted. To Strone he said, furiously: 'Is this the kind of discipline you have here? Are they allowed to insult everybody that passes?'

'Not everybody,' replied Strone, calmly. 'Her? Yes. If my job depended on it, Mr. Carstares, I wouldn't open my mouth to protect her.' He had to close his eyes and hold on to the car, so violent was the sickness of hatred that possessed him. 'She insulted my wife. Margaret,' he added, attempting to smile, 'is not well. If she outlasts this summer, the doctors will be cheated.' As he spoke he looked up at the trees, as if in that one anguished glance he saw them budding, bursting into leaf, harbouring birds, turning bronze, and becoming stripped again.

He stared at Carstares, almost as if in search of compassion, or at least understanding. 'She insults everybody,' he said. 'Even her own child.'

The men were now silent, except for some suppressed laughter.

'Yet,' murmured Strone, 'every day, at four precisely, she's under the larches outside the school, waiting for the girl. Today she's miscalculated. It's after four now. I understand, for all her punctuality, she never has a kind word for the girl.'

'Is the school far?' asked Carstares.

'About half a mile. It's beyond the hotel.'

'I'll see you in the morning,' said Carstares, and drove off fast.

Strone gazed after the car. 'A hero,' he muttered. 'A hero. With a dead wife.' At first he did not know what he meant by that addition. Doubtful and confused, he seemed to have just woke up and found himself there on the road by the lochside, in the dripping dusk. He thought the desolation was really in his mind, caused by Margaret's death. When big Rab McKerrol then began to sing an obscene song, he was going to scream to him to stop it, but in time he realised that Rab's singing so filthily was proof Margaret was still alive. Though she would be fighting for breath, with her lips as blue as her eyes, and her hair damp with sweat, she would nevertheless be able to greet him with a smile and take his warm hand in her cold one. It was as if Rab in some way had saved her, and he felt so grateful to the big, brutal, lustful man, whom usually he despised, that he walked over to the lorry and said: 'I think we'll knock off for the day, Rab. Give them a shout.'

McKerrol, high on the logs, roared like a rutting stag.

That roar was heard by Carstares and Constance Kilgour as they stood by the car, two or three hundred yards along the road. Carstares was trying to apologise. His very eagerness made it difficult.

'It won't happen again,' he assured her.

She had stopped when he had hurried out of the car to speak to her. She had been running, and still panted. If he had had a gun in his hand, instead of his great eagerness to propitiate her, she could not have watched him more warily. She seemed, too, discouraged, sad, and even a little afraid. He would not have been surprised had she begun to sob, but whether in sorrow, or anxiety, or anger, or desperation, he would not have been able to say. He wanted to take her hand and console her.

'I think,' he said, 'Strone's a bit demoralised about his wife. She seems to be ill, dying, from what he said.'

She showed no pity for either Strone or his wife.

'Otherwise,' he said, 'he'd surely have—'

'He thinks I insulted her.'

He nodded, and waited for her to exculpate herself.

'I asked her not to interfere in my business,' she said.

'That's fair enough,' he said, though he felt disappointed. 'But we'd be drier in the car. You must let me drive you home.'

'I don't like anyone to interfere,' she said.

'I'm not interfering. I want to be your friend. I hope you'll let me.'

She shook her head.

'At least as far as the school,' he coaxed.

She glanced towards his car. 'I'm rather wet. I'm afraid I'd soak your cushions.'

'Oh, never mind that. Please.' He took her arm. 'In you go. I'd be honoured; really I would.'

She yielded suddenly. 'Thank you.' Stepping past him, she entered the car.

Hurrying round in delight, he got in.

'My name's Carstares, by the way,' he said.

She stared in front, with her hands clasped on her lap. Had she been seated before a large fire, in slippers and warm, dry clothes, she could not have looked more at ease.

'You've been heralded, Mr. Carstares,' she said.

'I suppose so.' They would probably know about Marion, perhaps about the money, certainly about his limp and medal. Strone, to indulge his wife, would tell her everything; and she would tell everybody else. Like Miss Kilgour, he, too, might have to ask Mrs. Strone to keep out of his business.

'This is the hotel,' she said.

He had already seen the sign, and caught a glimpse of the building, as he drove past.

'It'll not take me a couple of minutes to drive back,' he said.

The road forked, turning left along the head of the loch. He knew that was his road, for he saw two children on it, hand-in-hand, with schoolbags on their backs. One was a little girl. He slowed down, wondering if she was Miss Kilgour's, but Miss Kilgour did not speak.

Then they were at the school. With the schoolhouse beside it, it stood under some tall larches at the very edge of the loch. There was a swing in the playground. The schoolhouse window was lit. Other lights could be seen farther along the road, where the scattered village of Kinlochgarvie began. As he switched off the engine he heard in the distance the whistle of a locomotive, and saw, on the far side of the loch, a moving row of lights, very bright against the blackness of the forest.

'When I said I wanted to be your friend,' he said, 'I meant it.' As he glanced aside at her, so strange and yet so inexplicably familiar, he could not control himself, so that his words rushed out. 'I'm going to be stationed here for a while. I'll need friends, too. Mind you, I understand your attitude – I mean, about wanting people to mind their own business. It's not sympathy, or even interest, that makes them interfere; it's greed, they like to feed on other people's griefs. Vultures. I've said myself I prefer trees. They mind their own business all right; they can be trusted; they know their place; they never pretend to be what they aren't.'

She did not reply, but sat gazing down the dark loch, as if content merely to be with him. They could hear the rain patter on the roof of the car. It seemed to him that they were sharing the rain, the darkness, the loch, the insults; why not, therefore, the child they had come to meet, and the life beyond this dreich night?

He laid his hand on her shoulder. 'I used to think I had had enough of the sun,' he said. 'I longed for this,' he indicated the scene outside. 'But I'm not so sure now. Christ knows, it's a dour country most of the time. No wonder those brutes insulted you the way they did. How could they help it? Yes, I think I'd like to get back to the sun. Perhaps I will. There are any number of forestry posts abroad, in Burma, say, or Malaya.'

While he was speaking a lorry had been approaching from behind. Now it rattled past. In the cabin beside the driver sat Strone, and on top of the logs cowered several men. A minute or so later three cyclists followed.

During that minute they had sat in silence, with his hand

lightly but apprehensively on her shoulder. When the bicycles were gone, she said, with cool amusement and determination: 'I'm obliged to you, Mr. Carstares, for the lift; but I shall be even more obliged if, like your trees, you know your place and keep it. You will find I know mine.'

Weakly he tried to prevent her getting out. She shook off his hand.

She was at the schoolhouse gate when the door opened and a stout woman appeared. Her voice was dry and even antagonistic: 'Is that you, Miss Kilgour?'

'Yes, Miss Carmichael. Has Alison gone on?'

'No, she's here.'

'Wouldn't she go home with the village children?'

'She would, but I saw fit to keep her here.'

Miss Kilgour seemed amused. 'What if I hadn't come for her?' she asked.

'You've always done so up till now. If you hadn't come I would have telephoned.'

'Is she ready to come now?'

'She's ready. Alison,' she called, sternly. 'Miss Kilgour's waiting.'

'I'm just coming,' cried a child's voice, timid and anxious.

'She'll be giving the cats a last stroke,' said the schoolmistress. 'Maybe she envies them their ease, as I do myself. You don't like cats.'

'Did she say so?'

'She wasn't clyping; telling tales, I mean.'

'I've heard the word before.'

'Do you like them?'

'Not particularly.' Miss Kilgour seemed to be smiling.

Then Alison, tiny in her red coat and hood, hurried out. She wore spectacles.

'I'm sorry, Connie,' she whimpered.

'Why, dear? Why should you be sorry? I'm the one who's late. Thank you, Miss Carmichael. I hope you've thanked Miss Carmichael for her kindness in looking after you, Alison?'

'She made a fuss of my cats,' said the teacher. 'For me that's thanks enough. Good-night, Alison.'

'There are three,' said the child desperately. 'Tiger, Sooty, and—' she could not remember the third.

'Sambo,' said the teacher, in what for her was a tender voice.

'Yes, Sambo. He's the one with white paws, Connie.'

She was still prattling about the cats when she set off with Miss Kilgour along the road. They did not take hands.

Carstares had come out of the car, and had been watching the scene in joy, perplexity, and alarm. It tormented him that the child should sound so afraid; that Strone was right in this matter was impossible. Yet the teacher's tone, grimly affectionate towards Alison, was towards Constance consistently hostile. No doubt injustices, insults, and humiliations, had embittered Constance; but he was surer than ever that hidden in her nature were warmth and brightness.

He could not bear them to go, and went running after them. He must banish their unhappiness.

'Wait a minute, please,' he cried. 'Wait.'

Alison turned to stare, but she was roughly pulled on.

'Wait, please,' panted Carstares, walking behind them.

'I asked you to leave us alone,' said Miss Kilgour.

'But I want to help you,' he cried. Suddenly he seized the child and crouching down pressed her to him. At that moment she represented, as no tree could ever do, the need for love, both giving and getting. She was the sun to be sought; with her disillusionment ended, and hope began. 'I want to help you, too, Alison,' he said. 'You don't want to walk home in the rain and dark, do you? I'm sure you'd rather go home with me in my car. You and Connie.'

She tried to squirm out of his arms; it was evident she was still afraid of Constance.

Constance's voice was quiet, but furious. 'Will you let the child go? Are you mad, or drunk?'

'I'm not drunk.'

Alison began to weep miserably.

He was dismayed. His comforting was incoherent.

'Let her go, you drunken fool,' said Miss Kilgour. Pulling the child out of his grasp she dragged her along the road.

He crouched where they left him, still smelling the child's rubber coat, and feeling it cold against his face. 'I'm not drunk,' he shouted. 'I just want to help you. I know I could, and the little girl, too.' He rose up; he could still see them on the road. 'I've got a right to help the child. And I will, too. You can't stop me.'

There came no answer, except for the calling in the distance of a curlew. He stood in the centre of the road, not quite understanding what he had been shouting, and pressing his hand against his drenched hair.

Three

From her schoolhouse door Miss Carmichael had watched and listened. Outwardly neutral, in her tight-mouthed, schoolmistressy way, she was in reality anguished by a mixture of envy, hatred, and another ingredient peculiar to herself, which she could not have named. Here, in the rainy gloaming outside her school, was being enacted a scene in which the three participants, the man, the woman, and their child, were being irremediably and justly unhappy. She ought to have been grateful for her hearthside cosiness and integrity; instead, she laid her hand on her bosom, as on a thing wasted, and in her heart writhed this knowledge of exclusion.

So Margaret Strone had been right, and she herself wrong. Alison's father had not been killed in the war. With her eyes wide with that clairvoyance which Miss Carmichael could neither understand nor despise, Margaret had declared many times he had not been killed. Perhaps he was still abroad, perhaps even legless in some hospital, perhaps married. But he was alive, and Constance Kilgour knew it. Otherwise why should she wait on in the big rotting house, why walk every day, rain or sun or snow, along the lochside in the direction he must come from? Helen Carmichael and Muriel Kirn, the proprietrix of the hotel, had in private agreed that Margaret must be recoiling from the idea of death, her own postponed winter by winter, and her child's, fifteen years ago, occurring with the most intimate treachery in her womb. Now her sentimental fancy had been proved true.

Helen Carmichael had wished and prayed that he was dead. Now his appearance, on the road in front of the school in which she had taught for twenty-five years, pleading on his knees to be taken back into the arms he had forsaken so callously, was as terrifying as a resurrection. There arose, too, in her mind a multitude of hopes and dreams long ago ruthlessly buried.

If a leaf fell in the forest, Strone told his wife; and she, without spite or rancour or malevolence, but with a great eagerness for life, passed it on to her friends. These did not always receive it in the same spirit. She had told them that Carstares, the new District Officer, was a widower; his wife had died while he was in Burma; she, a member of the Branter biscuit family, had left him quite a fortune; he had won the M.C. and had been badly wounded in the thigh; and since his return he had been worrying his superiors with his drunkenness and insubordination. What she had not told them was that, by the kind of coincidence that would have delighted her, as showing God's interest and kindness, he had been Constance Kilgour's lover, and was Alison Weir's father.

His wife must have been alive when he had made love to Constance Kilgour. That he had been unfaithful was simple, easily credible: it had happened during the war hundreds of thousands of times. What was less simple was that, in some profound sense, he had been unfaithful to Helen Carmichael, too, not as she had been during the war, but as she had been thirty years ago, bonnier than Constance Kilgour, more intelligent, and with a finer figure.

After standing on the road, muttering to himself, he came limping back towards his car. She made no effort to go in and peep out from behind the curtains; hers was not the curiosity of a sniggering old gossip. When he saw her he paused, and then hurried up to the gate.

'Have they far to go?' he asked.

His humbleness made her heart hard. Had he been arrogant, she might have stayed out of his business, although it was her business, too; she might have shut the door upon him and gone inside to the fireside, where she would have sat with her cats, as remote as they.

'If you mean, to the house,' she said harshly, 'far enough, on a night like this.'

She could hear his sad breathing. He glanced along the road.

'In another sense,' she said, 'they've got a very long road ahead of them.'

'Yes, I know.' Opening the gate he came eagerly up the path. 'I'd be obliged, please, if you would help me.'

Seeing his face clearly for the first time, she recognised the resemblance to little Alison: there were the same brown eyes, freckled brow, and too delicate mouth. He could have offered no more unforgivable insult. From him, too, exuded powerfully that odour, which Margaret Strone and Muriel Kirn in false embarrassment said didn't exist: the odour of maleness. It was not to be confused with the smells of shaving soap, tobacco, beer, or whisky. An old gamekeeper had once told Miss Carmichael that he could tell just by sniffing whether a fox had passed through the wood recently; so it was with her and men. No doubt a woman who slept every night with a man, as Margaret Strone did, or associated with them daily in the course of business, like Muriel Kirn, had that faculty sated and so dulled. Other women, Miss Carmichael knew, would call Carstares attractive; to her he was destructive, for he was her own life unfulfilled.

'If you would help me,' he repeated, 'I'd be very grateful.'

'How can I help you?'

'Just tell me about them.'

'I don't know very much. Come in.' As she went into the house before him she was aware that what she was about to do was evil. Her cats, therefore, asleep on the hearth rug, not only reproached, they even menaced her.

'Sit down,' she said.

When he sat down by the fire she was, as she had feared, arrested in her intention to revenge herself on him. Outside in the rain and dark, under the great dripping larches, he had been a creature of her imagination, moulded as her resentment wished; here in her quiet parlour, with the cats asleep and the children's exercise books on the table waiting to be corrected, he was changed into a human being, a young man who might have been her son, and whose unhappiness ought to have made him immune to her malice. That other faculty, of being able to see in any man or woman the child betrayed and corrupted, now disconcerted her. To punish the man, even if his punishment was deserved, was in some hateful way to dishonour again the child he had been. In Carstares's case, too, despite the wrong he had done, she with her white hair could have been his mother. Because of what she had intended to do, what indeed she might still do, that imaginary relationship itself seemed evil, as if incestuous.

As if to taunt her, he bent and stroked Sooty. She noticed he had his packet of cigarettes in his other hand.

'If you wish to smoke,' she said, 'you may.'

'Thank you.' He pushed one into his mouth like a starving man. 'I'm dreadfully sorry,' he said, a moment later. 'I should have offered you one.'

'Perhaps you took it for granted that I wouldn't smoke.'

He noticed the huffishness in her voice, and looked surprised.

'The first thing you'll want to know,' she said, 'is why she sent the child to an insignificant school like this.'

'No, no.'

'There was a time in Scotland, Mr. Carstares,' she said, with deliberate bitterness, 'when it was the custom for the laird's son to sit on the same bench as the son of his father's humblest servant.'

She refused to be mollified by his smiles and nods of agreement.

'My qualifications are as good as, if not better than,' she said, 'those of the governess *she* had at the same age.'

He followed her glance to the photograph on the sideboard. No doubt he saw the graduate's gown and hood, and scroll; she saw the confident smile, the uplifted head, the fine bosom.

'I'm sure the child's in very good hands here,' he said.

'Yes, she has been; it wasn't for that reason she was sent here.'

'I suppose they couldn't really afford to send her anywhere else.'

'There was that; but there was something else.'

Perhaps it was his smile of trust and optimism that provoked her into decision. She crossed to the sideboard, unlocked the drawer, and took out a child's exercise-book.

'What else, Miss Carmichael?' he asked, boldly.

'I shall tell you. It was what you came in here to find out. You have a right to know, so I have a right to tell you. What you make of the information is for you to decide. Miss Kilgour did not send the child here out of respect for my professional qualifications, nor out of any humble belief that the village children are as worthy as her own. For none of these reasons, Mr. Carstares.'

He waited, as if whatever reason she gave he would turn it to his lover's credit. Therefore, she exaggerated.

'She sent the child here to be hurt, humiliated, and disgraced.'

He shook his head. Now that he wanted Constance Kilgour back he would believe no ill of her.

'Look at that,' said the teacher, handing him the sum book open at the place.

He took it with a peculiar interest that she did not understand. Again she saw the resemblance to Alison, and for a moment wished to snatch the copy-book back, not for his sake or even for the innocent girl's, but for the relationship between them. Herself barren, she believed resolutely that parenthood redeemed any creature, rat, weasel, or man.

Not sure what he was expected to find on the page, Carstares at first was amused by the array of sums, neither neatly set down, nor correctly worked out. He supposed they were Alison's work. Then, at the foot, written through one of the sums in faint, untidy writing, he made out: 'Alison Weer is a basterd.'

She saw he had at last seen it; but he was not as shocked or angry as she had expected.

'I take it,' he said quietly, 'if they write it, they say it, too?'

'Yes, they do.'

'Do the sheep bleat it?' he asked, with a curious, sad smile.

'In this glen, and the next one, too. Miss Kilgour hasn't gone out of her way to win the sympathy of the people hereabouts.'

'Why should she?'

'It's none of my business, of course, but it would seem to me foolish to antagonise people, when you are so vulnerable.'

'You mean, they were bound to take it out on the child?'

She did not answer. He was so uncannily calm, she thought, because he was sure he had come in time to make amends. Now that he was free, with plenty of money, he could marry Constance Kilgour, and so rescue Alison. It was what she, so strict a moralist, should have piously approved and encouraged; but she could not; on the contrary, she prayed his appeal would keep on failing, as it had already failed that evening.

Again he stooped to stroke one of the cats.

She said, in agitation, what she had meant never to say. 'I ought to warn you I know your secret.'

'My secret?'

'Do you think I'm blind, and deaf? I saw and heard what happened out there in the rain this evening. You were on your knees to her, to them. And let me warn you, Mr. Carstares, if you intend to keep it a secret, you will have to go away again, and not show your face. I saw the resemblance at once.'

'What resemblance?'

'Between you and the child.'

His attempt at astonishment was soon abandoned; his intention to protest quickly died, too. Joy and pride flushed his face.

'As I said before,' she said, 'it's not my business; but I would like to remind you that Alison's already suffered a great deal. You mustn't let her be used as a weapon.'

What he did then shocked her more than if he had jumped to strike her: he rose, and before she could prevent it took her hand. His smile was so gentle it alarmed her.

'I promise you,' he said, 'Alison won't come to any harm. Not because of me,' he added.

She could not withdraw her hand. 'There's someone else to consider,' she said.

'Yes. But I don't think you need be afraid of what may happen to Alison.'

She wished to scream that his smile of confidence and faith was insane.

'I hope not,' she murmured.

He let go her hand and went to the door. She followed him, in fascination, smiling herself, she felt, insanely.

'Good-night,' he said.

'Good-night.'

He hurried down the path and across the road to his car. He stood beside it for almost a minute, staring along the road towards the village.

'Good-night,' he cried again, joyously.

Climbing into the car, he turned it skilfully and sped off towards the hotel.

For a minute or two longer she stood by the door, shivering, more than ever certain that a change was coming in the weather, too. It would be dry and clear before dawn, and there would be snow on the tops. Weather for reconciliation.

When she at last went into the warm, cosy, empty living-room she smelled the cigarette smoke. As she stood, waving it aside in distaste, and gazing down at the cats, a desire grew in her to rush over, press her feet upon them, and crush the sloth, remoteness, and soft contentment out of them. They represented her whole past life. Once or twice she had awakened out of that deadly somnolence, but had she not, like Sooty a few minutes ago, snuggled down again, thankfully, avoiding risk, cold, fear, and loss.

She forced herself to go down on her knees to fondle them. One awoke and with its eyes closed licked her hand; the others slept. Then, rising painfully because of the varicose vein in her right thigh, she went out into the lobby and picked up the telephone.

Four

Miss Muriel Kirn, proprietrix and manageress of Kinlochgarvie Hotel, in spite of her robin-like tininess, her pink-faced efficiency, her permed grey hair, her honest flat bosom, and her fifty-six years, was one of the war-god's nymphs. Her most precious possession, unknown by everyone but Helen Carmichael, was a small silver statuette of a warrior, nude, bearing shield and uplifted spear: Achilles, Helen with her customary quick contempt had said, Achilles with his lust appeased. But in Muriel's secret mind soldiers who fought for God and glory could never be lustful, lecherous, or obscene. Those Commandos who had been quartered for a while in Garvie House had gone roaring down to Caldoon in search of women; like rutting stags, Helen had said; but Muriel, who had heard their roars, and even had seen their inflamed eyes, had resolutely looked on every one as her lover. Her services as gas-mask distributor, organiser of the parcel fund, and knitter of khaki scarves, had not satisfied her: worthy, necessary, and patriotic though they were, they had seemed in the secrecy and daring of her imagination menial, when compared with that other service which Briseas had done for the great Achilles. In neither war had she any opportunities; in the second age, and in the first a puritanic upbringing, had prevented her. Now, when she had heard that Captain Hugh Carstares, M.C., hero of Burma, was coming to live in her hotel, she thought she saw her chance; so much so that when preparing his room, the one with the finest view over the loch, she had made the bed herself and had for minutes, smoothing the pillows, indulged in dreams that, in spite of Helen Carmichael, she refused to consider wicked. Resisting Helen, too, she vowed that if Carstares, wounded, widowed, lonely and sorrowful, were to find comfort with Nancy, the big-bosomed maid, she would not object. She would not see herself as brothel-keeper, as Helen would; no, she, would see herself far more gloriously as a kind of goddess supplying a Briseas for an Achilles.

She had expected him at three, but it was after five when she saw the headlights of his car sweep up the drive. As she rose from the desk in her office, glancing in the mirror above and patting her hair, the telephone rang. She supposed it would be Margaret Strone, with one of those thoughts that occurred to her, as strange and doomed as a deer in her husband's forest. Usually she listened, fascinated, in pity and wonder, for Margaret, in bed always, seemed to live in communion not only with deer but also with tree-like spirits that moved greenly in and out of silent sunshine, and spoke strange wisdom. This evening, however, resisting Margaret's spell, she resolved to put her off, gently but firmly.

But it was not Margaret, it was Helen Carmichael, imperative as ever, but hoarse and, it seemed, curiously reluctant.

'Is that you, Muriel?'

'Yes, Helen.' She tried not to sound impatient, though the car had now stopped outside, and in a few moments he would be entering. She had looked forward to being on the steps to greet him, despite the rain. 'Is anything wrong?'

'Why should there be anything wrong?'

'I just thought, you sound as if you've caught a cold, Helen.'

'Has Achilles arrived?'

Muriel frowned and replied with dignity. 'If you mean Mr. Carstares, yes, Helen, he has just arrived. As a matter of fact, I was just going out to welcome him.'

'You're an innocent, Muriel. I know your dreams, but in spite of them you're an innocent.'

'I really don't know what you're talking about, Helen.'

'Yes, you know. I want to warn you about Achilles.'

'Please, Helen.'

'He's Constance Kilgour's lover; or was; and wants to be again.' So distorted her voice now, like an old drunk woman's,

Muriel couldn't be sure what she had said. 'He wants it, Muriel, with the rage and passion of a tiger.'

'Tiger?'

'Should I say, of a rat? In them it shows as the filth it is.'

'Really, Helen, I don't know what you are talking about.'

He had now come limping into the hall, carrying a bag and smoking a cigarette. He was smiling.

'Alison Weir's his child, Muriel; his and Constance Kilgour's. They lay together, as the Bible says. You and I know, Muriel, what that means.'

It must be, thought Muriel in horror, a sexual brain-storm, a long-delayed symptom of an illness tormenting for years. Margaret and she had once or twice discussed it in awed whispers.

'I don't think, Helen,' she said gently, 'that can be right. After all, Margaret would have known—'

'Do you think she knows everything?' It was a scream, with spits of madness in it; and it went on to speak about Margaret and her husband so obscenely that Muriel, whimpering with compassion, held the telephone away from her ear. But still she listened. 'I saw them meet again for the first time in years, in the rain, this very evening, on the road outside my house. The child was between them, weeping. They will never be reconciled. I would hold Christ guilty for the rest of time if they were reconciled. So would you, Muriel; you hate her.'

Carstares, having rung the bell, was admiring the two stags' heads. He seemed, in contrast with Helen, patient, sane, and cheerful.

'No, no, Helen, you mustn't say that. I don't hate her or anyone.' But it was not true: her dislike of Constance Kilgour might be inexplicable, it was none the less real.

'Don't be a hypocrite, Muriel.' The rest was again filth, hoarse and horribly urgent. Helen, a goddess among children, now sounded like a nasty, greedy child gobbling sweets in haste lest others should come for a share.

Quietly sobbing, Muriel put down the telephone. She had suspected such stuff was festering in Helen's mind; but even over the telephone she could not bear to hear it ooze out. Besides, who knew who might be eavesdropping?

Jock, barman and handyman, had come in response to the bell. Miss Kirn was somehow comforted; yet Jock should never have been allowed to welcome Carstares to the hotel: a small, shrewd, grey-haired Glaswegian, he had in early manhood seen many medals in pawnshop windows and was cynical about heroes.

Carstares, though, was laughing. As she came out of the office, foolishly wiping her hands with her scented handkerchief, she tried hard not to see him as Constance Kilgour's lover.

From what in her perturbation seemed a great helmeted height he smiled down at her.

'Welcome to Kinlochgarvie, Mr. Carstares,' she said. 'I'm Miss Kirn.'

'The boss,' said Jock, with a cringe of terror and a wink of insolent affection. He was a persistent and eloquent winker, and she had never been able to cure him.

'Your hostess, Mr. Carstares,' she said.

'Thanks.'

As he spoke he grinned, and ended her incredulity: the resemblance to Alison Weir was undeniable, indeed was so convincing that she wanted to turn away from him and cover her eyes with her hands. Suddenly she knew he was doomed: not because of Helen Carmichael's wicked spite, or Margaret Strone's voracious interest, but surely because of his love for Constance Kilgour. All at once she saw a dozen different signs of that doom on his face, his hands, his body.

'Have you got a garage?' he asked.

So prosaic the question, she could not understand it.

'Waterproof, too,' replied Jock. 'Would you like me to put your car away, sir?'

Carstares considered. He glanced at his watch, at the stags' heads, and at Miss Kirn. 'No, just leave it,' he said. 'I might want it later. I might be going visiting. But you could bring in the rest of my stuff. Here's the key.'

'Yes, do that, Jock,' said Miss Kirn. 'I'll show Mr. Carstares to his room.'

As she went up the stairs in front of him, she had to resist the wish to turn and plead with him to take care, for he was in danger. When she did turn it was only to sympathise with him for having so unpleasant a day for his journey. He smiled then as if for him the day could not have been more splendid. Yet had Helen not said that he and Constance Kilgour had not been reconciled? It must be he saw hope, like a green glen, before him. She saw it, too, but she could never enter it, she must wander for the rest of her life through the desert and across the stone hills of lovelessness.

Outside the door of his bedroom she hesitated. In the morning when he drew the curtains he would look out over the loch, and would see, on the far side, amidst its wood by the river, Garvie House, where Constance Kilgour lived, and where she in her turn could stand by the window and gaze across to the hotel.

'In here?' he asked, cheerfully tolerant of her old maid's mysterious pauses.

Blushing, she flung the door open. 'It's one of our best rooms, Mr. Carstares. I hope you find it comfortable.'

'I'm sure I will.'

Throwing his grip on to a chair he strode across to the window and pulled the curtains aside.

'It's to the front,' he said. 'Good.'

'Yes. You'll have a very fine view of the loch.'

The exultation in his voice and in his hand, too, as it clutched the curtains weakened her physically, so that she had to sit down. For a moment she shared Helen's vicious spitefulness.

'Do you mind?' Even as he asked he had pulled the window open and had thrust his head out into the rain.

From behind him she could hear the roaring of the Garvie River, as it surged in spate past its islets of rock. It, too, exulted, and against her will she had a vision of supreme and indestructible happiness: in it the sun glittered on Vorlich's snowy peak, the great larches were a marvellous green against the blue sky, anemones spread like snow in the wood under Garvie

House, and there Constance Kilgour and Carstares walked
with their child, hand-in-hand, reconciled.

When the vision passed it was replaced by her former
foreboding, dark and bitter as this night of rain.

She was relieved when Jock came staggering in, with two
heavy cases.

'A phone call for you, mistress,' he gasped. 'Mrs. Strone.'

'Thank you.' Yet she did not wish to go and speak to
Margaret, who by this time perhaps had heard Helen's news.
'Well, Mr. Carstares, if there's anything you want, please
mention it.'

'I will,' he said, laughing.

She feared and hated the very rain-drops on his face. I must
be going mad, she thought; Helen must have contaminated me.
Yet, unlike her, I have a choice, I know what I'm doing, I can
stop myself if I wish, my mind is not diseased.

'Jock, there's always work to do,' she said, sharply, as she
made to leave.

'I'd like a word with Jock, if you don't mind,' said Carstares.

'Of course. But he'll be required in the bar shortly.'

When she was gone the two men stood grinning at each
other; there was no need to speak. Jock winked, not at Carstares really, nor at Miss Kirn's unpredictable spinsterishness,
but rather at erratic, malicious, and amusing fate, with which
he had an understanding, and from which in his time he had
had many generous tips. Otherwise he attempted, but not too
earnestly, to conceal his agile self-interest under a cloak of
obsequious respect.

Carstares sat on the bed and smoked.

'What's a Glasgow man doing in this wilderness?' he asked.

'On a civilising mission, would you say, sir?'

Carstares laughed, savagely. 'By Christ, they could do with
civilising. What are they really like? You see them drink. Let's
have the truth.'

With conjurer's humorous skill, Jock caught the two half-
crowns flicked to him. Then he stood with his finger-tips
together, and meditated.

'A bit slow on the uptake,' he suggested, 'because of the heather in their ears, maybe. Not good at catching the point o' a joke wi' a shade o' subtlety in it. Limited In their discourse. Suspicious as sheep. Beneath it all, decent enough; pretty much the same as folk everywhere.'

'I got the impression,' said Carstares, 'that they're a shower of nasty-minded bastards.'

Jock disguised his surprise by clicking his heels together as neatly as a Polish colonel. 'As I said, sir, the same as folk everywhere.'

Carstares remained serious and angry.

'I gave a woman a lift this afternoon,' he said. 'As you know, it's been a bitch of a day.'

'Still is, sir.'

They listened to the rain spitting against the window.

'I'd have offered a lift to a tinker's grannie in such weather.'

Jock waited, pretending that his was the humility which refused to seek after his superiors' motives for anger or passion or sorrow. In reality his wits in his head were as alert and inquisitive as weasels. Carstares, he saw, had the true superior's reluctance to confide in an underling, but was now in a humour to confide in a beetle, far less a barman.

'Before I gave her the lift,' said Carstares, 'she passed, a lorry. A forestry squad was loading it with logs. I was talking to Strone; he's the forester.'

Jock nodded. 'His wife is ill,' he murmured.

'There was a big red bastard like a gorilla on the lorry.'

For an instant Jock was himself; he scowled. That gorilla was no doubt Rab McKerrol, whose guts he hated, and whose fair-haired tranquil wife he pitied.

'They went out of their way to insult her,' went on Carstares, quiet in voice, but furious in manner. 'Even Strone. Christ, were they all mad? She gave them no cause. She just walked past.'

'Did you hear her name mentioned, sir?'

'Kilgour.'

'I thought so, sir. Miss Kilgour, from the big house. She's no favourite hereabouts.'

'Why the hell should she want to be?'

'Just so, sir.' Jock grinned: this was a more slippery situation than he had supposed. What game was the big yellow-faced sahib up to?

'Do they talk about her in the bar?'

A man less practised than Jock in interpreting distorted speech would never have made out that question; a man less resourceful in mind would never have been able to answer it safely.

'In my bar,' he said slowly, 'as far as lies in my power, every woman's sacred, even that tinker's grannie you spoke about.'

'I'm not joking.'

That would have been obvious to an Edinburgh bobby, never mind a Glasgow barman. Jock wondered if it was just a simple case of one nob defending another against the gossip of scruff. He felt perverse.

'Mind you, sir,' he said, 'they pay for their beer, and they tell me this is a free country.'

Carstares glowered at him. 'Just let them know that if any of them as much as speaks her name in my hearing, I'll have the bastard flung out of the glen.'

What, wondered Jock, if the bastard was a shepherd, like one of the McKews, say. Over them Carstares, for all his medal, had no jurisdiction.

Unexpectedly Carstares began to laugh. 'What the hell do they matter?' he asked.

'Very little, sir, I'm sure.'

'She's worth ten thousand of them.'

Jock smiled, humouring the exaggeration. What way was there of measuring the worth of human beings? Miss Kilgour certainly had style, breeding, and appearance: in an old dirty raincoat, for instance, she looked far more of a lady than Nancy would, dressed in new mink. Nevertheless, did she not lack meekness and consideration for her fellow creatures? Those were serious deficiencies. Because of them Miss Kirn did not like her. It was a good reason for liking Miss Kirn herself. Judicious manoeuvring could turn that liking into something more enterprising.

For a moment Jock had forgotten Carstares.

'Is there anything else, sir?' he murmured.

'No, not in the meantime. But I'd like another talk with you soon about these savages you came to civilise.'

'At your service, sir, any time.'

With dignity Jock withdrew. Outside the room he paused, took out the two half-crowns and winked at them. What he meant was that if his integrity as a barman was to be bought, there would have to be negotiations first. The price might not be easily settled.

Five

As he gazed out at the dark loch it seemed more and more to
Carstares that by wishing to befriend Constance Kilgour and
her child, he was not in any way betraying Marion, or revealing
as superficial and transitory his love for her. On the contrary,
those two, and he himself now, lay under Marion's protection.
She it was who had made him feel compassionate towards
Constance walking alone in the rain beside the loch; it was
Marion's indignation he had felt at the insults flung by the
forestry men; and surely it had been her love of children,
especially of those unborn children of her own that she had
written so often about, which had made him see in little Alison
Weir the means of resolving his grief at last. Marion had been
as fair as Constance was dark, simple and hopeful where the
other woman was complex and stoical; yet in a strange way they
were so much alike that as he made to recollect the one it would
be the other who came into his mind. It was almost as if
Constance was Marion transformed and still imprisoned by
death; it would be his duty and delight to set her free.

As he was unpacking, happy because he had decided in an
hour or so's time to telephone Garvie House and make his
peace with Constance, a knock was heard at the door. When he
called 'Come in', a maid in a black uniform entered.

He could not help giving her a grin of surprised and amused
admiration. Her hair was so fair as to be almost certainly dyed;
but there was nothing artificial about her breasts, or her
bottom in its tight skirt.

'Excuse me, sir,' she said, almost lisping as if to suit the little
blue ribbon in her hair; both lisp and bow were weapons of
coquetry. 'I'm just in to see if the fire's all right.'

'The fire's fine.'

So it was, too, with the oak log glowing red among the coals, but it was not as hot as she. It was easy, and pleasant, to imagine the whistles of homage she'd win from any lorry-load of soldiers, of whatever nationality. How long, he wondered, would John Ballantyne have been in the hotel before putting her provocativeness to the ultimate test? No more than a night.

'Maybe I'd better put another lump on it,' she said, giggling, 'just to make sure it doesn't go out. Miss Kirn says you've to be made comfortable. Very comfortable,' she added, with another giggle. 'As comfortable as possible.'

There was no doubt what she meant. As she stooped over the coal scuttle he could imagine her plump bottom blushing with temerity. Her legs in their nylons were not only shapely; they were also strong, for repelling or entwining.

'You see, sir,' she lisped, as she stood rubbing her palms voluptuously up and down her buttocks, 'I'll not be in to look after it later on. There's a dance at the village hall tonight.'

'Are you going?'

She answered by seizing an imaginary partner and waltzing.

He sat on his bed and watched her. 'Do they go in for the real Scottish country dances here?' he asked. 'You know, "Kiss-me-quick-my-mither's-coming"?'

'Not that stuff,' she said scornfully. 'They're awful dancers here. Do you dance sir?'

She peeped at his legs to see which was the one would prevent his dancing.

'I can shuffle around,' he said.

She considered the admission. 'They're an awful coarse lot in Garvie altogether,' she said.

Well, he thought, hands that wielded axes or rutters or ploughs all day would lack gentleness, especially when excited by the lust she would be proud to rouse and no doubt reluctant to appease. For all her apparent ingenuousness she looked a girl with a high price.

'What's your name?' he asked.

'Nancy, sir. Nancy McBlane.'

That's it, Nancy, he thought; make them squirm and sweat.

'Are you a native of Kinlochgarvie?'

'Not me.' She made use of the extravagant disclaimer to show off her full red mobile lips. 'They're a coarse lot. They've got heather growing out of their ears; that's what Jock says. Is everything all right, sir? To your satisfaction, I mean?'

'Yes, I think so.'

'This is a nice room, sir.'

'Yes, it is.'

'Miss Kirn specially chose it for you.'

'That was kind of her.'

'It's because you were a soldier, sir. She's daft about soldiers. She's got one in her room. That size.' She held her hands about a foot apart. 'It's got no clothes on, and her an old maid. It's made of silver.'

'I'm afraid I'm not as precious as that.'

'You've got a lovely car, sir. I like maroon. You should see the old bone-shaker I'm being taken to the dance in. Sometimes it's used to carry sheep.' She was so indignant she could express it only by giggling.

'I was sure you'd have a boy-friend.'

'He thinks he is. Me? No, thank you.'

'A forestry-worker?'

'No, he's a shepherd; which is worse. Better to smell of trees than sheep-dip. And he's as good a dancer as one of his own tups.'

On her way to the door she suddenly approached the bed and pressed it to demonstrate its springiness. 'Spring interior,' she said, and waltzed to the door. There she paused. 'If there's anything you want, sir, you've just to ask.'

'All right, I'll ask.'

'Miss Kirn said, anything at all, sir. Don't be bashful.' Then with a giggle she was gone.

He stared after her, smiling. There were names for her kind, and some of them sounded in his mind, uttered by voices he remembered with fondness: Ballantyne's, for instance. As a result he felt towards her a tolerance and even liking. She had her place in a world where Constance Kilgour was alive.

As he went on with his unpacking his hands became weak as they anticipated the lifting of the telephone when he went down to ring up Garvie House.

As he went down the stairs, joy heightened Carstares' perception more than fear once had done; and this time he cherished, as then he had hated, everything he saw. There was a bad painting on the landing wall, of a band of Jacobites hiding in the hills after Culloden. In trying to portray their continuing loyalty to a lost, foolish cause, the artist had made them look like bloodstained dolts; but in his brief glance as he passed, Carstares seemed to know each one of them, with a sympathy and affection that did not consider right or wrong, victory or defeat. Then in the hall, noticing the smears like tear-marks under the eyes of the stags, he saw the great, beautiful creatures alive again on their high hills, and felt that his own life was similarly restored.

From her office Muriel Kirn watched him. She knew he was coming to telephone, and had no doubt it was Constance Kilgour he was going to call. Hence his joy. Yet Helen Carmichael had said that he had been left sobbing in the road, on his knees indeed, pleading in vain. Constance Kilgour had spurned him more arrogantly than she had everyone else. Whatever her feelings towards him had once been, she despised him now. She would enjoy demoralising and humiliating him. In his love for her, and in their child, she had weapons able to destroy Achilles himself.

It was surely not possible, as Margaret Strone had prophesied, that there would come a spring in Constance Kilgour, too: that she would become a happy and beautiful woman, gracious and kind. She and Carstares would marry, and their little girl would have parents and a home at last. When making that joyful fecund prophecy, Margaret had wept; she was a sick woman who must flatter life and invent happiness.

Miss Kirn sat till he knocked and came in.

'Do you mind if I use your phone?' he asked.

'Of course not, Mr. Carstares.' Despite the provocation of

his cheerfulness her voice was calm and friendly. 'Any time you wish.'

Already he had his hand on it, waiting for her to go. A child presented with a new toy in a box couldn't have been more rudely impatient.

She lingered. 'I see it's still a nasty night.'

But for him it seemed the moon shone serenely in a clear sky.

'My friend, Miss Carmichael, the schoolmistress – I believe you've met her – thinks – and she's the best weather forecaster in these parts – it's going to clear and be fine and dry, for days, perhaps for weeks. Fire-danger weather, as you'll know.'

'Yes,' he said. But she knew he wasn't really listening to her. She was an old nuisance to him, all he wanted of her was that she would go and let him telephone.

'Almost every year we have a spell of it,' she said, 'at this time. I've seen it last all April, and into May. It's very beautiful. The air's so clear you can see the deer on the hilltops from the road. It dries your lips.'

He still had his hand on the telephone.

'I dislike the telephone,' she said, with a genuine shiver. 'A human being's not just a voice. Sometimes I imagine it's like speaking to the dead.' She had been thinking of Margaret Strone, whose voice often was a dead woman's voice, but realised he might think she was hinting at his own dead wife. 'Of course, that's just a silly prejudice of mine,' she added. 'I'm afraid I have many of them.' As she went out, she added, aloud, but to herself, bitterly: 'An old maid's hallucinations.' And glancing up at the stags' heads with their great antlers she saw them as symbols of beautiful masculinity. It was not too late after all, she suddenly felt; and her whole being, her shrivelled womb included, seemed to open like a fragrant rose. Carstares, waiting with the telephone at his ear, thought by his indifference to degrade her to less than a woman; but he could not, she who had wished an hour or so ago to be a goddess in beneficence towards him, was now one for her own delight. Human scruples, therefore, being meaningless, she stood inside the lounge where she could spy on him without being seen.

What she saw she had expected, and was confirmed in her triumphant divinity. She felt an urge to pull off all her clothes and run out into the rain, where under the silver fir, the most lovely of her trees, a satyr waited to give her joy. She could not, however, try as she might, prevent his face from being that of Jock.

It was a man's voice who had answered, barely that, for it was so soft, tired, and ludicrously refined; what seemed an element of self-caricature redeemed it a little. 'Cap'n Kilgour speakin',' it said.

'My name's Carstares, Hugh Carstares. I'd like to talk to Constance, to Miss Kilgour.'

Kilgour was astonished. 'To Connie? You a friend of hers?'

'Yes.'

'Carstares, did you say? Carstares? Can't say I've ever heard her mention you; but then, good Lord, there was a time once she wouldn't even tell me the names of her pet squirrels. Not that I mean you're a squirrel, old man.' He guffawed, rather sadly. 'Where are you speakin' from?'

'The hotel.'

'Kinlochgarvie Hotel, you mean? Little Jenny Wren's place? I mean Miss Kirn, of course.'

'Yes.'

'Not bad whisky there. I understand the food's all right, too. Are you here for the fishin'?'

'Is she at home? May I speak to her?'

'Connie? Yes, she's at home. She got another soaking today. What does she want to walk in the rain for? So you want to talk to her? Don't be surprised if she won't have anything to do with it. Connie's a recluse now. She's cut dozens of old friends. But you might be lucky. If you like, I'll let her know.'

'Yes, let her know.'

'Don't be too hopeful.' Laughing, Kilgour shouted her name. 'Keep your fingers crossed, old man. Here she comes.' Then he could be heard explaining. She replied, quietly. He expostulated, laughed, and spoke to Carstares again, with a kind of schoolboy malicious relish. 'No go, old man. The lady wishes to remain exclusive. Now if you were a hedgehog or a squirrel, she might talk to you. Are you by any chance a hedgehog or a squirrel? She says she doesn't know you, by the way. Carstares. That's right, isn't it?'

'Hugh Carstares.'

'I'm afraid I didn't mention the Hugh part. It didn't seem worthwhile.'

Carstares closed his eyes, fighting to control himself: all the frustration and despair of the past three years would over-whelm him, in a panic, if he gave in now. This was not just Constance Kilgour denying him, but Marion herself; this was not merely exclusion from one woman's friendship, it was rejection by all humanity.

He almost whispered into the telephone that he was Alison's father.

'Still there, old man?' chuckled Kilgour.

'Yes.'

'Thought you'd sneaked off for a whisky. Wouldn't mind joining you. This is a bit of a poser, eh? What are we going to do about it? Of course, I believe you know Connie. Damn it, you wouldn't have come all this way to see her if you didn't know her; and another thing, if she didn't know you, she wouldn't have put on her Medusa-look. Did you expect her eyes would light up when I mentioned your name, old man? I'm afraid they didn't.'

'Ask her again.'

Kilgour paused. 'Now, do you really think I ought to? I don't know what was between you and Connie, and I don't want to know. Was it during the war? Do you know about Alison? Never mind, I shouldn't have said that; that's Connie's own business. I say, shall we leave her alone? That's what she wants. Lord knows where it's going to get her, but it's what she wants, and neither you nor I, old man, has any right to interfere. But if you're going to be at the hotel for a day or two there's no reason why we shouldn't meet. I could have lunch with you tomorrow, if that suits you. One thing though, you'd have to promise, no discussing Connie. There's plenty of other things to discuss: fishin', for instance. I know all the burns and lochs around these parts. I should, shouldn't I? I was born here. In fact, to tell the truth, I used to own them; or at least my family did. When I was Alison's age – what I mean is, they were mine in prospect: I was the hopeful heir. Now. you might call me extinct. There used to be ospreys nesting on one of the islets in the loch. You can see the one from the hotel. Some fool rifled their nest, and since that day they've never come back. Same with me, you see; my eggs were rifled, too.' He chuckled, but seemed to be almost in tears. 'I take it you were in the army, old man? Let's understand this, like friends: as far as I'm concerned the war's dead and buried. Don't let's dig it up.'

'I'll come to the house,' whispered Carstares.

'No, no, I wouldn't do that, old man. Apart altogether from Connie, we're in no position at present to entertain guests. Sorry, but there it is; goes right against our traditions of hospitality, but there's no alternative. Shall I see you at the hotel tomorrow, in time for lunch? Connie won't mind eating alone, I assure you. One o'clock suit? I don't run a car at present, but it'll do me good to walk down, take some of the fat off.' He chuckled wistfully. 'As a matter of fact, old man, I think I must be the thinnest of all the Kilgours, from the beginning of the family in the reign of James I – the Scottish James I, I mean, not the hybrid.'

'I'll call at the house,' repeated Carstares, and put the telephone down.

As he came out of the office Miss Kirn appeared briskly from the lounge, carrying a daffodil.

'Get through all right?' she called.

He nodded; his fist, as yellow as the flower, was pressed hard against his cheek. She almost threw the daffodil away to clutch him and. beg him to give up this fatal affection for Constance Kilgour, who so obviously had again rejected him. Though she had never conceived, Muriel Kirn refused to accept that as a consequence her maternal intuitions were all withered. Now, indeed, they were in full flower of sympathy for this young soldier who, denied a body that he had once been allowed to caress, acted like a small boy bravely but precariously enduring toothache. She was surprised, and delighted, by the mature nature of her pity.

Nevertheless she felt slighted when, without a word to her, he turned away down the lobby that led into the bar. Tapping her cheek with the daffodil, she was on the point of calling to him that that way was private, that if he wished to drink he could order in the lounge. Before he had come she had pressed upon Jock that tact and perseverance must be used in dissuading him from drinking more than he should. When Jock, with his satyr's wink, had replied that the profits would suffer, she had rebuked him sternly. Now, with her heart beating strangely fast, she repented that sternness.

Six

Grave as a priest in his white smock, Jock stood behind the bar, polishing glasses. The only other occupant was an old man seated by the fire, grumbling into his glass of beer.

When Carstares came in, through the staff entrance, Jock was surprised and interested. At once, behind his mask of service, he set about diagnosing. Was this anger still directed against big Rab for affronting Miss Kilgour? Or had Nancy's breasts had time to come into it? Or was it, simply, the dead wife?

When Carstares ordered a large whisky, Jock at once set it up. Dissuasion could hardly begin yet. Besides, Carstares was not only upset, he was even vicious, desperate, liable to burst into rage. Well, Jock had known men who could drink themselves into benignity. If Carstares happened to be one of those, would not dissuasion be unwise and unkind? So, with experimenter's smile, Jock filled up the glass when bid.

'Where the hell are they all?' asked Carstares.

'It's a bit early yet, sir. In any case, this is blind Friday. You'll know forestry people are paid every second Friday. This isn't it.' He pointed to a notice which stated no credit was given. 'The rule's not rigid,' he said. 'I use my discretion; but ninety per cent of them don't get it.'

Deciding to carry the experiment further, he leant across and whispered: 'See that chair by the fire, sir? The one with the arms? They call it the throne. Know who sits in it? King Rab. Aye, your big red bastard in the lorry, sir. You should see them loup when he comes in, men twice his age, with grey hairs and grownup families. "Here's your chair, Rab; been keeping it warm for you." They slap his back, sir, they even go the length of standing him pints. But they know, and he knows, and that bird up there knows' – he nodded towards a buzzard in a glass case affixed to the wall – 'and I know, he's a man of sawdust, a braggart, a coward. They've got a word in Glasgow suits him. Maybe you've heard of it, sir. Crapbag.'

'Has nobody ever taken a punch at him?'

'Not as far as I know. Mind you, sir, he chooses his victims. But all the same I've served in pubs where men half his size would have crowned him all right with a beer bottle. I'll tell you what the trouble is here, sir. They're still feudal.'

Again Jock paused, considered, and decided to risk continuing with the experiment.

'Yes, sir, that's it: feudal. Hear them laugh at Captain Kilgour, behind his back. To his face, what do they do? Touch their caps, even lift them. The Kilgours, you see, have been lairds here for centuries.'

'What's Kilgour like?'

'The Captain, sir? Well, he wears a kilt.'

'What's wrong with that?'

'Nothing, sir, nothing at all. I used to wear one myself, when I was ten, under the age of protest. It's just that the Captain's legs are the thinnest I ever saw.' Jock could have added, but did not, that Miss Kilgour's legs on the other hand redeemed the family.

Carstares changed the subject. 'How does McKerrol get on with Strone?'

'Like a dog with a weasel.'

'Which is which?'

The most neutral of winks was Jock's answer to that. 'I'm expecting visitors,' he confided. 'Folk you might be interested in, sir: the McKews from Creagan. You'll have heard of the McKews?'

'I've heard of them.'

Jock had to admit that the whisky wasn't making for benignity. Maybe it would be safer not to discuss the McKews.

'I must say,' he said, 'in spring and early summer this is the most beautiful countryside in the world.'

'What about these McKews?'

'Wild men, sir.'

'In what way, wild?'

'Great hefty bruisers, all five of them, including Faither, which is what they call the old man, who's got a beard like a fleece. Clannish as wolves. You'll have met Nancy, the maid here? One of them's courting her. Will. He'll be in shortly to take her to the dance. To be fair, I should say he's the only one of the crew with a glimmering of civility. You wouldn't think it, though, to look at him. Coarse-looking? Got a face hacked out of rock. A quiet man, Will, but I wouldn't like to cross him. Big Rab, for instance, as you know, is filthy where women are concerned. You'll not hear him say a word against Nancy. Why? Because Will would break his neck.'

'Will seems fonder of her than she is of him.'

'That's often the case, isn't it, sir?' Then Jock had to hurry on. 'I've warned her she's playing a dangerous game. He's serious about her. He worships her.'

'As a tup worships a ewe?'

'I don't know what a tup's feelings are towards a ewe, sir. But I do know Will's determined to marry her. Every other man in these parts daren't look at her, for fear of offending him.'

'But she's been well-tupped in other fields?'

So, reflected Jock, had Miss Kilgour from all accounts, with a pretty little lamb to show for it. He did not say so.

The gong sounded through in the hotel.

'Dinner, sir,' said Jock.

Carstares ordered another drink.

As Jock poured it out they heard a car approach and stop outside.

'I thought,' said Carstares truculently, 'shepherds were meek, gentle men, carrying lambs in their arms.'

Jock could not help grinning: 'Ask the McKew collies about that, sir,' he murmured.

'It's a big farm. They'll have plenty of money.'

'The war was a Klondike for them.'

'Why then does Nancy not grab hold of Will?'

Jock smiled at that whisky irony. 'She wants to marry money, sir; but she'd prefer it good-looking.'

Then the door opened noisily and he had to switch on his host's smile to welcome the three large uncouth men who came clumping in.

'It's yourself, Alec,' he cried, 'and you, Will, not to mention Tom. Dirty night for the run over from Creagan, But there's a good fire, gentlemen, draw up your chairs, and make yourselves at home.'

They wore, like a uniform, clumsy blue serge suits, thick woollen pullovers, striped shirts, dotted ties, and checked caps. They were alike, too, in appearance, tall, straight, brawny, with enormous fists and heavy, bronzed faces. It was easy, from Jock's description, to pick out Will. His thick lips, squat, powerful nose, shaggy hair and brows, and ears large and thick as fungi on a tree, combined to form a remarkable yet attractive coarseness. He was the only one of the trio to smile back at Jock.

They hung their caps on a row of pegs along the wall. Will left a peg empty between his cap and Alec's; the latter moved it, so that all three caps hung close together.

They sat down by the fire and ordered beer and whisky. The old man got up and shuffled out. He had greeted them sycophantically, but they had ignored him.

'Dinner, sir,' urged Jock. He didn't like the belligerence with which Carstares was glowering at the newcomers. Nor did Alec McKew, the eldest, like it either.

'You'll ken us next time you see us,' he said.

'I shouldn't wonder,' replied Carstares. 'Once seen, never forgotten.'

Alec's beer, halfway to his mouth, returned slowly to the table. He thought hard. His brother Tom grinned moronically. Will muttered words of restraint.

Alec got up and swaggered over to Carstares.

'Mean onything in particular by that?' he asked.

Jock made an effort; he pretended this was an ordinary social meeting. 'Alec, meet Mr. Carstares, the new District Officer for Kinlochgarvie; Mr. Carstares, meet Mr. Alec McKew, of Creagan Farm, which is the largest sheep farm in the district. How many thousand is it now, Alec?'

There was no hand-shaking. Alec, the better to concentrate, picked at his nose. 'So you're the new D.O.?' he said. 'We've heard o' you. Sure we've heard o' him, boys?'

'Sure,' roared Tom, though it was obvious he didn't know what his brother was talking about.

Will stared at Carstares with what, on another face, might have been interpreted as a wish to be friendly, to admire even, to sympathise with.

'I see you're no' wearing your medal,' remarked Alec.

'That's right. But you're wearing your sheep-dung, aren't you? There's a stink of it, anyway.'

Jock appealed by an urgent look to Will, who hurried over and pushed his brother back.

'We don't want trouble,' he said to Carstares. 'Faither said, nae trouble.' Then, despite his brother's snarls, he held out his hand.

Carstares looked as if he was going to vomit on it. 'If you don't want trouble,' he said, 'keep your bloody sheep out of our trees.'

Will strove to remain reasonable. 'You ken sheep,' he said. 'They smell the green grass. They get in.'

'They get in because you bloody well throw them over the fences, and open the gates.'

'No.' Will shook his head. 'That's what Strone says. It's not true. Faither would like to see you. He says he's willing to give a new man a chance.'

'That's handsome of him.'

Will frowned. 'You've no' to say onything aboot Faither,' he said. 'That's one thing we'll no' allow.'

'Let me mak' a mess o' his yellow face,' snarled Alec. 'I'll show him what kind o' a hero he is.'

'I'll come and see your father,' said Carstares.

'You've no' got the guts to come to Creagan,' sneered Alec.

'Whit's the maitter?' shouted Tom from the rear. 'Your beer's getting cauld.'

'That's right,' said Will eagerly to Carstares, 'you come. But don't bring Strone wi' you. Faither doesn't like him.'

'He says he'll shoot him on sight,' said Alec.

'I'll come by myself.'

'Make sure you're sober,' sneered Alec. 'Faither willnae speak to a man that's drunk.'

'Where's Murdo?' asked Jock with anxious joviality. 'Don't tell me he's not going to the dance, and him the best dancer in the district.'

'Murdo's coming,' said Alec. 'He'll be there. We McKews stick thegether.'

'Like sheep's turds,' said Carstares.

Jock later laughed at the neatness of the remark. Then he was horrified. 'Dinner, sir,' he urged.

Alec was struggling to get past Will. Tom, at last aware his loyal brawn might be needed, heaved to his feet.

Carstares calmly emptied his glass, grinned at them all, grimaced as at a nasty stink, laughed, and went out, not too steadily.

Seven

Miss Kirn had decided, for his own good, to let Nancy loose upon him; indeed, she had kindled her maid's erotic ambition by hinting to her that Miss Kilgour was a rival.

So Nancy had arranged a love-nook in the dining-room, lit by a lamp with a red-fringed shade, warmed by a large electric fire. Though she still wore her uniform, under it she was bathed, powdered and perfumed. Her brassiere so emphasised her bosom she had giggled at it herself, not in embarrassment, but in pride and wonder; she had felt a desire to be male, so as to be able to enjoy and tame those aggressive protuberances. Earrings, shaped like clusters of forget-me-nots adorned her ears, while her fingernails glistened like cherries. She had changed her coiffure. Vexed by not knowing the style in which his wife had worn her fair hair, she had tried several styles; the one she had chosen was, she thought, the right mixture of glamour and dignity: the blue ribbon had been removed.

She did not fear Miss Kilgour's competition. The latter, she was sure, had as much sexual attraction as a tree. Didn't she walk in the rain with a raincoat fit for a scarecrow, and with her head bare, so that her hair fell over her pale brow like black rats' tails? Weren't her legs chafed and red at knees and ankles? Didn't she use no lipstick or nail-paint or even scent? And above all, in spite of the child which was said to be hers, wasn't she regarded by every man in the district as a kind of freak, not a woman at all, whose breasts were as hard and unreachable as the stones on Ben Vorlich's cairn? Yet, in spite of that poverty of sex, far worse than any lack of money, she had once, meeting Nancy on the road, repulsed her sisterly smile with a glance of utter indifference.

Here then, in Carstares, was presented an opportunity to triumph, not only over the whole village which derided her ambition, but also over Miss Kilgour who thought herself a lady. It was an opportunity, too, that Nancy felt equipped to take advantage of. Carstares was depressed and confused by the loss of his wife. Well, she could comfort him; and if, in that comforting, she had a child by him, she would have gained either him or at least a good part of the fortune his wife had left him.

She knew he had just come from the bar and likely had seen Will there. She would not bring up that subject herself, but she would not be discomfited by it if he brought it up; indeed, she would be pleased. She would be able to claim chastity, as far as Will anyhow was concerned. Nowhere, not among the bronze or saffron bracken, or in the flowering heather, or under the red rowans, or even in the high sheep-fank at Ardruie, Will's favourite place, had she let him do more than play with her breasts. She had roused his lust, only to subdue it by reminding him that he wished to marry her. Sometimes, after making him talk about the money that would come to him after his father's death, she had thought it might be good policy to let him tup her; but when she had shown herself willing, indeed eager to see how he would perform, he had refused, with a long, intense, foolish explanation that she had not been able to understand. Apparently, though, he wished to marry her first: it was a condition to be laughed at, but also, in spite of that laughter, respected, too. If Carstares had not come, she would have been willing enough to marry Will; and, of course, if this scheme to catch Carstares failed, Will would still be there to fall back on.

At first Carstares was quiet and sullen as he ate. Attending him, she strove, until her belly and thighs ached, to exert a sexiness that must overpower him. With hand, elbow, hip, and bosom, she nudged him. Her scent was so strong it must surely have flavoured his soup. She marvelled that he could remain so unresponsive, especially as drunk as he was. Had she been a man she would, she felt sure, have yielded almost immediately. What would she have done, as her first move? While she was wondering, Carstares suddenly, with what sounded like an oath, gripped her buttock and squeezed it hard.

She gasped, but tholed the pain. 'I bruise easily,' she said. 'All purple and yellow.' She wondered if she should say that a kiss would cure it.

He kept squeezing. 'I've just been talking to your handsome boy-friend,' he said.

She could not help giggling. 'Handsome?' And then, in surprise: 'My boy-friend? And who may he be?'

'You know damned well. Will McKew. He's in the bar waiting to take you to the dance.'

'Let him wait.'

'It must be his money you're after. He's an ape.'

'He's no oil-painting,' she agreed.

'If he's not your boy-friend,' he said, leering up at her, 'by all accounts you're his favourite ewe. Is that the arrangement, Nancy?'

'There's no arrangement. I wouldn't let him touch me with his little finger.'

'Now, Nancy, I doubt that; I must say I doubt it very much.'

'It's true.'

'Don't tell me you're virtuous, Nancy. I couldn't stand the disappointment.'

'I'm just particular.'

'Ah, so that's it? Particular. What about me, for instance? Would you let me touch you, with my little finger?'

'Maybe, if you wanted to.'

'Maybe I do want to, Nancy.'

She put her hand on his, which still pressed her buttock. 'All right,' she whispered, excited almost beyond control. She wanted him to start pulling off her clothes there and then.

'Not here,' he said, laughing.

'In your room.'

'I've still got my coffee to drink.'

'In half an hour.'

'Half an hour? Yes, I think I could wait that long. Can you, Nancy?'

She smiled, not sure what he meant.

'What about the dance?' he asked.

'I don't want to go.'

'Will'll be disappointed.'

'What's that to me?'

'He'll be jealous, too.'

'That's nothing to me.'

'Good. And it's nothing to me. All right, Nancy, it's a tryst, in my room, in half an hour.'

Then he let go her buttock, and proceeded to finish his rice and prunes.

Half an hour later Carstares was lying, fully dressed on his bed, wishing to smoke, but not able to because his fingers had let his packet of cigarettes fall, and he had not the will or the physical control to recover them. Stounds of pain kept shooting through his leg, though the surgeons had assured him it was now healed: any pain felt would be in his mind. He moaned in pity for himself, but once, hearing the moans, he raised his head to see who was in the room with him, making them. He expected someone, but he could not remember who.

Huddled in the lounge, almost asleep, he had this sense of appointment, and had staggered upstairs to his room, trying to remember who was coming. Once he found himself wandering into a distorted memory of childhood: a tall, thin boy of ten stood in front of a locked door, with his face as expressionless as it. He could see where his reluctant breath misted it, and by his side his hands hung maimed and paralysed with helplessness. Within that room his mother had lain dead; now, within this present room, more than twenty years later, he could not be sure it would not be she who would soon enter. Or perhaps it might be the mother of the Japanese soldier whose tranquil hands so often frightened him in dreams. It would be a woman, he knew that; and he hoped it would not be Marion come with the ruthlessness of the dead to tell him gently so many things he knew already. Nancy he had quite forgotten.

When, therefore, she tapped on the door, opened it, and

entered with a whirl of her new dark green tartan skirt, he gaped at her in astonishment and morose disappointment. She was not surprised or discouraged; she had half expected to find him sound asleep. The two top buttons of her white blouse were unfastened to show more of her breasts, white and fragrant as roses. Calm now, like a wife, she adjusted her forget-me-not earrings, and then began to stroke her thighs with a kind of voluptuous regret, as if not even he, an ex-officer and wealthy, was worthy to deflower them. Then, suddenly shy and uncertain as a bride, she turned and faced him.

'Well?' she whispered hoarsely.

With his mouth foolishly open and his eyes goggling, he was on the point of slipping into impotence. She had to be quick and resolute. Kicking off her shoes, she slipped over to the bed, lifted his hand, and though it twitched and was icy cold, pressed it against her naked bosom. Cool again, expert and observant as a doctor, she saw the symptoms: despite his drunken sleepiness, desire swelled in him, even in the veins in his throat.

'A minute,' she whispered, and hurrying across snibbed the door. Then she returned, resolute and capable. She had deliberately taken no precautions, and neither, she was certain, had he. No simpleton, she was well aware that if a man made a girl pregnant he was not obliged to marry her. Alec McKew, for instance, had had two bastards and was still a bachelor, while the grand Miss Kilgour had one and would die an old maid. But a brat whose father had been an officer and possessed a fortune of thirty thousand pounds would be a good investment in itself.

Nevertheless there was no need for extravagance. Her skirt was new, rumpling would spoil its pleats. Dexterously she stepped out of it. When she saw her legs, so long, smooth, warm, and swelling, in their transparent nylons, she felt not only pride, but desire, too. Often she gazed thus at her own nudity to taste that desire.

So far he had not moved; his hands remained foolishly idle. But she knew there were men who even if sober as a priest and strong as a stallion, liked to be helped. At the same time she had learned that impatience on her part might humiliate him into impotence. Luckily, there was no need for hurry. Will would wait in the bar till it closed, and then he would wait outside in the rain. She liked this picture of him waiting, as dour and stubborn as one of his own tups; and if she succeeded tonight, he would have to go on waiting for the rest of his life; that was to say, if what he had said, or rather had sung through his blackened teeth, was true: that she was the only woman he would ever marry and he would wait for her till a' the seas went dry. She had found out later that that was a quotation from a Burns song.

Half-nude now, with a last glance in the mirror, she turned towards the bed. His loud breathing alarmed her for a moment: she thought he had fallen asleep. But no, he was still awake, and was watching her. His nostrils quivered and his neck was thick with lust. He looked scarcely more handsome than Will. Bulls and tups and cocks, she had noticed, remained calmer and more dignified than men, before, after, and during.

Boldness was necessary. At any moment he might remember, with typical masculine conceit and fear, that he was in Kinlochgarvie as District Officer, a person of authority, whose career might be damaged if he was to be caught in bed with her, a skivvy. Once the intercourse had taken place, of course, it would be in her power to threaten him with that damage.

As, hand soft on bruised buttock, she approached the bed, he struggled up to a sitting position.

'Are my fags on the floor?' he muttered.

The question stopped her.

'Hand them up, will you?'

She tried to smile, wondering what his game was. Stripped thus, to do him any service but one would make her look and feel ridiculous.

He held out his hand, impatiently, expecting only his cigarettes.

Stooping, she picked up the packet, took one out, and placed it in the cleft between her breasts.

'There's one,' she whispered. 'Take it.'

He did so, as if from a packet held by another man. As he lit it, she still tried to smile, but she was trembling and feeling very cold.

He smoked in silence, not avoiding her, but making no sign he saw her. Her toes writhed on the carpet and the bruise on her buttock throbbed. She would have snatched up a garment, or at least used her hands, to cover her if she had not been afraid that that act of modesty would have made this insulting of her more conspicuous.

So abruptly that her breasts panged with hope, he scrambled off the bed, muttering hoarsely; but he did not make for her. Instead, he made for the window, opened it, and thrust his head out. At first she thought he must be feeling sick and wanted fresh air. Then it occurred to her he might be looking for the lights of Garvic House.

Now she did blush. With her back to him, unsteady with anger, she stepped into her skirt.

When he turned round with a face like a madman's, she was fastening her suspenders, as casually as she could, to conceal her shame and resentment. Indeed, she hoped she might still provoke him or at any rate exact some preliminary revenge by reminding him of his fair-haired wife who must often in the privacy of their bedroom have thus fastened her suspenders, with her pale thighs visible. It seemed to some extent she was successful. He groaned, and sitting, on the edge of the bed covered his face with his hands.

Then she realised in time she had better say nothing that would end the game for good: this was merely suspended, while drink and sorrow and whatever peculiar emotion he felt for Constance Kilgour was making him insane, or at least incapable. Later that night, or tomorrow, or the next day, she could try again; spring was here, the season of perseverance, for birds and frogs and maids.

Therefore, as she left she was smiling as if it was she who in pity had decided on a postponement.

'I'll look in after the dance,' she said softly, before she closed the door.

Eight

Having pushed Will McKew out into the rain, and locked the outer bar-room door, Jock, in Rab's throne by the fire, with his feet up on the table, was enjoying his nightly sacramental dram of whisky when his employer hurried in.

As he got to his feet he looked at her in as much reproach as astonishment. She knew his opinion, that the bar was no place for a lady, even if she did benefit from its profits.

She sat down at the table upon which his feet had rested so dominantly a minute ago.

'Jock, Mr. Carstares's car is still outside in the rain,' she said.

He nodded, wondering why she had had to come into the bar to tell him that.

'Sit down,' she said.

He did so, rather uneasily. She wore a smile that baffled and almost embarrassed him.

'It's been waiting out there all evening,' she said.

Again he nodded.

'Finish your drink, if you wish,' she said, with that peculiar smile intensified.

He took a sip.

'Didn't he say he was going out in it later?' she asked. 'We both heard him, didn't we?'

'Yes.'

'I think his plans must have been changed.'

'I'm not surprised,' he said. 'It's still pouring.' He thought of Will McKew huddled outside, waiting for Nancy. Was she, perhaps, the cause of Carstares's change of plan? And did that explain this odd suggestive smile, which excited but also displeased him?

'Where is he?' he asked.

'Upstairs, in his room, I believe. In bed no doubt.'

Those pauses were deliberate and significant. Was she insinuating he was in bed with Nancy? And did her smile imply she was delighted, not to say thrilled, by that exceedingly quick little bit of houghmagandy under her roof? Jock's own sexual system began to tingle, though he still felt displeased and uneasy.

'If he's in bed,' he said cautiously, 'he'll certainly not need his car.'

'That's just what I thought.' She chuckled. 'So perhaps you should go and put it into the garage.'

'Very good. But don't you think I should go up and ask him first?'

'If you think you should.' Again she chuckled.

He wondered if she hoped he would surprise Carstares and Nancy in the act.

'By the way, Jock,' she said, with a sudden severity that was evidently not genuine, 'you didn't do as I asked you; I mean, discourage him from drinking.'

'He's a hard man to discourage.'

'Is he? There's someone able to discourage him.' She stood up.

He rose, too. 'Discourage him from drinking, d'you mean?'

'No.'

Did she mean then, from coupling? But hadn't she already hinted that Nancy and he, with her blessing, were at that very minute cosily on the job?

'It was Garvie House he intended to visit,' she said.

He understood, and was relieved. So Miss Kilgour was the discourager. Well she might be. Some of the folk in the district blamed her for delaying the spring.

He followed his mistress out of the bar into the hotel. His hand experimentally bumped against her. The result disconcerted him. She turned and gave him a glance of such simpering equivocation he wondered if she'd been drinking herself. Certainly her face was oddly flushed.

'I'm not my brother's keeper,' he muttered. 'What I mean is, if he finds it easier to get to sleep with a dozen whiskies inside him, what right have I to deprive him of them? Didn't he have a hand in killing Japs? I should think they'd make bad ghosts. And he's got his dead wife to bury, every hour.'

As they stood at the foot of the stairs, gazing at each other's feet, Nancy came running down, wrapped in yellow oilskins.

'Oh Nancy,' said Miss Kirn sweetly, 'is Mr. Carstares asleep?'

Nancy laughed. 'How should I know?' She winked at Jock, who frowned.

'Will's waiting,' he said, 'and I doubt if he's pleased.'

'He'll be less pleased yet,' she replied. At the outer door she turned. 'Has he got the car outside?'

Jock grinned. 'No. Alec insisted on taking it up to the hall.'

'Does the fool think I'm going to walk there in the rain?'

'You'd better go and ask him.'

'I certainly will.' She banged the door in a temper.

'Do you think they'll marry?' asked Miss Kirn, very quietly.

'Will and Nancy? Not if he's got any sense.'

'Why should he not? She's a beautiful girl. And he dotes on her.'

He made a face.

'Would you deny love, Jock?' The question was accompanied by a peep of birdlike impertinence into his very soul.

He found himself blushing. 'I wouldn't say that,' he muttered.

'I should hope not. Now up you go and ask Mr. Carstares about his car. The coast's clear.'

As he went up, he pondered over that last remark. What in God's name had got into her? He had tested her breath and was sure she hadn't been drinking. It must be something else. Love? Certainly it was on her mind. For whom though? Well, wasn't he the only man around, at all eligible? He tried, but failed, to make a joke of it; he liked her too much. He knew that in the bar jokes were made about the grim schoolmistress who was finding her virginity as it decayed hard to endure; but he had not thought that cheerful, spry, capable little Miss Kirn was suffering from the same torment. Nor did he want to think it; indeed, he was angry with himself for having even let the suspicion into his mind. Why should it not be real affection that had caused those smiles? And why should that affection not be for him? For his part he had liked her from the day she had engaged him; and liking, like whisky, matured best in secrecy. Besides, was it not in all the kids' story-books, princess marries woodcutter's son, or in modern terms hotel proprietrix marries barman? If in the old versions the woodcutter's son always turned out after marriage to be a prince abducted at birth, why should not the barman turn out to be a born hotel-keeper?

During these reflections he had knocked on the door. When no answer came he entered discreetly. The light was on. Carstares was not in his bed. He was crouched in an ambiguous position by its side: either he had been trying to pray, or else he had collapsed through drink and weariness.

Jock felt pity. 'Mr. Carstares, sir,' he murmured, taking him by the shoulder.

Carstares sighed.

'Mr. Carstares, Miss Kirn wants to know if I'm to put your car away. It's nearly ten o'clock, and it's still raining.'

Carstares showed his face. Jock's pity increased, though embarrassment contaminated it a little; he had not thought Carstares was the kind to weep, even when drunk.

'The mistress thinks you won't be needing it after all, sir.'

Carstares did not understand.

'Your car, sir. It's still out in the rain. Do you want me to put it away for you? But in the meantime I'm sure you'd be more comfortable in the chair. Allow me.'

With a dexterity that was as much a part of his trade as the pouring of liquids into glasses, Jock seized the big man, coaxed him, and at the right moment heaved him up into the chair. Then, puffing a little, he contemplated him, sadly: more piteous than a man destroyed was a man in the process of destruction, especially a young man in spring-time. Suddenly Jock caught a glimpse of himself bloom from barman to host.

'Would you like me to help you into bed, sir?' he asked.

Carstares seemed to notice him for the first time, 'What's up?' he muttered, and then cried: 'Is there a message for me?'

There was, of course, from winking fate; but that was not the message he meant.

'No, sir,' said Jock. 'Not a message exactly. Miss Kirn wants to know if I've to put your car away. It's still pouring outside, you see. You said earlier on you might need it, but we thought—' Jock had to stop; he could hardly go on talking so compassionately to a man who had begun to smile as if he had just been told the most glorious news.

'What time is it?' asked Carstares.

'Nearly ten, sir. Bar's closed. Owls are hooting. Time for bed.'

Miss Kirn's bed had a spread and quilt of scarlet: the colour of sin and passion. He was fifty-six, she fifty-three or thereabouts. They would make as dapper a pair on the kirk steps as any finches in a nuptial tree.

As Jock grinned at that picture of comedy and innocence and affection, Carstares rose, stood steadying himself, and then walked across to the wash-hand basin where he began to splash cold water over his face. It had an extraordinary effect, for when he turned round, that smile, of ecstasy and hope realisable only in heaven, had returned. It was the true drunkard's smile, seen by Jock only once before in his career. To see it twice was not lucky. The first time had been years ago in a pub in Glasgow. A small man of about sixty, a stranger, who had been sitting in a corner decently drinking his beer, had startled everybody by suddenly rising and shouting. His face, a moment ago quite unremarkable, was now made forever memorable by an imbecile radiance and expectation; he had stood weeping in that prodigious joy. Later, it was discovered he had left his wife lying in the kitchen at home, a hatchet sunk into her skull, and her blood refreshing the roses on the walls. What he had seen or thought to be so full of joy all of a sudden, neither Jock nor anybody else could say, then or afterwards. Still, a man whose fingers were still cramped from clutching a hatchet stained with the blood of the woman who'd slept in peace and trust with him for thirty-five years might be expected to behave in an unorthodox way. What, equivalent to that murder, had Carstares done? Perhaps in his case it was still to do. Big Rab McKerrol? Or Nancy? Certainly, now one came to think of it, the room stank with her scent. Jock became alarmed.

'Are you for going out, sir?' he asked.

Carstares was fixing his tie. 'Yes,' he replied. 'Yes, I'm going out.'

'I know it's not my place to give you advice, sir, but do you really think you should? It's a dark night. There are bad places on the roads: sheer drops into the loch, dangerous corners, hollows that flood. If I were you, sir, I'd wait till the morning.'

'I can't wait,' said Carstares, and went out.

Jock followed him smartly, lest the victim should after all be Miss Kirn herself.

She was waiting at the foot of the stair.

'You needn't have come yourself, Mr. Carstares,' she cried. 'Jock would have put it away.'

Behind him Jock pretended to be steering a car with drunken hands.

'I don't want it put away,' said Carstares. 'I'm going out.'

But when he took his coat off the hallstand he had such difficulty in putting it on that Jock good-naturedly helped him.

Miss Kirn got between her guest and the outer door.

'I'm afraid I can't let you go out, Mr. Carstares,' she said. 'You're not fit to drive a car. I'm sorry to have to say it, but it's true. If you don't kill someone, you'll kill yourself. As the proprietrix of this hotel, it's my responsibility.'

He smiled down at her.

'The road to Garvie House especially,' she cried, 'is very bad. It's full of pot-holes. Isn't it, Jock?'

'Hundreds of them, all deep enough to drown a baby in.'

Carstares pushed her gently out of his way. She would have

resisted, but Jock put a hand upon her that surprised himself with its affectionate dominance.

'Let him go,' he whispered. 'What's for him won't go by him.'

'Yes. Do you know, I've got such a strange feeling about him.'

'Better have it about me,' he murmured.

'Look at him now,' she cried. 'He's stopped. He's coming out. What's he going to do?'

At first Jock had thought Carstares, in a drunk man's way, had remembered the needs of nature and had got out to attend to them in the headlights of the car. He had been about, therefore, to turn Miss Kirn round to save her modesty. But Carstares, once out of the car, had gone running across the lawn towards one of the life-size china rabbits, which were Miss Kirn's pride. He picked it up and tenderly carried it back to the car.

Jock laughed: the amiabilities of drunkenness were not only unexpected, they were also irresistible.

Miss Kirn, however, was not sure whether she should be touched or alarmed.

'He's taken Milkwort,' she cried. 'What's he going to do with her?'

Throw her into the loch, Jock hoped: Milkwort and her friends caused Miss Kirn to be laughed at, therefore he did not like them. 'One thing he'll not do,' he said cheerfully, 'is light a fire in the woods and cook her for supper.'

'I know why he took her,' she cried.

Carstares was now back in the car. Next moment it was off again, tearing along the curved drive towards the gate. It did not creep out into the public road as the notice advised, but swung out fast, and faster still rushed along the lochside.

Jock breathed into his mistress's neck. It smelled far sweeter than Nancy's. Well, the night's little drama was over. Bed was next: the question was, one or two. He felt like a weasel about to kill a rabbit.

'So you know why he took her,' he whispered.

'Yes. Yes, I do know.' Like the doomed rabbit she had not withdrawn an inch.

'Tell me.'

'I don't know whether I should.'

'Is it a secret?'

'Yes, it is really.'

'Am I not to be let into it?'

'It's for the little girl,' she whispered, with a strange shudder, 'Alison Weir, Miss Kilgour's child.'

'A drunk man's offering?'

'No, I don't think so. As far as she's concerned he's more than just a drunk man.'

'I'm still not in the secret, Muriel.' It was the first time he had ever used her name to her face, and the odd thing was he spoke it sternly. 'What's all the mystery about?'

She was silent, and then she began to sob.

He relented at once. 'What you need, little lady, is a nice cup of tea, and that's what you're going to get. We have our own destinies. Don't let us forget that.'

He led her towards the cosy kitchen, and she went so docilely that in him fondness got the upper hand of ambition. Ought he to take advantage of this weakness of hers? Besides, let him remember that if he did win a share of her hotel, and a place in her bed, he would at the same time lose a great part of his freedom. There was no doubt she was an able, alert, enterprising, little woman, not at all backward in scheming to get her own way. She might well, after marriage, turn domineering and exorbitant. True enough a tap would knock her down, relentless opposition would quickly break her spirit; yes, but he had too subtle a mind, too delicate an appreciation of the tricks of fate, too clear a perception of what in life was fit for laughter, and above all too great a respect and affection for her, to resort to any kind of violence against her.

'D'you think,' he asked, calmly, as he switched on the electric kettle, 'he met Miss Kilgour during the war?'

He had made her sit down. 'Yes,' she whispered.

He saw she was fascinated by the masculine assurance of his

hands as he set the tea things on the table. She was for the first time seeing him not as an underling whom she rather liked, but as a man who could, for all his smallness, if she consented to be a woman, make her flower, save her from the bitter everlasting winter of her friend the schoolmistress.

He spoke, with apparent irrevelance; but his smile was pertinent.

'Right enough,' he said, 'odd things happened during the war. I think I told you I worked for a spell in a steelwork. There were some fellows played football every day during the dinner break. Not with a full-size ball, you know, one about so big, the size of a smallish melon. Well, one day as it got kicked and headed about it fell among some scrap metal, where there happened to be an iron ball, solid through and through, pretty much the same size and colour. What did this joker do? He picked it up and shouted: 'Heid it, Tam,' and tossed it into the air. Now this Tam was a football exhibitionist: the kind that heads the moon in his dreams. So he rushed to head it before it should drop to the ground. He managed, too, and woke up four days later in hospital.'

It was not, he well knew, an orthodox courting speech, but its effect was as if he had havered about love and devotion and the birds in spring-time. She sat and stared at him yearningly, so much so that he was not sure whether he too wanted to leap up and head the moon, or whether he should hang his head in humbleness and shame.

'I'll tell you what's between them,' she said, 'between Mr. Carstares and Constance Kilgour.'

'Take it easy, little lady. After all, whatever it is, it's their business. As I said, we've got our own destinies to consider.'

'They were lovers during the war. The child's his. I don't know how many times they were together. It takes only once to make a child, doesn't it? But he was married at the time, you see, and now his poor wife's dead, and he's come to claim the child, and her, too, if she'll have him, although she won't, she's already refused him twice this evening.'

He went towards her. 'All right. So the child's his. So they were lovers. Why should you weep? Why should you break your heart over them. Let him go and try again. Good luck to him. He's been through a lot. So has she, I'm sure. Let's wish them well, Muriel, both of them, and the child, too. For us the world's going to be a very happy place. We want everybody else to be happy, if they can.' Even big Rab, he added, to himself.

While he was speaking he had gone down nimbly on his knees before her, and had taken her cold hands in his.

She wore an expression such as Tam the steelworker must have worn at the instant of impact.

'A man and a woman,' he said urgently, 'aren't made of wood, they're not like a couple of trees content to stand beside each other in the forest for years, and bear the same leaves every year, every spring, until they rot and die, or are cut down. No, they'll pull up their roots, sooner or later, whether it takes ten or fifty years, and they'll come together in the end, in love.'

Even in a countryside of trees, it did not make sense, but it came to him so easily and so spontaneously that he thought, with a sense of shock, that he must surely mean it all.

As for her, she still sobbed, not only for grief at human love thwarted and wasted, but now also for joy and terror at love much nearer and still to be tested. When he began to caress her legs, with infinite delicacy, as if they were liqueur glasses, fragile and precious, she gasped as if his hands were red-hot; but she did not stop him. For many, many years her legs as far as the knees had been thought attractive; thereafter they had remained too thin, and refused to blossom. Now surely they were beginning.

The kettle boiled, making rude but cheerful comments. Not at all discomposed, Jock flitted across to switch it off. Later, say in half an hour, over tea that would not taste like tea they would talk about the change which by that time would have taken place in their relationship. He was confident he would pour out, most potently, like a host.

Nine

If only he saw her soon, that very night, within the next hour, the words to explain, atone, reconcile, and re-establish his love, would be available: that was the assurance that had made Carstares rejoice like the insane murderer in the pub. Suddenly, it seemed, presences which since childhood had given him pleasure and sustenance, possessed his mind; or rather their essence did: blackbirds singing in gean trees, mountain burns, solitary pine-trees, beds of blueberries above the sea, and glens of wild roses, these and many others, representing sunshine and friendliness. Under great green sunlit larches, like those above the schoolhouse, people walked about purged of meanness and desire for revenge. They hailed one another in voices as cheerful and sincere as those of larks in the blue sky; and their hands as they beckoned were as innocent as flowers.

In the car the cushion of the seat where Constance had sat that afternoon was still damp. As he touched it, with reverence, he remembered the insults shouted at her, the gross gesticulations of McKerrol, and the careful vindictiveness of Strone. He was able now to forgive even these, not through any exertion or magnanimity on his part, but because they, too, were included in the amnesty and transformation. Everyone was to be given the chance to start afresh, and all had admitted their indebtedness to one another.

The china rabbit was cold and wet. As he carried it to the car, he hugged it close, for it reminded him of Alison, to whom he would give it as a pet. Tenderly he settled it where Constance had sat, turned round so that it seemed to be smiling up at him with its blue, trustful eyes. Alison's eyes, he thought, were brown, like his own; Constance's were blue. So, even if Miss

Carmichael was wrong and he was not the child's father, yet he might have been, and indeed still could be.

It was Alison he thought about as he drove past the schoolhouse where all the windows were dark, through the village, and past the dance hall where he could hear accordion music. Nancy would be among the dancers, waltzing with her faithful sweetheart Will McKew. He wished them both well.

A gate barred the private road leading to Garvie House. He saw it as the barrier separating him not from the house only, but from the people in it. So eager was he then to remove it, he got out of the car faster than his legs could manage and sprawled face downwards on the road. From waist to chin his belly was soaked and chilled in a large puddle. Laughing at the foolish accident, he scrambled up and made for the gate. It had no latch and leant against the post. He lifted it easily but when he made to swing it round he found it wasn't attached to the far post either, both hinges being gone, so that its weight and sliminess pulled it out of his grasp, and it fell with a great splashing of water and mud. Immediately he crouched to lift it up and drag it out of the way. His hands and clothes became splattered and slippery with mud and with slime off the gate, but with patience and cheerfulness, despite tearing his hand on a nail and cracking his knee-bone against the gate, he managed, after five minutes' struggle, to prop it against the hedge at the side of the road. There he stood for another minute, drenched by the moisture knocked off the hedge and by the rain which was still falling heavily, with his hand on the gate, proudly yet affectionately, like a hunter holding the antlers of a stag he had just shot.

Returning to the car he noticed his hands were now rather dirty for visiting, and carefully wiped them with the rag for cleaning the windows. The rest of him he did not notice. In front the way was now miraculously clear. There, sad and defeated, leant the gate, the barrier, the symbol of obstruction. He felt pity for it in its defeat.

From the gate up to the house the road was pocked with potholes, some more than a foot deep, and others stretching from verge to verge. The car bumped and lurched. He had to drive with one hand too, the other being needed to prevent the rabbit from sliding off the seat. To his surprise, he began to feel sick, until when he was in sight of the house he was forced to stumble out and vomit among some dark bushes that waved in the wind and confused him. Some vomit fell on his clothes; it smelled horribly. This would have to be cleaned off, he realised, and painstakingly tried to do so with his handkerchief.

Ahead, on a rise, stood the house, huge and dark. Not far away among the multitude of young trees the Garvie River roared in spate. Rain still hissed on the leaves and the road. But there were now breaks in the sky through which stars could be glimpsed. Throwing his handkerchief away, he went back to the car, still squeamish, very unsteady, and tired, but as confident as ever that within the next two or three minutes he would be welcomed and absolved by Constance.

Even in the headlights of the car the neglect and dilapidation of the house could be seen. Weeds and grass grew a foot high against the walls and over the drive. There were windows with broken glass. From a gutter water splashed down. The house looked roofless and abandoned, especially then, in the silence after he had switched off the engine, for amidst that silence the gutter made loud, weeping, desolate noises, as if expressing the shame and surrender of this great house, once magnificent and seemingly impregnable. He pitied it so much he sobbed, too, and kept murmuring he had come just in time.

With the china rabbit carefully under his oxter, he stepped out, and was trying to steady the ground that swayed and tilted under him, when the door opened with a screech and a tall man in a kilt came out.

'So you did come after all, old man?' he cried, like a small boy delighted and appalled by another's daring.

Timidly he ventured out from the doorway on to the terrace, where the rain fell on his bare head.

'Got to be careful,' he cried. 'Damned bad earache, if my head gets wet. Not like Connie, she's a nymph of the elements.' He laughed shrilly. 'I wondered if you would. You seemed

damned stubborn about it on the phone. I've been watching for
hours. Nothing much else to do. Had just about given you up,
though. Of course, you'll find it a fruitless quest. Connie's
chosen to cast you into limbo, and there's no limbo like
Connie's, I can tell you.' Again he laughed, with the same
shrill, sad, conscious insanity.

Carstares had been delighted to hear that human voice; it
was the beginning of the welcome he felt sure of. He straightened himself, hugged the rabbit, let go the handle of the car
door, took one joyful step towards the house, and collapsed
heavily on his face, bumping his mouth painfully against the
ground. Chips of gravel were embedded in his lips. When he
spat them off he spat blood, too. 'Shorry,' he muttered, and
laughed at this second droll accident within half an hour.

Kilgour had come running down the steps in a knock-knee'd
panic of concern.

'Hurt yourself, old man? Got to be careful, the place is full of
holes. Is that a bottle you've got there?'

Carstares, getting to his feet with great difficulty, found that
speech, too, needed extraordinary effort. His tongue was foolishly thick, and his lips were stiff and sore.

Kilgour, helping him, saw the rabbit. 'Jove, it's not a bottle,'
he said, in disappointment. 'I heard it clink, but it's not a
bottle.'

' 'S a rabbit.'

Kilgour touched it and shuddered. 'Is it one of those obscene
things that sit on the lawn in front of the hotel? What made you
bring it here, old man?'

'Ish for Alishon.'

Kilgour was sniffing. 'Haven't you had what they call a
skinful, old man?' he asked, with a giggle. 'You know, if
nothing else did, that would fairly set Connie against you.
She can't abide the stuff now; even the smell disgusts her. Odd
thing that, eh, in a Highland laird's sister?'

Carstares was trying to climb the steps and Kilgour was
trying as politely as he could to prevent him.

'I think, old man,' gasped Kilgour, 'you'd do better to get

back into your car. I'll sit in it with you and have a chat, if you wish. There's really no point in going into the house.'

'Mush talk to her,' said Carstares, affably. 'Mush give rabbit to Alishon.'

Kilgour was losing the struggle. 'But I've warned you it's no good, old man. She'll not see you. Don't think you know her. I don't care how well you knew her in the old days, you don't know her now. Connie's changed. I know we all do, some of us for the worse; but Connie's tried to change, and I'm sorry to say she's managed it. You'd never know her. For one thing she never laughs now. She used to; you'll know that.'

While he was speaking he was being pushed by the eager Carstares up the steps on to the terrace. The door was still open, and Carstares, like a child too young or too spoiled to take a telling, made for it.

'All right,' said Kilgour, no longer restraining. 'Go ahead, old man. Now that you're here, it would be criminal to send you away again, without at least inviting you in. Not that you'll enjoy your visit. There was a time when there would have been a dozen servants, and a piper, too, to welcome you in.'

He followed Carstares into the large, dimly lit hall. There were no carpets and no pictures. The only relics of the past splendour were the large tiles with which the floor was covered; some of these, though, were loose, and some missing.

'I must apologise,' said Kilgour, 'for the state of the house. I don't have to tell you it wasn't always like this. Look up there.' He pointed up at the lofty ceiling, where dark blotches could be seen. 'Footprints. In red paint. They're all over the house, in every room. Commandos were stationed here during the war for a spell. Their idea of a joke, you know: some monster with bloodstained feet walking about the ceilings. Take some nerve, I suppose, putting them there. No doubt,' he added, with a sigh as at retribution necessary but unfortunate, 'most of them got their heads blown off. What did you say your name was, old man? Carter, was it?'

Carstares tried to pronounce it with the most careful and

solemn articulation. 'Carshstares.' Then he spelled it, just as solemnly.

Kilgour could not help giggling. 'Mine's Ronald Kilgour,' he said. 'How d'you do, and all that. Welcome to Garvie House.'

Carstares insisted on shaking hands.

'Did you know you're plastered with mud, old man?' asked Kilgour. 'Are you sure you didn't crawl all the way on your hands and knees, like a fellow escaping from a prison camp? And your mouth's all bloody. Really, Carstares old man, do you think you're in a fit state to visit a lady, even one who would be glad in other circumstances to see you, which, by the way, Connie is not?'

Carstares, hugging the rabbit, looked as if he was about to rush singing into the interior of the house.

Kilgour gripped his sleeve. 'I say, did you know you've been sick all over your coat? I hope you don't mind my mentioning it?'

But Carstares laughed in a good humour as foolish as the rabbit's under his arm.

Kilgour then asked the question he did not want to ask. 'Were you in the army, Carstares?'

Carstares at once drew himself erect and saluted with mock solemnity. 'Captain Hugh Carshstares,' he said, and then added, 'M.C.'

Kilgour was sadly pleased. He honoured courage, though he possessed none. To hear it mocked was more bearable than to hear it praised. As he stood, scratching his thigh and frowning, he noticed that the rabbit was grinning, as if to imitate him. Its teeth, too, protruded like his own; its eyes were blue and vacuous; it was a by-word for silly timidity. Perhaps it had been brought along, not as a present for Alison but to bait him.

'We all know,' he said, in a peeved voice, 'that medals fall where they shouldn't; but really that's no reason for making fun of them.'

Then he saw Carstares was not listening to him, but was staring past with a joyful grin, that made him a third in inanity. Constance had come into the hall at the far end, and stood at the foot of the stairs. One hand rested on the banisters. With her shawl over her shoulders, her old tweed skirt, her spectacles, the red slippers on her bare feet, and her hair combed down her back, she looked at that distance like any other woman, just come from sewing by the fireside, to gaze with interest at the visitor.

But Kilgour knew better. 'Wait here, old man,' he whispered to Carstares. 'I'd better explain first.'

When he hurried along to her he saw there had been no marvellous resuscitation of her old humour and mercy. Years ago she would have been content to tease Carstares for his foolish, drunken optimism and his grinning rabbit. Tonight she would freeze him with her contempt.

'Now, Connie,' he whispered, 'take a joke. Of course he's drunk. Of course he shouldn't have come. But I think at heart he's not happy. For my sake, Connie, if not for your own, or his, say a friendly word to him, and then I'll get rid of him. I think he's really a good sort. It won't do, Connie, to cast off all our friends. The trees get their leaves again, now it's spring. Why should we stay bare? Please, Connie.'

He was interrupted by Carstares rushing forward. There came with him, as well as the ludicrous rabbit, the stink of vomit and whisky. Kilgour had to admit he looked and smelled hideous; what made it worse, too, was his idiotic laughter. He seemed to think Connie was going to throw her arms round his neck and kiss his bloody mouth.

'Miss Kilgour,' he cried. 'No, Constance. I'm going to call you Constance.'

From behind her spectacles she stared at him with a hatred that turned her face curiously tense, austere, and beautiful. A chill seemed to rise from her. Though tall for a woman, she was slight and small besides Carstares; yet she seemed charged with a strength witch-like in its source, while he was feeble and defenceless. Indeed, Carstares like a child had gathered all his trust together, represented by the china rabbit, which he was now offering as a symbol of reconciliation. At the same time he broke out into a long, passionate appeal, incoherent and unintelligible, but inconceivably hopeful. The only parts Kilgour could make out for certain were that Carstares' wife Marion was dead, and he was now prepared to adopt Alison as his own child.

Constance stood as still as one of the rocks in the Garvie waterfall. Her hand on the banister was like a dead woman's. She let him finish; then, as he waited panting for what he seemed sure must be her approval and acceptance, she said, with calm malignity: 'I told you this evening I did not wish ever to speak to you again. Why should you think I did not mean it?'

As she went up the stairs, slowly, her brother called after her: 'Now, Connie, that won't do. Mr. Carstares's my guest, if he isn't yours. I invited him in. Why do you shame us, Connie?'

She did not reply, but kept going up the stairs, slowly, remorselessly. He thought she supposed she was thus keeping the world at bay, striking back at it; but it seemed to him she was surrendering to it, in the most horrible, destructive way she could.

At the top of the stairs, before disappearing along the corridor to Alison's room, she turned and looked down. Carstares had sunk on to his knees, and was slobbering in entreaty. She smiled as if in triumph, and then was gone. Her brother, with one hand on Carstares's shoulder, wanted to call after her not to think that the world which she hated could ever be represented by a single unhappy, drunken man, even if that man during the war had known her well enough to sleep with her.

Ten

After much effort Kilgour got Carstares away. For a minute or two, after the car was gone, he lingered on the drive, shivering in the wind that blew keenly from the snowy mountain-tops, and gazing up with eyes that watered at the stars now shining brightly in a vast cleansed sky. For once he did not feel sorry for himself, rejected and despised; on the contrary he felt great relief; in Carstares he thought he had found one even less courageous and resolute than himself. Ridiculously soon after his boast of winning the M.C. poor Carstares had grovelled on his knees, beating his fists against the stair on which Connie had stood. It had been an exhibition of demoralisation worse than his own, and with far less excuse. Connie's hostility, though it should last till the grave, was not so hellish a breach of nature as those few days on the Normandy beaches. To see a man with his head torn off and a spout of blood in its place was a terror not to be compared with seeing Connie's toe so contemptuously still in its red slipper. Therefore he not only felt gratitude towards Carstares for his greater cowardice, but also pity, and even a deeper, warmer, happier feeling of community, akin to love. He and Carstares could be friends; they would not be ashamed in each other's presence; they would not talk about the war or Connie; they would be able to be silent together, without the one feeling the other's contempt as icy as this wind.

He began to feel his ears ache with the cold, and hurried into the house. As he was turning the key in the rusted lock, he heard the telephone ring. He thought he had heard it before while he was outside, but since he could think of no one wishing to telephone at that time of night, he had supposed himself mistaken. Now as he went to answer it he wondered who would be so persistent and anxious. It could certainly not be Carstares, who would not have reached the hotel yet. Perhaps it was someone with the wrong number. He hoped it was not one of the miserable anonymous calls they sometimes got, saying nasty things about Connie and Alison, and himself.

He picked up the telephone. 'Hello,' he said, cheerfully. 'Garvie House here. Captain Kilgour speaking.'

There was silence, and then the person at the other end seemed to start grunting in a curious way, as if dumb.

'Well?' he asked, encouragingly. 'Who's speaking?'

'Has she confessed it yet?' said a voice then, croaking as if to disguise itself. He could not be sure whether it was a man's or a woman's.

'Confessed to what?' He laughed. 'See here, let's cut out the mystery. What are you talking about? If you don't tell me right away who you are, I shall put the telephone down.'

'Your sister, the whore—'

'Now, now!' he cried.

'Has she confessed that the father of her child is this man Carstares who came to Garvie Hotel today?'

It sounded such nonsense he laughed in scorn. 'I say, whoever you are, isn't it rather late for such filthy nonsense? Good-night, and pleasant dreams.' He was about to put the telephone down when an outburst of quite meaningless obscenity was sobbed into it, in a woman's voice. He was so shocked he kept it at his ear. Words that had to do with sexual organs, and intercourse, and excrement, were repeated desperately, as if saying them was to empty the mind thinking them.

He was fascinated, horrified, and yet touched with a strange pity. Someone in the village then was as unhappy and as unnatural as he; someone, no doubt, whom he had passed on the road and envied for her apparent security of position in the community. If there was one such, full of a misery and sickness now breaking to the surface, likely there were others: he was not so isolated in shame as he had thought.

The voice sobbed into silence.

He spoke gently. 'I suppose I ought really to inform the police. You really can't say such things into the telephone, at least not when there's someone listening. Go into the forest. You'll be alone there. You can say what you like. The trees won't mind. You won't shock the deer.'

'You're a fool,' said the voice, suddenly sane and authoritative, 'and a disgrace to your country.'

Then the speaker hung up.

He was so disconcerted he could not put the telephone down; he had forgotten how to. As he stood with it in his hand he was trying to obliterate the pity he had felt a few moments ago; but he could not. The possibility that every second man and woman met on the road were tormented by private shames must at all costs be preserved.

When at last he managed to set the telephone down, he did not know where to go. Irresolute, he stood scratching at his naked thigh. To go into the little sitting-room at the back of the house where, the fire was lit would be to be confronted by himself. He would say aloud to himself, again and again, the words expressing his own peculiar agony of mind; two would now be added, since Carstares's visit: 'Military Cross.' But if he did not go into the sitting-room, because he feared the loneliness there, it would be even more dangerous to go outside and walk in the garden. There loneliness would take the voices of the leaves under his feet, and entice him to go and stand above the deep pool under the hazels, where a way to end his unhappiness would be suggested to him by some spokesman of nature, a fish plopping in the pool, perhaps, a star twinkling through the dark branches, a fox barking on the hillside, a railway engine whistling in the distance, or an owl hooting.

He needed someone to talk to, and there was only Connie. Likely she had gone to bed. He shuddered as he imagined the outward calm of her undressing and her lying down: thus every night she contained her terrible frustration. She would not moan or whimper or even cry out in bitterness. She would lie like a nun on a bed of penitence in a solitary cell; only it would be hope of revenge which would keep her quiet, not the nun's promises of glory.

The china rabbit lay on its side on the bottom stair. He stooped, set it upright, and stroked its cold, smooth ears. It was lucky; it did not have the terror of weasels to keep it awake.

He climbed the stairs with sad slowness, as if a piper at the foot was playing a lament. Connie often accused him of being in a kind of perpetual hibernation; like a hedgehog, she had said, with all his quills pulled out. He had not been insulted: those and other little creatures had given him much pleasant companionship when a boy, and now, on the dark, cold stairs, remembering them, for a few moments he did not feel alone and deserted.

As he passed Alison's room the spell was restored. Not only did he not know why he was there, in that sinisterly familiar house, but he could not be sure who he was or what was the connection between him and the child sleeping within. Everything that had happened to him had been long ago, even Carstares's visit and the filthy telephone call: Connie had been dead for years, and Alison was an old woman who had forgotten him.

He knocked quietly on Connie's door. 'It's me, Connie.'

Her reply was without passion or interest. 'What do you want?'

'Just to talk to you.'

'What about?'

'Anything. I'm feeling very lonely, Connie. It's all right about Carstares, you know. He's gone. I saw him away.'

She did not answer, and he entered diffidently. Thus had he entered his cave under the crags of Ben Sithein many years ago. There he had had a candle which cast shadows like these in this cold room, and there, too, Connie had been waiting, an intruder, or usurper rather, seated on the throne he had imagined out of a curious ledge. She would gaze at him mysteriously, and then suddenly break into laughter which made the cave a hundred times more thrilling, or else sneer with deliberate disenchantment. She had been only ten then and ought not to have been on the hill alone.

Now this evening, with the whole house become a cave, he entered again, with that old uncertainty. She was seated in a chair in front of the dressing-table mirror, but no one would have thought she was admiring herself. The room was cold, yet she had not troubled to throw her dressing-gown over her shoulders; these, like her arms, legs, and feet, were bare. She wore a faded pink slip. Her very fingers and toes seemed to have thinned to a strange ascetic loveliness, and her bosom by no means dessicated lacked grossness. She was very beautiful, he saw, and yet she was dying like a tree whose supply of sap had been cut off. The time would come, perhaps soon, when that withering would show: her face now so fine would become haggard, her eyes still calm and resolute would be desperate, and her body from soft and graceful would turn tight and barren.

He felt pity and affection for her. Not once had she accused him of betraying his responsibility as head of the family and upholder of its traditions. Never had she blamed him for their poverty. Perhaps she did not think him worthy of that great blame. Nevertheless, he was grateful to her.

He sat down on the edge of the bed.

'What is it?' she asked, smiling at his sorrowful reflection in the glass.

He tried to smile back. 'Did you hear the phone?'

'Yes.'

'It rang twice.' He waited, but she did not ask who had called. This conquest of curiosity was, he thought, the secret of her endurance. 'It wasn't him,' he added, and then realised he had been precipitate in mentioning the telephone call. He might have to tell what it had been, not because she would ask, but because he would not be able to contain it.

'It was someone with the wrong number,' he said.

'I don't think so.'

'What do you mean, Connie? Surely I'm at least capable of knowing when a caller has made a mistake.'

'You're not capable of telling a lie efficiently, Ronald,' she said.

'Is that a matter for congratulation?'
She smiled.
'Well, it wasn't him,' he muttered.
'So you have already said.'
'I don't know who it was, Connie. She didn't give her name.'
'She?'
'Yes. I'm sure it was a woman's voice. At first, though, I couldn't say.' He grew excited. 'My God, Connie, it was shocking. Whoever she is, she must be off her head. What filth! What absolute filth!' He remembered the cold, sane ending, and tried to laugh.
'What did she say?'
'I couldn't repeat it, Connie.'
She seemed amused.
'Sex,' he muttered.
'Was it Miss Carmichael, the schoolmistress?'
'Miss Carmichael! Good Lord, Connie!' Then incredulity went out of him in a gasp; that last reprimand might well have come from the schoolmistress's stern lips. 'Why should you suspect her, Connie?'
'She suffers from obsessions.'
He felt so shocked by this easy acceptance of such a dreadful degeneration in a fellow human being that he blurted out: 'She mentioned one of them. By Jove, she did.'
'Did she?'
'Yes,' He punched hard at his bare, bony knees. 'All right, Connie, I'll tell you. You've a right to know. But don't blame me. I'm just passing it on. After all, you've asked me.'
'Have I? I wasn't aware of it.'
'She said – don't get angry with me, now – she said Carstares was Alison's father. Of course, it's a shocking lie, but she said it; it was part of the filth.'
When he glanced at her, in the mirror, he saw she was still smiling, but her left hand was clutching her right breast with an increasing tightness.
'I told her I ought to inform the police,' he said, hoarsely.
Still she smiled, and clutched her breast. He wanted to seize

her and strike her and make her tell him what she was thinking and suffering. He could not bear to be left out of her pain.

'Who is he, Connie?' he asked. 'It won't do to say you don't know him. A man doesn't come all this way for nothing. He certainly thinks he knows you, very closely. Did you meet him during the war? Have you forgotten him? Is that it, Connie? God knows, there were many I met, whom I've forgotten.' But if Carstares was Alison's father, how could she have forgotten him? She must have slept with him, 'I admit he's a drunkard,' he said. 'No doubt he imagines things. For instance, he claimed to have won the M.C.'

'Did he say so?'

'Oh, yes, the poor fellow pretended it was a joke, but it was a very curious joke, don't you think?'

'He did win it.'

He gaped at her, and then tried to laugh. 'No, Connie, I won't bite.' But as he spoke he was wishing he really was a salmon in the hazel pool. 'You used to catch me that way, but not now.'

'In Burma.'

He got to his feet, and found himself strangely affected by Carstares's drunkenness. He could scarcely stand or speak. 'I don't believe it,' he said, with great difficulty.

'It's the talk of the village. They were expecting a hero.'

'A hero? Good Lord, did you see him on his knees down there in the hall? Did you hear him weeping, like a child that won't get what it wants?'

'No, I didn't.'

Her mildness baffled him. 'Well, I certainly did. If he's a hero, then I'm— No, Connie, it won't do. Take it back, please.'

She smiled and shrugged her shoulders. 'He won it.'

'For bravery?'

'I expect so.'

'For killing Japs? It would be for killing Japs if it was in Burma.'

'No doubt.'

He stood swaying and sick behind her. When he put his hand on her shoulder he found it icy-cold.

'Don't,' she said.

'You know a lot more about him than you'll admit, Connie. Did you know his wife? She was called Marion, wasn't she?'

'So he said. No, I didn't know her.'

'Are you sure, Connie? Tell me this, has he any money? He's got a fine new car, anyway. And what did you mean when you said they were expecting him? Who were expecting him?'

'The forestry people.'

'Why should they have been expecting him?'

'I suppose because he's to be their new District Officer.'

He reeled back and sank down on the bed again. 'You mean, he's here to work?'

'Yes.'

'I don't understand this, Connie.'

She smiled.

'If you think I'm going to believe that it was just a coincidence, you being here—'

'Think what you please.'

'Yes, Connie, I certainly will; and I think you know what I am thinking.' He was thinking that in spite of her denials Carstares was Alison's father.

'Do you think so, Ronald?'

Again her mildness frustrated him. Usually her anger was hateful, but now he wished it rather than this ominous placidity.

'Has he got money?' he demanded.

'They say his wife left him some.'

'But she must have been young!'

'I suppose so.'

'It must have been her people who had the money.'

'Yes. I believe they made biscuits in Edinburgh.'

'How much do they say, Connie?'

'Thirty thousand.'

He gasped. 'Thirty thousand! That would do, that would do all right, Connie.'

'Perhaps it would.'

Not just the words but the way she said them, with so strange a smile, made him look at her in terror. She was his sister and he loved her; yet he thought at that moment she was evil.

'I don't know what you mean, Connie,' he said, 'but what I mean is this. Think of Alison. She's got to grow up in a harsh world. Whether you like to admit it or not she's got a stigma. Perhaps we all have, but the difference is she's blameless. At least she's blameless now, later I don't know. Other people's guilt becomes your own in time.'

'What are you talking about, Ronald?'

'Don't be so sweet, Connie.'

'Sweet?'

'Yes, sweet. There's no sweetness in your heart, I see that.'

'You mentioned a stigma. How do you recommend it be removed?'

'You know what I think. You must have loved him once. He's brave, isn't he? He's handsome. He's rich. He's fond of her, and he's crazy about you. It's worth considering. Isn't it, Connie?'

She stood up. 'Yes, it's worth considering,' she said.

He would have said her face was radiant, but with malignity.

'What are you going to do, Connie?' he whispered.

She stared at herself in the mirror. 'Telephone Mr. Carstares,' she said. 'Apologise to him. Arrange to meet him. Do you approve, Ronald?'

'Yes. Yes, I suppose so.'

'Well then.' Smiling she picked up her dressing-gown and put it on.

'Now?' he cried.

At the door she turned. 'Yes. Why not?'

'Why not?' he repeated. 'But, Connie,' he muttered when she had gone out, 'you can't marry him because you hate him.'

As he said it he knew she not only could, but would. Was it his duty to warn Carstares, or ought he to remain snug in his hibernation? He followed Connie down to the telephone, sighing in perplexity.

Eleven

When she had first seen him in the car, looking at her with that condescending male pity and admiration, her very breasts had ached in resentment. In so many swift, inevitable ways had he resembled Francis Weir, and as she walked on she imagined, against her will, more and more points of resemblance until in her mind, as misty with bitter memories as the loch with rain, the two men, the one dead and the other newly alive, had become one, at least in their culpability towards her. Under the sodden, budded alders, smelling his whiskied breath and seeing the typical calculation in his eyes, she had been irresistibly reminded of the night she had told Francis about Alison. In the small blacked-out room, far from the hills, they had been in bed. Immediately he had stopped in his love-making, raised his head above hers, and muttered in an anguish stolen from her: 'Oh, Connie, for Christ's sake!' She had made no effort to console him or recriminate, but had lain watching as he had got out of bed to look for his cigarettes.

Clad only in his pyjamas top, he had been pitiable, foolish, and obscene. With breasts of agony she had listened to him repeating, with more and more petulance: 'For Christ's sake, Connie,' and in the end mumbling that she'd better see some-body who'd do the trick for her. Before he had left he had tried to apologise, or at least explain, almost in tears. 'I'm as sorry as hell, Connie. There's no good talking about getting married. That's not for me. Don't ask me why, it just isn't, not now. Christ, you can't rise from making love to go off and burn and obliterate its fruits without a scunner getting hold of you. You know the Scots word 'scunner', Connie?'

She had known it well.

Two nights later his plane did not return.

She had not seen anyone who had done the trick for her. She had let the fruit of love ripen within her; ripening with it had been a whole orchard of humiliations. An officer in the W.A.A.F., she had left the service temporarily, and had returned, leaving Alison in a child's home, where most of her companions were like herself, penances not graciously borne.

After the war she had taken the child home, to find the house derelict, but not more so than her brother. There she had lived, with little money, while the house crumbled away, and Alison grew more and more like Francis. She could not have said why she had stayed: it wasn't just that she had a bitter loyalty to this place where she had been born and which she had once loved; it seemed also, even to herself, as well as to a sentimental onlooker like Margaret Strone, that she was waiting, but for what or whom she could not tell.

While she had been away, an army of trees had been planted on hillsides once as familiar to her as her own face, but now strange and inimical with these small green intruders, whose silence and endurance mocked her own. As for those trees which had been planted before the war, occupying the approaches to the house like a Lilliputian garrison, they were now grown taller than she, and were full of menace.

Alison at times she loved, but always with a love desperate with restraint; at other times she hated the child, as symbolising the humiliation, not only of love rejected, but of humility enforced.

Now Carstares had come, with his fantastic drunken claiming of Alison; it was almost as if he was impersonating Francis. She did not know his motive in making that claim, but she saw that in forcing him to justify it could be her revenge and escape. Not only did he represent his sex and generation, he also represented the trees which she had grown so obsessively to hate and fear, and wish to destroy.

She spoke into the telephone with a charm and vivacity that surprised and amused her: 'This is Miss Kilgour, of Garvie

House. I'm very sorry for disturbing you at so late an hour. I wonder if I could speak to Mr. Carstares, please.'

It was Jock who answered, risen with bare feet from a bed in which his Muriel was weeping hysterically, whether for joy or shame at virginity lost he could not say. Whatever her reaction, the losing had not been for him a smooth, uncomplicated pleasure. He had felt like a burglar successful with a lock of extraordinary intricacy, but so tired and edgy after the effort he lacked the will and curiosity to open the door.

'Mr. Carstares hasn't returned yet, Miss Kilgour,' he said.

'I see.' Smiling, she hoped he hadn't had an accident: there would be no escape for her in that kind of purposeless destruction. 'He left here about half an hour ago.'

'Three-quarters, at least,' whispered Ronald, now beside her.

'Well, he's not back. Do you want to leave a message for him?' Jock's temper was as short as a housewife's threatened by visitors in the midst of an extra-special spring-clean. There were so many things to be seen to before his universe would be tidy and comfortable again.

'Yes, thank you,' said Constance. 'Would you please tell him I called? And would you ask him to call me tomorrow morning?'

'Any particular time, Miss Kilgour?'

'Let's say after breakfast.'

'Very good, miss. Will it be all right if I don't manage to tell him tonight? I mean, I've just come from my bed.' Listening with his other ear, Jock thought he could hear that weeping. My God, he thought, I've heard of stirring up a hornet's nest, but here's one I've gone and hung round my neck. Yet he could feel no bitterness or regret: he realised he must surely love her.

'Yes, I think that will be all right,' said Constance, though Ronald was shaking his head and whispering: 'While the iron's hot, Connie.'

In any case, Jock was thinking, he'll be so pissed drunk it won't matter a cow's turd whether I tell him or not.

'If you do happen to see him tonight,' said Constance, 'will you please tell him? I think he'd like to know.'

Ronald scratched ruefully, and nodded: if this was a plot, he was in it, too.

Love? Jock wondered. Am I in a forest of it? Then remembering Muriel, he knew there must be in that forest clearings of peace and sunshine and greenness. 'Very good, Miss Kilgour,' he said. 'If I see him I'll tell him.'

'Thank you.'

What though, he added to himself, if I happen to see him in bed with our Nancy?

'Good night,' she said, with an affability that had him clawing his rump in surprise as he hurried away to find Muriel sitting up in bed, fondling the little silver statuette that Jock had thought not quite decent or natural.

Ronald followed his sister to the foot of the stairs. 'Well, Connie,' he asked, with his silly smile, 'what's the programme?'

She picked up the china rabbit.

He watched her, expecting her to drop it again and break it; but instead she lightly kissed it. For whose sake? he wondered. Alison's or Carstares's?

'What's the programme, Connie?' he repeated.

'What do you mean?'

'You know what I mean.' He still wore that smile; he knew it was foolish, but could not change it. 'When you speak to him tomorrow, what are you going to say?'

'Does the lady not leave the initiative to the gentleman?'

'Don't try to put me off, Connie. This isn't a joke, you know.'

For answer she kissed the rabbit again.

'I don't understand you, Connie. Perhaps I never really did, even when we were children; but tonight, now, you're going even farther away from me. I don't like that, Connie. Good Lord, in the circumstances ought we not to keep close together?'

'What circumstances?'

'You know very well,' he cried. 'No, no, don't go up yet. I want you to tell me something.'

He paused, hoping she would ask what it was he wanted her

to tell him; but she just smiled. It was a smile that could have done with some of his silliness in it; it was too knowing, too sure, too resolved.

'The rabbit, Connie,' he said, touching it, 'are you going to give it to her?'

'To Miss Kirn, do you mean?'

'You know I don't,' he cried. 'You know very well I mean Alison. Wait, Connie.' He seized hold of her dressing-gown to keep her from going upstairs.

She waited.

'All right,' he cried, 'you're not going to give me any encouragement. I'll speak without it. Now, Connie, you've not to be doing anything you'll regret. I mean, Carstares is really a decent sort of fellow. A man who gives himself away the way he did here tonight hasn't any bad in him. I'll even admit he might very well have won a medal, and deserved to win it.'

Still she waited, in silence, with the rabbit in her arms.

'Do you know what I think, Connie?' he asked softly, with tears in his eyes. 'I think you love him. You used to, I know. You still do, but you won't admit it. Admit it, Connie. Give in to it. This could be the chance to rebuild your life, Connie, and Alison's. Take it. Don't be bitter. Don't nurse old grudges. What's past's past: that's a proverb in every language.' It was a lie, too, he knew, in every language, 'Don't worry about me, Connie. Think only of yourself and Alison. I'm extinct: we know that. So it doesn't matter where I go, does it? But you should go away, you and Alison, and Carstares. Let the house become a ruin. Let the nettles grow over it. Let them plant trees out there in the drive, blocking up the windows. The forest will eat up the house, like in a fairy-tale. It will eat me up, too, but you and Alison will have escaped.'

She turned to go upstairs. This time he let her go.

'I don't quite trust you, Connie, you know,' he cried, laughing and weeping to mitigate that distrust. 'You're too deep for me. You always were, even when you were Alison's age.'

She went up steadily.

'When I said I don't quite trust you,' he cried, 'I meant

you're capable of going after him, not because you want him, but because you want to get him at your mercy. You've never forgiven him, Connie. I know you've suffered, and perhaps he was the cause of it; but forgiveness is good, Connie, not just for the one forgiven, but for the one forgiving, too. You never practised it, Connie; that was the trouble.' She had now gone and he was shouting to the empty house. 'You could have practised it on me, but you wouldn't. My mother noticed it.'

Then he remembered his mother, whom he had trusted, had been dead for twenty years, and with his face pressed against the banister he wept at her loss.

Twelve

Muriel had been soothed asleep, and was lying on his arm in a way that was cramping it sorely, when he heard the car stop outside. It was so late, almost two o'clock, he thought Carstares must have gone to the dance. Therefore he wasn't surprised to find Nancy had come back with him. What did surprise him was that Will McKew had allowed her. Last night, at such a cynical and prompt desertion, Jock would merely have winked, thinking the ewe had louped the fence to go to another tup. But tonight, in this hallowed bed, he felt pity not only for the man deserted, but also for the woman deserting him, and even for the man responsible.

For Muriel's sake, he had to pity them: she, so sweet, so demure, so prim, brought up in a strict household, had before falling asleep confessed to him, not deeds, but dreams of vice and passion and lust, more suitable for the French heroine of a banned book. While she was sobbing her confession he had remembered that a lugubrious drunkard had once confided to him over the counter that women with flat breasts were in their imaginations raging debauchers; but he had dismissed the memory as absurd and insulting. The truth was he felt, with his heart as tender as scaled teeth, that every human being, from murderer to saint, was at the mercy of passions, desires, and appetites that crept out of the dark forests of the mind like ravenous wolves; the darker the forest the fiercer the wolves. With Muriel absolved on his numbed arm, he thought, Christ pity us all, but especially those like Carstares in whom even the wolves seemed lost.

The car was left outside. Carstares was either too tired or impatient to put it into the garage. From the amount of stumbles and giggles it seemed Nancy was having to cleek him upstairs. Likely, too, she would be urging him to keep as quiet as possible, lest Miss Kirn be wakened; neither of them knowing that so recently had Miss Kirn been startled out of a sleep of thirty years. Again Jock grinned, caught in a complicity of indulgence. Let them sneak up to bed, let them fornicate to their hearts' content. The bounds of his sympathy had been so extended, his mind now felt as vast and bright as the sky above Vorlich after the clouds had cleared. In it the fornication of Nancy and Carstares, and the betrayal of McKew, were specks, no larger than larks or hawks. It was exhilarating, but it was also a little frightening, to be so relaxed and Godlike in tolerance; luckily it was bound to be temporary, otherwise as barman, host, or husband even, he must meet with disaster.

He had promised Muriel to go to his own room before morning. Therefore, as soon as the hotel was quiet again, he began slowly, with masterful tenderness, to withdraw his arm. She sighed and shivered, but did not waken. Tholing the pain of his arm, he gazed through the curtains at the stars over the hills; he winked at them as an equal, for his own eyes were stars tonight. As he was pulling on his trousers, he remembered Miss Kilgour's message for Carstares; and while he was chuckling at the idea of going up now to deliver it, he heard another car come up the drive. A man whose eyes were stars could not be dense. He knew instantly who were in this second car: Will McKew and his brothers, in pursuit of Nancy and her abductor.

He was out on the steps, cool, resourceful, peacemaker and protector, when the car stopped and Alec McKew, followed by Will and Tom, scrambled out. Murdo, the neat dancer, the fox of the family, remained inside; he never struck a blow until many had been struck and the victim was helpless.

'On the late side for a visit, gentlemen,' said Jock. 'Don't you think?'

Alec had a bottle of whisky in his hand, whether as a comforter, like a baby's bottle, or a weapon, Jock could not be sure. With slavering profanity he suggested that Jock should get out of the way.

It was Will who restrained him, and by no means gently. The wolves were desperate in Will. Yet he tried to speak reasonably.

'We're not going to cause trouble, Jock,' he said. 'I just want to speak to Nancy.'

'It's late, Will. Can't it wait? She'll be in bed.'

'And wha's in it wi' her?' roared Alec.

Will turned and grabbed him by the throat. 'Don't say that. Don't say that. I'll let naebody say that. Brither or no', I'll tear your throat oot if you say that.'

'Christ, Will,' spluttered Alec, 'it's the truth. A'body kens she's juist a whure; a'body but you.'

There was a thud as Will struck him hard, and a crash as the bottle fell. Alec staggered back, growling oaths, but before he could recover himself to retaliate, Murdo hurried out of the car and seized him.

'Let Will handle this in his ain way,' he said. 'He's got to learn. Mind what Faither said. Into the car, Alec; and you, too, Tom. If we're needed, we'll be here.'

Alec, mumbling, let himself be pushed into the car. Tom, who had been squatting to see if any whisky survived in any hollow bit of glass, was ordered to follow, and obeyed, licking his finger.

Jock was left confronting Will only. 'Now, Will,' he coaxed, 'be sensible. It's after two. Sheep on the hills are asleep.'

Will strove to be calm. His fists, though, roved in front of him, hungry for a victim. 'I'm being sensible,' he said. Then he groaned so unexpectedly that Jock had to grin, despite his superhuman pity and tolerance.

'You ken I'm going to marry her,' said Will.

'I've heard you want to do her that honour, Will. But this isn't the time or place to discuss it; and I'm not the man either.'

'I'll kill him,' whispered Will. Then he touched Jock, with ominous gentleness. 'Tell her I'm here.'

'I think she'll know that, Will. Alec wasn't what you'd call quiet.'

'Tell her.'

But, Will, Jock might have said, at this very moment she's clasped in Carstares's arms; but he did not say it.

'If you don't go and tell her, as sure as Christ I'll go myself.'

He would, too, though the door was locked, and Jock had the key in his pocket. In this humour Will would go through a forest on fire to get at her.

'All right,' said Jock, 'I'll go, but on one condition, Will. If she refuses to come, you'll go quietly.'

Will was silent. Over his head Jock saw the stars. Well, he thought, were they not the guardians of shepherds?

'I'll go,' said Will.

'Good. Tomorrow's another day, Will. I'll not be long.'

Jock slipped inside, adroitly, lest Will attempt to enter with him, locked the door, and then, before going upstairs, crept along to Miss Kirn's room to reassure her if the hubbub had wakened and alarmed her. She was, however, so sound asleep he felt not only fond but proud: though he had taken her out of her backwater and launched her upon the wild ocean, he had seen to it she was prepared for the voyage.

Then off he stole upstairs. The thought occurred to him that in his white smock and bound on such an errand, he might be regarded as an attendant in a kipshop conducted on hygienic and humanitarian principles. At once he suppressed the thought and the chuckle it had roused. This was no longer just a hotel in which he worked, it was now his home. Nevertheless, he had to chuckle again when he found himself about to knock on Carstares's door. Nancy he wanted, not Carstares: why should his impudent fingers expect to find her in here? Smacking those fingers with his other hand, he continued up until he reached the attic under the roof where Nancy, the blonde crow, had her nest. Upon that door he let his fingers display all their impudence. There was no answer, of course. He called softly: still no answer. The door was locked, but he had an assortment of keys, one of which fitted. A flick of the light-switch showed the bed was empty. Under the pillow was the nightdress of black transparent nylon. As he fingered it he remembered Muriel's, of thick, pink flannelette, long enough to keep her toes warm; this one would scarcely keep the heat in Nancy's knee-caps. Yet as he gazed at the emblem of silly lust, he felt for its owner only an amused pity. It could easily be, he knew, that Nancy, for all her perfumed well-rehearsed breasts, her seductive nightdress, and her tormenting of Will McKew, was innocent, or at any rate shallow and commonplace in her guilt.

He was on his way across to the door when Nancy trudged in, carrying not only her yellow oilskin but her shoes, stockings, suspender belt, skirt, and brassiere; that left her, so far as he could see, wearing just her blouse, breeks, and earrings. Her hair flowed down her back. She did not seem to him much contented; indeed, he had seen many a shipyard worker come home after a heavy day's work, with overtime, too, looking more spry and satisfied. Had Carstares gone to sleep on her? Or worse still, had only part of him, the indispensable part, decided to slumber? Or had she successfully sold what goods she had to offer, only to find the price much below her expectations?

'What are you doing here?' she demanded.

'Bringing you a message, Nancy.'

She dropped her clothing on the floor, and sitting on the bed started to stroke her big, goose-pimpled thighs. It was as if Carstares hadn't done the job properly. Several times she yawned. She was only twenty-two or three, he thought, young enough to be his and Muriel's daughter. For a moment, to experience the sorrow of that paternal disappointment, he pretended she was.

'Nancy, Will McKew's downstairs, outside. He wants to speak to you.'

'Tell him to go and jump in the loch.'

The pretence was abandoned. Jock spoke crisply. 'Is that your answer?'

'Or climb a tree. He's more like an ape than a fish.'

There were forests under the sea, Jock reflected, where creatures of unimaginable ugliness dwelled; beside them, Will was a gorgeous beauty. All, of course, were God's creatures.

'He's hurt,' said Jock.

'Are you going to get out of here and let me get to bed?' she grumbled. 'I thought,' she added, sneering, 'it was wee Prim's bed that interested you, not mine.'

He refused to be provoked. 'He's a man who could be dangerous, Nancy.'

'Him? If I did that,' she patted her thigh – 'he'd slaver like a poodle. When I want him, he'll come running, with his tongue out.' She grinned lecherously, and loosened the buttons of her blouse.

In his white overall he felt now like a surgeon about to examine her for cancer in the breast. Again he was overcome by that ridiculous pity, which comprehended women with cancer, hideous fish, jealous shepherds, and amateur whores.

On the point of opening her arms wide to strip off her blouse, she suddenly paused. 'What's the Kilgour bitch's name?' she asked.

Astonished, he shook his head.

'Is it Constance?' she asked, with a curious whine of bitterness.

'I believe it is; either that, or Catherine. It begins with a c.'

Viciously, Nancy uttered a word that began with a c. It could hardly, though, be Miss Kilgour's Christian name.

In a spasm of fury and indignation she was about to confide in him, but changed her mind; instead she said that word again. After it she said another: 'Get.'

Jock, so fresh in love himself, understood: in some way Miss Kilgour had interfered with the love-making. Perhaps, instead of gasping 'Nancy', as the circumstances required, he had gasped 'Constance' or 'Catherine' or whatever the name was. No insult, he supposed, could be more insupportable.

She had by this time removed her blouse; only her pink breeks and her forget-me-not earrings saved her from naked-ness.

Chuckling, he felt for the stethoscope in his pocket. 'Good-night,' he said, and as he went downstairs he thought of Geordie McKendrick's kye in the green meadows on the banks of the Garvie; they, too, were splendidly uddered.

At Carstares's door he paused and considered. Ought he to pass on the message from Miss Kilgour now? Or should he wait till the morning? After all, it was getting on for three, and there were still the McKews to be got rid of. Yet was this not his first taste of being host, and were not these excellent opportunities for him to prove his fitness?

He knocked.

'Oh, go to hell,' said Carstares, most sourly. It was evident he thought Nancy was back.

'It's me, Jock.'

'Just the same, get to hell.'

Jock smiled. 'Miss Kilgour phoned, sir.'

It was like letting a cat smell fish. There was a scurry within the room, and the door was dragged open by Carstares, clad only in shirt and socks. He reeked of whisky and Nancy's scent. His eyes were bloodshot, and there was lipstick on his cheek. Almost as red was the great thick scar on his right thigh.

'She phoned?' he gasped.

'Yes, sir; about eleven, or thereabouts.'

'Was it Miss Kilgour herself?'

'In person, sir.'

'What'd she say?'

'Just that you were to call her in the morning, after break-fast.'

'That all?'

'Yes, sir.'

'D'she say what I was to call her about?'

'No, sir. You were just to call.'

Amazement and delight, of a pathetically ludicrous kind, now had Carstares laughing: he seemed almost an idiot, a saftie, certainly no hero, no saviour of civilisation from the yellow barbarians. Yet who, in socks and shirt-tail, could look wise?

'You're sure?' he asked.

'Positive, sir.'

Carstares, despite his joy, was like a child in great need of reassurance that this good fortune would not next minute be annulled, as perhaps it might be if Constance or Catherine or C— found out about Nancy.

'Good-night, sir,' said Jock, and went downstairs to face the McKews.

The night had turned frosty; stars burned in the sky; on the high hills, above the forest on the far side of the loch, snow gleamed. It was a night to sharpen grief, by making those who suffered it seem immortal, with their heads among the stars. Thus Will as he came from under the dark tree at the edge of the lawn was like a character out of an ancient tale of sorrow.

'Where is she?' he asked; even his voice seemed purged of grossness.

'She's gone to bed, Will.'

'She's not coming?'

'Not tonight, Will.'

Will fell silent, and suddenly Jock could hear the roaring of the Garvie River. Somewhere, too, a sheep bleated.

The spell was broken by Tom McKew who came out of the car to relieve himself. He proceeded to do it on the drive. Two objected, Jock and Alec.

'For God's sake,' said Jock. 'Remember this is a hotel.'

'Save it,' shouted Alec, coming out himself. 'I'll show you.' He staggered across to Carstares's car and made his water against it. Tom did likewise.

The river seemed to roar still more loudly, in contempt, Jock thought.

'Tell him to keep away from me,' said Will. 'Just keep away. Or sure as Christ, I'll hang for him.'

Then he began to run down the avenue, as if his destination was the bottom of the loch.

Murdo started the car's engine, and called on his two brothers. They hurried in, like firemen.

Murdo addressed Jock, calmly. 'Remind him he's to visit Creagan, will you? Tell him we'll be waiting.'

'We'll be waiting,' echoed Alec savagely.

The car drove off, and stopped down the avenue so that they

could coax their brother to come in. In its headlights could be seen two of the china rabbits.

As Jock went back into the hotel and locked the door, he was thinking that Carstares might find Garvie during the next two or three weeks a more dangerous place than the Burmese jungle. The McKews would be as ruthless and treacherous enemies as any Japs; Nancy, too, would be like a wounded tigress; and Miss Kilgour, who apparently was the mother of his child, and whom he seemed to worship, had it in her power to degrade him.

In that war, too, no medals would be issued.

Lingering in the hall, Jock winked at the stags' heads and the stuffed salmon. Tolerance without responsibility, sympathy without involvement, were barman's principles, and he could not see how, even for the wide world, they could be bettered.

Thirteen

The sunlight awoke Carstares. Turning away from its relentless radiance, he lay for a minute or two, not sure where he was;
only the headache and the taste of futility were familiar. Soon
he roused himself, lit a cigarette, and recalled the events of the
night before, with appropriate grimaces: the visit to Garvie
House, that deserved a wink borrowed from Jock the barman;
the dance in the village-hall, a grunt and a hunch of his
shoulders; the return with Nancy, a grin; and the abortive
love-making, a breathed oath. There seemed to be something
else, but he couldn't remember what it was. Perhaps it was his
appointment with Strone, the forester. Well, Ezra could wait;
and so, too, could the big foul-mouthed McKerrol. It was the
latter who reminded him of the message from Constance
Kilgour.

He tried not to think about her or about his visit. A bird sang
outside; he listened to it; but as he imagined it on its branch it
had her face, beautiful but hawk-like. Even now he could
hardly rid himself of the feeling that he had expected to find
her here at Kinlochgarvie, waiting for him, with her child
Alison. He no longer confused her with Marion, though;
somehow Nancy's fair hair last night had cured him of that.

Cautiously he got out of bed, noticed he was wearing a shirt
and socks, and inspected himself in the mirror. Lipstick, which
at first he took to be blood, smeared his right cheek. Constance
was pale-lipped. God, he wondered, just what had he done and
said last night? What sort of bloody fool had he made of
himself? He was not sure he liked her, but he wished to respect
her loneliness and pride.

When he turned to the window and drew the curtains, he

looked out upon a scene of such surpassing loveliness his mind seemed instantly cleansed. In the foreground, in the hotel grounds, indeed, was one of the finest silver firs he had seen; over a hundred feet tall, it soared with blue and silver grace to the blue sky. Admiring it intensely, and envying it, he saw the beauty of the morning with its calm, deep, patient appreciation. Here he, too, could be content. In the keen, bright sunshine loch and islets were legendary. Beyond it the trees of the forest, ridge upon ridge of them, had garlands of mist lying along their tops, while in a green field amidst their darker green cows grazed. Above all shone the peaks of snow.

As he turned from the window his determination to bait Strone, and to insist on the sacking of McKerrol that very morning, faded in him.

Miss Kirn herself brought him his breakfast. Though his recollection of her was of a brisk, cheerful, little woman, he was surprised by the quality of her happiness. She even reminded him of the magnificent tree: her roots held as firmly, and her head was as full of birdsong. Perhaps, at her age, with her hair grey and her neck loose and dry, her performance was a little ridiculous; but he enjoyed it.

She placed porridge before him like a benediction. Nancy, she said, was still in bed, with a bad headache. She smiled to show she knew how that headache had been got.

'I've got one myself,' he confessed.

She tapped him on the shoulder. 'What time did *you* get to bed?' she asked, and went away, laughing maternally.

Jock looked in, dapper and efficient in his fresh white jacket. 'Morning, sir.'

'Good-morning.'

'If you've been wondering about your car, sir, I put it in the garage, about six o'clock: to be out of the frost.'

'Were you up at six?'

'Before it.'

'But you were kept up late last night.'

'Half-past three when I closed my eyes, sir.'

Yet at half-past five, when he had opened them, they had

sparkled with keenness, confidence, humour, good-nature, and cheerfulness. What, wondered Carstares, is going on? Is it like this all the time? Or is this particular morning under an enchantment? He could not help laughing.

'You'll be remembering the message from Miss Kilgour, sir? That's really what I came in to remind you of. It was a bad time I chose to tell you, about half-past two, in fact. You've to call her after breakfast.'

Carstares nodded; he was reluctant to talk about that call.

'Tell me the truth, Jock,' he said. 'Did I make a bloody fool of myself last night?'

Well, replied Jock, speaking to himself, you'd have to ask Miss Kilgour that, and Nancy, too, wouldn't you? To Carstares he said, with a wink, 'I couldn't say, sir, to be truthful. I didn't see you come in. When I gave you the message you were in your room alone. Now can a man make a bloody fool of himself in his room alone?'

The answer, of course, was, yes: a man was usually alone when he drank arsenic or shot his brains out or just bit his nails.

'I think I went to the dance,' said Carstares.

'I believe you did, sir.'

'I have a feeling I didn't increase my popularity with the McKews.'

'Why worry about them, sir?'

Jock skipped off with the porridge plate. Seconds later he was back carrying a rack of toast and a pot of tea. Miss Kirn came with him; she carried a plate of bacon and eggs.

They were so alike in size, confidence, and happiness he could not help remarking upon it.

'What's going on?' he asked.

'Think there's something special going on, sir?' asked Jock. 'Something unusual? Something to suit the weather?'

'Yes, I do.'

'Maybe you're not far wrong, sir. Should I, Muriel?'

She hesitated, blushing; then she proudly nodded.

'We've got to face the wolves,' said Jock, with a chuckle. 'Not, of course, that Mr. Carstares is a wolf. Putting it briefly, sir, we wish you to be the first to learn that last night Muriel, Miss Kirn, and I decided to enter into partnership.'

'We're going to get married,' she said, still blushing.

'Congratulations.'

'Thank you, sir,' said Jock. 'So eat your ham and eggs, drink your tea, munch your toast: the first breakfast made under the auspices of the new joint managership.'

'I'm very glad,' said Carstares.

'You will find this, sir, not only an efficient hotel, but a happy one.' Mind you, added Jock, in private, certain liberties such as you enjoyed last night will not be repeated. Dear Nancy may make your bed, she will not occupy it.

'This has always been a happy hotel,' protested Miss Kirn.

'So it has, my dear; but it will be happier still.'

She did not deny that, and they went out into the hall to kiss with dignity and sincerity under the stags' heads.

'The phone's yours whenever you're ready, Mr. Carstares,' called Jock.

'Thanks,' he called back.

During the rest of the meal Carstares faced the problem of what to say when he did telephone.

He kept putting it off. When he had finished breakfast he strolled about the grounds and then stood for several minutes under the silver fir. He smelled woodsmoke, heard the ring of an axe and the bleating of sheep, and saw, through the branches of the tree, the chimneys of Garvie House across the loch. It looked, in the clear air, so close that telephoning didn't seem necessary; all he needed to do was to put his hands about his mouth and shout. What to shout, though? Though he smiled, he also shivered, not just because of the keenness of the air; an impression of Miss Kilgour remained in him, as deep as his bones, and as cold as the snow on the hills.

On Miss Kirn's desk, beside the telephone, was an object he hadn't noticed yesterday: a small silver statuette of a warrior nude but for his shield. He supposed it was a paper-weight.

It was Ronald Kilgour who answered, very promptly, as if he had been waiting beside the telephone.

'Kilgour speaking. Is that you, old chap?'

'It's me, Hugh Carstares.'

'Exactly. Who else?'

'I understand Miss Kilgour—'

'Now, now, why so distant? Constance, surely, at least.'

'I understand she phoned last night.'

'True. I mean, did she? Well, you never know just where you stand with Connie, do you? Here she comes. Do I now make myself scarce? Alison and I will take a ball into the garden and play at catching.'

Then it was his sister's voice, surprising and disquieting Carstares with its friendliness and detachment. He remembered how he had felt yesterday at the lochside that deep within her was a capacity for laughter and happiness.

'Good-morning, Mr. Carstares.'

'Good-morning.'

He was aware Nancy had appeared outside the office and was peering in through the frosted glass.

'Isn't it a beautiful morning?' said Miss Kilgour.

'Yes, it is. You asked me to call.'

'Yes. I thought perhaps there were too many misunderstandings yesterday. Also, I didn't think I had thanked you properly for rescuing me from the rain. It was kind of you.'

He could think of nothing to say.

Nancy opened the door. She wore her maid's uniform, with her white slip showing under the black skirt. Her hair was carelessly tied under her cap, and her eyes were puffy. 'Good-morning,' she said, with a mixture of tentative affection and defensive sarcasm.

'I suppose you'll have work to do this morning,' said Miss Kilgour.

'Yes, I've got some things to see to.'

'I hope I'm one of them,' whispered Nancy. She lifted the silver paper-weight. 'Where'd this come from? Has Miss Prim learned some decency at last?'

'I beg your pardon?' said Miss Kilgour, evidently smiling.

He signed to Nancy to get out.

She fingered the statuette. 'She used to play with it like this. That's true; I saw her. Shocking in a prim thing like her, eh?'

'I'm sorry,' said Carstares into the telephone. 'I didn't speak. I was interrupted.'

'You're still interrupted,' said Nancy. 'What am I going to tell Will McKew?'

'I was going to suggest,' said Miss Kilgour, 'that perhaps you'd care to visit us again, this afternoon, perhaps?'

'Ask her,' whispered Nancy, 'what it feels like to –' She was going to say, 'to have a little bastard', but thought he might not see the humour of the remark.

'Yes, I'd like to,' said Carstares.

Miss Kilgour laughed. 'You don't sound very sure. Did you see enough last night to make you doubtful of our ability to entertain?'

'No, no.'

'I'm afraid such doubts would be justified. The house is in a shocking state. But our river is as splendid as ever. There's a fine path up it, into your plantations. It looks like being a perfect afternoon for a walk.'

'Yes.'

Nancy giggled. 'You sound thrilled.'

'Is there someone there?' asked Miss Kilgour, with apparent mildness.

Again he signed to Nancy to go. This time she went, stroking her buttocks. At the door she turned.

'I think we could manage tea afterwards,' said Miss Kilgour.

'There's a good picture on tonight at Caldoon,' said Nancy. 'And it's a new picture-house. Would you like to take me?'

'Well?' asked Miss Kilgour, laughing.

'Think about it,' said Nancy, and went away.

'What about Alison?' he asked. The question surprised him as much as it did her.

'Alison?'

'Yes. I mean, would she care for a walk up the burn?'

'Perhaps not. But I really hadn't intended—'

'Why don't we all run down to Caldoon this afternoon, have

tea there, and go to the pictures? I understand there's a new cinema there.'

'I didn't think of you as a film fan, Mr. Carstares.'

'I like to see a good film. Of course, I don't know if the one showing would be suitable, for Alison I mean.'

'You seem determined to have her included?'

'Yes. And your brother, too, of course.'

'No, not Ronald.'

'Why not?' Carstares had thought Ronald would give his kilt for an afternoon out.

'It wouldn't appeal to him.'

Though she spoke pleasantly, Carstares felt sorry for her brother.

'Well, I'll ask him when I come round this afternoon.'

'When shall we expect you?'

'Two o'clock?'

'Yes, that would be suitable.' She paused, and he could picture her smiling; but what that smile meant he could not say. 'It's a beautiful morning,' she said.

'Yes, isn't it?'

'We often have quite long stretches of this weather: sunshine, keen winds, bright skies, frost at night. Sometimes it lasts for weeks.'

'I hope it does. Better than yesterday, anyway.'

'Do you think so? Yes, you did say something about wanting to get back to the sun.'

He had hoped she'd forgotten his outburst in the car outside the schoolhouse.

'Myself,' she said, lightly, 'I like the rain and mist. But I thought you forestry people weren't very fond of too much dry sunny weather, at this time of the year, before the new grass. Isn't there a danger of fire?'

'Yes, I suppose so.'

She laughed. 'You don't sound much concerned. Mr. Strone's fanatical over the danger of fire. He's got men posted in the watch-towers, day and night; and others patrol the road and railway.'

'That's his job.'

'There was a fire here last spring. Quite exciting while it lasted. You couldn't see the sun for smoke. Ash kept falling like snow. I'm afraid I found the reek of burning trees to my taste. Afterwards, too, the burnt trees were weird. Many of them still stood, as if unharmed, except that they were turned to the strangest brown. If you touched them, they fell to pieces. The birds avoided them. I rather liked walking amongst them. I found it in a way consoling.'

He remembered the suspicion that the fire she was speaking of had been deliberately caused.

'By the way, Mr. Carstares, you did say something yesterday about improving the discipline of the workmen here, didn't you?'

She waited for an answer. He gave it with his heart turned cold. 'Yes, I believe I did say something like that.'

'You were determined that the man on the lorry should be dismissed.'

'Yes.'

'His name's McKerrol, I believe.'

'Yes, I know.'

'I think he should be. Well, Alison and I shall expect you at two.'

'I'll be there.'

'Goodbye till then.'

'Goodbye.'

As he put down the telephone he told himself he was making a mistake. In spite of the McKews, and of her obvious scheme to ensnare him, it might be safer to go to the pictures with Nancy. He did not think he would ever become her prey; but he was not so sure about a woman who found it consoling to wander in a plantation of martyred trees, who condemned her brother to a solitude he feared, and who seemed determined to exclude her own child. As for her insinuation about McKerrol, he supposed she was justified; but he would have felt happier had her humour been one of forgiveness, in keeping with the brightness and hope of the morning. Was not, indeed, his own guiltiness towards her greater than McKerrol's? Yesterday he had let the elderly schoolmistress think he was Alison's father; likely she had already passed it on to her cronies. What revenge would Miss Kilgour think fit for him?

Before he left to drive along to Strone's hut at the forestry nursery, he sought out Jock and found him in one of the bedrooms with a vacuum cleaner.

Jock switched it off. 'Guests expected this evening,' he explained.

'Many?'

'Three. Fishermen. The season's starting.'

'Will you be busy during the summer?'

'Yes. You'll find it more cheerful with a crowd of people around.' And it wouldn't do the hotel any harm to have a wounded war-hero as a permanent guest.

Carstares wasn't so sure he'd enjoy company; but he grinned. 'I wanted to ask you about McKerrol.'

' "King" Rab?'

'Yes.'

'This morning, sir, the slate's wiped clean; for me, anyway. Rab's my fellow-man; a bastard, to be sure, but my fellow-man. I wish him joy.'

'He's married?'

Jock frowned. 'To as pleasant a young woman as you'd ever hope to meet; bonny, too, with hair that makes our Nancy's look like tarry rope.'

'Have they any children?'

'Four, and one expected. Rab's ripe for libbing.'

'They'll be young?'

'Eldest's seven, youngest about sixteen months.'

'Do they live in a forestry house?'

'They do. Let me say this for him, his garden's the best in the glen for a display of flowers. He's won prizes. Why should a man with so much nastiness in him be fond of flowers? Funnier still, why should they be fond of him, for they'll grow in his garden and die in his neighbour's? I've seen the day when I would have said it was because he's a concentrated lump o' dung, but this morning I'm for tearing my throat out and saying it must be because there's a streak of good hidden in him. Well hidden.'

'I see,' said Carstares. 'Thanks.'

As he turned away, Jock come after him. 'Excuse me for inquiring, sir, but is it in your mind to have him sacked, for his performance yesterday?'

Carstares glared at him.

'In a way it's legitimately my business, sir. I feel responsible. I've helped to set you against the man.'

'I was set against him before I ever saw you, Jock.'

'All the same, I did speak against him. I know you think I've already stepped well out of my place, so another jump will be neither here nor there. I'm going to ask you to let him off with a warning. Blast the two lugs off him, but don't drive him and his cleckan out of the glen. For your own sake, sir, partly. He's not liked hereabouts, but he was born in Kinlochgarvie, and his folks before him. It wouldn't be well taken, sir, especially if it was because of Miss Kilgour. If you'll pardon my saying so, she's not very popular, either.'

Carstares grinned. 'At jumping out of your place, Jock, you're a bloody kangaroo.'

'Except, sir, that I can jump backwards.' Humbly he returned backwards to his vacuum cleaner and switched it on.

Approaching the schoolhouse, Carstares decided to stop and let Miss Carmichael know the true relationship between himself and Constance Kilgour. As he came out of the car, under the gigantic yet delicate larches, he noticed that the road was speckled with their tiny red flowers. Everywhere was a fragrance of young living trees. The whole landscape gave the impression of earliness; for whatever had to be done, there was time.

As he opened the gate he heard a pheasant gabble in the forest behind the house. Somehow the sound confirmed the promise of the morning.

Miss Carmichael, guarded by her cats, was in the garden,

crouched over a strip of ground that had been prepared for seeds; these she was now planting, with a slow meticulousness not to be disturbed by him. He was beside her, close enough to be able to put his hand on her white hair, and still, unlike the cats, she hadn't looked up.

'Good-morning,' he said.

She did not answer.

'Flowers?' he asked. 'What kind?' Again she was silent, and he stooped to look at the packet of seeds on the ground. 'Virginia stock? That makes a pretty border.'

'Please don't speak to me as if I was a child,' she said.

'I'm sorry,' he said, taken aback.

'I prefer lupins,' she said, with what sounded like a chuckle.

He felt stupid. 'I see.'

'Old maids' favourites, they are sometimes called,' she said. 'I wonder why.'

He could have told her, but realised she already knew. Suddenly, increasing his embarrassment, she placed her hand upon his toecap; like a chubby pink frog it leapt there, and stayed.

The pheasant he had heard now appeared in splendour on the drystone dyke separating the trees from the little field that was the school playground. He was pleased he had been right in identifying the sound. As he watched, its drabber mate joined it; both kept swaying their tails ecstatically.

One of the cats slunk towards them, through the grass.

'What I came to tell you, Miss Carmichael,' he said, 'is that Miss Kilgour and I met yesterday for the first time.'

She seemed not to be listening. She gazed at the pheasants on the dyke. On her face was an expression, dog-like in its intensity and anticipation.

He found it difficult to say what he wanted to say. That plump hand on his foot confused him. He could not very well kick it off. Moving his foot discreetly was no good; the hand moved with it.

'Yes,' he said, 'we met yesterday for the first time. You were wrong, therefore, in your supposition. I'm afraid I let you believe it; at least I don't think I denied it as definitely as I should. It wasn't fair, either to you or to Miss Kilgour. But I assure you now, I never set eyes on Miss Kilgour, or the child, until yesterday.'

With a squawk the pheasants flew back into the forest. Chagrined, the cat stiffened in the grass. Miss Carmichael uttered a queer whimper.

'I had to come and tell you,' he said.

She rose to her feet and stood so close to him he had to step back.

'The whole earth's seething with procreation,' she said. 'Why be ashamed of your own little contribution?'

Was she mad, or ill, he wondered. Gazing down at her white hair and incongruous smirk, he remembered how eager and self-possessed she looked in the academic portrait taken at least thirty years ago. Despite his embarrassment and doubt, he pitied her: she had not been a willing traveller to this moment; for her this bright morning represented lateness.

'Even plant lice, smallest of visible creatures, make love,' she said.

'Do you feel all right, Miss Carmichael?' he asked, boldly.

'She has one bastard,' she said. 'Tell her I have had hundreds.'

'I hope you've understood what I've told you,' he said. 'You were quite wrong yesterday in thinking that the little girl Alison has anything to do with me. If I gave you that impression I'm very sorry. I hope you haven't told anyone else?' But as he spoke he was sure she must have confided in her cronies, one of whom was Mrs. Strone. The whole glen in a day or two would believe he was Alison's father. Miss Kilgour herself would hear of it. Apology would be awkward, and inadequate.

'This is Saturday,' whispered Miss Carmichael. 'The hotel bar will be crowded tonight. I know they talk about me.'

'No.' He shook his head.

'They laugh at me.'

'I'm sure they don't, Miss Carmichael. I'm sure they have great respect for you.'

One of the cats had come and was rubbing itself against her thick ankles.

'I sent her to get dressed,' she whispered. 'It is a serious operation for a female. Both her sides had to be opened. The scars can still be seen under her fur. What I want to know is: who sent me? I think it must have happened when I was asleep.'

There was no doubt in his mind now: she was on the verge of a mental illness. Perhaps the symptoms had been noticed before; hence the jokes in the bar. The schoolmistress spinster who had never had a man was a favourite subject of bawdy jokes, especially if, as in Miss Carmichael's case, she involuntarily showed indications of desire still smouldering after innumerable drenchings of professional morality and natural prudishness. Every man with a dram of whisky in him would feel towards her as immortal and beneficent as Apollo.

'Well,' he said, moving discreetly down the path, 'I hope it's clear now about Miss Kilgour and myself.'

As she stood staring after him she slowly began to lift her clothes.

At the gate he hesitated, not sure whether he ought to try and help her. She said nothing, just stood with her skirts held above her waist, like a small girl finding revenge in naughtiness.

He hurried away.

Fourteen

Strone's red-tiled bungalow stood by the roadside near the nursery of trees, about a quarter of a mile from the rest of the forestry community. His office-hut was within the nursery, joined to the house by a very narrow path through the tiny trees, of kind suitable, as Rab McKerrol often jested, for snares. Every morning at half-past seven, or in the dark winter at half-past eight, Strone would be seen unlatching the little gate separating his garden from the nursery. Like a tree himself, in his khaki uniform with its green facings, he would walk among the rows towards his hut, and when he joined the foreman there, or any workers reporting for new duties, this loneliness and remoteness, as of a tree walking and thinking, became even more conspicuous. It was known that often in the midst of the forest he would stand for hours in the same spot, spying on no one and disturbing not even deer or foxes. Once McKerrol had asked him if a bird ever made its nest by mistake in his pockets or hair.

Nor did his peculiarly undemonstrative worshipping of his wife weaken the illusion, for she, too, gaunt and doomed, was like one of the birches or oaks allowed to stand as shelters while the young interloping spruce were well-grown, and then ringed at the foot so that no more sap could be drawn up from the earth. Thereafter they sickened, and slowly, spring by spring, rotted to pieces, frightening even the birds. So in her house Margaret Strone was withering.

On the morning after Carstares's arrival in Garvie, Strone had come at the usual time to his hut to give the orders of the day to John McBraid, the foreman. Everyone had noticed how unsteadily he had walked among the young trees, trampling upon many. One man, kind-hearted but necessarily sycophantic for he was old and afraid of losing his job, asked shyly how Mrs. Strone was that morning. They all saw that it was the sycophancy rather than the kindness Strone wanted to notice, so that his answer need in no way compromise him; but after staring and grinning with contempt he had suddenly, with a gesture as astonishing in him as in a tree, put his hand on the old man's arm and said: 'She's bad, Angus. I've had to send for the doctor.' Then he had gone staggering through the trees, back to the house.

In the bedroom Mrs. Gibson, Margaret's aunt who acted as housekeeper, still sat by the bed, sobbing into her apron. He thought with a sensation of terrible relief that Margaret must be dead; but when he looked at the bed there she was, paler than ever, twitching under the torture, blue-lipped, and clammy. Every breath was of almost imbecilic difficulty, her tongue out, her throat convulsed like a poisoned creature. So she had been all night.

He signed to Mrs. Gibson to leave them. That he could not show his love adequately was humiliating even when he was alone; with another present the failure would have been intolerable.

Mrs. Gibson was reluctant to go. It was as if she feared he would do her niece harm. She sobbed that to her own dying day she would never be able to understand why the good Lord should ask so gentle and innocent a person to suffer such agony. It was to him comprehensible enough, but only if there was no Lord, good or bad. There was no after life, for rats or sheep or men or trees. When Margaret died he would endure her loss.

As he sat down by the bed he thought of Carstares, whose wife, too, had died, but who was able to console himself with other women, such as Constance Kilgour. Last night Helen Carmichael had telephoned Margaret to tell her that Carstares and Miss Kilgour had been lovers during the war, and the child Alison was theirs. It might have been the excitement of that news which had caused this latest seizure. Even if he had no other reason to wish them ill this would have been sufficient. That Margaret's excitement had been of joy made no difference.

With her eyes closed, to spare him the sight of the pain in them, she asked, in a series of hoarse, long gasps, whom he had seen at the nursery. He had to mention them all and suffer the ghastly smile of affection with which she greeted each name. He thought that this love, though as natural to her as fragrance to meadowsweet, had nevertheless in her illness helped to strain and weaken her heart. Even to a good woman goodness was a burden. When she had been able to walk about the village she had stopped to speak to every living creature, cat or bird or person, had knocked at doors behind which his name was hated, and had entered with gifts such as bunches of flowers or jam of her own making. Most people believed that her pursuit of philanthropy was really to ransom him. He had not been ransomed, though, because he did not wish to be; and perhaps his resolute conviction that most human existence was insincere and trivial had helped to kill her. Once for her sake he had made an experiment in trust: the result had been an immediate deterioration not only in his own character but also in those of his subordinates.

He never felt or looked at home in any room. Chairs, tables, chests-of-drawers, always reminded him of the trees they had been; the very floor boards under his feet in his imagination became again pine or spruce growing on hillsides far from any house. Now this bright spring morning, as he sat down on the chair by her bed and held her hand, he could scarcely realise this was a room in the home where he had lived for ten years.

The doctor had promised to come at nine. It was now almost half-past eight. In half an hour Margaret could be dead. Imagining that, he felt, only a thousand times more severely, the shock he always felt whenever a fine tree had to be felled. Every chip that flew from it during the laying-in by the axe and every puff of sawdust were like pieces of his own flesh; and when he saw the proud top sway, shiver, and begin to come down, with a rush of air like a great sigh, he sometimes had to close his eyes so that he only heard and felt but did not see the crash to the ground and the leaping of the branches in their death throes. But Margaret had always been infinitely more beautiful and necessary than any tree.

Suddenly she spoke: 'Ezra, has he come yet?'

She had not called him by that name for years. When they were courting and after they were first married, she had teased him by using it. He had never complained, but she had stopped of her own accord.

'Not yet, Margaret.'

'I want to speak to him.'

He had thought she meant the doctor, now he knew it was Carstares.

Her fingers in his hand were as agitated as a vole that he had once snatched up from its gnawing of a tree. He felt the same desire to crush them as he had the tiny, panic-stricken creature. The flicker of life in her, as in the vole, was too little.

He shut his eyes, sick with horror and despair.

'I knew it all along,' she whispered.

Opening his eyes he saw that though still shaken by stounds of pain she was trying to smile.

'Don't talk, Margaret.'

'I knew it.' She waited for breath. 'Muriel and Helen wouldn't believe me. I knew she was waiting in that big empty house. And now he's come at last.'

She was referring to Helen Carmichael's story about Carstares and Miss Kilgour. He was by no means convinced of its truth. A woman, especially one with white hair, who saw the contorted branches of trees as male organs, was likely to imagine strange loves and births.

'Don't talk,' he said again, and wished the doctor would come. Yet what help would he bring? A stronger drug at least to kill the pain.

'I've prayed for it,' whispered Margaret. She lay then so quiet and still, with so curious a smile, he thought she was dead, and in a panic was about to jump up and shout for Mrs. Gibson.

'I've prayed for it,' she repeated.

He wished to indulge her in this blessing of an enemy, but he found himself saying: 'I don't think it's true, Margaret. It's too big a coincidence. Helen sits by the fire with her cats, and dreams.'

'Dreams of all her children.'

He supposed she meant schoolchildren, but he was wrong.

'Sheila,' she murmured, and then repeated it, with a little sorrowful cry, not unlike the vole's squeal.

He grinned in anguish. Sheila had been the name of their still-born daughter.

'When she was a young girl she was lovely.'

He thought she meant Sheila, and was delirious.

'Poor Helen. Take care of her, Ezra.'

'Yes.' Though how to take care of a proud, grim school-mistress with sexual fantasies, he did not know.

Then in the nursery outside a song was started, in shrill, bad, cheerful Gaelic. He knew who the singer was: Betty McMasters, ex-landgirl, now as tough and coarse and capable as any forestry worker.

'She always was a cheerful one, Betty,' whispered Margaret.

He pictured Betty, stout, thirtyish, fag in mouth, squatting at her work, with her big frank buttocks bulging out her trousers. She certainly didn't suffer from Miss Carmichael's complaint, virginity too well preserved. He could never be disgusted with her, or blame her; in his eyes her gentleness in handling the infant trees redeemed her.

They heard the song stop and a shriek take its place, but only for a second. Likely someone had dropped a puddock down Betty's blouse, making three down there in all; and just as likely someone else, perhaps John McBraid, had reminded the jokers that their master's wife lay very ill.

Though he wished to despise them and reject their solicitude, Strone found he could not; indeed, on the contrary, against his will they seemed then in his mind to become magnificent and in some way immortal: Betty with her fat behind so often pinched and joked about, John McBraid with his large ears of authority spotted with blackheads, and old Angus with his slavers of flattery. Their hands were fragrant with the scent of the young spruces, and of the fresh earth; their faces were bright with pity and wisdom. It was in its own way as absurd and obscene a fancy as any of Helen Carmichael's or

Rab McKerrol's; but for a whole minute he could not prevent it from possessing his mind.

'He's with them now,' whispered Margaret.

Again he was slow in realising she meant Carstares.

'Go and see.'

Grinning, to hide his shame and despair, he went over to the window. Carstares's new maroon car gleamed in the sun beside the gate, and in the nursery, Carstares himself, bare-headed, hands in flannels pockets, was chatting to a group of workers. Old Angus had his cap in his hand and gazed up with a gape of reverence.

'Is it him?' asked Margaret.

'It's Mr. Carstares, the new District Officer.'

'You know I mean him. Please, Ezra, ask him in and offer him tea. Tell Angus.'

'He'll just be after his breakfast, Margaret.'

She was silent.

'But I'll ask him,' he added quickly. Yes, he would go and give Carstares his opportunity for revenge: yesterday he had insulted Constance Kilgour, now Carstares could insult Margaret. In his heart he knew Carstares would not, but it was a curious relief to think he would. The morality of tit for tat was all the world was worth.

'He's the master,' he said. 'I can't tell him what to do.'

'He'll come if you ask him.'

'You've got to rest, Margaret. The doctor will be here any time now.'

Then he saw that Carstares had left the workers and was walking towards the house.

'He's coming.'

'I knew he would.'

From behind the curtain he studied the younger man, seeking justification for hate; like a soldier with his enemy at a disadvantage he could find none. Carstares with so slight a limp walked among the small trees sadly. Once, too, causing Strone's finger on the trigger of hatred to uncurl, he stopped and stooped to examine with tender fingers some tree which had attracted his attention, perhaps because it too seemed diseased. As he rose and walked on again he unaccountably took on in Strone's imagination that same strange quality of grandeur; in his case it was made more credible by his youth, handsomeness, and sorrow.

They heard him ring the doorbell, after a long hesitation. Mrs. Gibson hurried to answer it, thinking he was the doctor. Why, wondered Strone, still with his hatred in abeyance, had he not waited at the hut and sent a messenger? Had he come himself to offer truce or even friendship?

'Ezra?'

'Yes, Margaret.'

They could hear Mrs. Gibson talking to him; she was cross because he wasn't the doctor.

'Ezra?'

'Yes.'

'There's a guest in the house.'

No, he thought, not a guest; you can't call a superior a guest without asking his sanction first. That was one of the elementary lessons Margaret had never learned.

Mrs. Gibson knocked on the door and came in. Before she could speak she glanced at her niece and at once burst into tears again. Strone looked, too, and saw, as if for the first time, how ravaged with pain and weakness his wife's face was. He wished to go down on his knees and weep. He could not; his legs were as stiff as branches of a tree, his face hard and dry. Mrs. Gibson out of her apron threw him glances of horrified reproach mixed with bitter sympathy. She, too, was a good, simple, stupid woman. Margaret's dying would be to her a separate sorrow, to be tholed with warm tears and afterwards in the churchyard on many sunny Sunday afternoons resolved. She did not see it as part of the tragedy and futility of existence. Everyone was involved: Carstares in the sitting-room embarrassed by someone else's grief; Constance Kilgour with the child she hated and loved; Miss Carmichael alone with her three dressed cats; Mrs. McKerrol sick with her new pregnancy, and big Rab exulting like a stag on the hillside. In the background, threatened, too, were the innocent trees; if they escaped the malice of fire, they would be cut down to make pit-props or joists for shoddy houses.

'Ezra, you know I want to see him.' Her appeal was in a small, tearful, feeble voice.

Tormented by his inexpressible and useless love, he almost shouted to her where were her pride and reticence, without which no one could live or die without being a fool.

'I'll see what he says,' he muttered, as he went out.

Carstares was turning over the pages of a forestry magazine. He got up as Strone entered.

'I shouldn't have come really,' he said. 'I know I'm in the way. But I thought I'd like to tell you how sorry I am.'

Strone grinned. Though he knew it was unjust, it relieved him to think that Carstares was speaking with the smugness of a man who, having suffered that same loss himself, was prepared to give advice on how to bear it.

'Sit down, Mr. Carstares,' he said.

'I'm not staying.'

'Sit down, please.'

Reluctantly Carstares did so. 'How is Mrs. Strone?' he asked.

Strone's answer was a smile. 'I suppose you'll want me to conduct you over the forest, Mr. Carstares?'

'That can wait.'

'Then there are the fire-danger precautions to be discussed. I have a system, but perhaps you will want to change it.'

'I don't think so.'

They could hear Mrs. Gibson sobbing.

'Mr. Foulds said you'd want to talk about the note I received.'

'Yes, but not now.'

'It's urgent, Mr. Carstares. Two days of this weather and any fool with a match could set a thousand acres ablaze.'

'I suppose so, but you don't want to talk about it just now.'

'I have three suspects, Mr. Carstares.'

Carstares looked at the carpet and said nothing.

'Murdo McKew's the first,' said Strone. 'You'll not have met him yet?'

Carstares shook his head.

'He's the sly one of the tribe. He would do it as a kind of joke.'

Carstares was forced to comment: 'So if it was him we wouldn't have to take it seriously?'

'I wouldn't say that. Burning us out would be the best joke of all for them. Then comes McKerrol, one of our own workmen. You met him yesterday.'

'Yes.'

The one word conveyed his opinion of McKerrol.

Strone grinned, remembering Rab's performance on the lorry. 'He thinks he has a grievance; he thinks he should have been made a foreman or ganger at least.'

Carstares could not help saying it: 'He's lucky to have a job at all.'

'I could not dismiss him on suspicion. Besides, he's a profitable workman. There's not his equal at draining.'

'And at filthy impudence.'

'Yes, Rab could have done it with a drink in him. He has a daughter at school. You would notice it was a page from an arithmetic jotter.'

'Yes.' Carstares had the note in his pocket, but he would not take it out. He had the feeling that Strone, for all his cool grinning, might at any moment start screaming in a kind of madness. Once a patrol he had led had found a Japanese soldier wandering in the jungle, screaming like a beast. Strone, so carefully calm, was also lost.,

'Murdo's got a younger brother still at school,' said the forester. 'So he could have got hold of the paper, too.'

There was a knock at the door and Mrs. Gibson came in, red-eyed and sighing noisily. 'Margaret's wanting you, Ted.'

Carstares jumped to his feet. 'I'll be going.'

'She wants you, too, sir.'

Carstares shook his head.

'I'm thinking,' she said, 'it'll be the last thing the poor soul is ever likely to ask you, or anybody else.'

Strone put his hand on his brow for a moment, and closed his eyes. Then he strode to the door, and held it open for Carstares. 'For a minute, Mr. Carstares,' he said.

'She'll keep naebody much longer than a minute,' sobbed Mrs. Gibson.

'I really think I ought to go,' murmured Carstares.

Strone touched him on the arm, as if about to appeal; instead he said, 'My third suspect's somebody you'd never guess: Miss Kilgour.'

He seemed disappointed and even alarmed by Carstares's lack of resentment. The latter merely looked surprised and still more uneasy.

They crossed the little hall.

'If it was her,' said Strone, 'we'd have to take it very seriously.'

Margaret had got Mrs. Gibson to tidy her hair, arrange the bed-clothes, and put on a fresh bed-jacket of pink wool; but the effect had been to accentuate her exhaustion and haggardness. As Strone gazed at her, he forgot Carstares, and even forgot her; instead he remembered a place in the forest where because of some peculiar sourness in the soil no tree grew. There he often stood, as now, as if he was a tree himself resisting that barrenness.

Margaret gazed at Carstares as if he was her son returned safe from war.

'I'm so glad to see you,' she said.

He was visibly disconcerted by her appearance and hoarseness. Mrs. Gibson almost pushed him into a chair. There he sat trying to find a suitable smile.

Strone stood by the window, betrayed again by the awkwardness that all his life he had not been able to overcome. Always his manners had lacked spontaneity and superficial warmth.

'I'm so glad,' repeated Margaret.

'Thank you, Mrs. Strone,' said Carstares.

'Welcome to Kinlochgarvie.'

Again he thanked her.

'In the spring especially it's very beautiful.'

'I don't think you should be talking so much, Margaret,' said Mrs. Gibson.

Carstares nodded eagerly; he felt guilty that this harrowing effort to speak should be on his behalf.

'I knew you would come.'

Though he was obviously puzzled he hid it behind a charitableness that chilled Strone's blood.

'I've prayed for you to come,' gasped Mrs. Strone.

Carstares smiled. It was this time a smile that Strone could not hate; he thought Carstares must be thinking of his own wife, not now of Constance Kilgour.

'Yes, I've prayed. For your sake, and the little girl's, and Miss Kilgour's.'

He nodded, was about to speak, glanced aside at Strone, shook his head slightly, and remained silent.

'Please . . .' She could this time say no more. She lay gasping, her tongue out on her blue lips, her eyes strangely asquint. 'Please.'

'For pity's sake,' wailed Mrs. Gibson, wringing her hands.

Strone had his hands thrust hard into his jacket pockets. He looked out of the window. His mouth kept twitching.

'Please ask her to come and see me,' said Mrs. Strone at last. Then exhaustion made her wince like a blow.

Carstares stood up. 'I'll ask her,' he said, and signed to Mrs. Gibson that he ought to go. She agreed and opened the door for him.

'Goodbye, Mrs. Strone,' he murmured.

This time she looked at him as if she had never seen him before; indeed, as if his strangeness frightened her. She began to make little whimpering sounds.

In the hall Carstares found Strone at his back. He was about to protest that he could see himself out when he saw that the forester had had to come, being unable to bear the sight of his wife dying. It was a sight he had been spared.

Through the opened door they saw the doctor's car arrive at the gate. Like Carstares's it was new, but green. When he came out carrying his bag he walked along to Carstares's car for a closer look. Obviously he liked what he saw. When he glanced towards the house and saw the two men on the doorstep he grinned contritely, and then came hurrying along, with brisk professional earnestness. A bird sang in a tree in the garden as he passed. He looked towards it with sudden reckless pleasure and gratitude.

'Good morning, Strone,' he called.

'Good morning, doctor.'

'Sorry about this. Came as soon as I could.' He stared curiously at Carstares.

Strone introduced them.

'I've heard of you, Mr. Carstares,' said the doctor. 'Honoured to meet you. You'd see me admire your car? It is yours?'

Carstares nodded uneasily.

'I had my eye on one its identical twin. Satisfied with it?'

Again Carstares nodded.

'How is Margaret?' asked the doctor, turning to Strone.

'I doubt this time if she'll get over it.'

'Don't say that, Strone. She's recovered marvellously before now. She's got too much interest in us to leave us.'

When the doctor had gone in Strone lingered with Carstares.

'Last summer,' he said, 'she was able on sunny days to sit out there in the garden. People came in to talk to her. But one person wouldn't come, though Margaret called to her.'

He paused and gazed into the sunshine. Cold with apprehension, Carstares waited.

'Miss Kilgour,' murmured Strone, and smiled. Then he turned abruptly and went into the house.

Going down the path Carstares stopped and looked at the road. He imagined Mrs. Strone sitting there, happed in blankets, interested in people and birds and insects; while on the road Constance Kilgour walked stonily past. As he walked on again he remembered his first impression, that within Constance was a capacity for happiness for a long time disused. Now he was sure he had not been mistaken. No one, he had often thought, was willing to do penance for the war; yet that great mountain of evil and putrescence remained in the world, infecting every mind. It might be that Constance Kilgour, unlike most, was not able to accept tamely that infection. Perhaps she thought, as he had done, that only in angry exclusion and renunciation lay cure.

Nevertheless, as he stood smoking in the roadway beside his car, he wondered if it would be wiser for him to avoid her altogether, and to begin by telephoning that he was sorry he couldn't take her to Caldoon after all. But even as he was thinking up a polite formula of cancellation, he knew he had no intention of using it. More than ever he wanted to get to know her. Indeed, as he stood thinking of her, some of last night's strange desperate anxiety to be welcomed into her life and her child's returned. Under its stress he got into the car and made to drive straight to her house; but he managed to convince himself that he had better wait.

In about half an hour the doctor reappeared. He almost ran down the path. Strone stood in the doorway, watching.

Carstares put his head out of the window. 'Doctor,' he called.

The doctor seemed pleased to come over. He stroked the car.

'How is Mrs. Strone?' asked Carstares.

'Pretty weak, I'm afraid.'

Carstares looked towards Strone still at the door.

'She'll be all right, though?'

'No, she won't be all right.' The doctor looked in at the dashboard. 'How many to the gallon?'

'About thirty.'

'Yes, just about what I get myself. No, I think it's really the end this time. I'm coming back this afternoon.'

'Too bad.'

'Yes. A fine woman. I don't know what Strone will do. He worships her, you know. He doesn't show, it. I don't think he can. But it's there.'

'Yes.'

'Well, I'll be pushing along. I hope to see you again, Mr. Carstares.'

'Surely.'

'Mr. McIan, your predecessor and I had a little arrangement, whereby I was permitted to do a bit of shooting within the forest.'

Carstares smiled. 'Deer?'

The doctor smiled, too. 'Well, maybe. But mainly rabbit, a pheasant, a blackcock, a grouse in season. All right?'

'Yes, all right.'

'Thanks, Carstares. Anything I could do for you in return?'

'No, I don't think so. But there is something maybe I should mention to you.'

'Yes?'

'You'll know Miss Carmichael, the schoolmistress?'

'I know Helen very well. Why?'

'I don't know whether it's any of my business or not, but I'll risk thinking it is.' He explained what had happened at the school-house that morning.

The doctor listen glumly. 'Aye,' he said. 'But what do you want me to do?'

'I don't know.'

'Sorry, Carstares. The trouble is, I don't know myself. This isn't new, you see, though I must say what you've just told me's the worst exhibition yet.'

'I thought, for her sake, I ought to mention it to you.'

'Yes, I know. All right, I'll make an excuse for dropping in to see her. But she'll be propriety itself. That's the trouble: her control most of the time's like iron. One of these days it's going to snap completely. There are places she could go into for treatment, but I somehow never get the chance to recommend that to her. As I said, with me she's propriety itself. It's damnable, for I like Helen; anyway, I respect her. But, who knows, she might get over it without anybody's help. Let's hope so, anyway.'

Carstares nodded. He noticed, as the doctor walked back to his car, that Strone no longer stood in the doorway. He had gone in to his wife.

Fifteen

Lunch was as subdued as breakfast had been cheerful. Miss Kirn had been to see her friend, and had returned red-eyed and curiously penitent. Jock, forgetting his elevation, tried to inform Carstares of the situation by a wink of the utmost tenderness and subtlety. A moment after he remembered, and used landlord's words of explanation, which were not nearly so eloquent.

'Miss Kirn and Mrs. Strone have been close friends for going on ten years,' he said. 'Mrs. Strone's a woman will be sadly missed.'

Carstares thought she must have died.

'No, sir, not yet. But it seems there's no hope this time. For the past three springs it's been the same, but there's got to come an end to the stoutest heart. For many people in this village, sir, the roses this summer will be black and their perfume will be the smell of sorrow.'

'Particularly for Strone,' Carstares could not help saying.

Jock nodded; he was no longer the landlord, but the barman for whom the glasses he had filled had been as microscopes to study human nature.

'There'll be dew on the roses,' he said, 'but he'll not shed a tear. Will it break his heart in two to admire what big Rab grows with love? It will, I'm sure of that. But so did his wife admire roses. She loved them, cream were her favourites. By putting our noses to a rose we prove we're dependent on one another. That's what some folk will never admit, though; and Strone's one of them.'

And Constance Kilgour, Carstares supposed, was another; at any rate according to Jock's sad, gentle wink.

'Oh, while I remember, sir,' added Jock, again the landlord, 'watch out for the McKews. Meant to tell you this morning. For some reason they've taken an umbrage against you. And our Nancy's not to be trusted, either.'

After lunch Carstares was about to drive off to Garvie House when Miss Kirn ran down the steps, waving to him to wait. She was weeping, and at first could not say what she so desperately wanted to say.

As he waited sympathetically he noticed Nancy watching from behind the glass door. She blew him a kiss.

'I've just been speaking to Mrs. Gibson on the telephone,' said Miss Kirn at last. 'Margaret's still sinking.'

Carstares thought of Strone.

'She never did harm to any living creature,' sobbed Miss Kirn. 'If ever anyone was sure of heaven, it's Margaret Strone.'

Her husband doesn't think so, Carstares thought; and yet he loves her more deeply than you, Miss Kirn, for all your tears ever could.

'But she thinks she hurt Constance Kilgour once. I'm sure she didn't, but she thinks so.'

So does Constance think so, thought Carstares, his heart cold.

'So she wants to see her, to ask forgiveness.'

Miss Kirn could not continue for almost a minute, during which Nancy again blew a kiss.

'Do you want me to tell Miss Kilgour?' asked Carstares, in pity.

She reached in and seized his hand. 'Not just tell her, Mr. Carstares. Plead with her. She will listen to you.'

He remembered he had already promised Mrs. Strone herself that he would bring Constance to her.

'She loves you, Mr. Carstares. I used to think, God forgive me, she loved no one, not even her own child; but she must have loved you at one time.'

He would not deny it.

'I'll explain it to her,' he said.

'She's not a stupid woman; she's not got that excuse. But let me tell you this, Mr. Carstares, whether she's going to be your wife or not, if she doesn't go this afternoon to see Margaret, just for a minute, then I'll always think of her as a cruel, black-hearted, spiteful woman.'

'She's not that, Miss Kirn.'

'Then let her prove it.'

He had to defend Constance. 'She might not think it right to excite Mrs. Strone.'

'The doctor's approved. He said it would do no harm, and might even do good. Yes, it might even give Margaret the strength to stay with us this spring again.'

He shook his head slowly, not quite sure what the gesture meant.

'I shouldn't say this, Mr. Carstares, but your own wife died. Think of Mr. Strone.'

For Christ's sake, he thought, don't bring Marion into this; let her stay dead.

'I'll speak to Miss Kilgour,' he said, rather curtly, and drove away.

Miss Kirn, weeping, and holding out her hand to find support in the sunshine itself, like a blind woman, crossed to the hotel door. Nancy, smiling, for she'd been thinking of the spittle in his coffee, held it open for her.

'Where's Mr. D.O. off to now?' she asked, 'Caldoon, for another night's boozing?'

Despite her grief, Miss Kirn had to reprove that impertinence. 'It's none of your business, Nancy, where any guest goes.'

Where that guest went last night, thought Nancy, was certainly my business. Outwardly she said, trying to make her voice sad: 'Has he gone to see how Mrs. Strone is?'

'He's gone to Garvie House, if you must know. I hope you're remembering we've guests coming at four.'

'Garvie House?' Nancy, yelped the words.

'Yes.' Then Miss Kirn rushed away to find Jock and weep guiltily in his arms.

Nancy lingered in the hall, bristling with affront. She swore aloud, and let spit form again in her mouth, savagely, not for his coffee this time, but his face. The only faces in sight, however, were the stags'; these had come out of his forest, and so she spat up at them.

'Wait till Will McKew's finished with you,' she said, 'Miss Bitchy Kilgour won't be thinking you're so handsome then.' But of course even if Will, helped by his brothers, waylaid Carstares as they had once waylaid another man, and almost killed him, he'd still be rich, and so still desirable to Constance Kilgour, whose need of money was so great as nearly to win for her Nancy's respect.

In the fank that afternoon, where sometimes live deer could be seen, she would tell Will how last night Carstares had forced her into his bed, after dragging off her clothes. As proof, she would show him the bruise on her buttock. The scene in prospect pleased and mollified her. How easy it would be, through his love, to rouse Will to hatred; and how exciting. Most of the time he was too patient for her taste, slow in mind as the clouds that floated above the hills where he watched his sheep. He was also far too anxious to see somebody else's point of view; a man as ugly as he couldn't afford that luxury. Then in his love of her he was always so irritatingly dutiful, talking of marriage and children. But once she had been given a glimpse of the ferocity hidden away in him, like a beast sleeping in its den.

As he drove along Carstares tried not to think about Constance and Mrs. Strone. Passing the schoolhouse he saw Miss Carmichael at the back feeding her hens. When she heard the car she turned and waved. The little gesture of sanity and friendliness delighted him and filled him with hope. He wondered what had restored her: the doctor's visit perhaps, or the shock of Mrs. Strone's decline. He could not help but think that the great company of trees, the multitude of young, dark-green spruces of the forest, and the tall, magnificent larches under which her house stood, must, too, have had their salutary effect. They represented not only patience and endurance, but also propagation as calm as it was puissant.

Past the village he reached the decrepit gate that barred the private way to Garvie House. As soon as he touched it he recalled something of his performance last night, and stood there in the road, touching the tenderness of his mouth, and trying to recall more. His overcoat would have to be sent to a cleaner's, to get the muck and spew out of it. His mouth was sore because he'd fallen. Where? And why, if he'd made such a bloody fool of himself, had Constance Kilgour changed her tune and become so sweet? According to every witness, she wasn't the woman to repent unkindness, particularly if it had been shown to a drunken lout stumbling into the privacy not only of her house, but also of her past. He'd be well advised to go very warily, like a stag with a stalker on the hill.

Seen in the vivid sunlight, amongst the trees, with flashes of snow-peaks beyond, the house did not look as dilapidated as he had expected. Square, high, and towered, with grey-green fortress walls four feet thick, it carried with dour contemptuous pride such blemishes as broken rones, bleached rotting wood-work, broken glass, and the moat of weeds. Some of the windows on the ground floor had been enlarged at some time, but otherwise the house externally was as it had been built in the seventeenth century. It was easy to imagine it guarded by fierce abrupt Highlanders, armed with dirks and claymores, and garbed in kilts and plaids of the family tartan. Inside, too, the walls would be hung with tapestries of the same tartan, and there would be a fireplace big enough to roast a whole stag.

Perhaps, thought Carstares, as he stopped the car outside the great iron-studded door, Constance would have been happier then: at least relationships with inferiors would have been simpler; certainly there would have been no McKerrol shouting insults, and no Mrs. Strone presumptuous in death.

Kilgour holding little Alison by the hand came out. Each wore a kilt of the same red and green tartan, his longer at the back than the front, hers very short, showing her pale, thin knees. She was dressed for the trip to Caldoon; in her dark hair was a bow of red ribbon, and to match her kilt she wore a fair-isle jumper in which the colours were vivid. Bright, too, though wary, were her eyes behind the spectacles.

Carstares went up the steps and crouched down in front of her. 'Hello, Alison,' he said, taking her hand.

Kilgour suddenly guffawed. 'Good man, Carstares,' he said.

Carstares gazed up in surprise.

'Hello,' replied Alison, smiling.

'You've got to like Mr. Carstares, Alison,' cried her uncle. 'Do you know why? Well, isn't he taking you to Caldoon?'

She seemed to understand him better than Carstares did. 'Thank you,' she said.

Carstares shook his head. 'You don't have to thank me, Alison. It's a great pleasure to me. Do you like cowboy pictures?'

She nodded, with sparkles of delight in her eyes.

'Of course she does,' cried Kilgour. 'And by Jove, so do I.' He laughed. 'That's the way to do it, eh, Carstares?' He brought his hand up quickly from his hip as from a holster, and pointed it. 'All the bad men dead at the finish, and the good men happy and flourishing.'

He still held his hand out, but somehow the joy and purpose faded from it. Carstares, glancing behind, saw in the distance Constance come walking up out of the trees that overhung the river. She wore a red bathing costume.

'Has she been swimming in the river?' he asked, in astonishment.

Kilgour nodded.

'Isn't it a bit early in the season?'

'Connie prefers it with snow on the ground, and with the river roaring, as it is now.'

They listened to the proud, fierce surge of the stream. Its waters, thought Carstares, must be icy from the high snows. Yet here in front of the house, out of the east wind, the sunshine was warm.

Now she was racing over the grass, in and out of the overgrown shrubbery of rhododendrons. Though her feet were

bare, and the long grass must have been littered with dried
cones, hard twigs, and withered leaves, some of holly, she ran
with a swift confidence that exhilarated him. He remembered
how in the rain he had imagined in her walk a lilt of courage
and humour.

As if he had been visiting daily for years, she waved and
called: 'Isn't it a glorious day?'

'Yes, isn't it?' He was fascinated to see how fine her figure
was, and how beautiful her black hair as it streamed down her
back. Looking for someone with whom to share his admiration
he noticed her brother giving him a strange grin that was
almost a leer of pity.

She reached the edge of the grass, found a pair of old tennis
shoes she'd left there, stepped into them, and came across the
pebbled drive. All over her, on face, thighs, breast, and
shoulders drops from the river glittered, like dew. He was
reminded of Jock's queer remark about the Kinlochgarvie roses
that summer being black.

As she came up the steps, pink-cheeked and laughing, he
hardly recognised her. Surely she was not the same woman who
yesterday had repulsed him with such harsh contempt? And
surely, too, everyone, including himself, was unjust in fearing
that out of some dark, bleak animosity she might refuse to go
and say a few friendly words to a dying woman?

'I'm sorry I'm not ready,' she said. 'I thought I'd have time
for a swim before you came.'

'If I'd known I might have joined you,' he said, laughing, and
shivering.

'Do you swim?'

'A bit.'

'There's a grand pool.'

'Gloomy as Hades,' muttered her brother.

'The sunshine strikes it like spears.'

'I like my sunshine more peaceful,' he said. 'Besides it must
be twenty feet deep, at least. You know, Carstares, if a person
who couldn't swim was to slip into it there'd be no hope for
him, none at all. It's not placid water, you know; it never is; it's

dark and savage. I've seen salmon this big in it.' He held his arms apart.

Constance laid her hand on Carstares's arm. 'You'll have to come and see for yourself, Hugh. I'll not be more than five minutes.'

As he watched her go into the house his arm tingled with her touch, and his ears sang with her saying of his name.

'When Connie says five minutes,' said her brother, 'she means five minutes. In that way she's unique among women.'

In many other ways, too, thought Carstares, and flung off restraint. To be with her all that afternoon and evening was suddenly a privilege and joy not to be given up though she were to deny a dozen Mrs. Strones. Now he saw that she was indeed the same woman as yesterday; then cheerfulness and hope had been extinguished in her, just as sunshine had been withdrawn from the loch, leaving it cold, dark, and deep. Compassion and fondness flooded his heart; she, more than Mrs. Strone, was the victim of spring.

Hand-in-hand with Alison he went down the steps and crossed the drive on to the grass.

Kilgour called after them: 'Take care. There are Injuns behind those bushes.'

'We're friendly palefaces, aren't we?' said Carstares to Alison.

He was surprised by the sudden vivacity of her smile; up to now she had seemed sulky and rather stupid.

'When the boys play at Cowboys and Indians in the play-ground,' she said, 'I'm always an Indian.' She fingered the ribbon in her hair as if it was a plume. 'I get killed.'

He found himself walking oddly on the grass; then he realised he was trying to walk where she had walked. Feeling foolish and strangely betrayed, he halted. Kilgour was inspecting the car; he hadn't seen. But Alison had, and was giving him a look from which liking kept out disappointment and scorn.

'Do you like school?' he asked.

She clenched her fist. 'Sometimes.'

'Just sometimes?'

'If Robert McKew wasn't there, maybe I would like it all the time.'

'Why, what does he do?'

'Calls me names, pulls my hair, and pushes me down.' She said it airily, with a smile, and looked very like Constance.

'Does he?'

'Yes, and he makes all the others call me names too.' She was contemptuous of those others bullied into being bullies.

'Doesn't Miss Carmichael stop them?'

She made a show of being fair to the schoolmistress, re-membering hard, with her brow furrowed. 'No,' she said at length, very firmly.

'But she must know they do it?'

'Yes, she knows.'

He was about to ask why the teacher didn't stop them when he remembered in time Miss Carmichael's malady. Perhaps, in some hellish way, the jeering at this child by the other children gave her relief.

'And what do you do when they're calling you names?'

She shrugged her shoulders. 'I just run to my tree, and stand with my back to it.'

'Your tree?'

'Well, I call it mine. It's a larch tree.' She laughed. 'They take hands and dance round it, singing that I'm going to be burnt. The boys throw cones at me.'

'Do the girls shout names too?'

'Oh, yes.' Constance herself could not have suggested the fact of feminine treachery and cruelty more coolly.

So far he had not dared ask what names, and she had not volunteered to tell. He decided not to ask, lest he should be told with devastating exactness.

'All the girls?'

'There are only six. Sometimes Peggy McKerrol doesn't.'

No doubt Rab's daughter, he thought.

'But she's afraid of Robert McKew. They're all afraid of him.'

'Are you?'

She nodded, with an honest matter-of-factness that he found moving. 'Especially when he tries to kiss me,' she added, in disgust.

This McKew cub, he thought, looked like being a credit to the pack.

'I kick him,' she said.

'Hard, I hope.'

'As hard as I can. I've got my school shoes on. They're heavier than these.'

'What age is this Robert McKew?'

'Twelve. He should be at Caldoon High School really, but he failed. He's a dunce. Miss Carmichael likes him.' She said that as if she was well aware of its improbability. 'When she's helping him with his sums, she sits beside him and puts her arm round his neck. Once –' she hesitated, smiling, as if the choice disclosure she was about to make might not readily be believed – 'she kissed him. On the head. We all saw it. He blushed and shouted. He was angry. Miss Carmichael blushed, too. But sometimes when he's stupid she slaps his head.'

Suddenly she pulled her hand out of his, and assumed her former sullen, taciturn expression. When he glanced towards the house he expected to see Constance, and did. Dressed in a tweed costume of dark green, and a blouse of lighter green, she looked so gay, confident, and lovely that for a moment he felt angry with this child who so innocently and yet so inevitably persecuted her.

Without looking up at him, Alison muttered: 'Please don't tell Connie I was talking about the school. She doesn't like me to.'

Kilgour reached in the car and pressed the hooter ring. 'All aboard,' he shouted.

Carstares was about to hurry over to Constance, but stopped, and insisted on taking Alison's hand. She was unwilling to give it.

'Must you two keep holding hands,' cried Constance, 'like Papa Bear and little Baby Bear?'

He felt the child's hand quiver, and knew she, too, was aware of the malice behind that laughing gibe. Though he shared some of the child's fear and resentment, his chief reaction was again pity: Constance loved the child surely, but somehow that love was under a spell that perverted it. He was reminded of Strone, and so of Mrs. Strone. He had not yet made up his mind whether he should tell Constance about Mrs. Strone's wish and Miss Kirn's appeal. If he did not tell her he would protect her from the blame of having heartlessly disappointed a dying woman; but perhaps she did not wish such protection.

'Well, shall we go?' she asked.

'Yes, of course.' With conscious defiance he touched Alison's head. 'We'll all sit in the front. Shall we?'

Alison nodded.

'Why crush ourselves?' asked Constance, laughing. 'Alison can sit in the back.'

Again Alison nodded, but there was a great difference in the two small gestures.

'There's plenty of room for the three of us,' insisted Carstares.

Kilgour was holding a door open, with little grunts of neutrality.

'Oh, very well,' said Constance, 'if you two are so set on sitting together, I'll sit in the back.'

In spite of her laughter, Carstares felt her amiableness was on the verge of ending. She gave Alison a glance of loathing; or so, shocked, he imagined. Certainly her knuckles and the bone at the bridge of her nose turned white for an instant. But had the loathing been of herself, not of the child?

He stood looking at her in dismay, compassion, and perplexity. What he did not want, he thought, what he must at all costs avoid, was to fall in love with her, and yet hate her sometimes, distrust her, and despise himself. Love ought to bring reassurance, whatever else.

'I'll sit in the back,' said Alison.

'That's what to do,' cried her uncle, and he lifted her in.

Constance and Carstares stood smiling at each other. In his smile, he realised, was a kind of regret, in hers challenge.

She held out her hand to be helped into the car.

'Sorry,' he muttered, and helped her in.

Kilgour was making brave faces in an attempt not to look sorry for himself. 'If you can remember, Connie,' he said, 'would you ask at Murchison's if they've got my pipe-reeds from Glasgow yet?'

'Bag-pipes?' asked Carstares.

'Yes, old man. I like a special kind. They said they'd get them for me.'

'We'll inquire,' said Carstares, grinning.

'Thank you. And perhaps, Connie, you might fetch me some cigarettes. Any brand really, I'm not particular.'

'Are you out of fags?' asked Carstares.

'More or less, I'm afraid.'

'Have these.' Carstares took out an unopened packet and handed it to him. He took it with fingers that trembled with gratitude and shame. Constance's smile of playful reproach he repelled with a fierce, angry scowl that bade her remember her own purpose was to fleece Carstares, not only of his thirty thousand pounds but of his happiness and peace of mind.

'Thanks, old man,' he said. 'I'll do the same for you some day.' And again he scowled at Constance, warning her that in her scheme to entrap Carstares she had better not depend upon him for help or even loyalty, unless she played fair by him. 'Well, enjoy yourselves.' He stepped back and waved as the car swung round and sped down the drive.

Only Alison, he noticed, kept waving to him till he was out of sight.

'It's a pity your brother couldn't come with us,' remarked Carstares.

'He could have,' murmured Constance. 'He didn't want to.'

Alison coughed, as if in subtle derision.

'Comfortable?' asked Carstares, turning to smile at her.

Constance smiled ahead.

'Yes, thank you,' murmured the child.

'Good. Now that we're friends, though, we'll have to decide what you're going to call me.'

'Mr. Carstares, surely?' said Constance.

'Too formal.' He shook his head. 'What's wrong with Hugh?'

'As you wish.'

He gave her a quick glance. 'What am I to call you.?'

They were now out of the private road and were driving through the forestry township. In the bright sunshine cocks crowed, washing gleamed, and woodsmoke scented the air. A few men were in their gardens; one was McKerrol. He stood with his foot on his spade, and flicked at his moustache as the car passed. He wore a flannel, collarless shirt, open at the front, showing his massive, hairy chest. Near him a small, fair-haired girl was pushing a pram with wobbling wheels.

'Constance or Connie?' asked Carstares.

She smiled but did not answer.

'Constance in the meantime?'

She nodded. 'Did you see Strone this morning?'

'Yes, for a few minutes.'

'Long enough, I hope, to arrange to have McKerrol removed?'

'I'm afraid we didn't discuss that.'

'No?'

They passed the schoolhouse. Miss Carmichael wasn't to be seen.

'He's vile,' she said.

'I could believe it. But he's got a large family.'

She said nothing.

'And a nice wife.'

'Yesterday wasn't the first time,' she said.

He frowned, 'Haven't you complained to Strone?'

'Yes.'

'And what did he say?'

'That he's got a large family and a nice wife. Of course, Strone doesn't like me.'

'Why?'

He softened the question with a smile; but that smile did not quite say it was ludicrous anyone should dislike her. He could not have given a reason for his thrawnness.

Her reply was surprising. In it was regret, carefully measured, not too much, not too little.

'I'm afraid I had to put Mrs. Strone in her place once.'

The snubbing must have happened before last summer. Mrs. Strone, though an invalid, had not been dying then. Would it have made any difference if she had been?

They were now approaching the hotel, and he saw that Miss Kirn and Jock were waiting at the gate. Jock skipped out into the road to stop the car; that done, he withdrew discreetly.

Miss Kirn came forward to the car. Her small face was stern with grief.

'How is Margaret?' she asked.

Carstares shook his head.

'Do you mean, she didn't go?'

'I thought, seeing she's so ill, it wouldn't be wise.'

Constance picked up a road-map and glanced politely through it. The conversation did not concern her.

Miss Kirn looked as if she was about to scream and strike. 'Black-hearted, as I said,' she sobbed. 'Cruel. I can scarcely believe anyone could be so callous.'

'I didn't tell Miss Kilgour,' said Carstares. 'You can't blame her.'

'Yes, I can, and I will. You didn't tell her because you were afraid. You were afraid that if you did she would refuse.'

Jock had come over. 'Easy now,' he murmured. 'It's not for us to judge.'

Constance continued to smile at the map.

'I'm sorry for you, Mr. Carstares,' sobbed Miss Kirn. 'You feel you must be loyal to her because she's the mother of your child, but like the rest of us you're afraid of her. I'm sorry for you, you've already suffered great unhappiness, but you'll suffer more, here in Kinlochgarvie. You should go away.' She tried hard to control her sobbing. 'Margaret will sleep in peace,' she said. 'I know someone who never will.'

Then she let Jock lead her away.

They made a queer pair as they entered the hotel gate.

Though he smiled after them himself, Carstares resented Constance's smiling; hers lacked liking and sympathy.

He drove on. She replaced the road-map.

'And what was all that about?' she asked.

He explained, trying to keep blame and resentment out of his voice.

'And what did she want to see me for?'

'Didn't you have a quarrel once?'

'No. I just asked her to mind her own business.'

'I see.' Perhaps the snubbing had been justified. 'Well, she may have felt she wanted to make it up, whatever it was.'

She was silent for almost a minute.

'Why didn't you tell me?'

'I thought she was too ill.'

'Did you really, Hugh? Wasn't it because you were afraid?'

He turned from her smile to look at Alison. She was staring at him as if, understanding and believing Miss Kirn's insinuation, she thought he was her father; but he could not say whether she was pleased or not. That decision was postponed, in a way that moved him greatly.

For a minute or two he concentrated on his driving. The road twisted alongside the loch, with a steep cliff on the other side.

'If I had told you,' he said, 'would you have gone?'

By the side of the road there was a copse of pussy-willows, thin, contorted, starved trees, yet now glorious with yellow catkins that blazed in the sun. She gazed at these and smiled in what he took to be gratitude; it seemed to him she was finding in their unlikely loveliness not only a present solace, but also a promise of companionship in the future. For the moment, at least, her rejection of humanity was not bitter; it was necessary, that was all.

'I suppose not,' she replied, at last.

Her hands rested, one on top of the other, on her lap. Their stillness moved him, so much so that he took one hand off the wheel to touch them. He did not speak or look at her; but he smiled as he stared ahead.

Sixteen

As if appreciating its escape from the tight, harsh hills, Caldoon
had made itself a relaxed, spacious, inland resort, with ivied
villas, genteel boarding-houses, and large hotels, all proud of
their gardens. In every street, especially the wide main street,
browsed a number of plump, domesticated trees, mostly elms
and limes. The river that flowed through it was as placid as the
cattle that grazed in the lush fields on either bank; no one could
have guessed that four miles to the north, as it rushed through
the gorge at the head of the pass, it roared as turbulently as any
in Scotland. Many bus-tours from Glasgow and Edinburgh
visited the town, which had had to learn how to be hospitable
without at the same time appearing mercenary or common.
The shops, for instance, were enterprising, their stocks large
and attractive, their prices high. The churches, particularly St.
Margaret's, the parish kirk, were fine, substantial, red-stone
buildings, cool in summer, cosy in winter, and at all times
reverent without fuss.

What pleased Carstares most about the town then was its
assumption, typically smug but nevertheless cordial, that he,
Constance and Alison, made up one of the comfortable families
driving in from their pleasant houses in the suburbs to enjoy an
afternoon's shopping and lounging. For the first time in years
he did not resent that invitation to conform. Indeed, as he came
out of the car, in the parking place among the cars of similar
families, he found himself smiling back with an acceptance and
gratitude he could not prevent. When Alison, delighted by the
same feeling of community, squeezed his hand with light
affectionate decisiveness, he understood immediately, and
looked with challenge at Constance, expecting her to be

contemptuous of his naïve surrender, but feeling confident he could justify it to her and even persuade her to share it with him.

He saw no contempt on her face, only what seemed to him a kind of sad dismay, as she glanced from him to Alison. Here, surely, in the cheerful street, she was remembering the catkins by the loch, and realising, against her will perhaps, that their companionship could not after all be enough. Making that inadequacy, and her acknowledgement of it, almost more poignant than he could bear, was the shabbiness of her green costume, noticed now for the first time. So lovely did she seem to him then, sad but on the brink of a happiness forsaken years ago, that he felt the bones in his body grow soft, so much so that he could hardly lock the door of the car. Miss Kirn's voice sounded in his head: 'Whether she's going to be your wife or not, Mr. Carstares,' and he answered it, 'Yes, Miss Kirn, she's going to be my wife, no matter what you or anyone else thinks of her.'

Unaccountably then, as he stood smiling across the car at her, a memory of the jungle occurred to him. Perhaps it was the green of her costume or the blood-like colour of the car that awoke it. At any rate, there in the welcoming street he saw again the body of Sergeant Scourie, who had been a member of his platoon. Scourie had been sent ahead to scout. He hadn't returned, and a day later they had found his body dismembered with almost facetious obscenity. There had been no need afterwards to hint to the members of that patrol that head-quarters wanted no prisoners to be taken.

'Is there anything the matter?' she asked.

'No.' He shook his head. 'No, no. Why?'

'You looked strange.'

Was it, she wondered, because he had caught a glimpse of that coldness in her mind, that icy chamber where love, and hope, and gladness, were frozen into contorted shapes of mockery? She could not blame the war, or Alison's conception, for it; no, it had been forming, with glacier slowness and sureness, since her own birth. Francis had glimpsed it, several times: his love of her had visibly degenerated into pity that had fear in it. Yet she had loved Francis, or had wished to love him. Carstares she could easily hate: he had humiliated her in the presence of the snivelling little hotel proprietrix, had insulted her by his feeble refusal to dismiss McKerrol, and now, in an offence she could never have named, he was outraging her with his attempt to win Alison's favour.

They began to stroll along the pavement, looking at the shopwindows.

'Are we going to get Ronald's reeds?' asked Alison.

'Should we get those first?' asked Carstares, laughing.

'We promised.'

Constance was smiling. 'If we forget we might be doing ourselves a favour.'

He grinned; no doubt Kilgour was a clumsy and melancholy piper.

Alison was not smiling. 'I like Ronald to play the pipes,' she said, 'especially when he's among the trees and I can't see him.'

Carstares laughed; yes, it might be better not to see those dejected, bulging eyes.

'All right,' he said, 'the reeds first. Then what? A present for you, I think. What's it to be?'

'Nothing, thank you.'

'Oh, it must be something. This is the first time I've ever been in Caldoon with you and Constance. So to celebrate I must buy you both a present.'

Though she obviously liked him, the child rejected his logic with scorn. She also glanced up to see Constance's reaction.

'It's a long time since anyone bought me a present,' murmured Constance. 'So I think I'll take you at your word.'

'Good. And here's the very shop.'

It was a jeweller's; in the window were clocks, watches, silverware, and rings.

He took Constance by the arm and pushed her gently towards the window.

'One of those?' he said.

'Those?' She bent forward. 'Aren't those engagement rings?'

'Yes. Yes, they are.'

'You must be joking.'

'No. Far from it.'

Again, to his dismay and amazement, he remembered the finding of Scourie's body. Was it the roughness of her tweed sleeve that had caused his mind to slip back so irrelevantly? Or was it because from Scourie's finger the ring, a keepsake from his wife, had been bitten off?

'We met yesterday for the first time,' she said coolly.

'I feel as if I've known you for years.' And it did seem to him that as he had lain sweating in the jungle he had thought of her, not of Marion.

'Others,' said Constance, 'appear to feel that too.'

He knew at once she meant Miss Kirn and the school-mistress, who supposed he was Alison's father. This was her first reference to it.

'Never mind them,' he said. 'I feel it; and I think you feel it, too.'

Yes, she thought, she felt it: it had been for him, or rather the release he could represent, that she had been waiting. In so short a time had he usurped Francis's place, even in her memory, that to her, as well as to the lecherous little gossips of the village, he was Alison's father. Once before, indeed, as Francis, he had stopped her like this in front of a jeweller's window to look at rings. 'Too bloody dear, Connie,' he had said, laughing, and pulled her away. Since then he had been burnt to death, and inherited a fortune from his wife. So vivid were her confusions, she thought really it was Francis who had had a wife, and that had been the reason for his unwillingness to marry her. His given reason that he could not marry while he was engaged almost every night in killing and maiming the fruits of marriage had been a characteristic equivocation. Had not Carstares that very afternoon, with the same kind of dishonesty, refrained from telling her that Mrs. Strone wished to see her.

'Well, do you?' he asked.

She nodded.

'I knew it,' he said, with joy, 'I knew it.'

Alison, she noticed, had moved apart with typical haughtiness and independence. She understood what was in the child's mind, and through her own breasts and thighs shot a pang of foreboding. Marrying Carstares might be like setting a match to a tuft of grass at the edge of the forest: a revenge impossible to control.

'I love you,' he said.

Though she smiled, she felt like striking him for that facile claim; it was like a child's boast.

'Yes, Constance,' he insisted eagerly. 'From the minute I saw you yesterday in the rain. I'll never forget how you looked.'

'My hair must have looked like a sea-lion's mane.'

He laughed. 'No, no. You were beautiful. More than that, Constance; I thought you looked – well, happy deep inside.' He tapped his own heart with his fist. 'I think you are often happy when you are alone, aren't you? I mean, in the pool this afternoon, for instance.'

Again she could have struck him for his crass, blundering pity.

'But you're not going to be alone any more,' he said. 'You'll have to take me to all your favourite haunts: the pool, to begin with. Heaven knows I've not been much in love with people myself in the past year or two; but I think I've got over my scunner now.'

'Scunner?' It was Francis's word.

'Yes. You know what it means?'

'Yes, I know.'

'So, you see, Constance, if you'll let me, maybe I could be the bridge, the way across to other people.'

'To McKerrol?'

He was taken aback; his enthusiasm fizzed out like fire with water poured on it.

'Well, no,' he said at length, trying to laugh, 'I'd scarcely expect that.'

'Why not? You seem to have a sympathy for him.'

'Not for him personally.'

She stared at the rings in the window. 'I thought you'd have dismissed him first thing this morning.'

'There were other things,' he muttered.

She waited for him to say what they were.

'Mrs. Strone. She was taken bad during the night. This morning she was dying. I spoke to the doctor. He thought there was no hope for her.'

'I can't see the connection between that and McKerrol.'

'No.' And then he himself saw the connection, but knew he could not make her see it; not now, anyway.

'Have you the power to dismiss him?'

'Yes.'

'You heard him yesterday. You saw him.'

She, too, then must have seen Rab's gestures. 'Yes, I saw him,' he said bleakly.

'I told you it wasn't the first time.'

He hated Rab, but not without some deduction from his love for her. He looked towards Alison for reassurance, but found her resolutely minding her own business.

Constance faintly indicated the rings in the window. 'If you're serious,' she murmured.

'I am serious, Constance.'

By shrugging her shoulders she asked him to prove his seriousness.

'I'll get rid of him,' he blurted out.

She paused. 'Didn't Strone encourage him? Or at any rate do nothing to discourage him?'

This quiet, persistent, vindictiveness was not her true nature, he thought desperately: she was being driven to it. In his uncertainty the love deducted was restored.

She seemed amused by his desperation. 'I'm not going to ask you to get rid of Strone.'

'I doubt if I could do it,' he said. 'He's been here as a first-grade forester for ten years. He's highly thought of at head-quarters. I've just arrived. I'd have to have something very serious against him.'

'Isn't it serious enough that he should stand by and allow an employee to shout filthy insults to someone passing on the road?'

'Yes, it is.'

'Supposing' – she pretended to be pushing on a ring – 'we did become engaged, could you really go on meeting him day after day, knowing what he thinks of me? Because, you see, McKerrol shouts what Strone wants him to shout.'

'No.'

'I think so.'

'I thought we'd go away, you and I, and Alison.'

She shook her head. 'I was born here; Strone wasn't. My people owned most of Kinlochgarvie for hundreds of years. Why should I let Strone drive me away?'

'Don't judge him too harshly, Constance. His wife's dying.'

'And McKerrol's is living, and pregnant. I should hope, if ever I became anyone's wife, he would never use me to hide behind.'

'Men are dependent on their wives, Constance.'

'I think, Hugh,' she said, smiling, 'we should move on and get Ronald's reeds. You were joking.'

'No, I wasn't joking.' He spoke, or at least tried to speak, with such sincerity that she glanced at him in disbelief. Safely insincere herself, she did not think this game in front of the shop window could be played otherwise.

'No, I wasn't,' he repeated, as if, she thought with some amusement, he had to convince some part of himself. 'Shall we go in?'

She nodded, and he turned to Alison, to take her in with them.

'No, no,' said Constance quickly. 'There's no need. Let her stay here.'

'I'd rather stay here,' said Alison.

'Are you sure?' asked Carstares. 'Will you be all right?'

'I'm five.'

He smiled. 'All right. We'll not be long.'

'I don't mind.'

As he conducted Constance into the shop he couldn't resist a glance back at Alison. She was staring at him with an expression in which alarm, regret, and vexation contended.

'She's jealous,' said Constance, lightly. 'You've made a conquest of her, you know.'

He shook his head: the child's trouble was more than jealousy.

The shopkeeper was a small man in a suit fit for church. Across his stomach was slung a thin, gold chain, which his fingers kept flicking, as if counting the notes it was worth.

He recognised Constance, and bowed his head in cautious homage, reminding Carstares of the Japs who had beaten their prisoners if these bowed either too low or not low enough.

'Good afternoon, Miss Kilgour,' he said. 'If I may be allowed to say so, you're quite a stranger in Caldoon these days.'

'Yes.'

'We'd like to see some rings,' said Carstares.

'There are several kinds of rings, sir,' chuckled the jeweller.

'Engagement rings.'

'Yes, of course.' Despite his training in dissimulation, he could not keep out of his eyes a sly astonishment. 'Certainly, sir. It will be a pleasure.' He began to set down trays of rings on the counter. 'That,' he said, 'is my entire stock at the moment.' Then he exquisitely hesitated and sighed. 'Except for what I might call my extra-special. Very expensive, I'm afraid.'

'Let's see them,' said Carstares.

The jeweller had to go into an inner room and open a safe. He returned, solemn as a priest, with a small box that contained three rings. He took one out and held it up, between fingers that apologised for their impudence in touching such delicate and precious loveliness.

'Beautiful,' he murmured, in awe. 'Platinum and diamonds.'

'How much?'

He moistened his lips before answering. 'This particular one, sir? It's the best in the shop. Five hundred and ten guineas. Would you care to try it on, Miss Kilgour?'

As Carstares grinned, remembering that Marion's, bought out of his own money, had not cost a tenth of that, Constance slipped the ring on her finger. It fitted perfectly.

'We could have it altered,' said the shopkeeper, 'but I must say it looks very much at home as it is.'

Carstares, admiring the ring on her finger, noticed that her cuff was frayed.

'Like it?' he asked.

'It's very expensive.'

'But you do like it?'

'It's very beautiful.'

'More beautiful than catkins?' he murmured.

'Catkins?'

'Yes.' Carstares turned to the shopkeeper. 'We'll take this one.

'No, no.' As she spoke Constance took the ring off and handed it to the shopkeeper.

He seemed almost relieved. 'I may say,' he said, 'that this is the finest ring I have ever had in my shop.'

'We'll take it,' said Carstares. He took it from the shopkeeper and put it on Constance's finger. She did not resist.

She could not have said why she had at first refused: certainly not out of deliberate coyness, designed to lead him further on; no, it had been spontaneous. Nor had it been because she was reluctant to squander his money. Had it really been his trust in her she did not want to endanger? She could not say, but the doubt, against her expectation, did not feed her desire for revenge. She found herself smiling up at him in an almost defenceless gratitude.

The shopkeeper, though beaming with congratulation, uttered a little cough of business, as respectful as the value of the ring required.

Carstares understood. 'My name's Carstares,' he said. 'I'm the new Forestry District Officer for the Kinlochgarvie area.'

'Ah, so you have replaced Mr. McIan?'

'Yes.'

How much did a District Officer earn, wondered the jeweller; not more than a thousand a year. And, of course, it was notorious that the Kilgours were beggars.

'Do you know Mr. Strone, the forester at Kinlochgarvie?' asked Carstares.

'Yes, I do. As a matter of fact he was in here a few weeks ago buying a bracelet for his wife. By the way, how is Mrs. Strone keeping these days?'

'She's not well.'

'A pity, indeed a very great pity: a most gracious woman, by all accounts. You do not mind, sir, if I get into touch with Mr. Strone?'

'No.'

'Merely routine procedure, you understand, where goods of such value are involved.'

Carstares was about to warn him Strone might not be available that afternoon, but decided not to. 'As you wish,' he said.

'Thank you, sir. I won't keep you waiting more than a minute.'

He went into the inner room to telephone, closing the door behind him.

'He might not get through,' said Carstares.

Constance was meekly admiring the ring.

'I mean,' he added, 'it's likely Strone's telephone will be busy.'

'Yes.'

He felt a strong surge of affection and sympathy for her.

'Well,' he said, smiling, 'does this mean we're engaged?'

She did not reply.

'Well?'

He put his hand on her shoulder. 'I just want the right to be in your company.'

She turned and faced him, her head raised. When he bent and kissed her, on the mouth, she closed her eyes, and shivered.

'I'm not worth it, Hugh,' she whispered. 'I warn you, I'm not worth it.'

He was gazing at her in a perplexity of love when the shopkeeper returned.

On the greater part of his face was pleasure at being able to resume such enjoyable and profitable business; but here and there was allowed to lurk a fastidious sorrow.

Carstares took out his cheque-book. 'Do I write you out a cheque?'

'Certainly, Mr. Carstares. By all means.'

'Five hundred and ten guineas. What's that in pounds?'

Constance touched him on the back. 'It's far too much, Hugh,' she whispered.

Cheerfully he shook his head at, her.

'A ring of such quality,' murmured the shopkeeper, 'is an investment.'

'How much in pounds?'

'Five hundred and thirty-five pounds ten shillings, sir.'

'So it is,' agreed Carstares, after he'd worked it out on the cover of his cheque-book. He wrote out the cheque and handed it over.

'Thank you, sir. Would it be presumptuous of me to wish you both the greatest of joy and good fortune?'

'I don't think so. Thanks.'

'Do you wish to wear the ring, Miss Kilgour, or shall I put it in a box for you?'

She looked at Carstares.

'Wear it,' he said.

She nodded.

'Very good,' said the shopkeeper. 'But you must allow me nevertheless to give you a box.' He chose one from a drawer; it was lined with purple plush. With a treachery of imagination, by no means customary, he was reminded of a coffin.

'I understand,' he said quietly, as he wrapped the box in paper, 'that Mrs. Strone is dead.' He paused in his wrapping, but that was as foolish and unavailing as if the gravediggers had stopped digging. 'Only half an hour ago,' he added, in horror.

'Are you sure?' asked Carstares, his hand on Constance's arm.

'Yes, sir. Mr. Strone was not, as you will appreciate, wholly coherent, but he did say she passed away at –' he peered at the many clocks on the shelves, all at different times – ' quarter to three: half an hour ago. Had I known I would not have troubled him.'

It had been a strange conversation over the telephone.

'This is Meikle, jeweller, Caldoon. I wonder, Mr. Strone, if you would oblige me?'

'Do you want your Christmas tree already?'

The shopkeeper was taken aback. With five hundred guineas involved, humour was far from his mind. 'No,' he replied, with a little laugh. 'A gentleman has come into the shop, claiming to be Mr. Carstares, your new District Officer. He has made a purchase, and wishes to pay by cheque. Now a considerable amount is involved—'

'How much?'

'I'm afraid, Mr. Strone, professional etiquette forbids me to say.'

'Is she with him? Is it for her he's bought it, whatever it is?'

'As a matter of fact, Miss Kilgour of Kinlochgarvie House is with the gentleman. I shall describe him briefly.'

'There's no need. If she's with him, he's Carstares. He won an M.C. in Burma.'

'Did he, now?' But winners of M.C.'s weren't all able to pay five hundred guineas for a ring.

'Whatever it costs, he can pay. Didn't you know his wife died and left him thirty thousand pounds?'

'No, I did not know that.' But it was knowledge to make the eyes gleam.

'Mine died half an hour ago. Do you take back bracelets?'

'Did I understand you to say Mrs. Strone is dead?'

'Aye. And left me nothing. Nothing at all.'

Then Strone had cut off the conversation.

The jeweller saw his customers to the door. 'If there's anything else you require, Mr. Carstares, or you, Miss Kilgour, I am at your service.'

Out on the pavement Carstares stood gazing at Constance. 'So she's dead?' he said.

She gazed anxiously at him, as if she was afraid he was going to condemn her. In a gesture which she could not have said herself was deliberate or involuntary, she brought her left hand up and pressed it against her breast, with the ring conspicuous. It could be, she knew, an appeal for mercy.

Looking at the ring, he remembered Mrs. Strone's bracelet; then he saw Scourie's finger, chewed to the bone.

'Am I to blame then?' she asked.

He shook his head. 'No. How could you be? It's not your fault in any way.'

During the war millions of people had died unreconciled. What difference would one more make?

They had forgotten Alison.

'Are we going for Ronald's reeds now?' she asked, with a patience whose sweetness made Carstares smile.

'Yes,' he said, taking her hand, 'we're going for them now. You lead me straight to Murchison's.'

Seventeen

As if the engagement was genuine, and she a young girl dazzled by love and its expectations, Constance could not help that afternoon and evening glancing frequently at the ring on her finger. In the street, in the shop where Alison with stubborn affection refused to let Carstares buy her a doll, in the hotel where they went for tea, and in the cinema, she found herself looking at it, and feeling it, in wonder always, sometimes in bitterness and self-contempt, but often, too, in a gratitude so simple as almost to make her own mind unrecognisable.

On those last occasions it seemed to her possible, indeed inevitable, that she should fall in love with Carstares, marry him, and enjoy a happy life with him and Alison either in Kinlochgarvie or anywhere he wished. She could find nothing ulterior or derogatory in his swift love for her; that it was inexplicable was in the nature of all love. Whatever wrong Francis had done her could not sanely be blamed on him. His generosity and his fondness for Alison were not gestures of penitence and reparation. As for his scruples about dismissing McKerrol, these had not been fabricated in order to thwart her and keep her within his power; no, they had really sprung from compassion. But if he loved her, he would surely never forgive McKerrol, and would, if she insisted, get rid of him, despite pity for his wife and children.

During those moods of awkward, unaccustomed optimism, the ring seemed to be on a finger she had never seen before; it and the rest of her body, even the face reflected in the shop windows, were strange and new. Paradoxically, the stranger she felt the more familiar did Carstares seem: his laughter as he teased Alison, his slight limp as he climbed steps, his good-natured, confident manner in the grandiose hotel, and his occasional companionable smiles at her, seemed not only as well known as if she had been seeing and hearing them for years, but also were necessary to her, so that she would wait, with an anxiety she could neither understand nor subdue, for him to turn and smile at her. Indeed, once she caught herself feeling jealous of the very ash-tray into which he was tapping the ash from his cigarette. At that peculiar treachery tears almost came into her eyes; but even if she had shed them, and they had gone stumbling down her cheeks, seen by him, the spell would still not have been broken.

Perhaps it was because those tears were not shed that there were other times when the sight of the ring, rather than making her seem a stranger to herself, made vividly and hatefully familiar what she had been for years trying to forget, the humiliations of love, birth, and motherhood. His teasing of Alison, and the girl's happy, pert replying, brought back the grotesque bloatedness and the agonising loneliness of pregnancy. She hated him then with a force like a blow in her stomach. His limp somehow became as obscene as McKerrol's fingering on the lorry, and his smiles were not for her at all but rather for his dead wife whom she for the time being was allowed to represent. Most insulting of all, the ring, bought with the dead woman's insolent money, trapped her within that woman's personality, so that she felt her own being contemptuously taken from her and that of the daughter of the biscuit-maker substituted. This sensation was so overpowering that in order to resist it or at least appease its strange terror, she asked him suddenly, in the cinema, if he had a photograph of his wife which he could show her. At first, astonished, he hesitated and seemed as if about to feel in his pocket, but changed his mind and shook his head. He had destroyed them all, he said. Then the lights went down, Alison clapped her hands, and Constance was able to escape again into her own thoughts which unaccountably were again hopeful and even happy, like a river, the Garvie River itself, flowing out of deep, slow shadows into surge and sunshine.

The film was noisy with the shooting guns. Alison's fingers kept flying from eyes to ears, and back again. Once Carstares stretched across her and pressed Constance's hand. He was curiously agitated.

'When I said I'd destroyed Marion's photographs,' he said, 'I meant it. It's true.'

She nodded, and pressed his hand lightly.

'She's dead,' he said.

Though her blood chilled with pity for him, she took her hand away from his.

'You must have been very fond of her,' she said, with deliberate callousness.

'Yes.'

But so, she thought, was Strone fond of his wife; and McKerrol is no doubt fond of his, as witness the new pregnancy. Did love prove anything but its own futility?

'I'd like you to tell me about her.'

'No, no.' A minute later, as if sorry for that sharp refusal, he added: 'Well, maybe later.'

He did not, she noticed, ask her in return to tell him about Francis.

By the time the programme was finished, Alison was tired. She walked so stiffly downstairs, and yawned so sleepily, that Carstares picked her up and carried her. On the way round to the cinema car park they met the doctor.

He looked dressed for golf, and was very affable, with the scent of gin off his breath. He seemed delighted to see them.

'Picture any good?' he asked. 'Doesn't really matter if it isn't. I'll confess: I'm mad about Westerns. My wife says I'm worse than a boy of ten. But maybe it's because it's a refreshment to my spirit to see folk pass on without a modicum of fuss.' He laughed, with a little pride, at that diagnosis. 'Everybody keeping all right at the big house, Miss Kilgour?'

'Yes, thank you.'

'Good. Well, I'd better hurry if I'm going to see the start. Goodnight, all.'

He had gone about ten yards when Carstares called after him: 'By the way, doctor, what's the latest about Mrs. Strone?'

The doctor came back. 'She's dead. I thought you'd know.'

'We've been here all afternoon.'

The doctor had been told by a weeping Mrs. Gibson about Miss Kilgour's refusal to visit the dying woman. He was interested but neutral.

'Yes, she left us about three o'clock. I wasn't surprised. I told you this morning, didn't I?'

'Yes.'

'Nothing could have saved her this time, nothing at all. Poor Strone. He'll not show it, you know; but deep inside he'll bleed. Don't misunderstand him, Mr. Carstares. He's a good fellow really.'

Then, he hurried away towards the cinema.

Reaching the car, Carstares made Alison comfortable on the back seat; she was asleep.

Constance sat waiting. When he was beside her, ready to start the car, she said quietly: 'Do you think Strone will be deeply hurt?'

He was startled. 'Yes, surely.'

'I don't think so.'

'As the doctor said, he won't show it, but surely he'll be hurt deeply?'

'He won't show it, not because he's incapable of showing it, but because he's incapable of being hurt deeply.'

He started the car. 'That's a harsh judgment, Constance.'

'I can make it because I happen to be like him, in that respect.'

'Incapable of being hurt deeply?'

'Yes.'

He turned the car out into the road. 'I don't believe it, Connie. You were deeply hurt once; you still are.'

She knew he was referring to Alison. 'No,' she said. 'I was humiliated.'

'Is there a difference?'

'If one's deeply hurt, does one look for consolation in revenge? If one's humiliated, one does.'

'Revenge against whom?'

'Against the leaves on the trees, against the pebbles on the shore of the loch.'

He drove in silence for about half a minute.

'You think Strone's just humiliated?'

'Yes.'

'But in God's name, Connie, how can somebody's death, somebody you loved, humiliate you?'

She did not answer.

'Was I just humiliated?'

Again she did not answer.

'I admit I thought Strone an insufferable little lump of conceit the moment I saw him; I admit, too, he's got a reputation of harshness as an employer. But conceited men, and harsh men, can suffer deeply when their wives die. I think that's true, Connie.'

Still she said nothing.

'Surely you admit it?' he asked.

'If they suffer, it's because their pride's been hurt. Isn't suffering supposed to ennoble? Strone will be even more conceited and harsh.'

'And I suppose that's why I drank so much I was sent here as a cure?'

'I don't know, Hugh.'

'I'm afraid you have a hard heart, Connie,' he said, laughing to temper the accusation.

'I hope so.'

He stopped the car.

'Do you recognise this place?' he asked.

She peered out. It was where he had overtaken her yesterday.

'Do you?'

'Yes.'

'I just don't believe the woman I met here yesterday is hardhearted. I'll never believe that, Connie, whatever you say, or do. Do you know what I thought? I still think it, too. You were singing to yourself; your heels lilted as you lifted them off the road. I expected to find a laughing, rosy-cheeked Highland girl when I made up on you.'

'Perhaps you were thinking of your wife.'

'No, Connie, I wasn't.'

'I have the impression she was a happy person. Was she?'

'Yes,' he replied, after a long pause.

'I'm afraid I'm not.'

'But you could be, Connie, you will be. I was thinking of you, and I've been thinking of you ever since.'

'All the time?'

He remembered his encounter with Nancy last night; even then, yes, he had been thinking of Constance.

'All the time with approval, I mean?'

'Approval's got nothing to do with it. I love you, Connie.'

This time she did not feel any impulse to strike him for his use of the word. Instead she felt wonder, pity, and even the wish to love him in return.

'And whatever you say,' he went on, smiling, 'I'm going to keep on loving the Connie I see. It's no good your trying to put me against her, for it's my Connie that's the real one.'

'You'll have to tell me about her.'

'I will, I most certainly will.'

'And what about Ronald's Connie?' she asked, with a ruth-lessness that only increased his love.

'I don't know her.'

That was scarcely true, she could have told him; he knew the Connie who would have refused to visit Mrs. Strone, and who insisted on McKerrol's dismissal.

'And Alison's Connie?' she asked, her voice higher than she meant.

Such self-awareness, and such calm self-condemnation, were not possible, he felt sure, without intense suffering. Pity for her illuminated in his mind her relationship with the child, from the latter's birth, and even before it. He felt he knew her profoundly.

'You know what I mean,' she said.

'Don't you?' she added.

'Yes, but you're not being fair to yourself.'

'She's afraid of me.'

It would have been dishonouring her own truthfulness to deny it.

'If you prune a rose-bush,' she said, 'cut it almost to the ground, you won't do it any harm; on the contrary, its roses will be larger and more beautiful. You're an expert on trees; you should know that. Did I think I was doing that with Alison's affection? Was my mistake in cutting it too far back?'

He knew he was listening to a confession that no one else had heard. That she was speaking in a calm, apparently clinical, manner did not deceive him: she was confessing that she had been guilty of a terrible wrong, and surely she was also asking his help to remedy it.

'It's not too late,' he murmured. 'We can make it up to her.'

'We? You've done her no harm.'

'She thinks I have. She heard what Miss Kirn said this afternoon.'

Yes, Constance could have replied, she heard it, and listened all the more attentively because this morning when she asked me if you were her father I would not tell her you weren't.

'That's why she wouldn't let me buy her the doll,' he said. 'She's not sure yet whether I ought to be forgiven.'

'For leaving her in my clutches?'

'Just for leaving her.'

'I ought to warn you, she's very like me in many ways.'

'I know that,' he said, laughing. 'Listen, Connie.' He put his arm round her and pressed his lips against her head. 'I think you and I can do it. We've entered into each other's lives and there's no leaving. Every beautiful thing I see, a silver fir, catkins, a cloud in the sky, remind me of you. For your sake, I'd get rid of McKerrol with as little compunction as I'd squash a beetle.'

She did not try to withdraw from his embrace, but she could not keep from shivering once or twice. As he spoke, with his lips touching her hair, there seemed to be within her a frenzied reluctant love with, at its quiet centre, hatred and revulsion.

She even thought, in that frenzy, that she might let him make love to her that night, either here in the car with Alison asleep, or afterwards in the house with Ronald prowling about, playing without pipes a lament for the lost honour of the Kilgours. She could not be sure whether that thought originated in the love or the revulsion: it would take the act itself to make that clear. In order to prepare for it at any rate, she had to kiss him; and this she suddenly did. Still she could not have said whether she was kissing him out of liking and gratitude, or out of resentment deeper than those.

He trembled with happiness and concern for her.

'From now on,' he said, 'it's just you, and Alison, and me.'

She did not answer, and when, a minute or so later, the car began to speed alongside the loch, he, too, was silent. Could it really be, she wondered, that in his mind everything was as simple and complete as he made it appear to be? She did not know whether to envy or despise that simplicity: her own mind seemed by comparison like the loch, deep but constantly restless, and dark in its deepest parts when the sun was bright.

Eighteen

Passing the hotel, Carstares noticed there were more lights on than usual. No doubt the anglers had arrived and Miss Kirn, despite her grief for her friend, was having to make them at home. She would have Jock to help her, and Carstares could not help smiling as he recalled breakfast that morning, when they had told him of their engagement. He wished them well, although they might not in return wish him and Constance well.

Their happiness, indeed, based on their trust in each other, was a refuge into which he could not resist escaping for a moment or two. It was like a holiday for his mind to contemplate a love so simple as never to suspect that its other side was hatred. Even with Constance beside him, he grieved again for Marion.

There were no lights in the schoolhouse. Either Miss Carmichael brooded in the darkness with her cats, or she was out visiting some other friend of Mrs. Strone, with whom, with all the voracity and spitefulness of lust repressed, she would discuss Constance's callousness.

'Have you ever thought of sending Alison to another school?' he asked.

'Often.'

'Is there a suitable one in the district?'

'It depends on what you call suitable. There's one in Caldoon. It's private. For children of the local gentry.'

Those children, he thought, would have more refined accents than the children on Miss Carmichael's school, but they would find the same words to say.

'Why not send her there?' he asked.

'What about transport?'

'I could run her down in the morning, and back up in the afternoon. I'd enjoy doing it.'

'Would they let her in?'

'Why shouldn't they?'

'They cherish their respectability.'

'To hell with them,' he muttered.

They had by this time driven through the village and were approaching the gate that barred the private road to the house.

'You see,' he said, 'if we were married, how it would help her.'

She saw, but she saw, too, that he was not entirely sincere. Passing the hotel and the schoolhouse, where two of her detractors lived, she had been aware of his momentary withdrawal from her, and had guessed its cause. Nevertheless, when at the gate he stopped the car, took her in his arms, and began to kiss her with all the desperation of that impaired sincerity, she did not resist, but coolly kissed him back.

When they were interrupted she felt as annoyed as he, but for a different reason. She had undone the top button of her blouse, as a first move towards tempting the curious, sobbing continence of his embrace.

Will McKew stepped from under the trees at the side of the road, and tapped on the window.

They came apart. Constance discreetly fastened her blouse. Carstares glared out at McKew, and turned down the window to ask him what the devil he wanted.

McKew, with his left hand, touched his cap to Constance. 'Sorry, Miss Kilgour,' he muttered. To Carstares he said, with slow ferocity: 'I want an explanation frae you.'

'Are you drunk?' asked Carstares. 'Get out of the way.'

'I'm no' drunk,' said McKew. He took a step backward, not in retreat, but to level a shotgun at Carstares. 'I'm in earnest, mind that.'

'What's the matter with him?' asked Constance.

'Drunk.'

'I've been here for three hours,' said McKew, 'and I've no' even had a drink o' water.'

'If he's not drunk,' she whispered, 'he must be mad.'

'Likely enough,' said Carstares, and opened the door.

Involuntarily she seized his jacket. 'Where are you going?'

'I'd better get out and talk some sense into this fool.'

'No. Better stay here.' McKew, she thought, wasn't likely to shoot while he remained in the car.

He stared at her, almost angrily, as if he did not believe her concern was genuine.

'We don't want Alison wakened,' he said.

'I am wakened,' said the child behind them.

They turned to look at her. She was yawning and apprehensive. 'What's the matter? Why are we stopped? Are we home?'

'We're nearly home,' he replied gently. 'Just lie down again. I've got to go out and push this gate back.'

'Do you want me to help you?' she asked, rubbing her eyes.

McKew took a step forward. 'I want Miss Kilgour to hear what I've got to say.' He addressed her beyond Carstares. 'Maybe you know, Miss Kilgour, that I'm engaged to Nancy, who's a maid in the hotel.'

'No, I didn't know that, but of course I know Nancy. Is she here?'

'No, miss. She'd to go back.'

'For God's sake,' said, Carstares. He had been half out of the car. Now he swung his legs in, and was about to slam the door in McKew's face when the latter crashed the muzzle of the gun against it.

Alison screamed.

McKew sobbed as he spoke. 'I don't want to frighten you and the wee girl, Miss Kilgour. My family's always had great respect for yours. Faither taught us that. When he learned Robert was being bad to your little girl at school, he leathered him wi' the big strap that hings behind the kitchen door. But this fellow here, he's a stranger in Kinlochgarvie; he thinks because he won a medal and has lots o' money he can come here and dae whit he likes.'

'Can't you see you're terrifying the child?' asked Carstares.

In Alison's weeping, though, was interest as well as fear.

'I'm sorry aboot that,' said McKew, in great agitation. 'Last night, Miss Kilgour, he came into the dance, doon at the hall there. Wha did he choose to dance wi'? There were ither lassies wi' nae partners. But wha did he choose? Nancy, though he kent she was at the dance wi' me.'

'I hardly think,' remarked Constance, in a voice smooth with contemptuous amusement, 'that that was a crime.'

'I'm jealous o' the wind that blaws in her hair,' he said. 'I cannae help it. But it wasnae the dancing; that was juist the beginning. Whit did he whisper into her ear?'

Constance chose to answer that rhetorical question. 'I'm sure I've no idea,' she said.

'He whispered he'd tak her away and marry her. He whispered he'd lots o' money.'

'That's a bloody lie,' muttered Carstares.

'But she had to pay the price. You'll ken whit that price was, Miss Kilgour.'

She seemed even more amused by his fervent naïvety. 'Did she pay it?' she asked.

He could scarcely answer for the grinding of his teeth in anguish and rage. 'She changed her mind,' he said at last.

'So she didn't pay it, after all?'

'For Christ's sake,' breathed Carstares.

'He forced her, Miss Kilgour. I don't want to say this in front of the wee girl, but he forced her, pulled the clothes off her. She said he thought he was still an officer, doing whit he liked wi' a native woman. Nancy's only twenty-two, you see; it was easy for him to tak advantage o' her.'

'I doubt that,' said Constance.

'And then this morning, he walked past her as if she was a tree without feelings or memory. I'm going to marry her, Miss Kilgour; but first I've got to settle things wi' him. I'll hae nae peace till I do.'

'Will you have peace if you shoot him?'

'Maybe I wouldnae,' he admitted. 'But,' he went on, in another surge of rage, 'if he was ever to tak advantage o' her again I would shoot him, as I would shoot a fox at my lambs. You see, he's not saying onything.'

'I doubt if there's anything for him to say.'

'He could deny it.' That was really an appeal to Carstares to deny it, even if it were true.

'I suppose he could,' she agreed, and waited.

'I don't know what happened,' muttered Carstares. 'But it's a piece of damned nonsense for him to make her out an innocent virgin.'

'So I understand,' she said.

McKew hadn't heard. 'You were rotten drunk,' he said, partly in angry accusation, partly in agonised justification.

'Well, I don't think there's any point in prolonging this,' said Constance briskly. 'I'd be obliged, Mr. McKew, if you'd put that gun down and be so kind as to open the gate for me.'

'For you, maybe,' he muttered.

'It's the least you can do, after damaging the car.'

'Whit did he damage?'

'Nothing that wasn't damaged before, I'm afraid.'

He understood, and agreed, for in his sudden rushing at the gate and dragging it out of the way was again that incontrollable anguish at the maculacy of his sweetheart.

'Thank you,' called Constance. 'Would you allow me to give you a piece of advice, Mr. McKew? Don't believe everything she says.'

Carstares started the car and drove on towards the house.

'What did happen?' she murmured. 'Or is that indiscreet to ask?'

'I told you I can't remember. He was right, I was rotten drunk.'

'You went back to the hotel with her?'

'Yes.'

'Intending to sleep with her?'

At first he would not answer. She waited.

'I suppose so,' he muttered.

Then he remembered what had happened. There had been an attempt at love-making, determined and cross on her part, abortive and maudlin on his. He had persisted in calling her Constance, so that in chagrin she had pummelled the pillow.

'It's none of my business, really,' said Constance. 'We weren't engaged last night.'

The car had no sooner stopped outside the door than Ronald hurried out, as eagerly querulous as a neglected child.

Constance was first out of the car. With an eagerness that had Carstares staring after her in dismay and foreboding, for he did not believe it genuine, she raced up the steps to show her brother her ring, calling to him that she and Hugh were engaged.

Ronald pulled her inside the house, out of Carstares's hearing.

'He can't see or hear you, Connie,' he whispered. 'So there's no need to act. What's happened? Did you remember my reeds?'

'We're engaged.'

'To be married?'

'What else? Look. Do you know what it cost?'

'Surely it's not the money value of such things that count, Connie?'

'Five hundred and ten guineas.'

As he boggled she added : 'But it's got to be paid for.'

'What do you mean? Has he just put down a deposit on it?'

'I think I have him, Ronald.'

'It looks like it.'

'I intend to make certain tonight.'

He was suspicious. 'I'm not stupid, you know, Connie.'

'Then show it by keeping out of the way.'

Goaded by her cynical guile, of which he felt as much a victim as Carstares, he said: 'You were caught once, Connie.'

He thought for a moment she was going to strike him. He would have preferred the blow to the laughter that took its place.

'This time the bait's thirty thousand pounds,' she said.

'While you're playing the whore,' he said bitterly, 'what do you expect me to do?'

'Play your pipes.'

Then Carstares came in, carrying Alison. The child opened her eyes and saw her uncle. She smiled. 'We've got your reeds, Ronald,' she said, and added, 'Connie's got a ring.'

'Upstairs, dear,' said Constance softly.

Carstares looked at her strangely and then set off down the hall.

'I understand I have to congratulate you, Carstares,' called Kilgour after him.

Carstares did not reply.

Constance followed him slowly. Her brother came close behind.

'Play the pipes, Connie?' he whispered, 'So that's to be my rôle?'

She did not answer. At the foot of the stairs he seized her. 'How can I play the pipes? You haven't even given me my reeds.'

'I expect they're still in the car.'

'You know what I mean,' he said peevishly. 'If you liked him, Connie, I could bear it; but you don't, you despise him, you want to get your own back through him. I saw it last night, and now I'm seeing it again.'

She smiled. 'You'll get your share,' she said, and ran upstairs after Carstares. 'It's the second door on your left, Hugh,' she called.

'I wouldn't touch a penny of it,' cried her brother, 'but I'll take you at your word, I'll play the pipes all right.' Even as he uttered the threat he put up his fingers and twiddled them: the lament he played could never be reproduced on any pipes.

Constance was close behind Carstares as he carried Alison into the bedroom. She switched on the table-lamp.

'Put her down on the bed, please,' she said.

He did so, and she began to undress the child. 'Draw the blinds, will you, Hugh?' she asked. 'Be careful, or they'll fall to pieces.'

At the window, before pulling down the blinds, he gazed out over the forest at the dark hills, with the stars bright above.

'I'm sorry, Connie,' he muttered, with his back to her. A feeling of frustration and futility twisted and grew hard in him. He wanted to blame her for her repulsion of him last night, and to blame Marion for dying: it seemed useless to blame himself or Nancy. 'She meant nothing at all to me. She told him a bundle of lies. He's too good for her.'

Just as you're thinking in your heart you're too good for me, she thought. On Alison's leg she saw the imprint of his tweed jacket. As she bent to kiss the mark, she felt in the one fierce spasm of emotion the need to hurt Carstares and to love him. It was the malice that seemed able to forgive him for his fornication with Nancy; the love could not.

He pulled down the blinds and turned.

Alison was now undressed and under the bedclothes. She opened her eyes. 'Where's Hugh?' she asked.

'He's here.'

'I want him to kiss me good-night.'

He looked at Constance. 'Tomorrow, maybe,' he said. 'You're too tired now.'

'I'll not sleep if you don't.'

Still Constance would not nod permission.

'Tomorrow,' he repeated.

Alison tried to rise up. 'Are you angry because I wouldn't let you buy me a doll?'

'I'm not angry with you, Alison.'

'Why will you not kiss me, then?'

Quickly he went over and kissed her on the brow. Constance sat on the bed, smiling.

'Was the man going to shoot you?' asked Alison.

'I don't think so.'

She shook her head, suddenly shuddered, sighed, and turning away from him seemed to fall asleep at once.

'So you still don't know why she wouldn't let you buy her the doll?' murmured Constance.

'I think I know.'

'I'm afraid I haven't the slightest idea myself. Why was it?'

'She thinks I'm her father.'

'I can't see the connection.'

He thought he could, but he did not want to try and explain it.

'Shall we go?' she whispered, taking his hand.

Outside in the corridor she did not hesitate but led him towards the next room, her own. As soon as they were inside, with the door closed, she let out a gasp, as if of pent-up desire, and embraced him, pressing very close.

Surprise, and perhaps suspicion, made him awkward and reluctant in returning the embrace. She seemed not to notice, or at any rate not to mind, for next moment, in a quick, smiling, apparently innocent excitement, she had turned from him and begun to take off her clothes, first her jacket and then her skirt.

'Connie, for God's sake,' he muttered, putting his hand up to his eyes.

In what seemed tender astonishment she stared at him. 'What's wrong, Hugh?' she asked softly.

He shook his head.

When she went over to kiss him again, he involuntarily repulsed her. He tried to do it gently, but his agitation was too great, so that his hand struck her mouth, quite hard, bringing tears of pain to her eyes. When she put her finger up to her lips it came back tipped with blood.

Then he broke out into a remorse as incoherent and passionate as last night's.

Her blood cold, she thought he was going to drop on his knees and weep.

'You're rather rough in your love-making, Hugh,' she said.

She continued undressing, and in another minute, save for her ring, was naked.

'It's cold,' she said, smiling.

But it was not the chilliness of the room that caused her to shiver: it was the knowledge that this game of seduction was dangerous for herself. Shame could turn this scene into a present and future hell of abasement, and it was not so well under control as she had thought. Let it escape, and she would blush to her breasts. She would see herself as a whore like

Nancy, amateur and inexpert; and she would see him as Francis, all the more hateful because of his long absence among the callous dead. If on the other hand she remained resolute and unashamed she would have him at her mercy, to do with as she wished; but some genuine love for him seemed strangely necessary.

It was somehow not difficult to achieve, that love. He was looking at her with such shy admiration of her body, such almost childlike anxiety about her motives, and such obedient love.

From below, outside on the drive, were heard the first despondent squeals of Ronald's bagpipes.

The silly sounds might have made her see her nakedness as absurd and debasing had it not been for their effect on Carstares.

His doubt and timidity went.

'I love you, Connie,' he said, 'and I want you to love me.'

'Don't I? Surely I must?'

It was all amazingly easy after that. The mortification that she expected to have to endure was never felt, perhaps because she did not, as she had intended, ask him during the act to remember his promise about dismissing McKerrol. Nor did she mention either Nancy or Mrs. Strone.

Somewhere in the grounds, under the stars, Ronald kept playing his coronach.

Nineteen

In the days following Mrs. Strone's death the weather continued keen and brilliant. Out of the wind, behind drystone dykes, at the gables of cottages, or in hollows amid the forest, the sunshine was as warm as midsummer; but take one step out of shelter and the wind from the east dried the skin on the face, gnawed at the ears, and cracked the lips. Nevertheless, even in Kinlochgarvie where the funeral was impending, smiles were frequent, for the invigoration of the air and the glitter of new leaves were irresistible. Shepherds for their lambs' sakes were glad; and those forestry-workers, too, were pleased, who were taken from such hard monotonous tasks as planting and draining to the more restful vigilance of fire-watching. If the weather lasted, as was expected, everyone would have his turn of manning the towers at night, which meant money, at overtime rates, for merely keeping awake. To their wives, the sparkle of the countryside was a challenge; they wished to bring that sparkle into their homes staled by winter, and were delighted to find that bedsheets, curtains, and carpets, hung out to dry in that translucent, exciting, alpine air, regained the freshness they had when new, and in addition acquired a fragrance as of pine-trees and primroses.

From those primroses in their numerous clusters on damp banks to the snow on the hill-tops, the eyes were dazzled by that cool radiance; while last year's grass, by the sides of the road and in the forest everywhere at the feet of the stoical trees, crouched and gleamed and crackled like an invasion of white-furred, sharp-toothed animals.

In the little graveyard, not half a mile from Strone's house, the very tombstones looked as if they had been cleaned and newly inscribed for the purpose of the burial. Even the earth heaped up by the side of the open grave was beautiful; it seemed as if the hands of spring, rather than the weary spade of Tam McIndoe the gravedigger, had thrown it out: dark-brown, gleaming, fertile, it deserved the finest seeds, as old Tam obscurely felt, rather than the dead bones even of a good woman.

About that goodness everyone who talked about it agreed, and so many people asked Strone if they might attend the funeral that, despite Mrs. Gibson's protests, he had decided to make it public: anyone who wished could walk behind the coffin from the house to the graveyard. It was taken for granted that he would have a proper hearse from Caldoon to carry the coffin in, but no, he had the forestry cart scrubbed and burnished, so that you could see your astonished face in the hubs of the wheels, and on this, drawn by Nell, the old half-blind white horse that Mrs. Strone had been so fond of, the coffin was to be borne. Nell was shampoo'd for the occasion, her harness waxed and Brasso'd, and her shoes polished. Unfortunately she had never in her life before pulled a coffin behind her with a corpse in it, and when the time came, half-past two on Monday afternoon, she refused, with shrill terrified neighs, that made tears flow in eyes recently dried, and also in eyes up till that moment bravely dry. No one, not even Strone himself or Alec McDowall her usual driver, could soothe Nell or persuade her to obey; and in the end it was decided among the mourners to carry the coffin themselves, in relays, six at a time. This meant that when it was the forestry-workers' turn they had to find people in the procession to whom to hand their fire-brooms, for Strone had only consented to let them attend on condition they brought those brooms with them, in readiness for the bugle-call that might at any moment be heard from any of the eminences round about on which watchers were stationed.

On Monday morning, before the funeral, Carstares found Strone working as usual in his hut, perched on a high stool that gave him a good view of the nursery out of the window.

'I just looked in,' he said, 'to mention I'm on my way to Clashmore. I telephoned Brodie I was coming.'

'There was no need to warn him,' said Strone. 'There's never a twig out of place at Clashmore.'

'Good.' Carstares smiled.

Strone stared out at the workers; these were particularly busy that morning, because they knew of his grief.

'Mr. Foulds telephoned to say he's coming tomorrow.'

Carstares nodded: it was like the good-hearted Foulds to come all that way to attend a function he would not enjoy.

'Will you be there yourself, Mr. Carstares?'

Carstares did not reply at once. He had mentioned to Constance he would like to go, if invited. After almost a minute's smiling she had asked him if he thought it right, considering their engagement, to do anything to increase her isolation or at least make it more conspicuous. He had not argued.

'I would be honoured,' murmured Strone. 'You know what Margaret thought of you.'

'I'll be there.'

'Thank you. I promise you the work of the forest will be upset as little as possible.'

'I don't think that matters.'

'To me it does. I think you will have noticed I have put the fire-danger precautions into operation.'

'Yes.'

'The grass would burn like straw. I have men patrolling the roads on bicycles, and two others patrolling the railway. Then I have a squad planting at the top of Glen Shian, one draining at Laggan Burn, and another bottoming drains at Loskin. Those are all good look-out points, and work can be combined with watching. That is my usual procedure.'

Carstares was fascinated by that cool competence. It was hard to remember Strone's wife lay in the house unburied. Why, he wondered, did Constance and Strone hate each other? In a profound way they were akin.

'I have taken another precaution, Mr. Carstares, perhaps the most important of all. You may not approve of it, nonetheless. It is connected with the note I received, threatening to burn the forest.'

While speaking he had been looking out of the window, with glances at the watch open on the desk in front of him. Now he pulled the window open and shouted, without any apparent censoriousness, to John McBraid, the foreman, who was in charge of the nursery squad: 'John, that's the third time in an hour and half that Donald Thomson's gone under the bridge.'

The bridge carried the road across a burn. It was used, Carstares supposed, as a latrine.

McBraid came hurrying along, solemn with explanation.

'Donald explained to me, Mr. Strone,' he called. 'He's got a touch o' diarrhoea. Something he ate, he thinks; or maybe a chill. I warned him to make it no' too often.'

'I think you'd better tell him he'll be easier in his mind at home. There he'll have better facilities, and forby he'll not be getting paid money he's not earning.'

McBraid tugged at his large ear in doubt. 'It's no' a habit wi' Donald,' he said.

'I should hope not, for his own sake.'

'And maybe you've noticed he works all the harder in between times to make up for the time lost?'

'That shouldn't be possible, should it, if like an honest man he's doing his best all the time?'

That logic struck McBraid in the mouth like a stone. He grimaced, tried to smile staunchly, shook his head, and shambled away. They watched him make for the bridge.

'I have nothing personal against Donald Thomson,' said Strone. 'My job is to look after the interests of my forest. In the same way, I have nothing personal against Miss Kilgour.'

'Miss Kilgour?'

'Yes. I think I told you, on Saturday morning, that I suspected her of sending that note.'

'I thought you were upset when you said that.'

'Upset? You mean, not in my right mind?'

'Put it that way if you like,' said Carstares dourly.

'I am almost convinced she sent it.'

'Almost.' Carstares was trying to curb his anger: this then, and the baiting of the foreman, were Strone's ways of grieving.

'If you were in my place, Mr. Carstares, and you were convinced she was the one who'd threatened to destroy the forest, what would you do?'

'I'd wait for proof.'

'In this case, would not proof be the forest blazing, and she caught with the match in her hand? Last year we had a fire. I understand she was in tears of triumph. I can't take any risk this year.'

'And what do you propose doing? Have her arrested on suspicion?'

'No. I am having her watched.'

'Watched?'

'Day and night. If she leaves the house, she is followed. For her own good.'

Still Carstares controlled his anger. 'What authority do you have for that?'

'To save the forest, Mr. Carstares,' said Strone slowly, 'I would have a watch kept on the dead.'

Carstares looked at him then for signs of nervous strain; but there seemed to be none. Yet surely this was a kind of insanity.

'I'm afraid, Strone,' he said, 'I'll have to countermand your order. You'd better call your dog off, immediately.'

Instead of replying Strone watched Donald Thomson go into the shed, come out again with his piece-bag slung across his shoulders, and trudge miserably up the path towards the gate, where he picked his bicycle out from the others left there, mounted it, and rode away, sitting without comfort on the hard saddle.

Strone turned to Carstares. 'It's difficult for you to be the judge in this matter, Mr. Carstares,' he said.

'No, it isn't. If it was anybody in the village I'd have to tell you to call it off. Surely to God you see it isn't legal?'

'Is it legal to set the forest on fire?'

Carstares lost his temper. 'I'm warning you, Strone, that if I find anybody snooping around, or following her about, I'll bloody soon put an end to it. Who is it? Who's your dog?'

'Rab McKerrol.'

'For Christ's sake!'

'He seemed to me the best man for the job. He knows every path in the district. If you were a weasel, you couldn't move without him knowing.'

'Especially if you were a female weasel.'

Strone grinned, as if accepting that description of Constance.

'I might as well tell you,' said Carstares furiously, 'that I was going to speak to you about McKerroI. I meant to wait for a day or two, but you've brought it up yourself. I want him sent to hell out of it. Friday's pay day. He finishes then. Understand?'

'I understand, but I don't agree. He's a good workman. He and his family have lived in Kinlochgarvie all their days. He served in the Army for four years. He's married, with four children, and an expectant wife. I can't agree to dismiss him because Miss Kilgour has a spite against him.'

'She's got a bloody good reason for having a spite against him.'

'You have only heard her side of the story.'

'I heard him, that was enough for me. The bugger was standing on the lorry, shouting at her, wasn't he?' Carstares, too, was shouting.

'He's a handsome man,' said Strone quietly.

'What the hell's that got to do with it?'

'More than you think. And virile, too. Like yourself, I don't care much for him personally; but among the women I believe he's in demand.'

'What do you mean? What are you talking about? Are you hinting at anything? I know, Strone, your wife's dead, and I'm making allowances, but for Christ's sake don't go too far.'

Strone remained very calm. 'You know Nancy, I believe? She works in the hotel. She couldn't resist Rab; though Will McKew doesn't know it.'

Carstares seized Strone by the arm roughly.

'Say what you're thinking, damn you.'

'When you let go, Mr. Carstares.'

Carstares let go.

'Miss Kilgour was another of Rab's conquests.'

Carstares struck him on the mouth. 'You're a bloody liar,' he cried. 'You're full of poison, Strone, because your wife's dead. That poor bastard with the diarrhoea—'

'There's another bastard in the case, Mr. Carstares.'

Already Strone's mouth was swelling from the blow, but he made no effort to protect himself as he uttered that insinuation about Alison. As a result, Carstares could not strike him again.

'We'll leave it for Mr. Foulds to decide,' said Carstares. 'But McKerrol's dismissal won't satisfy me now.'

'Mine, too?'

'Yes, yours, too.'

'You won't object if I produce witnesses?'

'Every man and woman who works for you, Strone, is a witness against you. Ask any of those poor bastards out there.'

But the forester was so aloof, and in his grief so inviolate, that Carstares could not keep back the fear, or terror rather, that the accusation about Constance and McKerrol had a seed of truth in it. He remembered his own doubts as to her motives when she had enticed him into making love to her: those doubts were still not allayed. Perhaps, in some fiendish hope of revenge, upon herself and upon the community's hateful morality, she had let McKerrol – kiss her . . . fumble with her . . . bestride her, even? He could not keep from groaning as he imagined that encounter: some-where in the forest, upon a day as bright as this, with spiders in the grass.

'By the way, Mr. Carstares,' said the forester, as if that other subject was closed for the time being, 'I've had a report that the McKew sheep are amongst our trees in dozens at the Creagan march. The gate was left open. It's no good telephoning the McKews, or writing to them. Either you or I, or perhaps both of us, will have to visit Creagan and protest very strongly to the old man. I think he should be warned that we are considering police action.' He paused to grin. 'It could be an exciting visit.'

'I told them I'd go and talk to them.'

'So I can leave it in your hands, Mr. Carstares?'

'Yes. And there's another thing you can leave in my hands. I'm going to find McKerrol, and tell him to get to hell out of it. And I don't think I'll be at the funeral.'

Carstares had already left the hut when he said that, and Strone called after him: 'Remember Mr. Foulds is coming tomorrow. He said he wanted to have a talk with you.'

Carstares did not answer. As he left the nursery and got into his car, he made a great effort of charity. Looking towards the house with its blinds drawn, he tried to become fully aware that in it Mrs. Strone lay dead, so that he might be able to understand what was going on in Strone's mind. It should have been easier for him than for most men: he had suffered the same loss. Yet he could not do it: that Mrs. Strone was dead was easy enough to realise, for her face in his memory was that of a dying woman; but what that death might do to her husband's narrow, tyrannical yet uxorious mind, he could not even conjecture. The failure dismayed him, not only because it let doubts regarding himself and Constance rush through his mind, as if the dam holding them back had broken, but also because it made him feel like a man lost on precipitous hills who for a few moments had seen the way to safety, only to find the mists sweeping round him thicker than ever.

As he set off along the road towards Kinlochgarvie House, he could not rid himself of the feeling that this approaching encounter with McKerrol was a test, out of which he might emerge either happy and confident or bitter and destroyed. The result was not an increase of hatred for McKerrol, but rather a strange sympathy for him, as if they were both involuntarily involved in the same predicament. That predicament could not be defined; it could only be endured.

Twenty

Carstares left his car hidden in the private road. He was sure McKerrol would be somewhere in the wood in front of the house. From there, with binoculars, he would be able to look over the house and see anyone leaving it by the back and entering the forest. Reminded, he turned back to the car for his own binoculars.

As he went through the wood, stealthily, not only its loveliness, but also its prodigality of life, was revealed to him as never before. He could not prevent that revelation. When, overwhelmed and exhausted, he leant against a huge boulder and tried to find relief by making himself as insensible as it, he saw instantly, with that torturing vividness, not only the delicate beauty of the lichen on the rock, but also, on the silver birch above, the many catkins, with the male dangling as though in submission and the female upright in a green arrogance. He closed his eyes and felt the sun warm on his face, remembering his own submission to Constance and wondering if his life with her would grow to be as beautiful as this birch in full leaf. He remembered, too, the great Burmese scorpions of which the female after consummation had torn the male to pieces. There were no scorpions here, but there would be in summer many clegs; of these it was the female that drank blood, the male being satisfied with the juices of leaves.

As he went on again, over grass that crackled with last year's leaves and under red-flowered larches, he tried to laugh at his own despondency. Perhaps, he thought, when he found McKerrol he would be able to understand him with this same clarity, and so in some way from his love for Constance this foreboding would he removed.

Above the river was a knoll surmounted by a few small pines. There, on his stomach, concealed among the trees, he prepared to search the wood for his enemy. Every tree, every patch of blue sky or green hill, every bird, every stone, that came into his vision was infinitely beautiful, and sad. He was not surprised: this was surely the final confirmation of a feeling that had haunted him in Burma, during battle. He could not bear to look towards the house.

It took him ten minutes to pick out McKerrol. On the other side of the river, on a green craggy rise, he lay propped on his elbows, gazing at the house through binoculars, and kicking the air idly now with one foot and now with the other. Suddenly both feet were left in the air, and his gaze grew more concentrated. Swinging his own glasses round towards the house, Carstares saw Constance come out with Alison. She and the child began to play on the grass, throwing a ball at each other. Now and then, as she waited for Alison to run and retrieve it, she would gaze towards the loch, taking in the knoll on which he lay and the crag where McKerrol seemed now to be twitching with some hideous copulatory joy. Carstares thought he could hear her: above the roaring of the river, above the wailings of gulls and the scream of a hawk, and above the yelpings of his own jealousy, he heard her cool, amused teasings of Alison who time after time failed to catch the ball.

He was now in a frenzy to cross the river and join McKerrol. Yet he could hardly bear to descend into the gorge of the river where he would not be able to see her, so that, unprotected by his gaze, McKerrol's would devour her. Panting, he ran and slid down to the river, splashed across without looking for an easy ford, and climbed straight for where he thought McKerrol was. Despite his desperation, he must instinctively have taken care in his approach, or else McKerrol was too absorbed in his erotic fancy; at any rate, he reached the crag unnoticed, scaled it, and crouched resting, less than twenty yards from McKerrol, whose tackets he could see and hand-knitted socks. With his binoculars in one hand, McKerrol in the other held a sandwich which he was eating with enjoyment.

Carstares was reminded of an incident in Burma. Then, too, he had come upon an enemy who didn't know he was watching: six Japanese, manning two machine guns. Like McKerrol, they had been eating in peace; one had cracked a joke, and the others had quietly but merrily laughed. Sten gun at the ready, Carstares had been unable to shoot. The corporal with him, a small, resolute Glaswegian, had nudged him and winked. He had winked back, and next instant the corporal's gun had flashed and stuttered. The six men had lain sprawled over their guns, the food still in their mouths, the laughter in their eyes. Going up to them, as he was going up to McKerrol now, to make sure they were really dead and so not dangerous, Carstares had felt no hatred of them but only a pity that was reconciled to its own uselessness. The corporal had felt, it, too. 'Poor bastards,' he had muttered, after the nod of satisfaction that they were dead.

'Well?' said Carstares.

McKerrol turned quickly, was astonished, but at once concealed it in a chuckle of amusement. He was indeed, Carstares saw, a handsome man, with immense relaxed strength; yet his hands were neither coarse nor clumsy, and his face too had an unexpected refinement, with its tan, white teeth, and neat, auburn moustache; it had also a cheerful lecherousness, proud rather than furtive.

For a moment Carstares saw him as dead.

'Well,' he replied, grinning.

Carstares sat on a stone. 'Enjoying the view?' he asked.

'Sure. You might say that's what I'm doing. You can't say it's not worth enjoying.' He glanced over his shoulder towards the house.

'I've just been talking to Strone.'

McKerrol looked about as if expecting to see the forester.

'In his hut. About you.'

'Were you talking about promoting me? I'll be grateful, if only because it'll quieten the wife. You know how it is, she's always saying there's John McBraid foreman, and Andrew Brown ganger, and yet you're just an ordinary worker, though you've got as much experience as any of them and are a better workman than most. That's not me bragging, you understand, that's just what the wife says.' He spoke of his wife as if, in a composed sultanic way, he loved her.

'Why weren't you promoted?' asked Carstares.

'That's just what I couldn't tell you. It looks as though Mr. Strone just hasn't appreciated me.'

'Yet he picked you for this job.'

'I've got good eyesight.'

'Are you sure there wasn't another reason?'

McKerrol seemed to reflect. 'He's a close man, Mr. Strone,' he said; 'and of course all the closer now.'

'What did he tell you to do?'

'Come here and watch.'

'Watch what?'

'Miss Kilgour.'

'Surely he said why you'd to watch her?'

'He did mention it was a part of the fire precautions.'

'Didn't that strike you as odd?'

'It did.'

'Didn't you ask why you'd to watch her?'

McKerrol glanced at Carstares shrewdly, as if he'd become aware of the tension behind those questions. ' "Theirs not to reason why" ', he said, with a grin. 'I had four years in the army.'

Carstares found the temptation to like him fascinating and terrible. He saw McKerrol as a soldier, a comrade, cool, resourceful, brave, and loyal. Perhaps his fault the other day in shouting after Constance consisted only in forgetting this was peace-time, when lewdness could no longer be loud and honest.

'As a private, of course,' added McKerrol.

Carstares overcame the desire to ask him about his war experiences. 'If Miss Kilgour left the house, what were you to do?' he asked.

'Go after her.'

'Didn't you object to that?'

'It seemed better than bottoming drains.'

'And more interesting?'

'Sure. Have you ever bottomed drains? There's only one job in forestry worse; that's weeding in the nursery, on your hands and knees, with Strone watching you from the window. If you stop to sneeze, he's liable to shout.'

Still Carstares found his anger inert. 'Wouldn't it have been easier on your conscience to bottom drains?'

'Conscience?' Laughing, McKerrol waved his hand, embracing trees, rocks, loch, river, and hills.

Carstares felt priggish and ineffectual. 'Some men would find it objectionable being asked to follow a woman about.'

'It would depend on the woman, wouldn't it?'

'In your case.'

'In everybody's, if he's going to be honest. We've all the tup instinct.'

Carstares glanced briefly from him to the house where Constance and Alison still played.

'I'll be honest, McKerrol,' he said. 'I've told Strone you finish here on Friday.'

'You mean, I watch till Friday and then go back to draining or planting?'

'I mean, after Friday you get to hell out of it altogether.'

'I'm to be sacked?'

'That's right.'

'For this?' McKerrol jerked his thumb towards the house.

'It's got something to do with it.'

'Well,' said McKerrol, laughing, 'I was going to say I was just obeying orders, but weren't there Germans hanged for obeying orders?'

Carstares could not keep bitterness out of his voice, though he felt it was unmanly compared with McKerrol's humorous acceptance. 'Were you obeying orders when you stood on the lorry yonder by the lochside, and shouted at her as she passed?'

McKerrol smiled. 'I knew that was it,' he said, in the same almost friendly tone. 'What did I shout? "Good afternoon, Miss Kilgour. Dirty weather."'

'It was how you shouted it.'

'"Good afternoon, Miss Kilgour. Dirty weather."'

'No, it wasn't like that, McKerrol. And what were you doing with your hand when you were shouting?'

'My hand?' McKerrol glanced at it resting on the grass. As if it was a creature out of his control it began to contort itself into the jumping gesture it had made on the lorry. 'This,' he said, 'signifies victory. You know who used it.'

'It signifies something else.'

'Maybe victory just the same.'

Carstares made to rush at him. McKerrol sat at ease, his fingers still making the sign.

'Miss Kilgour and I happen to be engaged to be married,' said Carstares.

'So I heard.'

'So you'll appreciate that I don't enjoy filthy insinuations about her.'

McKerrol smiled at him. 'This is a new spring,' he said. 'You wouldn't want to pick up all last year's leaves and stick them back on the trees, would you?'

That, of course, was what Carstares did want: Marion still to be alive, the war never to have taken place, Constance Kilgour not to exist. McKerrol's attitude was adult, his own childish and petulant. In a fit of vicious envy he said: 'You're in a forestry house, aren't you?'

'Yes. You've seen me in the garden.'

'How long will you be allowed to stay after you leave the forestry service?'

'I think a month's the allowance.'

'You'll get your month, not a day longer. Now there's a squad bottoming drains at Loskin. You know where that is?'

'When I was a boy I fished in the loch there.'

'All right, you can finish the day there.'

Slowly McKerrol rose, and with movements as calm as those of the clouds in the sky buckled his piece-bag, slung it over his shoulders, and thrust his binoculars into his large pocket.

'I'll have to go to the house first to get my Wellingtons,' he said. 'That all right?'

Carstares nodded.

'Do you think,' asked McKerrol, as he was going, 'that it's on the early side yet for me to tell the wife she's got to flit?'

'That's up to you,' replied Carstares, but he knew that McKerrol, who went away laughing, was sure he would not have to flit at all, but would still be there, in his native place, long after Carstares was gone.

Carstares watched him go down into the river and spring across it from boulder to boulder, with a surefootedness like a stag's. He did not turn to look back, but went on up through the wood, below the house, in and out of sunshine and shadow. In his going there was not a trace of self-pity, yet Carstares, watching with an eagerness that seemed about to flower into love, found his steadfast solitariness among the trees intolerably moving. When he had disappeared into the forest, to reach his home in the village by a short-cut down a ride, it seemed to Carstares that for a minute or two over the whole scene came a cessation, the river roared but did not flow, a hawk hovered, and the trees waited. When he turned towards the house and saw Constance racing Alison for a ball, the spell of suspense was ended; but nothing moved in just the same way as before; river, hawk, and trees, were changed.

Perhaps he, too, was changed. He could test it by going up to the house, hearing Constance's denial or confession, and loving her all the more whatever it was. But there would be no change in her: she would still wish him not to go to the funeral tomorrow, to persist in his dismissal of McKerrol, and to be tactful and limited in his show of affection for Alison. She would not weep; like the river in his vision a moment ago her pity had ceased to flow. If ever it flowed again her whole being would burgeon like this wood, in a great greenness of generosity and joy, which he would share.

Twenty One

Jock was again in Muriel's bed.

Though it was only their third love-making already she showed an aptitude, possessiveness, and instinct to dominate, that astonished, alarmed and delighted him. When it was over, too, and he was lying beside her, winking into the darkness with a quizzical regret that he could not himself have interpreted, she began to speak in a manner he had never heard her use before, so much so he found it incredible that the toes now mastering his under the bedclothes were the same that two nights ago he had kissed for their very shyness; and what she had to say more than suited that new tone of matriarchal authority.

'We must get rid of him,' she said.

She meant Carstares who had been drunk that evening and rude to the other guests. Also in the bar his refusal to attend the funeral, his striking of Strone, his dismissal of Rab McKerrol, his seduction of Nancy, his danger from the McKews, and his being the father of Alison Weir, had been excitedly and drouthily discussed. For a Monday night the takings were exceptional; although at one point drinking was suspended, mouths being wide-open, when McKerrol had remarked that the reason why he'd been sacked was because Carstares seemed to suspect that he, Rab, had tupped the Kilgour ewe, or at least had nosed her a bit. There had been a hubbub then. One old fellow, Archie McDavid, whose forefathers had worked for the Kilgours, had gone off, scandalised, not forgetting, however, to drain his glass first. But the rest, thrilled, envious, and obsequious, had asked Rab many questions, which he had royally disdained to answer.

Jock, rash and incontinent with love, had told Muriel. Now she was telling him.

'But I thought you said, Muriel,' he murmured, with conscious malice, 'you'd forgive a hero anything.'

'He hasn't brought Milkwort back yet,' she said, with a grim irrelevance that he noted anxiously. Too much of that could make even love dizzy.

'If you're patient, my sweet,' he said, and paused to taste the word tried for the first time, 'he'll leave of his own accord. Aren't they going to get married, like us? He'll go to live in the big house then. He'll use his money to do it up.'

'And then she'll fling him off like a squeezed lemon! No, I can't have him drunk every night, disgusting my guests.'

'I wouldn't say he disgusted them, Muriel. Mr. Jamieson said to me, "Well, Jock, you can't kill Japs for four years and come back as meek as trout". '

'We'll have lady guests soon.'

And what, wondered Jock, would those lady guests think if they knew that the prim, efficient little proprietrix was every night demonstrating her primness and efficiency in bed with the jolly barman? He smiled in love. 'I suppose we could drop a hint he'd be happier in the inn at Clashmore. That's more of a boozing howf than a hotel.'

'We'll not hint anything. We'll tell him to his face he must go.'

'But, Muriel, didn't you say you wanted to protect him?'

'He doesn't want to be protected. In any case, how can you protect a man who's in love with an evil woman? Will you tell him, or shall I?'

'With what authority could I speak, my dear?'

'With the authority of my future husband.'

Off his guard, Jock sighed. 'All right, I'll speak to him. God knows how I'm going to put it, but I'll try to find the words.'

She was silent. 'Are you regretting anything, Jock?' she asked at length.

'No, no. Never.' In haste his hand, which had demanded its freedom from hers as the conversation proceeded, returned to captivity. 'If I sighed, Muriel, it was because I like the young fellow, and I am sorry for him. After all, his wife did die when he was thousands of miles away killing men who had wives, too.' Put forward to appease her, that ill-luck of Carstares's appalled him. Almost it made him believe in God.

She pressed his hand and then lay in a silence that at first reassured him but soon had him apprehensive. He felt ice forming on the ceiling.

'Remember this,' she said hoarsely, 'I'm in deadly earnest.'

He thought she was still harping on Carstares.

'It's Helen,' she said, with a long, sad groan.

He had known about Helen long before she had: it had been the subject of much bar-room banter.

'What can we do to help her?' she asked.

'That's hard to say, Muriel. I understand the doctor's treating her.'

'Who told you that?'

'I heard it from somewhere.'

'Didn't I make you promise never to defile our bed with dirty bar-room gossip?'

'I mentioned it, dear, because I thought it was a helpful thing to say.'

'What can he do? What did he ever do for poor Margaret? She's dead, isn't she?'

He expected more passionate grief, but none came. Muriel lay very quiet. The ice thickened on the ceiling.

'Jock?'.

'Yes, dear?'

Again she was silent. Her hand, though, gripped his as if her intention was to torture rather than caress.

'Is there anything would cure Helen?'

Startled, he almost blurted out the cure advocated in the barroom. 'I expect there are places she could go to for treatment,' he murmured. 'I believe it's a fairly common complaint among women of that age.' He could hear randy laughter as he so circumspectly put it that way.

'I suffered from it,' she said boldly. 'Not so badly as Helen, though.'

He hoped not. If the bar gossip could be believed, Helen was now at the stage of lifting her skirts, like a drunk kiltie.

Muriel said, through clenched teeth, 'What cured me, could cure her.'

'It could, dear,' he replied, with drowsy amiableness; and then he became fully aware.

'I'm shameless to talk like this,' she said.

'No, no.' Those were feeble denials.

'But I don't care. Helen's my friend. There used to be three of us. Now there are only two. I won't desert her. She should never have stayed single. There was no need for it, in her case, When she was a young woman, she was beautiful, with a bosom as fine as Nancy's, and it wasn't artificial, either.'

Neither is Nancy's, he almost said. What he did say was: 'Like many another good woman she sacrificed herself for her career.'

'Would it cure her?' she demanded fiercely.

If her teeth had been clenched in his neck, the question couldn't have perturbed him more; if a little bawdiness was allowed, it could be answered, perhaps; without it, never.

'Would it?'

'I don't know. It's what you might call experimental surgery, isn't it?'

'Don't make a joke of this, please.'

'I wouldn't dream of doing such a thing, Muriel.'

'She'll be arrested, that's what will happen.'

It was likely enough, he reflected: some women with boys at the school had reached the stage of talking about telling the authorities.

'Her career would be ruined. If she was disgraced, I'd never be the same woman again. That, on top of Margaret's death, would break my spirit. I'd give up this hotel and go away.'

He considered the cure in theory: difficulties were as thick as trees in the forest. First, who would oblige? Much amusement had been caused in the bar by nominations offered; there had been estimation of the fee. Secondly, would the invalid agree to the treatment? Thirdly, since it couldn't be kept secret, what would the Education Authority say, the children's mothers, the surgeon's wife?

'You're not being helpful.'

'I've been thinking it over, Muriel.'

'Well?'

Once as a small boy learning to dive in a Glasgow public baths, he had climbed to the very top of the diving-platform, stood for a minute with knees knocking, and then recklessly had dived. Nervousness, as well as inexperience, had made that dive a real belly flopper. Now he remembered the occasion so vividly he felt that round the corner was the tenement where he lived and where his mother would be toasting bread for tea. He could almost smell the warm toast. Yet his mother had been dead twenty-five years.

'If Helen's willing—' he began.

'This is a medical treatment, remember.'

'I'm remembering, Muriel; but sometimes patients don't agree, they won't take the medicine.'

'She would.'

'Then I suppose the next question is: who'd do it?'

'Don't put it so crudely.'

He was flabbergasted by such injustice; he had used a caution like a fox's round a henhouse. 'How would you put it, Muriel? Words have got to be used, after all.'

'It's a matter of mental health.'

'Yes, of course.'

'And I didn't think you needed to ask who.'

Could she really have Rab the bull in mind?

'That's pretty important, Muriel.'

'It's more than important; it's sacred.'

Humbly he agreed.

'So there could be only one man I'd ever consider. You.'

'Me?' Again he rushed back to those childhood baths. Once he had dived too steeply, into water too shallow, and had lain on the bottom, stunned, with a lump on his head as big as one of the schoolmistress's ducks' eggs.

Suddenly she heaved up and flung herself upon him. 'Yes, you. You, you, you.' She had this time her teeth actually in his ear.

Whatever Carstares had got his M.C. for, he thought, it was a picnic compared with this.

'You don't know what you're saying, dear,' he managed to say. 'I'll be your husband. Helen will always be your friend. How could she ever come visiting us afterwards?'

'You can be both our husbands.'

Smothered in flannel, with his ear bitten, he still grinned at that entrancing picture of himself, Mohammad Jock McDermott; he'd have to take to wearing a turban. Next moment he saw it wasn't so funny; indeed, he realised there was now a likelihood he wouldn't have even one wife. Sorry for young Carstares entrapped in love's complications, he found himself in a worse tangle. Perhaps he would be packing his bag some dark night soon, stopping a lorry, and cadging a lift back to Glasgow.

Then she was no longer biting his ear, was instead weeping, breaking her heart, cowering away from him as if he had been bestially cruel to her.

To solace her he promised what he prayed he would never have to fulfil.

'No, no,' she sobbed. 'It's impossible.'

For him it was, he agreed; but for others perhaps not. There was big, skinny, Isaac McKay, who lived in a bothy by himself, a giggler, scratcher, nose-picker, and knee-creeper. He would probably oblige for a pound of tobacco, say; but Helen might well object, as nobody had ever heard of him taking a bath.

'Don't talk about it any more, ever,' she said, sniffing now, and drying her eyes with the bedsheet. 'It was just an idea I had, a silly idea.'

Not so silly, really, he thought. In a properly constituted society a spinster suffering from Helen Carmichael's complaint would be supplied, on prescription, with a big therapeutic navvy, just as today, for her headaches, pills were prescribed. But, of course, in such a society there would be no spinsters vexed with unwanted virginities.

He lay smiling at the absurdities of society perfect and imperfect, while she, still turned away, sobbed afresh, but more naturally now, for her other friend who was dead.

Twenty Two

Foulds, accompanied by the Conservator, arrived at the hotel about half an hour before lunch. They had motored from Glasgow, and wore dark suits with black ties and expressions whose solemnity became less conventional when they learned from Carstares that he wasn't going to the funeral. It appeared they hadn't yet seen Strone.

They had the lounge to themselves, the anglers being out on the loch. Carstares insisted on ordering them drinks; they consented to take sherries; he took whisky.

'Strone didn't expect you,' he said to McAndrew.

'No. I thought I wouldn't be able to manage. I'm glad I could.'

'I suppose you thought it a good opportunity to see how I was getting on? Well, the report's startling, you'll have to say that for it. Yesterday I punched Strone in the mouth, in his hut, more or less in the presence of our underlings.'

Foulds's glass at his lips seemed suddenly to contain the vilest vinegar, the Conservator's, in his hand, boiling water.

'So I'm not going to the funeral,' remarked Carstares, 'in case I should have to punch him again.'

With a frown of decision, the Conservator pulled his white handkerchief from his breast pocket, dabbed at his scorched fingertips, replaced the handkerchief, and then faced Carstares sternly.

'Assuming you are not, in some adolescent fashion, attempting to shock us with an outrageous falsehood, perhaps you would be good enough to offer some further explanation?'

'He called Constance Kilgour a whore.'

'Constance Kilgour?' In his perplexity the Conservator

forgot, picked up his glass, found it even hotter, and put it down even quicker.

Foulds was as miserable and embarrassed as a man whose dog, praised by him so highly, has just soiled his host's best carpet.

'Miss Kilgour of Garvie House?' he asked.

Carstares spoke with apparent great indignation: 'And the demented bastard set a man to watch over her day and night – the very man with whom, according to him, she'd done her whoring.' He glared at them, as if demanding they share his indignation.

'Demented—? Do I understand you to be referring to Mr. Strone?' asked the Conservator, incredulously.

'You do. Ezra the swine.'

'But, good God, Carstares, his wife's lying dead, she's to be buried this afternoon!'

'She's happier that way. She hid it well, but she must have led a hellish life with him.'

'But Mr. Foulds has frequently assured me Strone's one of our most dependable foresters.'

'He looks after the trees, if that's what you mean.'

'Yes, of course that is what I mean.'

Foulds made an effort to tidy up the mess. 'You surely weren't serious, Hugh, when you said you'd struck him?'

'I certainly was.'

'You did strike him?'

'You'll see the evidence when you see him, especially when he smiles.'

'I doubt if the poor man will be in any humour to smile this afternoon,' said the Conservator sharply.

'Oh, he'll smile, though Christ knows what it'll mean.'

'But why did you strike him, Hugh?' asked Foulds.

'I told you. He called Miss Kilgour a whore.'

'Yes, so you said. I may say it does not sound at all like Strone. But, admitting he said it, and admitting it was an extaordinarily indiscreet thing to say, in public especially, why should you *strike* him ?'

'Drunken chivalry, perhaps?' muttered the Conservator.

'Miss Kilgour and I happen to be engaged to be married,' said Carstares.

That was the biggest shock yet.

'You're not serious, Hugh?' asked Foulds.

Why not? You see, Miss Kilgour has a little girl.'

'Her own, you mean?' asked the Conservator.

'I think I said so.'

'Was she married before, and did she revert to her maiden name?'

'She was never married before, though I see the direction your mind's heading in.'

'Never mind my mind, Mr. Carstares. Let's be plain. The child's illegitimate?'

'That's the word,' cried Carstares. 'I'd forgotten it, but I knew you'd remind me. Illegitimate. So far her existence is illegal. But it's going to be remedied. Miss Kilgour and I are going to be married.'

'I'm afraid that would confer legitimacy only if you happened to be the child's father.'

'Exactly.'

'You mean, you are its father?'

'That's what I mean.'

'My God!' exclaimed the Conservator. Looking round he saw only Foulds, more mystified than himself, and therefore no deity to be consulted.

'But, Hugh,' said Foulds, trying to smile, 'when we were talking about the Kilgours in the office a few weeks ago you didn't mention a word of this.'

'Mr. Foulds, it's been my secret sorrow for years.'

'You mean you deliberately kept it dark,' said the Conservator, 'knowing very well that if we had known about it, we should certainly never have allowed you to come here?'

'Why wouldn't you? Don't you approve of our getting married for our child's sake?'

'I suppose I do, Carstares, but I certainly don't approve of forestry affairs being dragged into it.'

'Did Strone know about this when he made his remark about Miss Kilgour?' asked Foulds.

'That was why he made it.'

'What did you mean, Hugh, when you said he'd set a man to watch her?'

'Just that.'

'But why should he do such a thing?'

'Because he's got it into his demented head she's the one who sent the note about burning the forest. The whole countryside's hotching with people who'd burn Strone himself, and yet he has to pick on her. Why? Because she once told Mrs. Strone to mind her own business. Mrs. Strone, it appears, was one of those women who think themselves candidates for sainthood; everybody's business is theirs, and no one's to be offended. Constance was offended and told her so.'

'The woman is dead, Carstares,' said the Conservator.

'It does seem,' murmured Foulds, 'as though grief perhaps has temporarily distorted Strone's judgment.'

'Considerately put, Mr. Foulds. It would be truer and simpler to say he's an arrogant little twerp who likes only one thing on this earth.'

'And what may that be?' sneered the Conservator.

'His forest.'

'It does not happen to be his, Carstares. It's yours, too, and mine, and Mr. Foulds's; it belongs to the nation, as you may remember. I should say the man who is paid to look after it deserves commendation if he makes that looking after a labour of love.'

'The trees don't talk, think, suffer, shit. They're not human. That's why he likes them. I may as well tell you, while I'm at it, that I've ordered one of his men to be dismissed.'

'The man set to watch Miss Kilgour?' asked the Conservator.

'That's right.'

'But surely, as a soldier, you must appreciate he was only obeying orders?'

'Would you snoop after a woman if the Commissioner ordered you to?'

'Are you aware whom you're talking to, Carstares?'

'You must remember, sir, this is the woman I'm going to marry, the mother of my child.'

The Conservator was not sure whether that rather old-fashioned way of putting it was genuine, caused by deep emotion, or whether it was ironical.

'Strone's going to talk to you after the funeral,' said Carstares. 'You'll hear his version then.'

'I should certainly like to,' said the Conservator.

'Will you be there, Hugh?' asked Foulds.

'I don't know, Mr. Foulds. Probably not. Better not.'

'I think you should be, you know.'

'Undoubtedly,' said the Conservator.

'I'll consider it.'

Then the gong sounded for lunch, and Nancy appeared to summon them, looking by no means hospitable, for she, too, like McKerrol, was under sentence of dismissal. Miss Kirn, fornicating herself, could not any longer tolerate the presence of a younger, more buxom, and perhaps less blameworthy fornicator.

After lunch, driving to Garvie House, Carstares wondered why he had been so aggressively rude to his superiors; it seemed almost as if he'd wished to provoke them into removing him from the district. Also, why had he been so relentlessly and brutally unsympathetic to Strone and his dead wife? And towards Constance, too, his attitude had been, to say the least, equivocal; pretending to defend her, he had succeeded in making Foulds and the Conservator think of her as a whore and incendiary. If he had been trying to convince himself, was it of her guilt or innocence? Did he really love her, or was he merely fascinated, not by her beauty and loneliness so much as by the way she attracted to her all the misanthropic passions like hate, spite, envy, and resentment, by representing, indeed, that contempt for human motive and ambition which he had himself felt, but not so staunchly as she, since Marion's death.

Yet when he thought of Alison it was his old happy, optimistic love for Marion that revived; but this time that love was for Constance, or wished to be for her. If he were to lose her, and Alison, it would be like losing Marion for a second time, and he did not think he could bear that.

If he were to resign and go abroad, as he often thought of doing, he knew that for the rest of his life he would yearn for Kinlochgarvie more than for the places associated with Marion. Here a chance was being given him of escaping from the degrading torment of Marion's death. He could not give up that chance, whatever risk there might be in accepting it.

Constance came out to greet him. She seemed so healthily pleased, so sane and controlled in her movements and judgments, that he felt his own misgivings to be unjust and half-mad. He had to kiss her, in love and contrition, but his attempt would have been spoiled by his almost maudlin clumsiness had she not, with deft cheerfulness, co-operated. Nevertheless, he felt, as he had done even when making love to her, that he was being allowed, out of some peculiar charity, as far as the threshold of her being, but no farther. He could not believe McKerrol had ever been welcomed in. Perhaps no man had, not even Alison's father; or if he had, he must have done so much damage he was the last.

As if they had been affianced for years, she put her arm through his and led him across the drive on to the grass.

'I thought perhaps you'd gone to the funeral after all,' she said, smiling.

From there he could see the crag from which he and McKerrol had watched her yesterday.

'No. My two chiefs have arrived for it.'

'Didn't they think it strange you aren't going?'

'I suppose they did.'

'Ronald's been worried about it, too. You see, he still thinks of himself as laird of Kinlochgarvie. In the old days, not so long ago really, a representative of the family always attended funerals, as a duty. So I suggested why not go if he felt like that? He thought it would be more prudent to telephone Strone first. The answer was, I'm afraid, rather a ferocious snub.'

She must have known that snub was inevitable, yet she had enticed her brother into its way.

'All the same,' she added, turning to smile at him, 'I've decided to go myself. Not as a mourner, of course; as a spectator. Will you take me? There's a hill they call Lochmore, just above the village; it would make an excellent vantage-point.'

Before he could answer, he was shouted at by her brother who, dressed in dark jacket and kilt of sombre tartan, came out of the house and hurried towards them.

'Hugh, old chap,' he shouted, 'would you do me a favour?'

'Surely.'

'I'd like you to run me down to the village. Perhaps Connie's told you? Strone doesn't want me at his wife's funeral, but I think I should be there all the same. What do you think, old man? Good Lord, as I see it, it's one thing having no money and the house falling to bits, but it's another thing altogether ceasing to attend funerals; *that's* really a betrayal. Don't you agree?'

'But how can you possibly attend when Strone has forbidden you?' asked his sister, apparently amused. 'Even in the old days, Strone would still have been the principal, wouldn't he?'

'Are there such things as principals at funerals, Connie? I thought we were all equal at the grave.'

'In it, perhaps.'

'Anyhow, it's public. I can walk in the crowd.'

'But I've just asked Hugh to take me out.'

'Couldn't you drop me near the village?'

'Yes, of course we could,' said Carstares. 'What about Alison, though?'

Constance, still with her arm through his, swung round suddenly as if she was going to strike him hard, in enigmatic protest; just as enigmatically she turned the blow into a gentle affectionate tap on the cheek.

'I was waiting for you to remember her,' she said.

'That's only natural, you know, Connie,' blurted out her

brother. Though he was delighted by that naturalness, he was at the same time seizing the chance to revenge himself on his sister. 'And I can tell you this, Hugh. Alison reciprocates. Perhaps she won't talk very much about you, but by Jove she thinks about nobody else.'

'Where is she?' asked Carstares.

'In the house, in what we used to call the ballroom, playing.'

As he looked at the house Carstares saw not only its physical dereliction. He had to restrain himself from rushing to rescue the child, who seemed to be in as imminent danger as if it was visibly collapsing.

'I'll go and fetch her,' he said. He could not say it calmly, nor could he walk at an easy pace towards the house.

'He stayed away long enough,' said Ronald, 'but I must say he's making up for it.'

'Look how he limps,' she whispered.

He did not catch what she said. 'What's that, Connie?'

She would not repeat it, but gazed after Carstares with a curious intentness that he misread.

'So It's coming back, Connie? I knew it would.'

'What is coming back?'

'You know what I mean. Your love for him.'

He was sure he was proved right when she put her hand up to her face as if to hide her blushing.

'I owe you an apology, Connie,' he muttered. 'When he came in drunk the other night of course you were right to treat him as you did. He had to be made to atone. I can see that. I suppose that when love comes back it's like the circulation returning to an arm you've been sleeping on, very painful but very necessary.'

They watched Carstares come out of the house with Alison.

'One thing we've both got to admit,' said Kilgour, 'she's been much happier since he came. She doesn't show it much, but I feel she's got more confidence in the future now. It's not because of his money, either. I suppose, you know, I ought to regard it as a sort of reflection on myself. I mean, before he came, who was the hope of the Kilgours? Someone even a child of five could see through. You and Carstares will have to have a son, Connie; otherwise the male Kilgours will have ended with a whimper.'

Carstares, having installed Alison in the car, was waving to them. They walked across, Kilgour wishing to run, she hardly wishing to go at all.

'I thought,' she said to Carstares, 'we'd be going alone. Lochmore Hill's a lovers' tryst.'

'But if Ronald's going to the funeral who'd look after her?'

'Need he go? Or rather, should he go?'

'Yes, I should, Connie. Some people can afford not to overlook snubs, but I'm not one of them. I don't enjoy being cast out of the herd. Let me tell you this, too: never judge people by what they say or even by what they do; most of them have their secret heartbreaks.'

As the car went down the road Carstares chatted to Alison beside him about leaving Miss Carmichael's school. She became interested only when she learned he would be driving her to and from her new school in Caldoon.

'Don't build up her hopes,' murmured Constance.

He almost retorted savagely that she certainly had never done that; on the contrary she had fed the child, piece by piece, like a bird its young, with despair.

'Why shouldn't I?' he demanded. 'I hope she's got a lot to look forward to.'

'Hear, hear,' said Ronald. 'You sit still, Hugh, old man. I'll open the gate.'.

But Carstares got out and opened it with him.

'D'you think, Hugh,' whispered Kilgour, 'I'm doing the right thing?'

'Yes, I do.'

'I'm no hero, mind you. I just shrivel up when I'm among people who don't want me. But I felt I just had to put in an appearance this afternoon. You'll find, with Connie, one has to redress the balance. No, perhaps you won't find it. She's changing already.'

'Do you think so ?'

'Oh, yes. I notice it particularly in her attitude to Alison.'

Connie looked out of the car. 'Are you two going to be hanging over that gate all afternoon?'

Her brother laughed. 'Sorry, Connie. I won't come back in. I'll just walk along from here.'

With a wave to them he set off along the public road away from the village towards the forester's house. At first he walked sturdily with his head up, but when he caught sight of some people in front, on the same mission as himself, he began to hesitate and shuffle.

'It's early for midges,' murmured his sister.

Carstares glanced at her, hoping he had detected amidst the malicious amusement a seed of sympathy and affection.

She pointed in the opposite direction. 'This is our way,' she said. 'We climb up a back road above the village. It's pretty rough.'

'Do you really want to go?' he asked.

'Of course. Why not?'

'Very well.'

The track that led off the main road was narrow and over-grown with grass. In places the surface had been washed away by streams overflowing in winter out of the forest above. Below, too, cut off by a low drystone dyke green with moss, the forest of spruces dropped quite steeply down to the railway line, on the other side of which sparkled the loch. The village consisted of a row of small, stone cottages, some green fields, a shop, the station, and the purple-slated kirk with its graveyard attached.

'We'll take your glasses, Hugh,' said Constance.

With an eagerness that struck him as too naïve to be genuine, she led the way over the stile and up the path through the heather, among the small pines stunted by the sourness of the thin soil. He noticed that once, casually, she pulled from one of the trees a green tassel that represented a hard year's growth.

At the top she flung off her blue cardigan.

'Isn't it warm?' she cried, and stood, for a moment, with legs apart, and breasts thrust out, breathing in the scented air. 'You know, I can remember coming here when I was as young as Alison. It was different then. There were only a few trees, here and there on the hillsides, as trees ought to be.' She turned all round, seeing trees everywhere like a plague of silent devourers, in hollows, by the sides of streams, on ridge after ridge, to the very skylines. 'Don't you see, Hugh, why I hate your trees? They're between me and my happy childhood.' Laughing, she crouched down on the heather and trained the binoculars on the village below.

Carstares and Alison reached the top and sat down on his jacket. They began to point out places to each other: the hotel, the school, a boat on the loch, the fire watch-towers, and the house. They avoided the churchyard beneath, where a few spectators were already waiting, by the walls or under trees, and where the open grave could be plainly seen.

'Here they come,' said Constance.

Creeping along the road from the forestry settlement was the procession.

'They're carrying it,' she said. 'I thought it was to be taken on a cart pulled by the white horse they call Nell. Strone's in front of course. Those must be your chiefs on either side of him. I suppose most of the males in the district are here, but they don't amount to much, do they?'

From that height, and under so vivid a sky, the procession did seem very small, and also very inconsequential. Ants carrying the carcase of a fly, thought Carstares.

'I don't see Ronald,' she said.

'Yes.' It was Alison who spoke. 'He's at the end.'

'So he is, among the humble labourers. Your friend Will McKew's there, Hugh, with his father. Would you like to see?'

He took the glasses and soon picked out McKew, uncomfortable in his dark dancing suit. Beside him walked a tall old man with white hair and beard.

'I like old Faither McKew,' she said. 'He comes to funerals, not out of respect for the dead, or for the living either, but to defy death itself. He's almost eighty, and still strong.'

'He's got a boy at school, hasn't he?'

'He married twice.'

Then he saw Jock, no doubt representing Miss Kirn. Behind him strolled McKerrol, fire-broom over his shoulder; he represented lust and fertility, and far more effectively than old McKew's senile pride defied death. Raising his eyes from him, Carstares was overwhelmed by the magnificence of the countryside, and by his and Constance's transience amidst it.

He turned to Alison. 'Would you go down to the car for me, Alison?' he asked. 'I left some sweets in it. Will you bring them up? The door's open.'

She immediately rose and set off down the hill.

'You'll be all right,' he called after her. 'We can see you the whole way.'

Hardly had the child gone than Constance turned to him, and pulling him down on top of her kissed him with what seemed to him a passionate contempt.

'Was this why you wanted to be rid of her?' she asked.

He lay looking down upon her, seeing the blue sky reflected in her eyes and trying to see what else was there. 'Perhaps,' he said, and kissed her.

'You see,' she whispered, 'you should have let me keep her at home with Ronald.'

On the grass beside her he saw the tassel she had so wantonly plucked from the little pine. With his fingers he formed part of her hair into a black tassel, and tugged it.

'Do you know what Strone believes?' he said.

'That his wife's in heaven? No, I'll give him that credit; he doesn't believe that, whatever he believes.'

The very hair in his hand, so silky and black, became sinister with that reply. He was sure she had said it to mock him, and her, and this love threatening to take root between them.

'About you, Connie?'

'That I helped to kill her?'

'No, Connie. That you dropped a note into his letter-box, threatening to burn the forest. It was written on a page torn from a child's arithmetic jotter. Alison's got such a jotter, and there are pages missing.'

She opened her eyes and ran her fingers up his pullover like a spider.

'You seem to believe it, too,' she said.

'Is it true?'

'Yes.' She laughed at his dismay. 'Yes, I wrote it and dropped it into his letter-box. I must really be mad. Is that what you're thinking, Hugh?'

'Why did you do it, Connie?'

'To express my feelings, surely. You express yours by getting drunk and getting into bed with buxom chambermaids.'

'Be serious, for God's sake, Connie.'

'God is neither here, nor there.' She took her hand from him to wave it negligently down in the direction of the churchyard. 'How are they getting on, by the way? Have they reached it yet? And, darling, do use your elbow as a prop. I am not quite so pneumatic as Nancy.'

He turned from her and looked down. The coffin-bearers were entering the gate. The minister could be seen walking from the church to meet them at the grave.

'Well?' she asked.

'They're going into the churchyard now.'

'Then perhaps I ought to be looking. Foolish to come here just to watch the sky, and the disappointment in your eyes.'

'No, Connie.' He kept her from rising and bent passionately over her.

'Here, Hugh? With the words of the service being said below? And Alison peeping from behind one of your little trees? Well, if you don't mind, I don't.'

He glanced round to look for Alison. She was not to be seen.

Had this then been Constance's intention in asking him to come here this afternoon? As a gesture of contempt and loathing it would embrace the sky, the trees, the hills, the dead woman, the mourners, herself, and him. Perhaps her couplation with McKerrol had been a similar gesture.

'I know,' he gasped, 'why you hate McKerrol so much you want him sent away.'

'You should know. Haven't I told you often enough?'

'But did you tell me everything, Connie?'

'What else was there to tell you? You're hurting my breast, by the way.'

'Sorry. Have you ever let McKerrol make love to you, like this?'

Her eyes, so blue and bright a moment ago, suddenly closed; it was as if light had gone from the sky. She still smiled; her fingers clutched at the dead heather; and suddenly she shuddered, breast, belly, and thighs, as if under the toughness cultivated so long she had at last been hurt.

From below they heard the mourners begin to sing, with pathetic lugubriousness, 'Abide With Me.'

'Have you, Connie? It doesn't matter. I just want to know.'

'McKerrol?' So quietly did she say the name, it was like the wind rustling the heather.

'I was speaking to him yesterday.'

'About me?'

He did not reply, and after a silence she said, all banter gone: 'Get off.' He was too slow for her liking and she pushed him violently.

'So it's true?' he asked.

She lay on her stomach and gazed down at the scene in the churchyard.

'What happened before you came is none of your business,' she said.

'But Alison—' Even to her, then, he was pretending he was really the child's father.

'She's got nothing to do with you, and never has.'

'But she will have, Connie, when we're married.'

She watched the mourners disperse. McKerrol was amongst them, carrying a fire-broom, perhaps thrusting its handle between his legs obscenely, even there in the churchyard. She remembered how she had come upon him in the forest. He had been working by himself, stripped to the waist, chopping down old dying trees. When he had made his suggestion, or his offer rather, she would willingly have killed him with his axe; yet as she had rushed away, furious and revolted, she had also felt a crazy desire to go back and be degraded by him. Perhaps it was that admission which made her now feel towards Carstares a gratitude and commitment that astonished and alarmed her.

To find refuge she looked for her brother. He was speaking to the minister, no doubt too loudly out of a lack of confidence, and being overheard with disgust by those women now sneaking in to drop flower or pebble or piece of earth into the grave.

'Let's go home,' she said, and rising quickly raced down the hill.

'But if we go back now, Connie,' he called, 'we'll meet some of them returning.'

'Does that matter?'

'I suppose not.'

He gathered up his jacket, her cardigan, and the binoculars. When he reached the car, she was seated in front; Alison, behind, kept her lips tight,

'You didn't bring the sweets,' he said to the child.

She shook her head, and he decided to say no more. Perhaps she had gone up the hill with the sweets. What had she seen, and what was she now thinking? Even at five you were painfully and inextricably involved; but perhaps at that age stoicism was not the best reaction. He thought that even if Constance were to torment him until he was as embittered as herself, he still would not leave her, for the child's sake.

As soon as they came out on to the main road they were amongst returning mourners. There was a group of forestry-workers, laughing and juggling with their brooms; for them the funeral break was now a relaxation. McKerrol was among them.

As the car approached the road to the house Carstares caught sight of Strone, Foulds, and McAndrew in front.

'My chiefs,' he said. 'Do you want me to stop?'

'You'll be stopping at the gate anyway to let us off.'

'Don't you want me to take you to the house?'

'No, Hugh. I think you'd better be polite to your chiefs.'

'Shall I come and see you tonight?'

'If you wish.'

'You know I wish nothing more.'

Then they were at the gate where Foulds, McAndrew and Strone waited,, the first two uneasily, the forester with apparent calm.

Strone, though, was not allowed to predominate. Constance, being introduced, chose to be at her most vivacious, charming, intelligent, and patrician. They were obviously impressed. Strone, smaller than ever in his black indoor suit, was made to seem, despite his privilege of grief, plebeian and curiously hapless; his slightly swollen mouth seemed in no way to give him any advantage.

The Conservator was particularly attentive and affable to Alison; she was merely polite.

'Hugh will run you along,' said Constance. 'Alison and I are going to walk up to the house.'

'We don't want to deprive you of your transport, Miss Kilgour,' said the Conservator.

'You're not doing that. Goodbye, gentlemen. I'll see you tonight, Hugh.'

'Yes.'

Foulds and McAndrew raised their hats, and Strone made a strange little bow. They watched her as, taking Alison's hand, she walked through the gate and along the private road. She looked happy and confident.

Carstares, glancing from her to Strone, knew the latter was beaten. The Conservator, called upon to choose between the Miss Kilgour he had just met and the bewildered forester, who had so oddly and distastefully belittled his wife's death, would never hesitate.

McKerrol, it was clear, would find no one to defend him.

Twenty Three

On Friday afternoon at half-past four all the workers gathered at the hut for their fortnight's pay, except those engaged on fire-watching. Carstares was present, seated in a corner of the hut; Strone had suggested that since this was the first paying out since he had taken over the district he ought to supervise it. But nobody regarded it as an ordinary occasion. All week there had been rumours that McKerrol was going to be sacked, so that they were all waiting until it was his turn to go into the hut, summoned by John McBraid the foreman. The least anxious seemed Rab himself. Wearing Wellingtons caked with dried peat muck from the bottoming, he sat apart on a grassy bank, enjoying the sunshine in the same easy, masterful way he enjoyed their adulation in the pub. One or two in nervousness rather than friendliness called to him, but not to speak about his impending dismissal.

At last McBraid appeared in the doorway. They knew by the way he tugged at his ear that Rab was next. 'Rab,' he shouted, without a smile. Despite his big ears, and his tongue too ready to lick, he was not the man to smile at another's misfortune.

McKerrol rose and strolled towards the hut. Old Angus McFadyen tottered up to him, with advice that fear and slavers almost made unintelligible. 'Keep your temper, Rab,' he gabbled. 'They're the bosses, right or wrang. Violence doesnae pay.'

Some thought Rab would strike the advice away with his cap as he would have a pestering wasp, but instead he smiled, nodded, and glanced up from the silly, white-haired face to the bright clouds.

'Not in daylight, Angus,' he agreed, and then entered the hut.

Strone, wearing spectacles, sat at the desk, with the book

open in front of them that each payee signed. McBraid had the
pay packet ready in his hand.

The forester put his linger on the place where McKerrol was
to sign. McKerrol picked up the pen in his powerful fingers,
made to sign, paused, and looked up, grinning.

'Just what am I signing for?' he asked.

'Your fortnight's pay,' replied Strone coldly. 'Six pounds
sixteen and eightpence. You'll find it right.'

'I think I'll check it all the same, before I sign.'

'Did you ever find it wrong before?'

McKerrol took the packet from McBraid and emptied it on
to the desk. Carefully he counted.

'It's right, Rab,' said McBraid, in relief.

'Not much, though, for a fortnight's sweat, is it?'

'You've expressed that opinion before,' said Strone. 'You'll
be pleased to know then that, as from this minute, your
connection with the forest is finished.'

'Why should I be pleased?' asked McKerrol calmly.

'Surely you'll be anxious to go elsewhere where the wages are
more to your liking?'

'I have a house here.'

'You'll be allowed tenancy of it for a month from today.'

McKerrol laughed. 'And a garden,' he said. He glanced at the
pen in his hand. 'Isn't it written down somewhere why I'm
being sacked?'

'That isn't the practice,' said Strone. 'There are, others
waiting. Will you sign?'

As McKerrol slowly signed, he remarked, in an amiable tone:
'I doubt if I'd care to work for you any longer, Strone. You've
always been a hard-hearted, tyrannical, wee bastard, but now
you'll be a hundred times worse.'

'A horse's fart, Rab,' murmured the forester, 'means as much
to me as anything you say.'

McKerrol held the pen like a dagger and drove it into the
desk. He had his back to Carstares.

'Before I go,' he said, 'I'll think of a suitable farewell present.
Not to you,' he added to Strone. 'You've had yours.'

Then he strolled out into the sunshine, as assured as a king into his realm.

'Bob Davidson's next,' said Strone. 'Call him.'

McBraid muttered, 'Rab'll get nae sympathy. They're a' glad in their hearts to see him go. But his wife will; she's a good soul, is Jean. I'm sorry for her.'

'Why?' asked Strone. 'She's still alive.'

Later that night, about eight o'clock, when the pay-night celebrations were in swing in the hotel bar, Mrs. McKerrol, keeping in the darkness of dykes and trees, trudged slowly along the road and entered Strone's gate. She had been one of those who on Monday afternoon had dropped a flower into the grave, and now, plodding up the path to the dead woman's house, she felt the same warm-hearted pity for Mrs. Strone, but no envy at all. Sweetly, where he had been so concentratedly bitter, she agreed with Strone that despite her many troubles her one advantage of life compensated for everything.

As she rang the bell and waited, she hoped her family was safe in her absence, and the thought occurred to her that were she dead she would have this same anxiety for them. The difference was that now, if she ran in spite of her heavy belly she could be with them in twenty minutes, soothing their sorrows and terrors with her inexhaustible love, whereas if she were dead, even in the luxury and ease of heaven, she would never be able to go to them. But even that fearful prospect she suffered without bitterness or rebellion.

Mr. Strone, she knew, was living alone in the house; his wife's aunt, Mrs. Gibson, who had kept house for them, had gone away; some said she had been sent away. Therefore, she expected him to open the door to her; but she had not expected him to be wearing his wife's gold bracelet. It was almost the first thing she saw as he asked her to come in; and then, surprising her still more, she smelled the scent his wife had used. In her simplicity she looked round, prepared to see Mrs. Strone.

Strone was dressed in his uniform breeches, and a khaki

cardigan that his wife perhaps had knitted for him. He seemed strange and tender, as if he had been drinking. Most people believed that her Rab came home drunk and in a fit of lust forcibly made her pregnant; it was not true, often Rab was at his most gentle and loving when drunk.

'Do you want to take your coat off, Jean?' asked Strone.

It was the first time he had ever used her Christian name. Likely he was feeling tender towards all women, for his wife's sake.

'No, Mr. Strone,' she said, 'there's no need. I'll not be staying long.'

'That's a pity, Jean,' he said, as he showed her into the sitting-room.

At once she noticed the number of pictures of his wife; eight at least.

'Sit down, Jean,' he said, already seated himself on the arm of the settee.

That was not bad manners on his part, she knew. He was sensitive about his smallness, and she was almost a head taller.

'Maybe you'll have guessed what's brought me here in secrecy?'

He was gazing at her hair, as men often did. She was used to that admiration. Mrs. Strone's hair, she remembered, had been grey and dry; but no wonder, after the death in infancy of her only child, and after so long an illness.

'How many children have you, Jean?' he asked.

'Four.'

'But they'll soon be five?'

She could not resist putting her hand fondly on her belly. 'I hope so. It's for their sakes I'm here. No, that's not just true; I'm here for my man's sake as well.'

Too shy to look at his face, she saw only his hand with the bracelet. When she glanced up, quickly, it seemed to her that in a way she could not have explained he resembled his dead wife. Yet Mrs. Strone had been a bonny woman, whereas not even his own mother would ever have called him handsome.

'Rab's always been a good workman,' she said.

'He has, Jean, but it wasn't for his work he was sacked.'

She had heard rumours of the reason, and supposed they were true.

'Do you want me to tell you just why he was sacked, Jean?'

'It doesn't matter.'

'You know we have a new District Officer?'

'Mr. Carstares?'

'Yes, Mr. Carstares. It also happens he's the father of Miss Kilgour's bastard.'

She winced and shook her head. 'No child should be called that.'

Strone got off the settee and came closer.

'They met during the war, Jean, and the little girl was the result. I don't know how many times they had to lie belly to belly to get her; once can be enough.'

She blushed and looked at the carpet. His mouth was at her ear.

'And they're back at it again, Jean, every night in the big house. Do you know they were at it on Lochmore Hill while the funeral was going on under them? Bob Davidson was on fire duty, and he had the binoculars on them.'

'This is none of my business, Mr. Strone.'

'But it is, Jean, that's where you're wrong, it is. Carstares found out, you see, that your Rab's had her on her back.'

'Please don't talk like that to me, Mr. Strone. I don't think you ever talked like that to your wife.' As she spoke, with dignity, she was remembering what was whispered, that he and his wife had not come together sexually for years. Men deprived of that became like small boys in their self-pity and their eagerness to shock. 'I hoped you would be able to do something for the children's sake,' she said. 'It's the house, you see. It's their home; they were all born in it.'

Her reference to his wife seemed to have inflamed his lechery. He crouched on the arm of her chair and stroked her neck.

'For you and your children, Jean, I'd do a lot. But he's my boss, and the bosses above him, who were here on Monday, took his part as you'd expect.'

'What happened in a private way shouldn't be held against him at his work.'

'You don't understand the world, Jean,' he whispered. 'You're too simple, too good. But it happened in the forest, Jean.'

'Still, it was private.'

'Very private, Jean; maybe a puddock saw, a chaffinch, a spider, a deer even.'

'Don't do that, Mr. Strone.'

'Your neck's like many another woman's thigh, for smoothness, Jean.'

'I didn't come here for such talk, Mr. Strone. I came for your help and advice. I mean, if he was to apologise—'

'Rab, you mean?'

She nodded.

'But to whom would he apologise, Jean? Miss Kilgour? Can you apologise to a woman you've done that with?'

'It was a silly thing to say.' Yet, she thought, with her eyes closed, after so many times was the act of much more consequence than, say, a hasty slap on the face, which could be apologised for? 'You see, Mr. Strone, he's talking about working for the McKews, and I don't want that.'

'I heard they were after him, Jean. Sheep-drains. He's the best drainer in the district, is your Rab. They've offered him a cottage, too, eh?'

'Look where it is; in the heart of the hills. Would it do any good, do you think, if I went to see Mr. Carstares?'

'None at all, Jean.'

'Maybe I should go and see her.'

Then his control broke. He went down on his knees and crawled round to crush his head into her lap, sobbing to her to help him.

'How can I help you, Mr. Strone?'

With the desperation, incoherence, and cunning of a child he told her: if she let him make love to her in his wife's bed, Margaret would stop tormenting him; so many times, he confessed, he had denied Margaret, pretending he did not wish to risk injuring her in her frail condition, but really punishing herself and him, for what he could not say, perhaps just for being human beings, with bodies demanding appeasement in so filthy a manner, or perhaps because there had been in Margaret something that had made him impotent, her goodness, maybe, or what other people called her goodness.

Mrs. McKerrol thought he must be mad, and yet she could not look for usual sanity in a man whose wife had been buried that week. She wished to help him, if she could; and the thought even crossed her mind that if the use of her body for five minutes could restore him, why not give it to him? She was pregnant, and Rab often said that there was no better way of preventing birth than to have the womb already filled. A handkerchief could wipe away all the damage he could do. She did not think she was denying or belittling love; that seemed to her much more than the touch of bodies, and had to involve her children. It occurred to her, too, that here was an opportunity to get revenge on Rab, who had been unfaithful to her with women whom she had to smile to on the road or talk to in the shop; but her children would be humiliated.

Had she struggled and screamed, perhaps Strone would have persisted; but as he pawed her legs and thighs she merely sat with her hands clasped, gazing at him with her large blue eyes full of pity and wonder. He could not bear it, and got to his feet, holding out his hands as if minded to thrust them into the fire.

She rose too and without hurry arranged her clothes.

'That's what I'll do,' she said, as she made for the door. 'I'll go and see her. I have no pride where my children are concerned.'

Hiding his face with his fists he came over to her. 'I'm sorry, Jean. I'm off my head.'

'If I was to die, Mr. Strone, I hope my Rab would be off his. And so he would for a while, anyway; and that's all I would look for.'

They stood at the open door smelling the coolness of the loch and the sweetness of the young trees.

'Tell me, Jean, what do I do to get over this?'

She considered: in her own case her children would help her; but he had none. Then she remembered what others said in cynicism, that his trees were his children.

'You've got your trees,' she said simply.

In anyone else he would have suspected sarcasm, but from her it was the consoling truth.

'Good-night, Mr. Strone,' she said. 'I know you'd help me if you could.'

'I would, Jean,' and he meant it.

'What happened tonight is forgotten.'

'Thanks, Jean. Good-night.'

He watched her as she went down the path with cautious, proud, triumphant, pregnant gait; and remembering the new growth of trees, and the splendour of the whole forest in its spring-time resurgence, he stood shaking and sobbing with a great hope and relief.

One afternoon when Rab was over the hill at Creagan, seeing about his new job there, Mrs. McKerrol paid her visit to Garvie House. Peggy and Ian being at school, she had to take the two youngest children with her; Hector, the baby, travelled in the old buckled pram that had served his brother and two sisters, and Morag, aged three and a half, walked.

Mrs. McKerrol could not help being hopeful as she wrestled the pram along the rutted road to the big house. The sun, shining for days without faltering, had built up a warmth and radiance in the air that had her, once or twice, like the birds, humming involuntarily for joy. A moment after, of course, she remembered the serious predicament in which her family was, and she fell silent, frowning, gnawing at her lip, and sighing, in an attempt to show appropriate worry and indignation. But the birds, secure in their nests, went on singing; and in the pram little Hector, kicking up his pink heels in the sunshine, chuckled and seemed to be trying to catch chubby fistfuls of that delightful element which was making life for him so gleeful an experience. Even Morag, the dark-haired solemn one of the family, felt free that afternoon to be happy, and carried primroses in her hand as emblems of trust.

If the errand failed, it would be safer to keep it secret; but Morag was, as well as dour, a persistent purveyor of the truth. Often that characteristic had caused all the family to burst irresistibly into laughter; but once or twice it had caused awkwardness. Therefore Mrs. McKerrol sought some way of enticing her small daughter into promising not to say where they had been; the difficulty of finding such a way made her proud rather than annoyed. Smiling, she decided to wait and see how the interview turned out.

Just before they came in sight of the big house, Morag stopped and would not go further. She said she wanted to go back now; she didn't like that road; there were too many stones on it; those stones were spoiling her new shoes, as well as the wheels of Hector's pram. Her mother knew the real reason: the Private sign at the gate, which Morag could not read but understood very well, and also the inborn distrust all the village children had of the big house.

As she stooped to reassure her daughter, she remembered Miss Kilgour's own child, deprived of affection.

'Morag,' she whispered, 'your mummy's going up to see the lady in the big house.'

Morag was interested but still more suspicious. 'What for?' she asked.

'There's something I want to speak to her about.'

'Are you going to ask the wee girl to come to our house?'

That had been a proposal of Peggy's, timidly put forward. Rab had laughed, but Mrs. McKerrol still gravely considered it.

'For Peggy's party?' added Morag.

Peggy's birthday was in two months; already there was talk of a party.

Mrs. McKerrol nodded. Morag was satisfied. As Mrs. McKerrol rose and pushed the pram on again she thought how much happier and more suitable to the sunny afternoon that errand would be.

'If I leave the pram,' she said, 'will you look after it? It's too far for you to walk all the way to the house.'

Morag agreed. 'Tell her there'll be dumpling.'

'Yes, I'll tell her.'

'With things in it: a wee white doll, a ring, a silver three-penny, a button, and a thimble.'

'Yes.'

Then Morag stopped again. They had come in sight of the house. Mrs. McKerrol looked for a place to leave the pram. There was a flat plot of grass by the side of the road. She wondered if it would be seen from the door of the big house, for she did not intend to enter, even if invited, and so be out of sight and hearing of her children.

As she was arranging the pram, Morag said sharply: 'There's somebody.'

With her hand clasping the baby's foot Mrs. McKerrol glanced towards the house: on the terrace someone – Miss Kilgour herself, she thought – was sitting on a deck-chair, reading.

'She's reading,' said Morag, as if it was a shameful thing to do.

'Well, you read, too, don't you?'

'I'm not at school.'

'But Peggy teaches you, doesn't she? You'll look after Hector, won't you, pet?'

Morag nodded. 'But don't be long.'

'I promise.'

Reluctantly, she began to walk away from her children towards the house. Several times she looked back and waved. With a calmness that smote her heart more than any hysterical fondness could have done, Morag waved in reassurance. Mrs. McKerrol then walked on with a heart that remained light in spite of her expectation that Miss Kilgour would do nothing to help her, and might indeed be unpleasant in her refusal.

Constance noticed her approaching, but did not rise or even look up from her book. Mrs. McKerrol reached the steps and hesitated, not wishing to climb them without being asked. She saw the signs of dilapidation in the great house, even in the deck-chair whose stripes were faded and canvas torn; she saw, too, what she had been told about, the bullet holes in the door.

'I'm sorry for disturbing you, Miss Kilgour,' she said.

Constance looked up, raising her head unnecessarily high. She snatched off her spectacles, too, in what was meant to be an intimidating gesture. Somehow she seemed to be acting; but what her real feelings were Mrs. McKerrol could not say.

'I'm Mrs. McKerrol.'

'Yes.'

'I'll not keep you long, Miss Kilgour. You see, I've left my children yonder, Morag and Hector the baby; he's in the pram.' She turned, saw the pram and Morag, and was given courage to confront a hundred black-haired Miss Kilgours, all haughtier than this; but she was given no truculence, and did not wish any. 'I had better explain.'

'It would help.'

'It's hard to begin.'

Miss Kilgour did not smile.

'My husband works in the forest.'

'Do you not mean, used to? I understand he has been dismissed.'

Mrs. McKerrol was aware of the relish in the other's voice; she wondered if, for Rab's sake, she should reprove it.

'It's a great misfortune for my family,' she said simply.

That seemed to be reproof enough. Miss Kilgour's thin hand, with the diamond ring, clenched, and her pale lips tightened.

'Mr. Strone was always pleased with Rab, or Mr. McKerrol I should say. It was Mr. Carstares, the new District Officer, that said he had to go.'

Miss Kilgour made no comment.

'You see, it's not just the job, it's the house that goes with it, it's our home, all the children were born in it, and forby Mr. McKerrol's worked hard at the garden; they say his roses are the best in the countryside.'

She paused to smile in indulgence at her man's child-like pride in his roses; but the other woman was far from smiling in sympathy.

'I don't want to be impudent, Miss Kilgour, but I know you

and Mr. Carstares are friends. They're saying in the village you're. engaged, but that's none of their business, or mine either. I just thought that if out of kindness you were to speak to Mr. Carstares he might be willing to give my husband another chance. Whatever he did that was wrong, I apologise for him; whatever you would like me to do to put it right, I'll gladly do it, if it's in my power.'

Then she waited, without any noticeable defences, and yet somehow not without pride.

As Constance stared at her, contempt, disdain, dislike, resentment, and even anger, seemed unable to take a hold in her mind. There an unfamiliar emotion was roused, which she could not have named, but which seemed to have regret of some kind in it. Yet her attitude to this stupid, common woman ought to have been swift and unmistakable. Pregnancy, as insolent as the budding of the trees, and simple-mindedness that by expecting trust and forgiveness cheapened these and made them not worth obtaining: these things Mrs. McKerrol represented; and moreover, with her flaxen hair, landgirl's complexion, and voluptuous body, she was so obviously the willing victim of her husband's lust. Nevertheless, it was not easy to despise her.

'I'm afraid,' said Constance, 'there's nothing I can do.'

'I thought if you were to speak to Mr. Carstares—'

'You say you do not know why your husband was dismissed. Is that true?'

Mrs. McKerrol looked ashamed. 'No, it's not exactly true. I've heard talk. He hasn't spoken to me about it. He doesn't know I'm here.'

'If he did know, would he beat you?'

'He has never laid a hand on me in anger,' retorted Mrs. McKerrol, with a flash of anger herself. 'I know they say he does. Well, it's a lie.'

'Your husband insulted me, very grossly.'

Mrs. McKerrol glanced back towards her children. They were the results of Rab's love-making. Would Mr. Carstares's bear bonnier fruit?

'And he has been spreading the most filthy insinuations about me.' Constance was surprised at her own indignation. It must be that this woman's naïvety was catching.

Rather than being shocked by that imputation of her husband as an obscene liar, Mrs. McKerrol seemed to rejoice that here at least was one infidelity he had not been guilty of.

'It's his imagination,' she said, smiling. 'In many ways he's not grown-up. Most men are like that. He gets carried away. But I can understand why you feel annoyed, Miss Kilgour.'

'Thank you.'

That silliest of sarcasms was annihilated by Mrs. McKerrol's smile. 'If he was to apologise,' she said cheerfully, 'would you speak to Mr. Carstares?'

She did not seem to realise that her husband was an incorrigible brute, who would turn the apologising into another sexual insult. It amazed Constance that a woman could live with a man for ten years, be violated by him hundreds of times, in this case thousands, and yet know him so falsely. Love truly was blind.

Mrs. McKerrol was shaking her head, as if she had read those thoughts. 'My husband's misjudged,' she said. 'You've got to like him to know him. At heart he's really more content than I am, and I know it's a fault of mine. The children are as fond of him as they are of me.' She seemed to think that was proof anyone would accept.

Then they heard the sound of a car.

'I think this is Mr. Carstares,' said Constance. 'You can ask him yourself.'

Mrs. McKerrol was strangely unconfident. 'It's different with a man,' she murmured. 'I mean, a woman knows these things in the long run aren't important.'

Constance was astonished. Mrs. McKerrol had put the thought forward as incontrovertible wisdom, whereas surely it really represented the sexual submissiveness so typical of women of her class.

'What I mean is, Miss Kilgour, a woman just hasn't time to stop and make herself ill with jealousy; she's got the house to look after, and the children to protect. If she's the jealous kind, she'll suffer it rather than hurt them.'

Carstares had stopped the car and came out to speak to Morag.

'He seems to be fond of children,' said Mrs. McKerrol.

'He is.'

'Maybe then he'll do it for their sakes.'

Constance was on the point of retorting that Mrs. McKerrol seemed to be under the delusion that everybody had the same solicitude for her children as she had herself; but she recognised in time the peculiar fatuity of such a statement. Even so, she was surprised she kept silent.

The car came on again and stopped at the steps. Carstares was smiling shyly as he got out; he had two or three wilted primroses in his hand. They were a gift from Morag.

So, thought Constance, simple Mrs. McKerrol has transmitted to her offspring her own kind of cunning.

'I hope she wasn't cheeky, Mr. Carstares?' asked Mrs. McKerrol.

'Not in the least. Didn't she give me these?'

'I think maybe she was feeling a wee bit guilty at being there.'

'So you think they were a bribe?'

She laughed with him. 'She's one for bribes. Her father says she's a real woman.'

Carstares stood smiling at the flowers. The little girl had told him her mother was at the big house to ask Alison to come to a party. He could not believe it.

Going up the steps, he took Constance's hand, held and pressed it, glanced at the book she'd been reading, and then took up his position behind her chair, with his hand on her head.

'I ought to tell you what's brought me here, Mr. Carstares,' said Mrs. McKerrol.

He waited, smiling.

'I'm here to ask you to give my man another chance. Miss Kilgour said she'd be willing to let bygones be bygones, if you were.'

'I said nothing of the kind,' said Constance sharply.

Mrs. McKerrol looked puzzled. 'But I was sure you did.'

Carstares was embarrassed. 'I thought your husband had got another job,' he said.

'If you mean, sir, with the McKews, I'd much rather he didn't take it.'

'I understand the pay's better.'

'It's just temporary, and besides I don't want him to get mixed up with them. I was just telling Miss Kilgour that here in Kinlochgarvie is our home. All our children were born here.'

She was interrupted by Morag. 'Mummy, Hector's crying,' she shouted.

They listened, and heard the baby.

'So it would be a great benefit to us,' said Mrs. McKerrol, in some agitation at last, 'if we were allowed to stay here. I wouldn't like to be staying in a cottage in the depth of the hills, when my time came. Would you consider it, Mr. Carstares?'

She saw he might have, but when he bent over his fiancée's chair and whispered, Miss Kilgour at once answered loudly: 'No!' He straightened and shook his head.

'I'm afraid it's impossible, Mrs. McKerrol. I'm sorry.'

'I would go down on my knees,' she said, 'if I thought it would do any good; but—' She looked for several seconds at Miss Kilgour's face – 'I can see it wouldn't. You'll excuse me then if I can't find it in my heart to wish you both well.'

Then she hurried away, sadly, but with dignity.

'I suppose this is as good a time as any to tell you, Hugh,' said Constance, 'that your flattering suspicion regarding me and her bull of a husband is unfounded.'

'I never believed that, Connie,' he protested, but he could not keep the relief and joy out of his voice.

'Now it's your turn,' she said. 'Reassure me about Nancy.'

Huffed, he watched Mrs. McKerrol reach the pram and pacify both her children. He realised he had the primroses in his hand. As he bent to kiss Constance's head he dropped them.

Twenty Four

Two women, even though he was asked to sleep with only one of them, were too many for Jock; Muriel, without his sanction, had co-opted Helen Carmichael. Hitherto, when he was just her barkeeper and handyman, Muriel had consulted him upon almost everything, not merely upon what liquor to order; now, when he was preparing to be her husband and co-owner, she was making decisions that affected the inmost peace of his soul without letting him know. Nor did she keep him out lest he object; as her husband, objection was not going to be permitted him, he was too well-beloved for that. Helen therefore joined the board, and was neither as meek nor reticent as a woman in her condition ought to have been. Towards Muriel certainly she showed a subservience altogether different from her previous assertiveness, but in echoing Muriel's opinions and decisions to Jock, she spoke with a sergeant-major's snarl. The treatment which the doctor apparently was giving her, to quieten her nerves and keep her skirts down in public, seemed to make her avoid all other men, like a shy dog too often kicked; but towards Jock she became, with his mistress's indulgence, a snapping, querulous bitch. Soon his own nerves suffered: he could not pour without spilling, and lost the knack of telling when talk had become too blue to be allowed; in short he became tactless and short-tempered in the bar.

The subject on which Muriel and Helen hounded him most was the expulsion of Carstares from the hotel. Once when his mind was flabby with affection, he had promised Muriel he would see to it, and now she was determined to keep him to his promise. To protest that he liked the young District Officer and was sorry for him was to have Muriel go into a pet of jealousy, in which she accused him of not being as fond of her as their nightly actions made utterly necessary. Once she wept for her maidenhood so cynically filched by him; while Helen, so far kept out of that guilty bed, but allowed into its secret, sat by almost drooling with what seemed to him, despite the doctor's medicine, uncontrollable heat. They had both more or less dug up Margaret Strone and flung her, limb by limb, in his face; and Helen had, until hushed by Muriel, burst hoarsely into a description of Miss Kilgour and Carstares's love-making that, if written down, could have been sold in any pub in Christendom as authentic pornography.

It was clear to Jock, therefore, that if he remained in Kinlochgarvie, it would not only be peace of mind he would lose. Muriel, sooner or later, convinced of the therapeutic necessity, would have him in bed with Helen, and might herself fuss around to see that he applied the cure properly. So far that happened only in the nightmares he had while wide awake on his feet. When the time came for it to happen in actuality, then life and nightmare would be one. There was, however, still time to escape; but that time, like a worm disappearing into a bird's beak, was fast growing less.

But could he, in honour, escape? Had he not made, not just his own but Muriel's bed, too, and should he not lie on it? If he fled, what would be the effect on her? Not public shame, at any rate. So far only Carstares and Helen knew of the engagement; perhaps Nancy suspected the sharing of the bed, but then, she had been sacked, and people would think she was lying for revenge. Would there be much private shame, in Muriel's heart? Worse, would there be hurt and sorrow? He was not sure whether he loved her: if love was a matter of frenzy, of rushing to the tops of the snowy mountains to hallo her name to the sun and moon, then he did not; but if, allowing for his age, it could be a warm wish to cherish her, to protect and help her, then he did. As for himself, if he slipped away he would without a doubt nurse in his heart for many years a regret that, in the midst of beer and beer-drinkers, would smell as intolerably sweet as the wild roses on the banks of the loch. Yet if he stayed it was certain that those roses, before the summer was over, would stink in his nostrils.

He could not very well lug his suitcase to the station and flee by train. There were two for the south in the day, one at three in the afternoon, the other at half-past seven. It was still dusk at half-past seven, and with stealth he might be able to get to the station undetected; but there Harry Baker the stationmaster would be sure to recognise him when selling him the ticket, and always there were others hanging about just to get a peep at the lucky passengers who, in two or three hours' time, would be amidst the roar and lights of Glasgow. What he did not want, and what he would certainly get, would be questions put with the persistency and crudeness of rams battering a gate. The discreetest way would be by lorry, but few lorries went by in the dark, and some that did were bound for Falkirk or Edinburgh, whereas it was essential he went straight to Glasgow. In no other place would he get over this crisis.

He found an opportunity one day after lunch to mention his problem to Carstares. They were alone in the yard at the back of the hotel. Carstares was sitting smoking in his car. Two or three times before, Jock had been about to speak to him, but had always been put off by Carstares's obvious unwillingness for conversation. Indeed, Jock was inclined to suspect that the young man was suffering from the same foreboding as himself, and with more reason, for compared with a hawk-like Miss Kilgour Muriel was a finch, whose beak would take much longer to tear a soul to pieces.

That afternoon, though still subdued, Carstares seemed reasonably approachable. In fact, he was the first to speak.

'When's the wedding going to be, Jock?' he asked.

Jock, finger on lips, went up to the car. 'Never,' he replied, with a long, wincing wink.

Carstares grinned in surprise; every day he saw Miss Kirn growing more and more publicly possessive of her little bar-man.

'D'you mind, Mr. Carstares, if I take you into my confidence?'

'When I was in the army, Jock, I used to have to censor letters. I'm sure I can take it.'

Jock grinned sadly. 'Expect nothing sensational, sir. Maybe you'll have noticed I've been gey thoughtful this past week?'

'I think I have. I put it down to love.'

'Love, sir, is a frog that jumps in all directions.'

'I've heard it called many things, but never that.'

'The truth is, sir, I've decided I can't go through with it.'

It seemed to Jock, watching slyly, that Carstares's face darkened and the hand holding the cigarette trembled.

'Why not?' he asked. 'This is a pretty good hotel, Miss Kirn's a pleasant little woman. I'd say you'd landed lucky. It's not like a Glasgow man to kick good luck in the teeth.'

'Glasgow men, sir, like to call their souls their own.'

'Do they? They're bloody lucky. So at the moment your soul's your own?'

'I believe so, sir.'

'How d'you manage it?'

'I've been ordered about a lot in my time, sir. I'm not of the gaffer class. You could be a slave and yet possess your own soul. You could even be ordered to kill men in war, and still remain your own man.'

'Are you making Miss Kirn out to be a devouring monster?'

Jock pretended not to notice that burst of anger.

'In a way, sir, yes,' he replied.

'I can see little sign of it.'

With Miss Kilgour, thought Jock, it was different; everybody saw the signs in her.

'Don't ask me to explain, sir, because I couldn't.' He wondered if he should use the illustration of Muriel's naked silver statuette, but decided it would be disloyal.

'Does this devouring happen to everybody who gets married?'

So you're hot on my heels, thought Jock; then he remembered that Carstares had been married before, to a young and beautiful woman, who had left him a fortune. 'No, sir, I wouldn't say that. There are women who might hand you your soul back, improved.'

'A lot of men would say you're talking a lot of balls, Jock.'

'They'd be entitled to their opinion, sir.'

'I think I'm one of them.'

'As I say, sir, you're entitled to your opinion. Likely you're right, too, in the majority of cases. With me the position's peculiar. Now I'm going to ask you a favour, sir. Do you mind?'

'Ask away. If it doesn't suit me, I'll damn soon tell you.'

'What could be fairer than that? Will you be going to Caldoon some night soon? To the pictures, maybe? If I could have a lift I'd be very grateful. This is presumptuous, sir, I know; but though I maybe don't look it, I'm desperate.'

Carstares laughed. 'And when you get to Caldoon?'

'Bus for Glasgow, sir.'

'Well, I go to Caldoon every afternoon.'

'Yes, sir.' It was to fetch the little girl from her new school there. Everybody took it for granted he paid the fees. And why not, if he was her father?

'Sometimes I go down empty.'

Yes, it had been noticed Miss Kilgour did not always go with him.

'There's your chance then. You'll have luggage?'

'One case, sir. I travel light. The trouble is, I'd be seen.'

'You mean you want to sneak off without letting her know?'

'Desertion, sir; not noble, but the only way. Tell her, she'd weep, I'm here for good.'

'Christ, Jock, aren't you being morbid? As I see it you're both suited for each other. You'd be happy, and you'd make a success of this hotel.'

'Thank you for saying so, sir. On the surface it might be just as you say. But I'd become like a nut with no kernel. You'd have to crack me open to see the emptiness, but it'd be there.'

Carstares shrugged his shoulders. 'You're a mysterious little bugger,' he said, 'but it's your funeral. All right, I'll run you down to Caldoon any night you want. When is it to be?'

'Will it be all right, sir, if I tell you tomorrow?'

'You're still thinking it over?'

'I am, sir, but just for the torture of it. My mind's really made up. Thanks very much for your offer.'

'When she finds out, Jock, she'll be for throwing me out of the hotel.'

Jock smiled. 'That was another thing I wanted to speak to you about. She wants you to leave.'

'Why?'

'Don't ask for logic, sir. It's connected with Mrs. Strone.'

'I see.'

'I've done my best to dissuade her, sir, but she's stubborn. They'll be at you, whether you help me to go or not.'

'They?'

'Miss Carmichael, the schoolmistress, is an associate.'

'What the hell's it got to do with her?'

'Nothing, of course. But they're in partnership.'

'You mean she's got a share in the hotel?'

'Not in the hotel, sir. In its owner.'

'I think I'm beginning to understand, Jock.'

If you are, thought Jock, then why in God's name grin? This is serious; a man's heart and a woman's are going to be broken. Yet was there not in that grin more agony than amusement?

'Right,' said Carstares. 'Let me know when the escape's to be made.'

'I'll do that, sir; and thanks again.'

Then the car drove away.

As Jock walked slowly back to the hotel he was thinking that it wasn't at all unlikely there would be two of them escaping; perhaps three; for it wasn't Miss Kilgour that was keeping Carstares there, it was the little girl.

Twenty Five

Several times Constance had asked him when he was going to pay his visit to Creagan Farm. She explained she wanted to go with him, not as a protectress, of course, but because it was years since she had been at the farm, which used to be part of the family estate. It stood in a very lonely, beautiful glen.

He was reminded of her wish when Jock came up to him, the day after the conversation in the yard, and before saying whether he had decided to flee or stay, warned him that the three McKews had been in the pub the previous night, with McKerrol, and had bragged about what they intended to do to Carstares if they got the chance. In Jock's opinion the threat was serious, especially from Will and McKerrol. It seemed Nancy, having let Will taste the apple, had snatched it away as far as Oban, where no doubt somebody else was already nibbling. Will knew he had lost her, and he was as dangerous as a bull out of whose field the last cow had been taken. As for McKerrol, he hadn't said much, but he had smiled a great deal, like a deposed king comforted by dreams of revenge.

'So I'd look out, sir, if I was you,' said Jock. 'Don't let them meet you in the dark, on a lonely road.' As he said it, he was thinking that the road from Garvie House would be excellent for ambush. Perhaps Miss Kilgour would be finding her hero on her doorstep some bright morning, with his nose broken and his eyes needing poultices. Would she, wondered Jock, tend him lovingly?

'You'd have thought, sir,' added Jock, slyly, 'that there would have been some disapproval expressed. I mean, after all, isn't this a country of law and order and fair play?'

'Are you making out they'd all rejoice if I was beaten up?'

'There's a cruel streak in us all, sir. Now about that trip to Caldoon that I was speaking about yesterday.'

'Yes, what about it? When's it to be?'

'Never.' Jock grinned bleakly; he tried, but neither lid would wink. 'Even before I could swim, I preferred the deep end. You wouldn't think it to look at me, would you? So here goes.' And putting his hands together he pretended to dive. At the same time he did not miss the emotions that flitted, as fascinating as fish in a tank, across Carstares's face. Envy, was it, with its tinge of green, that swam past most often?

'I think you'll keep afloat all right,' said Carstares, rather sourly.

'I expect so, sir; but I doubt, mind you, if you're aware of all the currents.'

'Well, for God's sake, look happy, like a bridegroom.'

Jock appreciated the irony: Carstares, too, was soon to be a bridegroom. Ever since yesterday when Jock had dug up so many dead cats for them both to dissect Carstares had looked sick, unsure, perhaps even desperate; so Jock doubted whether he would ever reach the altar, or in his case the registrar's desk. He would be off one day soon, and in her tumbling castle Miss Kilgour would be left to sharpen her claws.

While thus meditating, Jock hid behind a bridegroom's glaikit smirk, in which his teeth protruded and his ears wilted.

Sane again, he said, 'But thanks all the same for the offer, sir.' He made to go. 'No fires yet in the forest?'

'No. Why should there be?'

The question was like a bull's rush; neat as a matador, Jock skipped aside. 'From what they were saying in the bar it seems a whiskied breath would be enough to set the dead grass in a blaze.'

'Strone's taken his precautions.'

'Yes, sir.' And one of those precautions, it seemed, had been setting a watch on Miss Kilgour, whom Strone suspected of being a potential arsonist. Yet, according to his workers as they relished their beer, Strone was almost racking his bowels in an effort to be cordial and fair to them. It was enough, one said, to

make you believe in spirits: Mrs. Strone, on the other side, still
unwearied by whatever it was they did there, was sending
messages of hope to her man, who was not only receiving
but also heeding them. A discussion had sprung up on spir-
itualism; but becoming bawdy, it had had to be stopped by
Jock, though he had been interested, and was on the point of
telling of the time he had seen his mother five years after her
death. 'I understand he's taking his wife's death much better
than was expected.'

'Yes.'

The word as spoken by Carstares meant, 'Get to hell about
your business, you sly little conceited bastard of a barman,' and
Jock, with a grin of acknowledgment, departed. In the kitchen
he found Muriel sharply instructing the new maid, who was
skinny, forty, sniffy, and skelly-eyed; she had got the job, he
knew, because she was no temptress.

Carstares drove straight to Garvie House. When Constance
came out he cried that he was going to Creagan now, if she still
wished to go.

She hurried down the steps and put her hand on his. She
seemed taken by surprise, as if she hadn't had time to choose the
attitude best suited to hide her real feelings. What he saw on her
face then struck him as genuine; he saw alarm and concern.

'According to Jock,' he said cheerfully, 'they've got their
hospitality ready, so it's time for me to go and enjoy it.'

'What do you mean, Hugh?'

'They were promising in the pub last night to beat me up.'

'The McKews?'

'And their new henchman, McKerrol. Our lover of roses, it
seems, is bloodthirsty.'

'Were they drunk?'

'They'd be drinking.'

Suddenly she smiled, and the woman he had met by the
lochside in the rain was lost again. 'It'll be interesting to have a
chat with old Creagan.'

'This is hardly a social visit, Connie.'

'For me it is. I used to be a favourite of Creagan's, in the old days. We had a lot in common.'

'Not, including, I hope, an urge to beat up District Officers?'

It seemed to him incredible that he should accompany that question with an appeal and challenge that were far from being facetious like it. How could he love her and yet believe, even for an instant, that she was capable, for some inexplicable motive, of wishing him hurt. Yet if she did love him, that might be her way of showing it. He had seen her in many little ways persecute Alison, whom he was sure she nevertheless loved. Love when it did not wish to confess itself could be more resourceful in its malice than hate.

She leaned in and kissed him lightly on the cheek. He gripped her shoulders.

'I love you, Connie,' he said, desperately.

'Are you really sure you do, Hugh?'

'Yes, Connie, I'm sure.'

'It doesn't seem to bring you much happiness, does it?'

'But you keep hiding yourself away. I just get glimpses of you. I know there are times, when you're alone, when you're not embittered, when you've managed to forget everything that's been done to you.'

'Is this intuition, Hugh, or compassionate insight?'

'At other times, like a barrier, you pretend to be hard, callous, cynical, merciless.'

'Words not usually found in the vocabulary of endearment.'

'Don't mock, Connie. I'm serious. If it is a barrier, surely you don't need it with me?'

As she stood smiling, her brother came out of the house. Joviality, he thought, was called for, and he tried to achieve it. 'Hello, Hugh,' he called. 'I must say it's a good job the trees grow by themselves. I mean, you're here rather oftener than you're in the forest, prodding at their roots, eh?'

'He's prodding at mine,' said Connie.

Kilgour sulkily dropped his pretence. Connie so often in a moment descended from terrifying haughtiness to dirt. 'Connie's roots,' he muttered, 'go back four, five hundred years.'

'You'll frighten Hugh if you tell him that,' she said, laughing. 'He prefers his women soft, simple, and uncomplicated, as if they were made yesterday. Like Nancy?' she added, to Carstares only, in a whisper. Aloud she said, 'What watered those roots, Ronald?'

'Tears often, I'm sorry to say.'

'And blood still oftener. The history of the Kilgours, Hugh, is a sordid tale of thieving, murder, feuds, violence.'

'That's the past, Connie,' cried her brother, 'long ago.'

'The present? Insolvency, illegitimacy, ignominy.'

As she uttered the three words, in a slow, light, teasing voice, she looked not at her brother, standing shocked and miserable on the steps, but at Carstares, gazing at her in puzzled, anxious love.

'Ignominy?' bleated Kilgour. 'That means me, doesn't it? And insolvency? That's father. You've no mercy, Connie, neither on the dead or the living. You never had.' He was almost weeping now. 'Carstares, be warned. Do you know your rôle in her scheme of things? You're marked down as victim-in-chief. She's going to get even with the whole world through you. That's her idea. She'll destroy you, Carstares, as sure as grass is green.'

Then Kilgour rushed back into the house.

'He'll sit,' she said, quietly, after a long pause, 'with the pipes in his lap, and the mouthpiece in his mouth; but he'll play nothing. He says the saddest laments are those that can't be heard.'

'You deliberately humiliated him, Connie. Why?'

'He was always a coward, even as a boy.'

'Have you been humiliating him then, all your life?'

'Heroes are magnanimous,' she said, with a sneer.

He smiled, and obviously annoyed her. It seemed to him that, despite her black hair and thin-nosed haughtiness, she resembled Nancy at that moment.

'Well,' he said, 'if we're going to visit Faither this morning, we'd better get started.'

She nodded.

'Will you let Ronald know? I mean, we might not be back for lunch. I thought we could go to some hotel.'

'There's no need to tell him. He won't wait for me. I doubt if he'll have lunch. There are days,' she added, as she slipped into the car, 'when he refuses to eat.'

'Why?'

'He thinks he doesn't deserve to.'

'Damned few of us do. We eat to excrete.'

She patted his knee. 'Who's being embittered now, Hugh?' she murmured.

He smiled, as he drove off. 'All right. Cheer me up by telling me all you know about Faither and his clan. How many District Officers have they hanged from the old rowan tree?'

Creagan Farm, at the head of its remote glen, was almost encircled by grassy hills. The only approach was over four miles of moorland track made by the McKews themselves, and barred by three gates each with strands of rusted barbed wire nailed along the top. Despite the loneliness, the glen and hills seemed as good for trees and sheep as the sky for larks. On knolls Scots pines grew; there was a wood of beech and sycamore; and the native birch and rowans flourished everywhere, but especially along the banks of the lucid streams. As continuous as the singing of larks and murmuring of water, was the bleating of lambs and sheep. In that place it was a curiously musical, tranquil sound.

Carstares stopped the car at the last gate, about a hundred yards from the house. On one skyline he noticed the tops of the trees of the forest coming up from the glen, beyond; they were like an army massing to invade. He could not help sympathising with the McKews, who were holding so dourly to their traditional way of life in spite of an isolation growing greater every year. Coming along the road he had counted at least five deserted cottages; perhaps it was one of them McKerrol had been offered.

'Well,' he said, 'do you want to go first to have your chat with Creagan?'

'Aren't we going together?'

'They'll think I've brought you to protect me.'

'Does it matter what they think?'

'No, I suppose not.' All the same he hoped Will wasn't at home; better have no wild talk about Nancy.

As they set off towards the house Constance gazed all round with a defiant pleasure. 'I like this place,' she said. 'I always have. It's an outpost, still holding out.'

'Against what? Civilisation?'

'Yes. Why not?' Her retort was sharp.

'Don't you think the McKews could do with a little civilising?'

'And become like the poodles in Garvie?'

'You prefer wolves, Connie?'

'Yes, every time.'

Carstares could see little difference between the dwelling-house and the outbuildings; all were squarely built of the same solid, lichened stone, with small windows, and roofs with thick purple slates.

Two black and white collies slunk out to glare up at them with lips curled back and tails drooping. One of them suddenly threw back its head and howled.

'Wolves all right,' said Carstares.

The howling stopped when a piece of wood, the handle of a shovel, flew from behind a shed and struck it on the head. It raced off, yelping; and its companion, itself crawling away, seemed to grin in canine malice.

The flinger of the wood was Tom McKew. As soon as he saw Carstares he jumped for the handle, snatched it up, and brandished it. A moment later he flung it down again and dashed away through the outhouses towards the hill.

Carstares looked after him. 'Gone to summon the clan, do you think?' he asked.

Sure enough, scrutinising the hillside up which Tom was now leaping with idiot's zest, he saw two men working at sheep-drains. They had stopped to watch Tom. One, who looked like McKerrol, rested on the broad handle of his rutter; while the other, Will McKew, stood with the pronged hawk over his shoulder.

As they crossed the cobbled yard towards the house, Carstares was thinking it was perhaps as well Constance was with him. He did not have to knock on the door. Old McKew himself opened it as they approached. He was a tall, bald, old man whose beard, curious on so fierce a face, was as soft and white as bog-cotton. He wore a thick knitted cardigan as shaggy as heather. Holding on to it was a thin-faced anxious woman at least thirty years younger.

'Mind you're no' to get angry, Faither,' she whined softly. 'Mind whit the doctor said.' She was too ashamed to look at either Constance or Carstares.

Her husband ignored her. He stood with one fist clenched on his belly, and the other swinging at his side as if holding a club or hatchet. He seemed ill, and before he could speak began to rumble and splutter in his throat.

'Where's your cloth?' cried his wife, and ran inside to fetch it.

He wiped the froth and slavers away with the sleeve of his cardigan.

'Hello, Creagan,' said Constance, very coolly.

He had been peering, and now it was obvious he must be almost blind, for he came forward with eager stumbling deference, holding out his hand.

'I ken that voice,' he cried. 'It's Miss Constance. I didnae see you. That skite of a wife said it was a stranger, the forestry fellow.'

'So it is, Creagan. This is Mr. Hugh Carstares, the new District Officer from Kinlochgarvie.'

Carstares was ready to hold out his hand, but soon saw it was useless.

'I hae never liked onybody frae the forest,' muttered McKew, 'frae the first day a tree was planted. I'd hae thocht you, too, had little reason to love them, Miss Constance.'

'Here's your cloth, Faither,' whimpered his wife.

Again he ignored her, and turned to Carstares. 'I hae naething against you for what you did to Wull,' he said. 'I was going doon to tup her myself to open his een. But' – here his voice rose to a hoarse roar and he shook his fist towards the trees on the bright hill – 'you're a tree man, and that's enough for me.'

'Faither,' whined his wife, 'mind the young lady's here.'

'Say what you've got to say, Creagan,' said Constance.

'Aye, by Christ, I'll say it,' he roared. 'They'll no be content till this hoose stands a ruin, like many anither, and a' these bonny hills that God made for sheep hae a' the substance sooked oot o' them by trees. Can ye eat a tree?'

By the end of his speech his fury, though not less in his heart, was dwindled in his throat to painful grunts and wheezings. He had to stagger back and hold on to the wall of the house.

'I've seen the day,' he muttered, 'when wi' my ain twa hands I wad hae torn up every tree you planted.'

'You should be in your bed, Faither,' cried his wife, 'like the doctor said.' To Carstares she said sullenly, 'You'd better go. The boys will be coming.'

But the boys had already arrived. Led by Will, still clutching his hawk, they came running into the yard. Tom had picked up his shovel handle again, and was spitting on it. McKerrol had no weapon. With them came three dogs, snarling joyously.

'All present but Alec and Murdo,' said Carstares. 'I expect they're tending the lambs.'

But Constance did not smile in companionship, or come closer to him; instead she walked two or three paces away, as if signifying that these consultations about sheep and trees were none of her business.

Will would have attacked Carstares with the hawk if McKerrol hadn't seized and held him back. 'This isn't the place, or the time, Will,' he said, laughing.

Tom, using the handle like a sword, thrust at Carstares's face; he had to knock it aside.

Mrs. McKew wailed and wept. The old man, still holding on to the wall, muttered furiously; his eyes were closed. Will struggled with McKerrol. The dogs snarled and growled at Carstares, and seemed ready to rush in and bite. Constance watched from the background.

'I was asked to come here to discuss some business matters,' said Carstares.

That display of contemptuous calmness maddened Will afresh. He hurled abuse so obscene that his step-mother, putting her fingers to her ears, ran into the house.

Again Carstares thought that Constance, smiling, resembled Nancy. He turned and tried to address the old man.

'Mr. McKew, it was you I came to talk to. It appears your sheep—'

Then Tom lunged with the handle and the jagged end struck Carstares's cheek, tearing it. Blood flowed down, on to his collar.

In glee Tom showed the end of the handle to Will and McKerrol, as if there was blood on it, too.

'If I was you,' said McKerrol, 'I'd go.' He was particularly amused by Constance's aloofness.

Will pushed his fist against Carstares's face. 'I'd hang for you,' he managed to say.

The old man seemed unable, rather than unwilling, to assert his authority.

Carstares thought he'd better go. Constance was already on her way to the car, walking slowly. He tried to deceive himself that she was thus urging him to follow her.

'I'll come again,' he said.

Will seized him by the front of the jacket. 'You knew I wanted to marry her,' he cried. 'How would you like it if I was to run after her' – he gestured with his other hand towards Constance – 'and drag her into the hayshed?'

'Maybe you wouldn't have to drag too. hard, Will,' chuckled McKerrol.

At that moment the old man collapsed. Tom first, and then Will, rushed to help him. They picked him up tenderly and carried him into the house.

Carstares was left with McKerrol and the howling dogs.

'So you've done for Faither, too?' said McKerrol. 'For a man who's been here such a short time, you've fairly made your mark. All it needs now is for the forest to go on fire. And, as you know, that's been arranged.'

He laughed as Carstares went away. 'Take care of yourself,' he called. 'Jean, my wife, tells me you're fond of children. I wouldn't like anything to happen to a man that's fond of children; and fond of getting them, too.'

Constance was waiting by the gate near the car. She watched him as he went down into a burn, dipped his handkerchief into the water, and went to the driving-mirror of the car to wipe the blood off his face. Neither of them spoke. Larks sang and lambs bleated.

At last he got into the car, ready to drive off. Still she waited by the gate.

'Coming?' he called.

With a sigh that seemed angry rather than penitential she came reluctantly to the car and got in beside him. She did not speak, nor smile when he, with sudden surrender and forgiveness, smiled at her. He tried to put his hand on hers, but she would not let him. All the way back to the house she remained silent, staring ahead, her mouth tight, her eyes intense, and her body trembling, as if she was the one who had been betrayed.

Twenty Six

When she had seen the jagged wood tear Hugh's cheek and make the blood flow, Constance, in the profoundest most bitterly protected parts of her being, had been betrayed. With pang after pang of agony every belief she had built up over years of resolution and renunciation was attacked, so savagely she felt physically weak. Her walking slowly back to the car was not deliberate; it was because she feared she might at any moment fall, like the sick old man. Most terrifying of all, those periods of tranquillity, previously endangered by Hugh's guessing at their existence, were now surely at an end. Hugh would soon go away from Kinlochgarvie, and from her, but she would never be able to forget him: that blow, delivered on her behalf by an idiot with powerful body, would be struck again and again, both in her waking and sleeping minds. Yet she shrank from the admission that she loved him, as from an adder unseen in the grass.

When she came out of the car at the house, she found herself still so weak, so afraid, and so desperate for comfort that could not be asked for, that she could hardly recognise herself; the very house seemed strange.

Holding on to the car, and trying to smile, she said: 'I think we ought to end this pretence, Hugh.'

'Pretence?'

'I think you know what I mean.' She gazed at his scratched cheek, though it filled her with terror and fascination. 'We've been deceiving ourselves. I never saw you before you came here; you never knew I existed. We're strangers, really. Alison's not your child.'

'She could be, Connie.'

'No, it's finished.' She pulled the ring off her finger. 'It was an expensive joke, Hugh. But it's not too soiled. You should get all your money back.'

He wouldn't take the ring, but seemed to find it hard to show on his face good reason why he shouldn't. Instead of feeling insulted, she felt love of him weaken her still further. With a clumsiness that looked like reluctance, she put in her hand, dropped the ring into his breast pocket, and then went up the steps, holding on to the stone parapet.

'Are you all right, Connie?' he asked.

At the top of the steps she turned and smiled. 'Yes, I'm all right, Hugh.'

'You don't look well.'

'This is the finish, Hugh. Don't come back. Goodbye.'

He did not, as she expected and hoped, hurry out of the car after her. Standing inside the door, she heard it drive away. This was the finish then. For his sake, she thought, she was glad; and yet, for her own sake, she wished to hate him for this destructive love he had provoked in her.

Ronald came out to meet her at the foot of the stairs. He looked drawn and peevish, as if he had eaten only the thin resolve not to eat.

'I didn't expect you back so early,' he said.

'No.'

'Has anything happened?' Suddenly he glimpsed her un-happiness; for a moment it was like a feast to him. 'Is it Hugh?'

'He's taken your advice, Ronald.'

'What do you mean?'

'He's seen through me. He won't be back.'

He frowned as if the feast after all was not to be enjoyed. 'What about Alison?' he asked. 'He's got to bring her back, hasn't he?'

She had forgotten. Now hope had to be kept back.

'Besides,' went on Ronald, 'isn't he her father?'.

She shook her head. 'No. I never saw him before he came here.'

'Do you think I'm going to believe that, Connie?'

She could hardly believe it herself.

'This is part of your scheme, Connie. Take care you don't go too deep. Good swimmer though you are, you can still drown.'

As she went up the stairs, with Ronald speaking behind her, she remembered the water in the burn where Hugh had wet his handkerchief. Never had water seemed so beautiful, and in its clear, steady flowing so symbolical of the sadness of life. When she reached her room she could not bear to look at herself in the mirror, lest the resemblance to Alison remind her too poignantly of him. Nor did she dare to look at the mark on her finger where the ring had been.

When he brought Alison home at half-past four, she had been hiding for over half an hour in the rhododendrons near the drive; but she did not rush out and greet him.

Ronald came out eagerly.

Hugh asked: 'Where's Connie?'

'I couldn't say, old man. Out somewhere. She doesn't leave notes, you know, to say where she's going.'

Alison marched sturdily up the steps into the house. It was as if she was aware of the wilful web of tension and misery in which these adults were trapped, and she was determined to keep out of it, or, if caught, too, to pretend not to be. Constance had often before been aware of the unhappiness of her small daughter, but never till now had admitted how desolating it must be. So proud of her own endurance, and so intent upon strengthening it, she had not realised that Alison, too, was enduring, with as much courage and far less bitterness.

Hugh had come out of the car and stood with Ronald in the sunshine, smoking. Ronald was speaking earnestly, perhaps was finding extenuations for her; but Hugh listened with an effort, as if the subject now wearied him; certainly he said very little. She was sure he had made up his mind, and was indeed finished with her. Her whole being curled within her, like the leaf in her desperate fingers, as she resisted the desire to rush out and plead with him.

At last he got into the car and drove away. Ronald, after a

strange salute at the sun, began to march with piper's precision from one marked point on the drive to another, turn, and march back again. He had done it at least eight times when she came out from among the bushes and strolled up to him.

'Is Alison home?' she asked. 'I thought I heard a car.'

He had stopped at attention, and was examining her face with an uncharacteristic cruel curiosity. 'Composing a lament, Connie,' he said. 'Know what it's called? Farewell to Kinlochgarvie. You know who I'm going to dedicate it to. Yes, Hugh. But I doubt if I'll have it finished in time.'

She did not speak.

'Why did you do it, Connie, for God's sake? He didn't say much, but I gathered you've wounded him to the depths of his heart. It's ignominy all round, Connie. There's still one way to get him back, Connie, but I might as well ask you to fly to the moon. Humility, Connie; genuine humility.'

'Did he say he was coming tonight?'

'There you go, as hard as iron with confidence. It never was justified at any time, Connie; certainly not now. No, he's not coming here tonight. I doubt if he'll ever come here again.'

'Did he say so?'

'No, but it was in his face. As for tonight, he's spending it in the Runacraig watch-tower. Not here, Connie; up yonder, alone.' He pointed to where above the forest the small tower could be seen against the skyline.

'I didn't think that was a duty for District Officers.'

'There you go again, Connie. You can't even understand humility in someone else. If you ask me, he wants to think it all over; and if you ask me again, I'll tell you what his decision will be. Farewell to Kinlochgarvie, Connie; that'll be it. I thought there was something very sad, and final, about the way he said goodbye to Alison. You had your chance, Connie, but you were too bitter to take it. You didn't even have the patience to play the spider, as you intended.'

She wondered what Hugh's motive could really be for wishing, to spend the night in the lonely tower. He had mentioned that the men manning the towers at night had been complaining about the cold, and regulations apparently prevented the use of oil-stoves, as one man in another forest had almost been asphyxiated. Perhaps that was the simple explanation: he had decided to investigate for himself.

'Was it you who scratched his face?'

The question was asked with a sudden shy savageness that startled her. 'Don't be ridiculous,' she said.

'It's not ridiculous, Connie. I thought you might have. You've got it in your heart to scratch faces all right, especially the faces of those you're expected to love.' Then he relented, and stared at her with affection miserably chasing from his face satisfaction at her unhappiness. 'You are fond of him, aren't you, Connie? You know, since he came back, you've shown gleams of joy; you've tried not to, but I've seen them. Things just don't go smoothly, do they? Maybe you were right after all. Maybe there are too many ghosts from the past seeking for revenge. History catches up, they say.'

She remembered that the tower on Runacraig was just over the ridge from the McKew land. Likely a view of the farm in the glen could be had from it.

'Pride's a good thing, Connie, but it oughtn't to be cultivated, as you've cultivated it. You've let a whole forest of pride grow in you; now you're lost in it. What's worse to be lost in, Connie, pride or ignominy?'

Trying to laugh, but groaning instead, he walked away towards the river.

That evening, after dark, she rang up the hotel. It was Jock who answered. When he discovered who she was he became, or so she thought, suavely impertinent. She tried to make herself believe that Hugh had let it be known he was finished with her; everybody in the hotel would already know, and soon the whole village would be sniggering. Hugh would feel safe among the sniggerers.

Jock's irony, however, was not directed against her, but against the freakishness of providence which had ordained that he and Muriel should last the course of love, while

Carstares and Constance Kilgour, handsome and young enough for daylight passion, should fail so soon.

'No, Mr. Carstares isn't in, Miss,' he said. 'I understand he's spending the night in one of the watch-towers.'

'Yes, I know. I thought perhaps he hadn't left.'

'About an hour ago, maybe a bit more. Said he wanted to reach it before dark.'

'Did he leave any message?'

'For you, miss?'

'Yes.'

He paused. 'I don't think so. But if you'll just hold on a minute I'll enquire of Miss Kirn.'

'Never mind. Thank you.'

'Glad to oblige, miss.' As Jock put down the telephone he was sadder than he had expected to be. Perhaps there was nothing to be hilarious about in his successful romance with Muriel, but if amusement was forbidden or improper, and continuous rapture only for birds in spring-time, what was there except amiable, thoughtful acceptance?

As he returned to the bar, whistling like a proprietor, to see how his recently acquired apprentice there was getting on, Constance Kilgour in Garvie House had again picked up the telephone.

When the operator asked the number, she replied briskly: 'Kinlochgarvie 25.'

It was Mrs. McKew who answered, in a voice like a series of plaintive sucks. 'Wha is it?'

'I should like to speak to Will McKew. Is he at home?'

'So it's you? I was wondering if ye'd let him alane. It's as weel for you Faither's ta'en a stroke and cannae speak or hear. He thocht ye must be efter Wull's money, which I think mysel' is no' fair to poor Wull wha's no' braw, God kens, but he's got the best he'rt o' them a'.'

'May I speak to him?'

Suddenly Mrs. McKew's voice was strengthened by an infusion of sharp sympathy. 'In ony case, lassie, whitever ye've done, whether ye're the seeking whure they say ye are, ye don't deserve to get trapped into this family.'

Then she was interrupted. Constance heard a man's voice, and next moment Will was speaking to her, with a hoarse, sobbing, fierce entreaty, which reminded her of the ferocity on his face when he had threatened Hugh that morning.

'Is that you, Nancy, my sweetheart? Whit made ye go away? I thought it was a' arranged between us?'

'This isn't Nancy. Never mind who it is. I thought you would be interested to know that the new District Officer is spending the night in the Runacraig watch-tower.'

'If he was spending it in hell, whit difference wad it make to me? Wha are you?'

'He'll be alone,' she said, and put the telephone down, with a gesture and smile meant to mock the humility Ronald had told her was needed.

Afterwards, lying on her bed, staring out at the stars, with her fists clenched on her breast, she kept thinking she could justify what she had done, if she wished; but she did not wish. She did not wish either to think of him walking alone up to the tower, but in spite of her he kept limping deeper and deeper into her imagination, with his smile like a torch illuminating every hideous feature of her tremendous treachery.

Suddenly, as punishment it seemed, love for him overwhelmed her. Falling like a spark, within ten minutes it was beyond her control; while she lay, watching the stars and moving not so much as a finger, it spread and roared and consumed in her.

At last, as if indeed racing from a conflagration, she hurried downstairs. In the small sitting-room Ronald was guiltily toasting bread. He had a table set for supper. It would be his first food since breakfast. He thought her agitation was scorn at his succumbing so soon again.

'You know I'm a fraud,' he muttered. 'Why keep on discovering it?'

'Hugh's in Runacraig watch-tower,' she said.

'I know that. It was me who told you.' But despite his peevishness he looked at her so long, in surprise, that his toast burnt.

'It's just above Creagan Farm,' she said.

'Now, Connie, don't start teaching me about the place I was born in.'

'That scratch on his face!'

He was suspicious of her difficulty in speaking; indeed, her whole performance since her entry was so unlike her, she seemed to him to be mocking her own customary, too-patient sanity.

'What about it?' he snapped. 'I saw it. Did you do it, after all?'

'It was Tom McKew, this morning at Creagan.'

'Tom? That's the big daft one, isn't it? I can remember him when we were both boys. He fascinated me by the way he used to pull the wings off bees. They stung him, but he didn't seem to mind.'

'They would all have attacked him, if I hadn't been there.'

'Connie the protectress! That's a new rôle for you.' Laughing, he impaled another piece of toast on the brass fork. 'But what are you up to, Connie? I know he's a forestry official, and they don't like anybody that has to do with trees, but I hardly think they'd go the length of assault.'

She realised he did not know about Will and Nancy. Then, picturing Nancy and Hugh together in the hotel, bed, she discovered that part of the justification which she had refused to define had simply been sexual jealousy.

'They hate him,' she whispered, not sure even yet that she herself did not in the midst of her love hate him, too, for having lowered her to Nancy's level.

'There you go, Connie. Hate! You see it as thick as bees in heather. It's really rare, you know. Ask Hugh. He was telling me he's killed men he never hated. People can't live on hate, Connie: it's a poison, not a food.'

'They know he's alone.'

He laughed. 'I think you should sit down and have some toast, Connie.'

'McKerrol's with them.'

'McKerrol? That's the fellow Hugh sacked? A brute, they

say; but, mind you, I've always found him respectful enough, touches his cap quite nicely.'

'I told them he was there.'

'Now what are you talking about, Connie? You've got me confused. What's your game? What are you up to?' Then he stopped, astounded, for he saw there were tears in her eyes; these were a resource she had never used before.

'I love him,' she said.

'I knew it all along,' he replied, after a pause. 'And he loves you. And both of you love Alison. And he's got enough money to keep you in comfort. Why weep then, unless it's for joy?' He could not think of her weeping for sorrow; she had not wept at their mother's grave.

'Yet I told them he was in the watch-tower, alone.'

He thought she must be bragging about her love. 'They say people in love will confide in beetles,' he said.

'I told them because I wanted them to go up there and hurt him.' She clenched her own fists. 'Perhaps I still want them to.'

Again his toast burned as he gaped at her. 'I'm afraid I don't follow, Connie,'

'My God, what am I to do?'

You are not to invoke God, for one thing, he thought: you do not believe in Him.

'I think really you should go to bed, Connie, after you've had some supper.' He scraped the blackness off the toast on to the hearthstone. 'You don't seem to know yourself what you're saying. You've got yourself into a tangle, that's obvious. You seem to be saying you told the McKews Hugh was in the tower, so that they would go up and attack him.'

'Yes.'

He gazed at her, in a kind of awe. 'You know, Connie, it's not incredible. It ought to be, but it isn't.'

She did not hear him; she had remembered that Strone's bungalow was in touch with the two watchtowers by telephone. If she hurried, and Strone agreed, she could warn Hugh. But as she was running upstairs to put on her coat, she stopped suddenly at the top, faced with the impossibility of asking

Strone for a favour. Only by reminding herself that Hugh was Strone's superior and this was Hugh's business, could she go on again. In her bedroom she quickly put on her coat, found a small torch, and then, all ready to go, just stood waiting, for more than five minutes.

Downstairs Ronald met her in the hall. He was munching toast.

'Are you going out?' he asked.

She ran past without answering.

'Surely you're not going up there to him?' he cried. 'It's dark, you know; and that whole hillside's gashed with precipices. Besides, Connie, where's your celebrated pride?'

By this time he had followed her out and was standing on the terrace listening to her run down the drive. 'Do you want me to go with you?' he shouted, but he knew the offer was foolish. Not only was she a more intrepid and safe-footed mountaineer than he, but it was also obvious that when she reached the tower and was reconciled with Carstares his own presence there would be even more ludicrously pointless than usual.

He went in to eat his supper.

To the forester's bungalow it was about a mile and a half; it took Constance almost an hour. All the way she had to struggle against her pride, which was fertile with reasons why she did not have to go and ask Strone. No doubt Will McKew and McKerrol hated Hugh enough to attack him; but would their malevolence endure all the way up the hill in the darkness, at a time when McKew's father lay dying? Besides, if she did get in touch with Hugh, and warn him, it would amount to a confession of treachery; thereafter the advantage would be with him. Better surely, therefore, to return home, and hope the McKews would stay at home, too. But she knew that if she did go home, she might not be able to resist the temptation to wish that the McKews and McKerrol were at the tower, agents on her behalf.

The bungalow was in darkness. She knocked several times without answer. Then she noticed there was a light in the hut in the nursery. When she went there and knocked, it wasn't Strone who came, but a middle-aged, grey-haired man called McLeish. He was yawning, but quickly closed his mouth and made some kind of involuntary salute when he saw who she was.

'I'm looking for Mr. Strone,' she said.

'I don't think he's at hame, miss.'

'I know that. Do you know where he is?'

'Aye, I think so. You see, miss, I've got to keep in touch in case o' fire.'

'Where is he?'

McLeish hesitated. 'He's visiting Miss Carmichael, the schoolmistress,' he said, ashamed to say it to her, although they said the little girl in the big house was her bastard. He had always admired her fine proud looks.

'Is it the hut then that's in touch with the towers?' she asked.

'Yes, miss. It used to be the bungalow, but Mr. Strone changed it; he thought it might disturb Mrs. Strone.'

'I should like to speak to Mr. Carstares, then.' She could not help putting the request arrogantly.

McLeish did not seem to resent it, he seemed instead to expect it; his quietness therefore was a rebuke.

'It's a regulation, miss, just to send messages about fire danger.'

'I hardly think it applies to District Officers.'

Likely not, McLeish thought. All the same, other young lassies in the village wouldn't mind coming for a chat with their boy friends in the towers. Why should District Officers be favoured?

'I don't think Mr. Carstares would be pleased,' she said, 'if he was to find out you'd so much as hesitated about letting me speak to him.'

This is you in the mood that got big Rab fired, thought McLeish; but he did not feel anger; it was, to his own surprise, pity he felt.

'I'd raither be at my ain fireside,' he said. 'But I could dae wi' a breath of fresh air. If you'd be so kind as to watch the phones for me while I'm away.'

'Which one is for Runacraig?'

'This one.'

'Do you know if Mr. Carstares has arrived in the tower?'

'Aye, he phoned to say he'd got there safe.'

'Thank you.'

As soon as he had gone, taking his cap with him to keep the frost off his head, she picked up the telephone.

'Hugh, this is Constance,' she said.

There were only crackles in reply. She said it several times, with the same result. Opening the door, she called to McLeish. When he came and tried, he too could get no response.

'That's unusual,' he muttered, as much to himself as her. Even if a man took diarrhoea from the cold or the loneliness, that was still no reason why he shouldn't be able to attend to the telephone; so Strone would think anyway. Of course Carstares was above Strone and could please himself.

They waited another ten minutes, trying several times, but the telephone remained silent. The man in the other tower was consulted, but could give no help; he had spoken once to Mr. Carstares, but that was about an hour ago. Maybe the line was broken, he suggested.

McLeish had another theory, which he kept to himself: Carstares had been wounded in the leg; maybe then, coming down the ladder to relieve himself, he had fallen and was lying up there helpless. Something of the sort seemed to have occurred to Miss Kilgour, too, he saw: she was as nervous and worried as his own wife would be, he hoped, if he was the man silent in the tower.

'Will you let Mr. Strone know?' she asked.

He scratched his head. 'Maybe I should.' He wasn't sure because, after all, Carstares was above Strone, and did an underling like himself tell one boss that another boss, still higher, was not attending to his duties? Besides, just why was Strone visiting the schoolmistress? There were already jokes about it among the men. Strone's wife, it was said, had asked him with her dying breath to look after her friend Miss Carmichael; well, there were many ways of looking after a

woman, but didn't everybody know the one she'd put first? So
the jokers said. What bothered McLeish personally was that
the schoolmistress was fifteen years at least older than Strone.

'What will he do?' asked Miss Kilgour.

McLeish, startled, realised a moment later she meant about
Carstares.

'Will he send someone up to find out what's happened?'

'I expect he might, miss.' Though it would be mortifying to
the man who struggled up there, with his eyes poked at by
thousands of unseen twigs, and his legs wet to the thigh
through falling in burns, to find Carstares not only unscratched
and dry, but also indignant at being sent help.

'At any rate there's no good waiting here,' she said. 'Good-
night.'

He watched her hurry down the path. His wife had often said
that the upper class was far more callous than the workers.
Having served the gentry for over ten years as a scullerymaid,
Maggie ought to know; yet it was his own private belief that,
being human, they suffered the same pains and griefs as everybody else. Here was Miss Kilgour now, prouder than most
because of the poverty and disgrace that had befallen her
family, weeping as she raced down the path, like any girl
worried about her sweetheart.

It would have astonished McLeish to know she was weeping
not just because she was anxious about Carstares, but also
because she had been insolent to him. He could never have
guessed that to her he had represented then, apocalyptically,
something she could never have named but which she knew she
should have honoured. Ronald was right in saying she was
doomed: having fed on hate so long, she was now irremediably
poisoned. To be pleasant to McLeish ought to have been easy;
she had found it impossible. Though she was now climbing up
through the dark forest to confess to Hugh that she had so
shamefully betrayed him, her pride was far from defeated;
without her permission, indeed against her will, it remained
cunning, ferocious, and resourceful in seeking to regain its
position, no matter what she might find at the tower. It would

sacrifice Hugh, Alison, Ronald, and her hope of future happiness, rather than surrender. Yet surely it was not invincible: her
love for Hugh could, with luck, overcome it.

At last, wet, sweating, dishevelled, scratched, and exhausted,
she emerged from the wilderness of trees on to the bare ridge,
along which the way to the tower was clear. As she approached,
shivering in the cold wind, she heard faraway the melancholy
cry of some nightbird, and below in the loch the quiet slap of
oars as a fisherman moved to try his luck in another place. The
tower itself, like a gigantic spider against the starry sky, was
silent and dark.

She was close enough to the tower to hear the whining of the
wind through its wire stays, before she became aware there was
someone on the concrete foundation beneath, leaning against
one of the great legs, and smoking. Afraid it might be McKew
or McKerrol, she hesitated; then, still more afraid it was Hugh,
she went boldly on.

It was Hugh, unhurt so far as she could make out, and
strangely happy. She halted a few yards from him, and held on
to one of the vibrating wailing wires. For a full minute they
stared at each other, without speaking, she tense and shy, he
relaxed and patient.

She could not restrain a long harsh sigh.

'They were here, Connie,' he said, laughing. 'Your hired
assassins.'

She pressed her fist against her breast. If he was going to
mock her, he had a right.

'Their hearts weren't in it, though,' he went on, in the same
amused voice. 'You see, Faither's dead; he died about half an
hour after you telephoned, in the middle of the murder pre-
parations, you might say. I saw them coming, and hid down
there among the trees. I could hear everything they said,
Connie; and I'm afraid they said a lot about you. It seems
you didn't tell them who you were, but they guessed all right. I
think even if they'd caught me they'd have let me off with a
black eye and a kick or two in the groin, not just out of respect
for Faither, but out of what you might call masculine sym-

pathy. At least I'm sure that was how Will felt. I can't speak for McKerrol, though; he's married to an honourable woman, as we know, Connie.'

Had he spoken with bitterness and disgust, she would have understood and agreed; but this light-heartedness was an unnecessary cruelty.

'I knew you were coming, Connie. I was speaking to McLeish on the phone about ten minutes ago. He was anxious about you; I was to be sure and let him know if you got here safely. Or perhaps it was the forest he was anxious about. For, Connie, what could ever harm you?'

He smoked for a little while, during which she grew very cold and began to shiver.

'I'm grateful to you, Connie,' he said.

She made to protest against that sarcasm, but could not.

'I mean it,' he said. 'Like yourself, I find it hard to explain. When I came here to Kinlochgarvie I didn't much care what happened. I didn't think anything could happen that would matter. I couldn't escape from a feeling that anything I did, or anybody did, was childish. I even went the length of thinking that what was needed was some sort of atonement.'

Again he paused and smoked.

'It's all right now,' he said, 'thanks to you, Connie.'

Was it humbleness, or contrition, that made her so obtuse? She could understand well enough what he was saying, but not his motive in saying it. Hope, too, had suddenly begun to leap and bark and strain within her, like a chained dog. Such was his manner, she would not be surprised if, in a minute or two, he wished her a goodbye as final as death, and then climbed up the ladder into the tower; but neither would she be surprised if he came across and punished her dreadfully with a kiss of love.

She did not know then what she wanted. To be rejected would be to suffer for the rest of her life, but suffering, she knew, was endurable; whereas to be forgiven, and loved, and forced to recognise not only the possibility of happiness but happiness itself would be for her to enter upon an experience for which she was not prepared and in which she might find a new kind of suffering. If tomorrow he left Kinlochgarvie for good, as Ronald had prophesied, there were secret places, in her own heart, and also in these native hills, where she could manage her grief; but if he stayed, and married her, her joy must become public.

'It wouldn't be easy coming up in the dark,' he said.

'No.' She tried to imitate his light tone, but she could not.

'Alison all right?'

'As far as I know.'

'I'm afraid that isn't as far as it should be, Connie.'

She felt then like screaming to him what right had he to believe his heart was cleansed, that atonement had been made? In what way had he atoned to her for debasing himself with Nancy? Until he did so let him never reproach her with her callousness towards Alison, let him keep his taunts about honourable women to himself.

All she said was, 'No.'

Then he was across at her, so suddenly she thought for an instant he was going to strike her. Instead he began to stroke her cold head and face in caresses that urgency made clumsy, and to tell her, almost bitterly, how much he loved her.

As she kissed him, the stars seemed close above his head. They were like a promise not only of an immensity of time in which to learn to cultivate love, but also of forgiveness if, in that cultivation, perfection could not be achieved.

POLYGON is an imprint of Birlinn Limited. Our list includes titles by Alexander McCall Smith, Liz Lochhead, Kenneth White, Robin Jenkins and other critically acclaimed authors. Should you wish to be put on our catalogue mailing list **contact**:

Catalogue Request
Polygon
West Newington House
10 Newington Road
Edinburgh EH9 1QS
Scotland, UK

Tel: +44 (0) 131 668 4371
Fax: +44 (0) 131 668 4466
e-mail: info@birlinn.co.uk

Postage and packing is free within the UK. For overseas orders, postage and packing (airmail) will be charged at 30% of the total order value.

Our complete list can be viewed on our website. Go to **www.birlinn.co.uk** and click on the Polygon logo at the top of the home page.